A NOVEL

A NOVEL

JEANNE TREAT

AHEAD OF THE HANGMAN PRESS
2 0 1 1

AN
AHEAD OF THE HANGMAN PRESS
BOOK
PUBLISHED BY
TREAT ENTERPRISES, INC.

Published and Distributed in the United States by
Treat Enterprises Inc.
PO Box 724, East Amherst, NY 14051

www.darkdestinythenovel.com
www.jeannetreat.com

FIRST EDITION

ISBN 978-1466478787

Manufactured in the United States of America

Cover design and illustrations by Charles Randolph Bruce - rebelking.com
Most interior character drawings by Jane Starr Weils - janestarrweils.com
Drawing of Gilbert Gordon by Charles Randolph Bruce- rebelking.com

This book is dedicated to my husband, who helped me to realize a dream, to my mother, who told everyone I was an author before it was true, and to dozens of seventeenth century Scots who lived in my head, guiding my pen.

SCOTLAND

A- Peterhead
B- Whinnyfold
C- Drake Castle
D- Huntly Castle
E- Forest of Deer
F- Abbey
G- Forres
H- Aberdeen
I- Inverurie
J- Turriff
K- Dundee
L- Moray Firth
M- Edinburgh
N- Glasgow
O- Dunglass Castle
P- Kelso
Q- Dunse Law
R- Stonehaven
S- Dunnottar Castle
T- Jedburgh
U- Castle Grant
V- Garmouth
W- Castle Skeen
X- Scone
Y- Perth
Z- Stirling
AA- Dunbar
BB- Inverkeithing

BERWICK

NEWCASTLE
DURHAM

WORCESTER

WALES

LONDON

ENGLAND

EDEN PLANTATION

GREEN SPRING
PLANTATION

JAMESTOWN

CHESAPEAKE
BAY

JAMES RIVER

VIRGINIA COLONY

Many people contributed knowledge of their respective fields of expertise and interest to make this a better and more interesting book. I wholeheartedly thank those who gave their time and energies to improve my writing and those who allowed me to use them as models for the character drawings. Among those are:

Gregory Gumkowski, Robin Schulmeister, Robert Davis, and Anne Simon – who spent hours proofing the manuscript.

Charles Randolph Bruce, Jane Starr Weils, and Lisa Langer – artists.

Cecilia "Bunty" Penny - my historian friend from Scotland.

My character models –
Allen Casler (Fang Adams)
Robert Davis (Lord Balmerino)
Kevin Hampe (Murdock)
Frank Kolarek Jr (Dughall Gordon – Lord Drake)
Ashley Toth (Keira Gordon)

Synopsis

DARK DESTINY IS THE THIRD BOOK
IN THE DARK BIRTHRIGHT SAGA.

It's 1648. The English civil war is over. The imprisoned King and his lieutenants are in trouble. Gilbert Gordon is one of them. What will the Gordon brothers do? You will meet the next generation - young Maggie, James, Luc, and George. James' supernatural abilities endanger his father and threaten the peace of the family. England executes the King and declares itself a Republic, but the Scottish government refuses to follow. The King's son tries to gain his thrones, starting with Scotland. Unfortunately, he was given a directive by his father to execute Lord Dughall Gordon. Scotland is in turmoil. Battles are fought and fortunes are lost. What will happen to the Gordons? Will they abandon Scotland for the British Colonies?

James Conan Gordon

Chapter 1
Abdication of Responsibility

October 25th 1648

APPROACHING THE ABBEY OF DEER,
ABERDEENSHIRE, SCOTLAND

Autumn had come early to the Highland forest. Golden leaves dropped like rain and oak spinners littered the narrow path. Fragrant pines stretched to the sky, providing refuge for squirrels and chattering birds.

Six riders rounded a corner and made their final approach to the Abbey of Deer. The two men in front were servants, dressed in breeks, shirts, and plain leather capes. They wore serious expressions and were armed with swords and dirks. These were followed by a trio of obvious stature, a Duke, a young Lord, and a boy dressed like a prince. Riding three black stallions, their clothes bore the tartan of the House of Drake. Behind them rode a servant bearing the standard of the Duke, a blue flag decorated with a golden lion's head.

The Duke was almost twenty-nine. Dughall Gordon had been a

husband, a father, and the Duke of Seaford for more than ten years. As a Lord, he led men into battle, fought real and supernatural enemies, and rescued his step-father from the jaws of death. Yet, this experience could not prepare him for what was to happen today.

The events of this day had been long anticipated. In a way, it was a repeat of previous trips where his son and daughter were tested. The apparent difference now was that the girl wasn't with them. Rightfully so, the boy was suspicious of the purpose.

Dughall reflected on those earlier visits, when both children were found to have supernatural abilities resulting from their unusual lineage. His daughter Maggie could sense the emotions and energies of people and animals. She saw colorful halos around bodies, which she used to identify mood and illness. She was a sensitive child with a voice like an angel; attractive, well-loved, and respected. His son James had multiple abilities. He could read the thoughts, feelings, and emotions of others; and employed this talent with no reservation. He used his mind to distort or move objects, especially when angry. In contrast to his sister, he was brash, inconsiderate, and feared by most.

The Duke's heart was a jumble of emotions as the Abbey came into view. The place had been a source of comfort and the Abbott was a dear friend. Dughall's lineage had a long history with these monks. Once again, they would be expected to save his family.

The Duke reached into the depths of his soul to summon courage. The task ahead was an ugly one and he feared the boy's reaction. He glanced to the right and watched his sons turn their horses towards the Abbey's entrance.

Luc at nineteen was a brawny lad, with straight brown hair and a winsome smile. Jamison had taken him under his wing after the adoption and trained him in horsemanship, weapons, and military strategy. In spite of his early trials, Luc had become the perfect son - loving, respectful, and loyal.

His natural son was another matter. James at ten was a handsome child with thick red curls and startling blue eyes. Highly intelligent but quick to anger, he was spoiled, manipulative, and hostile to authority.

Dughall had attempted to discipline the boy as a father should. But each time he'd been overruled by his wife who took the lad's side. He'd never been able to escape the fact that he wanted to end the pregnancy when the boy was conceived. His wife knew it, and he was convinced that the boy knew as well. Oh, he'd been proud when Keira gave birth to a male, and perhaps that was the problem. There had been celebrations, ceremonies, and outpourings of congratulation for at last he'd provided an heir.

His thoughts were dark. *Pride is the sin of sins. It transformed Lucifer, an anointed cherub of God, into the father of lies.*

He'd failed to give Keira more children so she wouldn't obsess on her son. The lass had no trouble conceiving or carrying a child to term. But each baby died within days of birth, struggling as its skin turned yellow, then blue. The cemetery was a shrine to these wee ones they'd named; Elspeth, Alan, Donald, and Jeanne. Four precious children and two broken hearts... Surely, the Morrigan had cursed them.

Dughall hadn't touched her in six months, to give her poor body a rest. The situation added to his frustration. He glanced at his sons. Luc engaged James in a lively conversation, allowing Dughall to seize a moment for private thought. Unless the boy was occupied, there was a chance that he could read his mind. Now he knew how others felt when he discerned their intentions. The boy was an expert at that.

Keira's interference has rendered me impotent, he thought. *The boy respects no man, least of all me.* He shivered as James glanced his way and then returned to his conversation. *He needs discipline so that he'll show respect. Perhaps Lord Skene will have better luck.*

It was imperative that James receive spiritual training so that his abilities could be used for good. The monks were the only ones who could provide it. The Abbey lacked the facilities to raise a boy, so the Abbott suggested that they foster him out to a local family, requiring them to bring him for weekly visits. Desperate for a change, Dughall had agreed, subject to his approval of the family. When Lord Skene's name was proposed, he could find no objection. The man was a respected Christian, wealthy, educated in northern Italy, and recently widowed with no children. No man would speak against him. Surely the Abbott knew what he was doing.

The morning had been heart wrenching. Keira implored him to change his mind, falling to her knees in supplication. She wept openly when she said goodbye, fueling the child's suspicions. Sensing the gravity of the situation, Maggie fled to her room in tears.

Dughall had refused to change his mind. His son's disrespect was bearable. But his hand had been forced when he found James kissing his sister with wandering fingers up her dress. He'd pulled them apart and struck the lad, sending Maggie into hysterics. The Duke recalled his dream after the boy was conceived, of the young man raping his sister. He had stopped hoping or fearing. The prophecy had become a part of him, like his vigorous young body or patent courage. It was time to separate brother and sister.

James turned and gave him a malevolent look. "Why is Maggie not with us?"

The Duke suppressed his thoughts using a trick that the Abbott taught him. Beginning with a chant of a vowel, he ran a vibration through his head that canceled thought.

James narrowed his eyes. "Ye can't do that for long!"

Dughall knew that the boy was right. His heart raced at the prospect of speaking his mind. The trick was to tell the truth, omitting inflammatory details. "The Abbott wishes to see only ye."

The lad's face reddened. "Ye're lying! Ye mean to leave me here."

Dughall's heart squeezed painfully. Since he struck the child, he'd been tortured with chest pains and headaches, and had begun to lose weight. If it didn't stop, he wasn't long for this world.

They arrived at the stone steps of the church and waited for the servants to dismount. Gilroy and Pratt tied their horses to a hitching post and walked away to explore the area. Upon their return, they had only one thing to report. Tied in a nearby woods was a black stallion bearing the red, blue, and green colors of the house of Skene.

James scowled. "I don't like this! What are ye up to?"

Dughall signaled for his sons to dismount. He increased the vibration in his head, switching to a memory of a screaming infant. It was one of the few things that confused the boy.

"Stop it, Father!" There was a cruelty about him that caused his brother to cringe.

"Hush, lad!" Dughall commanded. A crippling headache crept into his skull; a malady that occurred when he opposed his son. He grasped his chest as pain shot across his heart and radiated down his arms. He had no doubt that boy could inflict illness, even unto death.

Luc was startled. "Leave him alone, James! Talk to me, Brother."

"Ye're NOT my brother!" The boy turned to him and began a tirade. "Adoption is not the same as natural birth!" His eyes narrowed. "Mother understands."

Luc hung his head in genuine distress. "There's no need to say it. I gave up on Mother's love years ago."

Dughall's pain subsided. He was grateful for Luc's distraction and resolved to praise him later. He dismounted Black Lightning, straightened the saddle, and stroked the animal's mane. The horse nickered as he whispered in his ear, "Easy, Lightning. We won't be long."

"Blackheart?" Gilroy said. The burly servant stood by to take his horse. "Shall we accompany ye inside?"

Dughall stared. Why did they insist on calling him Blackheart? The name cut him to the quick. "Nay. Give the horses some apples. They are in my saddle bag."

Gilroy grunted. "As ye wish, my Lord." The servant went about the task.

Dughall, Luc, and James were about to ascend the church steps when the door at the top opened. The Abbott emerged from the doorway and descended the steps with a strange man.

The Duke looked up at his old friend. *Brother Lazarus looks frail,* he thought. The Abbott's skin seemed almost transparent and the corner of his mouth drooped. *I wonder if he suffered a slight apoplexy.* The monk looked fragile. Dughall was glad that the boy would be placed under the care of a younger man who had the stamina to face his challenges.

The two men arrived at the bottom of the steps.

Dughall was a bundle of nerves. "Greetings, Brother Lazarus. We are once again in yer debt."

The Abbott managed a lopsided smile. "Master Luc… my young friend James… and my dear Lord Drake…" He extended his aged hand to the Duke.

Dughall grasped it with both hands and squeezed affectionately. He was grateful for this man's support.

James' expression darkened. "What is *he* doing here?"

The strange man came forth from the shadows. He was a large man, well-muscled, with long brown hair and a beard and moustache. His forehead was lined with frown marks. "I am Lord Alexander Skene."

Dughall hesitated. There was a vibration about this man that disturbed him. Only once before had he felt this, in the presence of King Charles. At the time, he identified it as a whiff of evil. Obviously, in this case his senses had gone haywire. He remembered his manners and extended his hand, "Lord Dughall Gordon, Duke of Seaford."

Skene's voice was deep, "I am honored, Sir." He shook his hand and released it. "So this is the lad?"

"Aye. This is my son James."

"I won't go with him!" the boy cried. He held his breath and stomped his feet until the trees started to shake.

Luc placed a hand on his shoulder. "Brother, please. This is for the best." The lad was known for his attempts to calm his sibling.

James whipped his head around and bit his fingers. As Luc yelped in pain, he tensed his jaws, drawing blood.

"Desist at once, James!" Dughall cried.

The boy stopped suddenly, leaving Luc to cradle his hand in agony. Gilroy took charge of the injured lad, handing him a handkerchief to stop the bleeding.

The Duke had been inclined to delay the transfer, given his feeling about Lord Skene. But this was the final straw. He hoped that his intuition was wrong. "I would be grateful, Sir, if ye could teach this lad how to be a decent man. To be sure, I've failed at the task."

Lord Skene frowned. "He appears to be a handful. Yet I'm willing to take on the task. Do I have yer permission to discipline him?"

James sat on the ground and howled. The boy screwed up his face and stared at his father.

Dughall's chest pains returned with a vengeance. His thoughts were bleak. If they didn't separate, this child would be the death of him. He could barely breathe. The pain crept down his left arm, causing his hand to spasm. "Discipline him if ye must. Take him."

Lord Skene walked to the boy, bent down, and placed a hand on his shoulder. This was a brave move given what just happened to Luc.

"Come with me, lad."

To their surprise, the boy calmed and stood to join his new master. He looked up into the man's face… and smiled.

Dughall took a deep breath. The pain in his chest was subsiding. Skene and the boy seemed to be communicating on a level he didn't understand. "James…"

The boy turned. "Farewell, Father. Goodbye Luc. Tell Mother that I'll be all right." Once again he had turned from darkness to light. He looked up into Skene's eyes.

The Abbott came forth. "Good luck, Lord Skene. It seems that ye have a way with this lad." He turned to Dughall, "Not to worry, my friend. This man's good reputation precedes him."

Dughall was grateful for his intervention. He stooped and encouraged his son to come into his arms. To his amazement, the boy did. They embraced stiffly. "Be a good lad for Lord Skene. Mind yer lessons well."

"I will, Father."

" Yer mother and I will visit in a year. Write to us."

"I shall."

"Ye may keep yer horse." He signaled to Pratt to untie the reins of the stallion. The servant made haste and brought forth the animal, handing the reins to James. "Yer clothes are in the saddle packs."

Brother Lazarus smiled. "Lord Skene. I think it best that ye leave while the child is inclined to cooperate."

Skene nodded and proceeded to lead the boy into the forest.

Dughall watched as they walked into the woods. When they were out of sight, he turned to the Abbott. "Bless ye, Brother. I am in yer debt."

The Abbott embraced him. "This is the best thing for the boy. He needs to be free of his mother, under the tutelage of a man who can discipline him."

Dughall was ashamed of his failure, but at the same time he felt relief. "Will ye write to me about his progress?"

The monk smiled. "Aye. Lord Skene promised to bring him to us weekly. We will begin his training after the new moon."

"Good. Will ye train him yerself?"

"Of course." Brother Lazarus glanced at the sun. "I'm afraid that the morning has gotten away from us. Brother Luke is ill, so I must lead afternoon prayers. Farewell, my Lord."

In truth, the Duke was anxious to leave. The further away he got from James, the better off he would be. "Good bye, old friend." He watched the monk ascend the stone staircase and approached Luc.

The lad smiled through his pain. "Father."

Dughall removed the handkerchief from the boy's hand. There were bite marks that pierced his middle and forefinger. "He got ye good this time."

Luc winced. "Aye, but it's over."

"Thank ye for distracting him. Bless ye! The pains were so bad. I thought I was done for."

"Oh Father." Luc's eyes filled with tears. "Ye've been so good to me. To lose ye would be unbearable."

Dughall shuddered. "Ye must be glad that he's gone. He's been awful to ye."

"Don't say that! Those things that he said don't matter."

"He's spoiled and inconsiderate." The Duke sighed. "Would that ye were my natural son, Luc. Ye are far better suited to rule than that one."

The lad flinched. "Ye must never tell him that! Nay, ye must never even think it, for he knows what we think. He would kill me in my sleep."

Dughall knew the truth when he heard it. There was nothing he could say to allay the lad's fears. He embraced his son and filled his mind with the sound of a screaming infant, canceling the dangerous thought.

They separated and mounted their horses. As he guided Black Lightning away from the Abbey, he permitted himself to think. They would have to treat that bite wound as soon as they arrived at the castle.

Lord Skene

CHAPTER 2
OMEN

James Gordon led his horse through the thickening forest, following his new master. The large man's cape swayed as he took long strides and his boots crunched leaves underfoot. They reached his horse, a magnificent black stallion with a white mask. It snorted and pawed the ground.

Lord Skene untied the beast and took the reins. "Follow me, lad."

James cringed. The man's voice lacked the respect he was accustomed to. He followed dutifully as Skene led his horse in a southerly direction.

At the Abbey, he'd established a kinship with this man. Their minds had merged for a moment, sharing their desires and turbulent histories. He'd calmed instantly, succumbing to curiosity. The boy attempted to search the man's mind, but was met with powerful resistance. He was frustrated by his failure, but in a way he was fascinated. At last, here was a man worth challenging! He changed tactics and sent out a vibration to cause an excruciating headache. Again, Lord Skene seemed unaffected.

My father would be writhing on the ground, James thought. After walking for a mile in eerie silence, the boy got restless. He needed to take a piss, but wouldn't admit it. *This is no way to treat the son of a Duke.* His thoughts darkened. *Stinking old Lord! He thinks he can tire me out! We shall see.*

The man let out a loud fart, fouling the air behind him. The odor did not dissipate.

James fumed, *How dare he? Does he know who I am?*

Lord Skene's shoulders shook with laughter. He chuckled, and then laughed out loud.

The boy's anger flared. Months ago, he'd dissected a cat and examined its beating heart. He squeezed the incoming vessels, noting the agony it caused. A man was not much different than a cat. His father had been the proof of that. The lad gripped the reins and imagined that they were vessels surrounding Skene's heart. He applied an increase in pressure, a twist, and then a slow pull. To his surprise, there was no reaction. He gritted his teeth and gave the reins a vicious yank. The stallion groaned.

Lord Skene's voice was sharp, "Give it up, lad! Unlike yer father, I will hurt ye."

James narrowed his eyes. "Ye don't own me!"

Skene dropped the reins and whirled, backhanding the boy and splitting his lip. "For now, I do!"

James drew his breath in sharply. No one had ever treated him this way. He wanted to cry but was too proud. The boy sucked in his lip, tasted blood, and held his tongue. He looked around. Perhaps he could run away.

Lord Skene stared. "Go ahead... Run... I'll hunt ye down and beat ye 'til ye can't breathe!" He picked up the reins and continued walking.

James panicked. *I'll have to be careful with my thoughts from now on.* After a few minutes, they emerged in a clearing where a patch of sun came through. The boy noted something ominous. Skene's horse cast a shadow on the ground yet the man wasn't casting one. He heard raucous cries in the trees and looked up to see branches full of ravens and crows. His mother considered them a bad sign. "What's going on?"

Lord Skene turned to face him. "Ye're a quick study, lad. We've waited centuries for one with yer abilities."

James' skin crawled. He knew that he was in dire trouble. "Ye have no shadow! What are ye, Sir?"

Skene contorted his face into an evil grimace. "I'm a warlock, lad. Do ye know what that is?"

"Nay!"

"Ye will soon enough."

King Charles I

CHAPTER 3
ROYAL DEMISE

JANUARY 30TH 1649

THREE MONTHS LATER

LONDON ENGLAND

9:30AM - ST. JAMES' PARK

It was a bitter morning in London, with temperatures hovering in the low thirties. It was so cold that the Thames froze over. The sky was overcast, a harbinger of things to come.

King Charles knelt beside his dog; a brown and white spaniel named Rogue, and caressed his ears. "Never fear, my friend. Someone will care for you." The dog gazed at him with innocent eyes. Charles knew that he would never see him again.

"My King!" William Juxon cried. The Bishop of London looked stricken. "I would be pleased to take him to your family or keep him myself if need be."

Charles looked up. "Thank you, friend." The old man was a devoted companion. "May God smile upon you." The King stroked the dog's back and planted a kiss on his head. Then he struggled to stand, relying upon his weak ankles.

"Let me help, your Majesty!" The Bishop reached out to assist him.

Charles waved a hand. "Nay, let me do it." After a few more attempts he was upright, facing the Bishop. He gazed at the sky and sighed. "Such a beautiful morning."

Juxon raised his eyebrows.

The King smiled. "Ah… I know that it is not. Humor me. For it is the last morning that I will ever see."

"Oh…" The Bishop was close to tears, "I wish that was not true."

The King squeezed his shoulder. "Weep not for me. For this is my second marriage day. Before night I hope to be espoused to my blessed Jesus."

Juxon wept openly.

Charles barely heard him. Now that he'd said goodbye to the dog, he obsessed on events that led up to his predicament. After a long incarceration, he'd escaped to the Isle of Wight. Betrayed by the island's governor, he'd been confined to Carisbrooke Castle. From this location, he bargained with various royalist parties and signed a secret treaty with the Scots. His offer was simple. If they would invade England on Charles' behalf and restore him to the throne, he would tolerate Presbyterianism. Factions of royalist Scots invaded England, sparking a brutal second civil war. They were soundly defeated.

After failed negotiations, the King was moved to Hurst Castle in late 1648, then to Windsor Castle. For encouraging a civil war while in captivity, the monarch was accused of high treason. The House of Commons passed an Act of Parliament to create a court for his trial.

Charles had thought that this action would fail. It was dangerous to accuse a King of treason. Indeed, many potential commissioners refused to serve. Then the unthinkable happened. In early January, he'd been put on trial before sixty-eight commissioners who urged him to enter a plea. Charles refused, claiming that no court had jurisdiction over a monarch. He argued that his authority to rule had been given to him by God when he was crowned and the trial was illegal. Three times he refused to enter a plea! It was seen as an admission of guilt. The trial proceeded, witnesses were heard, and fifty-nine of the commissioners signed his death warrant.

The Chief Judge had delivered the sentence, "Charles Stuart is a tyrant, traitor, murderer, and public enemy to the good of this nation. He shall be put to death by severing his head from his body."

The memory infuriated him. *When the sentence was passed, I tried to defend myself. They would not hear me! I was taken from the court by armed soldiers like a common criminal.* He'd been granted a few days to make peace with God and say goodbye to his family.

The Bishop of London helped him to prepare for the ordeal, joining him for morning prayers and administering the Sacrament. He read the lesson for the day, 'The Passion of the Christ'. Charles found it reassuring. Like Christ the Savior, he was ready to endure this final humiliation to meet his maker. Some thought him guilty. But God would absolve him of wrongdoing.

His family was another story. His two oldest sons and younger daughter were living in Paris, under the protection of the exiled Stuart court. It gave him comfort that his son James had escaped parliamentary custody to travel to France, disguised as a woman. His bloodline would continue and eventually prevail. The only ones left in London were his wife Henrietta, his thirteen-year-old daughter Elizabeth, and nine-year-old son Henry. He hadn't seen his wife in more than four years. They'd quarreled over fundamental issues, one being her unfaithfulness. Therefore, he'd snubbed his wife and allowed only his daughter and son to visit.

Charles got revenge. His last words to his daughter were "Tell your mother that my thoughts never strayed from her, and that love should be the same to the last. I have always been faithful to her." This innocuous message pleased his children, but he knew that it would wound his wife. He'd investigated her infidelity and found that she betrayed him. He confronted her with evidence and extracted a confession about that traitorous Scot, Lord Dughall Gordon. He gritted his teeth. *How many more were there? French whore!*

Colonel Thomlinson approached. The uniformed man was in charge of the two companies of infantry guarding him. He stroked his beard nervously. "It is time, Your Majesty."

The King unconsciously touched his neck. *They will escort me to my death. Breathe, Charles! Dignity is required. You must not show fear.* He had dressed in thick underclothes so that he would not shiver from the cold. It could be interpreted as a sign of weakness.

"Your Majesty," the Colonel repeated. "The signal has been given. We must go." The guards raised the Colors and began to beat drums. A young boy accepted the leash and led the spaniel away.

The King's bowels churned. He'd eaten no breakfast, but instead had taken the Sacrament. Nothing more. He did not want to vomit. Oh, how he wished for a swig of laudanum! Charles looked around. He was surrounded by soldiers. No one would rescue him. There was no chance of escape. "I am ready."

Ah... But a handful of his supporters were there as well. He saw them remove their caps to travel bare-headed as he would. The Bishop, his attendant Thomas Herbert, and a few more... Such brave men.

Bishop Juxon placed a hand on his shoulder. "Come, your Majesty."

Charles watched as his partisans lined up before and after him. For an instant, he felt protected by his friends. The foot soldiers formed a barrier around them as they began to walk across the park with Colors flying and drums beating. The Palace of Whitehall loomed in the distance. He could see a large crowd gathered around it.

Charles held his head high. His outward manner was calm, but his mind was a raging storm. *How dare they do this to a King!*

The procession left the park and passed crowds of curious onlookers gathering to see the execution. They took the stairs up into the Gallery, then into the Cabinet Chamber. There the King continued his Devotion with the Bishop. To avoid fainting from hunger, he drank a glass of wine and ate a piece of bread at noon. Another hour passed.

Charles thought that it was cruel to make him wait. He'd been informed of a delay. The official executioner refused to do the deed. There then followed a frantic search to find someone to take his place. Finally, they'd located a man and his assistant who agreed to do it masked.

The King hoped that he knew what he was doing. An unskilled ax man could take three blows to sever a head. Charles swallowed hard. He wished that it was over.

***

1PM – WHITEHALL

Dughall stood near a platform that was located in front of the Banqueting House. He and Jamison had arrived at dawn to secure a close position. They were dressed as English gentry to avoid attracting attention. Their highly tailored clothes were made of silk and wool, and were complemented by polished boots.

Jamison scowled. "I hate these clothes. Give me a kilt and sporran any day."

Dughall nodded. "They're warm. I might keep the cape."

"Hmmphhh…"

Dughall surveyed the situation. Upon the raised platform was a scaffold which was hung round with black cloth. The ax and block was laid in the middle of the fabric, awaiting the condemned man. Pike men stood in front of the scaffold, stamping their feet against the bitter cold. Companies of foot and horse soldiers were gathering on one side of the platform towards King Street and on the other side towards Charing Cross. The horses' breath turned to vapor in the frigid air. Thousands of people gathered behind them, gentry and commoners alike. Others stayed behind windows or watched from icy rooftops. Dogs barked and peasants gossiped. The stench of body odor and piss was overwhelming.

Dughall hated the King, but wondered if it was wise to put a man of his stature to such a public death. He'd been in the city for a week and heard talk about it, ranging from disbelief to shocked outrage. Dughall had to be honest. He wanted to see the King die. The man had caused him a lot of trouble, some recent. Gilbert, deeply in debt, had returned to his estate in 1642. Ever the Royalist, he'd been persuaded to lead forces to restore the King to his rightful place. When the effort failed, he was arrested. Gilbert now sat in Edinburgh prison accused of treason. Once again, Dughall had assumed guardianship of Gilbert's son George and his two wee daughters. Bankrupt, Huntly Castle was under his control.

Their being in London was a fluke. One of the Duke's ships was heading there on a trading mission and he'd decided to accompany them. He missed the sea and found that his troubles vanished when he was upon the shining waters. When they arrived in London, they'd learned that the King was being tried for high treason. Days later, the monarch was condemned to death.

Jamison had suggested that they attend the execution. Now, he seemed to be enjoying it. "I've longed for this day. Too bad that Jenny couldn't see it." His wife had died a year ago in childbirth. He'd married a wet nurse within weeks to provide a mother for his three sons.

Dughall's conscience pricked. *Why must I see this? Is it morbid curiosity or do I have a reason?* He didn't like executions, though he'd presided over a number of them. Throngs of people experiencing strong emotions could drain a man with the Sight. This time it was complicated by personal emotions. He looked up at the scaffold and felt his blood boil. *I must see it! The King tortured my father and divided my country. He deserves to die!*

The crowd stirred and shouts rang out. Jamison stood tall to get a better look. "Look! They're bringing him out."

***

The King's heart was in his throat as he climbed the staircase of the Banqueting Hall. He walked slowly as visiting dignitaries and ambassadors had done before, beneath Rubens' paintings depicting the glory of his father's kingship. His thoughts were bleak. *How could I have fallen so far from grace? Will I get a chance to speak?*

They stopped at a door that would lead them outside. The Bishop embraced him and then proceeded to arrange his long hair.

Charles swallowed hard. "There is no need. Soon I shall put it under a cap to keep it away from the ax."

The Bishop stopped fussing, "Forgive me, Your Majesty."

The monarch sighed. "Let us proceed to the platform. This wait is torture."

Juxon stared. "Are you all right?"

Charles shook his head. "Of course not! I am innocent of the charges. Even so, I will walk in the same footsteps as Christ. Though abused, I will not abuse my enemies. I accept my lot."

The Bishop sniffled. "Spoken like a true martyr!"

"Do not let them forget, my friend." Charles didn't wait for the man to answer. He opened the door to the outside and stepped onto a platform that had been constructed outside the central windows. He noted that the structure was high off the ground, too high to address his subjects. A large crowd stared at him, no doubt awed by the display of public justice.

The King looked up at the sky. The sun had broken through the clouds, a sign, he thought, from God. Perhaps this was why the execution was delayed. His eyes widened as he saw the scaffold, draped in black fabric. In the center of the platform was the block of wood. It had attached ropes and staples in case he resisted and needed to be secured to the block. *Breathe, Charles. You must not resist.* A plain coffin lay to one side with a black pall to cover it. His heart pounded with fear. *So this is where I will meet my end.*

He wasn't alone. Standing on the platform were two hooded headsmen, Bishop Juxon, Colonel Tomlinson, Colonel Hacker, and three shorthand witnesses. They would record this unfortunate affair.

The King looked at the block where his head would lay. It was very low on the ground. He might stumble as he kneeled. "Is there no higher?"

Colonel Hacker replied, "No, Sir."

Charles balked. So now it was *Sir.* "How can I kneel at something so low?"

Hacker's eyes narrowed. "You shall lie face down."

Charles was mortified. *How undignified!* He knew that his subjects would not hear him, so in hopes of delivering a message, he addressed Colonel Tomlinson. "I doubt that my subjects will hear me. I shall therefore speak a word unto you here. Indeed I could hold my peace, if I did not think that holding my peace would make some men think that I submit to the guilt as well as to the punishment. But I think it is my duty to God first, and to my country, for to clear myself both as an honest man, a good king, and a good Christian."

The Colonel seemed uncomfortable, but motioned for him to proceed.

Charles cleared his throat, "I shall begin by saying that I am innocent. In truth, it is unnecessary, for all the world knows that I never did begin a war with the two houses of Parliament. I call God to witness - to whom I must shortly make an account - that I never intended to encroach upon their privileges. They began upon me: it is the Militia they began upon. They confessed that the Militia was mine, but they thought it fit to have it from me. And to be short, if anybody will look to the dates of commissions - of their commissions and mine - and likewise to the declarations, they will see clearly that they began these troubles, not I. So that as to the guilt of these enormous crimes that are laid against me, I pray that God will clear me of it." He coughed. "God forbid that I should lay blame upon the two Houses of Parliament. I hope they are free of this guilt, for I believe that ill instruments between them and me have been the chief cause of all this bloodshed."

Colonel Hacker frowned. "Enough. It is time, Sir."

"Wait!" Charles cried, and pointed to the Bishop. "This good man will bear me witness that I have forgiven all the world and even those in particular who have been the chief causers of my death. Who they are, God knows; I do not desire to know. I pray God forgive them. But this is not all. My charity must go further. It commands me not only to forgive particular men, but all men to secure the peace of the kingdom."

The headsman bent down to pick up the ax.

Charles flinched. "Blunt not the ax that will hurt me! It must stay sharp."

The executioner stepped back.

The King knew that they would not allow him to talk much longer. "For the people - and truly I desire their liberty and freedom as much as anybody - I tell you that their liberty and their freedom consists of having a government of laws by which their life and their goods may be most their own. It is not for having a share in government, sirs; that is nothing pertaining to them. A subject and a sovereign are different things. If I would have given way to an arbitrary way for to have all laws changed according to the power of the sword, I need not have come here. Therefore I tell you - that I am the martyr of the people."

Hacker frowned. "Desist, Sir! We must proceed."

Charles concentrated to keep his hands from shaking. He spoke faster, "I declare before you that I die a Christian according to the profession of the Church of England as I found it left me by my father." It was time. Turning to Colonel Hacker, he said, "Take care that they do not put me to pain." Then to the executioner, "I shall say short prayers, and when I thrust out my hands, do it."

The Bishop spoke in soothing tones. "Your Majesty. There is but one stage more. This stage is turbulent and troublesome. It is a short one. But you may consider it will soon carry you from Earth to Heaven, and there you shall find a great deal of joy and comfort."

Charles sniffled. "I go from a corruptible to an incorruptible crown."

The Bishop helped him put on a nightcap, tucking all hair underneath so that it would not trouble the executioner.

The King took off his doublet and handed Juxon the Badge of the Order of Saint George. "Give this to my oldest son." He then put on his cloak and reminded the masked headsman, "Wait for the sign... When I thrust out my hands like this... Do it fast."

Charles prayed with his eyes and hands lifted to heaven. Then with a pounding heart, he dropped down and laid his head upon the block. It was as cold as ice.

Breathe, Charles! Think of a beautiful garden. Your beloved dog is there.

Oh, why can I not see him? He couldn't control the scenes that flooded his mind. His overbearing father.... His exiled children... His wife servicing her Scottish lover! Terrible last thoughts. *My God, my God, why hast thou forsaken me?*

He swallowed hard and stretched out his hands.

***

Dughall watched the King speak. He couldn't hear words, but he sensed the emotions of a man steeped in self-righteousness. The monarch felt no regret for his actions. At last, the man dropped down and laid his head on the block.

Dughall couldn't resist. What would it be like to lose your head? He closed his eyes and felt a pervasive cold against his neck. The block was coated with ice crystals and the platform was not much warmer. He then saw what the King saw – scenes of his father, his children, and his wife betraying him. But with whom? The scoundrel's face turned and he recognized himself. The Queen had told her husband about them.

Anger consumed the monarch's final moments. That's when he stretched out his hands, signaling for the ax to fall.

Dughall was shocked. *The King knew about our rendezvous!* The monarch had summoned him several times after the first war. He'd wisely sent emissaries in his place. *Thank God I refused to meet with him.*

The bright ax flashed and with one blow, the King's head was severed from his body. Dughall flinched as their connection was broken. He opened his eyes and stroked his neck. "Oh, God."

Jamison placed a hand on his shoulder. "Are ye all right, my Lord?"

"Aye."

"We should return to the tavern and celebrate! The King is dead."

The executioner held up the head, displaying it to the spectators. The eyes and mouth opened slightly and blood dripped from the neck. A great groan went up from the crowd.

Dughall watched the executioners place the body and head in a simple casket and cover it with a black velvet cloth. With the help of the Bishop and Colonel Tomlinson, they carried the casket into the Banqueting House.

Colonel Hacker allowed spectators to approach for a price, so Jamison climbed the platform and paid to dip his handkerchief in the monarch's blood. Some thought that the blood of a king could cure illness, but the Duke knew what Jamison wanted it for. It symbolized freedom for the Scots.

Dughall was overcome with the crowd's emotions – shock, outrage, anger, and fear. Some were jubilant in a macabre sort of way. He felt sick to his stomach and stepped back from the platform. Suddenly, he sensed a different emotion – a girl sobbing for the loss of her father. She was being comforted by her mother. Could it be?

Time stood still as he scanned the crowd for the pair. Then his eyes lighted upon two petite women, disguised as upper class English gentry. Both wore plain black dresses and hooded capes. The younger one had her back to him and her shoulders shook with grief. Her mother was facing him. Unmistakably Henrietta, she held her daughter's face and comforted her.

Dughall had vowed to never see her again. But now he was torn. No matter what passed between them, she'd saved his father and uncle from a horrible death. It would be an act of decency to pay his respects. He took a deep breath and walked through the crowd to greet them.

Her face was serene, unlike what he expected for a woman who just lost her husband. When he arrived, she looked up at him with dark eyes that seemed to search his soul. He sensed a myriad of emotions – grief, sadness, and a bit of anger at him. Oh, aye. He'd rejected her offer to meet again.

Dughall bowed slightly and spoke in low tones, "My Queen."

Henrietta sighed. "I'm afraid that is not so anymore. My husband is dead." She turned her child to face him. "This is my daughter, Elizabeth. Mind your manners. Lord Gordon is a friend."

The young girl sniffled. "Pleased to meet you, Sir." She was the image of her mother.

Dughall felt her grief. Whatever the King had done, he'd been a beloved father to this girl. He reached in his coat and handed her a handkerchief. "I am sorry for yer loss."

Elizabeth accepted it. "Thank you, Sir." She turned to her mother and resumed crying.

Henrietta gazed into his eyes and spoke softly, "I would like to see you again. We leave for Paris tomorrow, where I shall reside."

He blushed. "I can not..."

"There are no more excuses. Ask for me at the Palais du Louvre."

Dughall's loins stirred as he sensed her intentions. They seemed to have a mind of their own, separate from his morals. My God, she was beautiful!

She held his eyes with her steady gaze. "He can't hurt you now," she whispered. "Come back to me, Lord Gordon."

Dughall didn't know what to say. He'd made a pledge to be faithful. Yet to say so would be inappropriate. She was a powerful lady. He didn't wish to snub her. Like an English gentleman, he took her hand and kissed it. "Farewell, my Queen. I will never forget the things ye taught me."

She smiled. "Nor, I."

He kissed her hand again, sending shivers through both of them.

She whispered, "I shall be free to marry again in a year."

Dughall had to get away before he did something inappropriate. He released her hand and bowed slightly. "I shall leave ye to yer grieving daughter."

The young Lord turned abruptly and walked to the platform to find Jamison. His conscience pricked. *I should have turned her down. What kind of man am I?*

***

Henrietta's mind raced as she watched him walk away. He was her most intuitive lover. The years had been good to him. She longed to ask him to accompany her to Paris, but it wouldn't be appropriate. Common decency dictated that she mourn the passing of her husband for a year.

Poor Charles, she thought. She'd been shocked by his appearance when he stepped onto the platform. There were obvious signs of strain. His face was haggard and his hair was thin and grey. Nearly fifty, he looked like an old man. *He tried to hurt me with his cryptic message,* she thought with bitterness. *But he failed. I wonder if he saw Lord Gordon in the crowd.*

Elizabeth hugged her tightly.

Henrietta stroked her hair. "Soyez courageux, ma cher. Ton père ne veux pas que tu pleures."

The girl patted her face with the handkerchief. "Je vais, ma mère."

Henrietta grieved for her. If nothing else, Charles had been a loving father. He'd been a good husband too until he got consumed by religious crusades. She hated to see him die this way, but on some level she understood the frustration of his subjects. England had been divided by civil wars for almost a decade. There was a bright side to this. Perhaps her son Charles would be restored to the throne. It wouldn't be hard to convince him to bring back Catholicism as the state religion.

Her thoughts returned to Lord Gordon. Was he still married? Widowed? She hadn't thought to ask. In any case, they could be lovers. Lovers… She hadn't made love in five years, since the birth of her last child. Charles had accused her of infidelity and refused to touch her after that. He even questioned the parentage of the baby. *I've waited five years. I can wait another twelve months.*

Lord Gordon had the body and temperament of a young man – strong, muscular, and willing. She smiled as she recalled what he said. "I will never forget the things you taught me." She'd recognized the look in his eyes – the look of a man who had been deprived for too long. It was a matter of time until he came to her bed.

Lord Huntly

CHAPTER 4
BAD NEWS

FEBRUARY 20 1649

3 WEEKS LATER

EDINBURGH SCOTLAND

8:00AM – EDINBURGH CASTLE

It was a cold morning in Edinburgh. A downpour had thinned to a drizzle and the sky was overcast. It was a fitting backdrop for news that arrived that morning.

Lord Huntly stood in his quarters, gazing out the iron-barred window. His thoughts were bleak. He'd just been informed that King Charles had been beheaded in London on the 30th of January. His stomach turned. "All is lost. With my benefactor dead, they will come for me."

Gilbert thought about the events that led up to his predicament. He'd been in prison for more than a year. When the King asked his supporters to restore him to the throne, Gilbert answered the call.

Against his brother's advice, he'd raised an army and fought Covenanters who were opposed to the restoration. Briefly joining with Montrose's forces, the royalist Gordons fought bravely. Lord Aboyne was killed and his brother Lewis wounded. Lord Huntly managed to escape with a few supporters. Relentlessly pursued by Covenanter troops, they lived in farm houses, dens, and on sequestered hills. Towards the end of December 1647, Gilbert was captured. Worn out with grief and fatigue, he was carried under guard to Edinburgh to await trial for treason. Prison had been difficult for him. The man looked like he'd aged twenty years.

King Charles had written to the Earl of Lanark, requesting that he make the utmost effort to save Lord Huntly's life. This act had kept Gilbert from the headman's ax. But now Charles was dead.

Gilbert sat at a desk and held his head in his hands. "Dear God! What will become of me?" He cried bitterly for the loss of his King, his freedom, and his beloved family. After a while, there were no more tears. Gilbert opened a drawer and took out writing paper, a quill, and an inkwell. He took a deep breath, inked the pen, and poised it to write. Soon, words flowed from his heart to the paper.

My dear brother, Dughall. I assume that ye have heard about the King's execution. As ye can imagine, this places my life in a precarious position. It will not be long before they try me for treason and put me to death. Do not worry about me. I have accepted my fate. My only wish is that ye bring Bridget and the children to me for a final visit. Do not tarry! I appreciate all that ye've done for me and my family. No one could ask for a better brother. - Love, Gilbert

He folded the letter and sealed it with wax. Then with a heavy heart, he rang for a guard to post the correspondence.

CHAPTER 5
TO RENEW A LOVE

MARCH 10TH 1649
18 DAYS LATER

DRAKE CASTLE, THE BATH CHAMBER

The Duke pulled on a shirt, fastened the pearl buttons, and stepped into his best kilt. As he pinned the garment, he pondered the events of the last few days.

***

Dughall had received a letter from Gilbert, describing his dire predicament. After recovering from the shocking news, he faced the unpleasant task of telling Bridget. His sister-in-law was devastated.

The Duke was an emotional mess. The government and cause he supported would now put his brother to death. He felt betrayed and utterly helpless.

Murdock had inspired him with an innocent remark, "I once heard a story about a woman who saved her condemned husband by exchanging clothes with him."

The Duke liked the idea and formulated a plan. Only one man knew about it – his faithful servant Jamison. There was no time to waste. He directed the captain of the Black Swan to provision the ship to sail to Edinburgh and beyond.

Dughall knew the risks. Gilbert was imprisoned in Edinburgh Castle. The fortress was a model of security. His plan was fraught with danger. There was a chance that he might not survive.

***

The Duke left the bath chamber and began to walk to the Lord's chamber. There was something important he needed to do. He might never see Keira again and he wanted to make love to her. It had been months since they'd been intimate. It wasn't her fault. She hadn't denied him. After four lost children, he'd avoided getting her pregnant.

Dughall longed for the love they shared before his illness, the war, and their lost children. In truth, they'd both changed. He'd been hardened by responsibility and tainted by his tryst with the Queen. She'd been affected by her brush with the Morrigan and an unreasonable obsession with their son. Could they put it aside and find love again?

He arrived at his bed chamber and knocked. When he heard her voice, he entered.

Keira stood at the dressing table, clad in a green silk robe which was tied at the waist. Her long raven hair was loose around her shoulders. She seemed surprised to see him. "Are ye leaving?"

Dughall came to her and stroked her cheek. "Not yet." He cupped her face and kissed her tenderly. "We have some time." He untied the sash of her robe and let it drop.

She blushed. "Do ye want to make love?"

"Oh, aye." He smiled. "But I have a favor to ask. Think of me as the lad ye met in the forest."

He voice was soft, "We were innocent then."

"Aye. It was wonderful. I shall think of ye as the lass I dreamed of." He pulled his shirt over his head and dropped it onto a chair. Next came the pin... the kilt... and the socks... At last, they were naked. He took her hand and led her to the bed. They lay down and faced each other.

Her green eyes misted. "It's been too long. I've missed ye, Husband."

Dughall held his breath as he stroked her breasts. The pregnancies hadn't affected them. They were firm, pink, and hardening at the tips. "So bonny... Oh, lass. Ye haven't aged a day." Doing what she liked best, he positioned himself above her and began to suckle them. First gently, capturing the buds between his lips, circling and caressing... Then firmly, nibbling and sucking.

She cried out, "Oh!"

Dughall's heart pounded with desire. Her skin was soft and she smelled like the essence of a woman. He ran his tongue between her breasts and moved lower. He entered her navel, making her shiver.

"Oh!"

The Duke's heart raced as he lowered his head to her mound. He spread her womanly petals and blew on them. "Do ye want this?"

"Aye!" Keira gasped. "But there is something that ye've always wanted. Tell me about it."

Dughall was stunned. Would she do what he wanted? His member throbbed in anticipation. He turned and faced her feet. There was only one way to tell her. "As I do for ye, ye must do for me." He could hear her take a breath as he spread her nest of downy curls.

"How, Husband?"

"Take it in yer mouth." He didn't wait for an objection, but parted her petals. His Sight guided his tongue to the bud and encouraged him to linger.

Then it happened. Dughall felt her grasp his manhood and take in her mouth. He groaned. To his surprise, she took it further.

They continued like this for a half an hour. When he could stand no more, he changed position and thrust his member inside her. There was no hesitation and no fear. A child could come if it was meant to. The lovers rocked until they climaxed.

Now they lay side by side, thoroughly exhausted. Dughall stroked her cheek. "Thank ye, lass. I will always remember this."

She touched a finger to his lips. "Shhhh... Must ye go?"

He sighed. "Aye. I must take Bridget and the children to my brother."

"Poor Gilbert. Will ye be in danger?"

Dughall couldn't lie. "Perhaps. Don't worry. Ye've given me the best gift. A reason to live... As the river returns to the sea, I shall return to ye."

She sighed. "Ah... Poetry. I've missed it."

Dughall nodded, "I want us to start over. Promise me."

"I promise."

He got out of bed and began to dress. "I must go now." As he pinned his kilt, he made a silent vow. *My sweet lass. Upon my heart, my body, and my soul... I will never again be unfaithful.*

As he kissed her goodbye, he came to a realization. *I must survive. She needs me more than ever. I just fathered a child.*

Lord Balmerino

CHAPTER 6
EXECUTING GILBERT

MARCH 21ST 1649

11 DAYS LATER

EDINBURGH SCOTLAND

4PM – EDINBURGH CASTLE

Lord Huntly had been tried for treason, convicted, and sentenced to death on the 16th of March. He was given a few days to make peace with God and visit with his family. A Catholic priest gave him last rites. Then by God's grace, Dughall arrived by ship with Bridget, the children, Jamison, and Connor.

Now, Gilbert sat in an overstuffed chair, visiting with his wife and children. Bridget looked bonny in a white wool dress. His eleven-year-old son George was clad in his clan's colors in a kilt, jacket, shirt, and sporran. His eight-year-old and six-year-old daughters, Anne and Mary, were attired in blue dresses with lace collars.

Gilbert held his daughters close and kissed them on the cheek.

He struggled to hold back his tears. "Promise me that ye will obey yer mother."

They stood back and spoke in unison. "We will, Father." The wee lassies hadn't been told about the impending execution.

Gilbert nodded to Bridget and she escorted the girls out of the room to their uncle. He stood. "Come closer, my son."

George approached his father with trepidation. He hugged him tight and then looked up into his eyes. "Is it true, Father?"

Gilbert tipped the lad's chin. "I'm afraid so. Tomorrow, they will take me to the Market Cross and strike my head from my body."

George flinched. "*Why*, Father?"

Gilbert held the boy's shoulders. "They say that I committed treason, but it isn't true. I fought to restore my King to his rightful place. Always remember – yer father is not a traitor."

The boy sniffled. "I will remember."

"Upon my death, ye will be granted the title of Lord Huntly. Uncle Dughall will serve as yer guardian until ye are old enough to fill the role. Until then, take care of yer mother and sisters."

"I shall."

Gilbert embraced the boy. "Be brave, my son. I love ye." After a few moments, they separated. "Join yer sisters and send yer mother in here." Tears sprang to his eyes as he watched him walk away. He would never see him again.

Bridget entered and hurried to him. They embraced tightly and ended with a desperate kiss. At last, they separated. "Oh, Gilbert. I don't know what to say."

He swallowed hard. "There are no words, lass. For tomorrow, I die." He stroked her blonde hair. "Don't cry. Let us make our last minutes together pleasant. He began to tell her what she meant to him, "My bonny lass... Ye have been a good wife and mother..."

***

THE HALLWAY

Dughall stood with Jamison, watching his nephew and nieces from afar. He'd sent them to the end of the hallway with Connor so that he could have a private conversation. The Duke was dressed to the hilt in the red and blue colors of the Drake clan. He wore a kilt, a shirt, an ornate cloak with a lion's head brooch, a sporran made from a fox's head, and a flamboyant hat that drew attention away from his face. He wanted all who saw it to remember the clothes, not the man. They were not armed, having left their weapons at the front gate. Jamison had spoken to the constable and convinced him to leave them alone.

The servant was agitated. "My Lord. Ye must not do this!"

Dughall stared. "I will if he agrees."

Jamison clenched his teeth. "This is too dangerous."

Dughall ignored his concerns. "We've discussed this. Ye know what to do."

Jamison's shoulders slumped. "Ye are as stubborn as yer grandfather."

"I shall take that as a compliment." Dughall grasped his arm. "Remember what we agreed upon. If I don't survive, take my family to Gilbert."

The door opened and Bridget emerged. She approached Dughall and spoke softly, "He wants to see ye." She started to cry and fled to her children.

"Poor lass." Dughall hesitated for a moment. Then he addressed his servant. "Ye've been a brave and loyal friend. No matter what happens, I've been proud to know ye."

Jamison swallowed hard. "It's been a pleasure, my Lord. Rest assured. I will do as ye wish."

Dughall left his servant and entered his brother's quarters. The man was sitting in a chair, sobbing. He approached him. "Brother?"

Gilbert stood and embraced him. "Forgive me for crying. I've been holding it back all morning. Bridget... My son... My wee daughters... I will never see them again!"

They separated, and Gilbert stared. "I've never seen ye dressed so strangely."

Dughall was solemn. "That brings me to my point. There is a way for ye to avoid this unpleasantness."

Gilbert's eyes widened. "What way?"

Dughall smiled. "I love ye, Gilbert. I do not wish to see ye executed. There is a ship waiting in the harbor to take ye and yer family to the colonies. A box of gold and silver is on board to sustain ye. All ye have to do is walk out of this chamber."

Gilbert frowned. "How?"

Dughall took a breath. "When we arrived, I took great pains so that no one would talk to me." He pointed to his hat and clothes. "It's likely that this costume is all they saw."

Gilbert's hands shook. "What are ye proposing?"

"Change clothes with me and leave."

His eyes widened. "Ye will take my place?"

"Aye."

"They will kill ye!"

Dughall knew that it was possible. For his brother's sake, he tried to dismiss it. "Jamison will stay behind. When they take me to the Market Cross, he'll tell them who I am. They won't execute an innocent man."

Gilbert paced the room. "Dear God! I was ready to die. What ye propose is dangerous! Why must I face this decision?"

Dughall squeezed his shoulder. "Are ye afraid to die?"

"Oh, aye."

"I am not."

Gilbert took a ragged breath. "I wish I had yer faith, Brother. In God and man. Are ye sure about this?"

"Aye." Dughall began to undress even though his brother hadn't agreed. "Give me yer clothes."

Gilbert stared for a long moment. "It's a cowardly act, but I will do it for my son." He began to undress.

The two brothers exchanged clothes without another word.

***

Gilbert left the chamber, disguised as the Duke of Seaford. With his hat tipped forward to disguise his face, they proceeded to the exit and claimed their weapons.

Connor, having been apprised of the situation, led his master and his family to the harbor, where they boarded a ship and sailed for the colonies. They stood on deck and prayed for the man who freed Gilbert.

***

Dughall looked down at his clothes. It had been a long time since he'd worn the Gordon colors or a garment this shabby. Gilbert had been incarcerated for more than a year. His clothing was thin and full of patches.

After an hour, he presumed that the escape was successful. No alarm had been sounded. No prisoners had been brought to this wing. No guard had burst in demanding an explanation. Now, he needed to work on his appearance so that he could fool them until his ship departed the harbor. He stood in front of a mirror, took a pair of scissors, and began to trim his beard to look more like Gilbert. Lastly, he chopped three inches off of his long hair. "There! I look something like him."

There was a knock on the door.

"Who is it?"

"McGee, my Lord. Come to bring yer dinner."

Dughall hurried to the chair and sat with his head in his hands. "I am praying for the salvation of my soul." He took a breath. "Please leave my meal on the table."

The door creaked open and a servant entered. Dughall heard him place a tray on the table.

McGee cleared his throat. "Forgive me, my Lord, but I will not see ye again. It has been an honor and a pleasure serving ye."

Dughall never raised his head, but answered in a husky voice, "Thank ye. I will not forget yer kindness." He kept his eyes covered. "Leave me to my prayers and my fate."

Dughall heard footsteps and the sound of a door closing. "Thank, God." He'd passed the test and bought time for his brother to get away.

He sat at the table, ate his meal, and then prepared for bed.

Dropping to his knees, he prayed to God. First in gratitude for the life of his brother... Then for his family who had no idea what he was doing... Lastly, he prayed for his soul. For tomorrow, he could be executed.

7AM – THE NEXT DAY

The Duke rose early and dressed in his brother's clothes. He didn't comb his hair. Instead, he messed it so that he could draw it around his face. There was a knock at the door. Dughall opened it a crack and heard a servant girl offer him breakfast. He refused it and sent her away.

At eight o'clock, the Magistrates of Edinburgh arrived to escort him to the Market Cross. The constable of Edinburgh Castle escorted them into Gilbert's chamber.

Dughall suspected that the constable knew Gilbert, so he kept his head low.

"Lord Huntly?" one man commanded.

"Aye."

"By order of the Committee of Estates, we are here to take ye to the place of execution." The man tied his wrists with a length of rope, while another placed a black hood over his head.

Dughall felt a wave of panic. He hated being in narrow spaces. It took some effort to swallow his fear. Then he felt himself being walked out of the room with a soldier on each arm. They traversed what seemed like hallways, stairs to a lower floor, and a flagstone courtyard. It sounded like a grille to a portcullis was raised. As far as he could tell, they were leaving the castle. Soldiers lifted him into a wagon, which got underway.

Dughall's heart pounded with fear. The Market Cross wasn't far. There awaited a block and ax. He was too young to die. He hoped that his servant would save him.

✳✳✳

Jamison stayed the night at a tavern, rose at dawn, and headed for the Market Cross. When he arrived at the market square, he couldn't get near the cross. Thousands of men, women, and children had gathered to see the execution of Lord Huntly. He elbowed through the crowd until he got within forty feet of the cross.

He stood tall to get a better look. A platform had been constructed, upon which a block and ax lay. Positioned around the platform were foot soldiers, pike men, and the executioner, identifiable by his large arm muscles. To the right were a small group of gentlemen; no doubt members of the Committee that passed judgment.

He'd racked his brain thinking about what to do. No matter what the risk, he would make a loud commotion, insisting that this wasn't Lord Huntly. If they wouldn't listen, he'd charge the platform with his knife. Jamison's nerves were on fire. "I must save him!"

The crowd buzzed with excitement as the Magistrates arrived driving a horse-drawn wagon with the prisoner in the back. His hands were bound and he was wearing a black hood. The crowd made way for its passage and it stopped in front of the Market Cross. The prisoner was lifted to his feet and onto the platform.

Jamison began to press through the crowd, stepping on toes and making enemies.

***

Dughall's heart was in his throat as they lifted him onto the platform. The ride through the market had been confusing. While the hood obscured his view, he'd heard mumblings and insults from people waiting to see him die. The wagon was unsteady and the smell of the crowd was revolting. At last, they removed his hood. He stared at the throngs of angry people.

"Let the traitor speak!" a man cried. "Let him speak!"

Dughall had to stop this charade. He wasn't Gilbert and had to let them know it. He held up his bound hands. "I am NOT Lord Huntly!"

"Boo!" "Liar!" "Traitor!" The crowd went wild. Obviously, they didn't believe him. A rock sailed through the air and landed at his feet.

Dughall scanned the crowd for Jamison. At last he spotted him, about thirty feet away. The crowd was thick and unruly. A brute of a man blocked his way, refusing to let him pass. The servant wouldn't arrive in time. Dughall dodged a rock and shouted at the top of his lungs, "Ye have the wrong man. I am NOT Lord Huntly!"

The executioner climbed onto the platform. "Time's up." He tucked Dughall's hair under a cap, pushed him to his knees, and forced his head onto the block. He growled in his ear, "Give me trouble and I'll take three strokes to kill ye."

Dughall's heart pounded with fear. "I won't resist." The situation was in God's hands. He said a prayer for his soul.

***

Lord Balmerino stood near the platform, waiting with the other Committeemen. He would be glad when this ugly business was over. He saw them lift the condemned man to the platform and remove his hood. The prisoner looked like a vagabond. His clothes were shabby and his hair was messed. Lord Huntly spoke words that he couldn't hear and the crowd went wild. They would have to get this over with soon or risk a riot. He signaled to the executioner to climb the platform.

That's when he heard the prisoner shout, "Ye have the wrong man. I am NOT Lord Huntly!"

Lord Balmerino climbed the platform just as the headsman raised the ax. "Wait!" He grabbed the prisoner's hair, lifted his head, and looked into his eyes. *By God! It's that idiot Lord Drake. The man has more courage than sense. I should let him die in his brother's place.*

Dughall spoke through parched lips. "Help me."

Lord Balmerino relented. Once, he himself had been condemned to death and pardoned at the last moment. As daft as he was, this man had stood up to the King and rescued two men from the Tower. He'd like to hear *that* story. He turned to the crowd and shouted, "This is NOT Lord Huntly!"

***

Dughall was taken back to Edinburgh Castle. There he was beaten by soldiers and interrogated for hours. He told them the truth, except about Gilbert's destination. He claimed that his brother boarded a ship for France, where the Gordons had relatives. At last, they escorted him to a private study and sat him at a desk.

Dughall took stock of his injuries. The beating he received made what his father did to him seem trivial. His ribs were bruised, possibly cracked. His left arm had been cruelly twisted, but it seemed to function. He couldn't count the times he was pummeled in the face and head. One man struck him with a chain.

Lord Balmerino entered the room and took a seat across from him. He stared. "I see that they roughed ye up."

Dughall shrugged. "It was worth it." He tried to smile, but it caused him pain. His lip was split.

"I knew that they would beat ye. There was nothing I could do about it."

Dughall grunted. "I owe ye my life."

"Ye do."

"If there's anything I can do for ye, ask."

Lord Balmerino put his fingertips together. "There's just one thing I want. Tell me how ye rescued those men from the Tower."

Dughall had promised that he would never tell another soul. But this man had rescued him from a horrible death. Perhaps he could keep a secret. "Will ye promise to never tell anyone?"

"Aye."

He started at the beginning, describing the visit he and Gilbert paid to the King. His trip to the observatory with the Queen... Her request to be his lover... Honoring that request was the only way to save his stepfather and uncle. He'd proposed a deal and she accepted. He became her sexual slave. Then he described the details.

The older man leaned back in his chair, a smile growing on his face. He slapped the desk. "Ye fornicated with the Queen?"

Dughall reddened. "Aye."

"Excellent! Ye cuckolded the evil bastard. Did he know?"

"Aye. He found out."

"Ha! Cuckolded by a Scot!" Lord Balmerino opened a drawer and took out a decanter and two squat glasses. He poured three fingers of whisky into each and handed one to Dughall. "Ye've got more courage than sense, but I like ye."

They talked awhile, mainly about the peculiarities of the King and Queen. Finally, Dughall asked the question. "Am I free to go?"

Balmerino smiled. "Aye. I'll escort ye to the gate. Yer servant has been frantic, inquiring about ye." They stood and shook hands. "Oh. There's one more thing. "Yer brother's lands are forfeit. He must never set foot in Scotland."

So Huntly was lost to the Gordons. Dughall felt a pang of regret. "I'll make sure that Gilbert knows that."

***

Dughall met Jamison outside the gate and embraced him. "I'm glad to see ye."

"My Lord!" Jamison stood back. "Ye look like hell!"

He loved this man like a brother. "I'm alive and whole. That's all that matters."

There was anguish in his voice, "I tried to save ye, but I couldn't get close."

"It's all right, friend. Sometimes God works in mysterious ways."

They started walking towards the market. After a few blocks, Jamison stopped at an inn. "It's best that we avoid the harbor. I've acquired two horses for the ride home. Not stallions, mind ye. But they'll have to do."

"Where are they?"

"Stabled around back. But first let's get a drink and a meal."

"I'm for that."

They entered the inn, grateful for their friendship and the fortunate turn of events.

Keira Gordon

Chapter 7
Homecoming

March 31 1649

9 Days Later

DRAKE CASTLE

It had been a long painful journey. The roads north were rough and many were flooded with water. The horses they acquired lacked proper shoes and had to be traded before they were halfway home. Most accommodations were primitive and they never found a healer.

The Duke suspected that his ribs were cracked. He experienced pain when he took a deep breath. It got worse when he bent or twisted his body. Nine days of pain had brought him to the brink of exhaustion. He had to get home so that his wife could wrap him.

Now, Dughall and Jamison were approaching Drake Castle. A sharp whistle went up when they were spotted, and the main gate opened.

"Blackheart!" Gilroy shouted. The burly man helped him dismount and took their horses. "Ye look awful."

Dughall knew that he looked bad. That morning, he'd glanced in a mirror. His bruises had turned a sickly yellow. "I'm heading for the surgery. Send my wife and mother to me."

"As ye wish, my Lord." The servant led the horses away and handed them to a stable boy.

Jamison frowned. "Shall I accompany ye?"

Dughall winced. "Nay, friend. It's been a long journey. Go home to yer wife and children." He watched him walk away and then entered the castle and took a flight of stairs. It hurt his chest to climb more than a few steps at a time. He desperately needed to rest in bed.

Murdock caught up with him on the second level. "My Lord!" He took his arm and steadied him. "Ye look awful. Let me help ye to bed."

The Duke took a shallow breath to avoid the pain. "Nay. Take me to the surgery."

Murdock guided him down a hallway and up a staircase to another wing. At last they reached the surgery and entered. No one was within. The servant lit an oil lamp on the sideboard. "Who did this?"

Dughall grimaced as he jumped up on the table. "Never mind. Help me get my shirt off."

Murdock unbuttoned his shirt and tried to slip it off his right shoulder.

"Ow! Cut it off."

The servant got a pair of scissors and proceeded to cut his shirt. "Ach! Ye're a mass of breaks and bruises. What happened?"

"It's a long story. I was beaten by guards at Edinburgh Castle."

The door opened and Keira entered. She looked relieved and frightened at the same time. "Husband!"

Dughall tried to smile, but his lip hurt. "Leave us, Murdock." The servant left the room in a hurry.

Keira came closer. The healer in her prevailed as she examined his chest. "I see cuts and bruises, a few of them deep. Her hand pressed into one of them. "Does this hurt?"

He gritted his teeth. "Aye! It hurts when I breathe. I think that my ribs are cracked."

"Then let's start with that." She extracted a roll of cloth from a drawer and cut it into long strips. "How did this happen?"

Dughall coughed. "I freed Gilbert. He and his family are on their way to the Colonies."

"That's good news."

"Aye. When the magistrates found out, they ordered the guards to beat me."

She clucked her tongue. "Can ye hold up yer arms?"

He smiled sheepishly as he did. "Perhaps, a wee bit."

She wrapped the cloth around his chest to immobilize the area. "I can't tie this too tight. Ye won't be able to breathe properly. Ye'll get pneumonia."

He grunted. "Then leave it loose. It feels better already."

Keira fastened the wrapping with a silver clip. "I'll make ye willow bark tea to blunt the pain and take down swelling." She began to attend to his face, sponging cuts with witch hazel. "What did they do to ye?"

"Ow!" It burned. "They pummeled me with their fists. They twisted my arm. A man lashed me with an iron chain. Ye haven't seen the half of it. Ow! Lord Balmerino rescued me."

"Thank the Goddess." She got out a needle and thread. "There is one cut that we should stitch."

"The one on my hairline?"

"Aye."

"Nay, bother. It's been nine days. Too long. I guess I'll have a scar."

Keira put down the needle. "What am I going to do with ye?" She kissed him lightly, being mindful of his injuries.

"Mmmmmm... If this is the cure, I'm going to like it."

She smiled. "Ye must be all right. Yer loins are swelling."

"Ha! At least my member's not broken."

Keira giggled. "Oh, Husband. I love ye."

"I love ye, too." He stroked her cheek. "I meant what I said. I want us to start over."

The door opened and Jessie entered. "God in heaven! What happened?"

"Gilbert is free. I'm alive and whole. I'll tell ye about it later." Dughall winced as he smiled. "Ow! What's for supper?"

Jessie grinned. "It's a good sign if his belly's complaining. Let's get him to bed. We will bring him supper."

The women helped him jump off the table and led him out of the surgery. He would spend the next few weeks recuperating.

Lord Drake

CHAPTER 8
A FRIEND IN NEED

MAY 20 1649

7 WEEKS LATER

DEER ABBEY

It was a fine spring morning, with clear skies and warm weather. The air was sweet with the aroma of apple blossoms and spring honey. Monks and servants scurried about, tending to their duties. The day was bright but the mood was somber. The Abbott of Deer Abbey was dying.

Their beloved leader was expecting a visitor, the Duke of Seaford, Dughall Gordon. Some said that he clung to life for this one purpose. Word had just arrived that the Duke was at the gates of the Abbey.

Three days ago, the Abbott suffered an apoplexy. When he woke that morning soaked in piss, he didn't have the strength to get out of bed. His arm was useless and one leg was lame. He prayed for Jesus to take him, but Brother Luke came instead. He'd been bedridden since.

This morning, the monk had gone to great lengths to sit up. They moved his chair by the fire and propped him up with stiff pillows.

Brother Luke provided him with a glass of honey wine to blunt his constant pain.

The Abbott tipped his glass. He sensed that the Duke was coming. "Pour me another."

Brother Luke stared. "Are ye sure?"

The monk managed a lopsided smile. "Are ye afraid it might kill me?"

Luke didn't answer. He refilled the glass and placed it before him.

The Abbott drank the wine in one gulp. "Ah. Mead. It's the only pleasure I have left." He set down the glass and coughed suddenly, bringing up a ball of phlegm tinged with blood. "Not again."

Luke was startled. "Has this happened before?"

"Twice this morning." He wiped his lips on a handkerchief.

"I'll send for the healer."

The old man shivered. "Nay bother. I'm not long for this world."

Luke had tears in his eyes. "What can I do?"

"I must see Lord Gordon one last time. Go now. Tell the Brothers to send him in."

"I can't leave ye alone."

The Abbott sighed. "Dear Luke. Ye've meant so much to me. Like a son..." He took a ragged breath. "Go about yer duties. I've taken enough of yer time." He was sad as the younger monk left the room. He might never see him again.

***

Dughall was solemn as he followed a monk to the Abbott's quarters. They'd received word at Drake yesterday that Brother Lazarus was dying. He and Jamison set out before dawn to honor the monk's last wishes. The young Lord knew why he was summoned, even though it was unspoken. During their visit, he would be expected to help his mentor cross over. They arrived at the Abbott's house, a modest stone structure with a narrow oak door. Thick smoke rose from the chimney in spite of the season.

Brother Adam had a slight paunch that showed through his white robe. "'Tis a great honor to be summoned to his deathbed. He's a rare man."

Dughall swallowed hard. "I know."

The monk squeezed his shoulder with affection. "Have ye done this before?"

"Aye. I was at my grandfather's deathbed."

"Good." The silence that ensued was uncomfortable. "The Abbott said that ye are interested in bee keeping. I would be pleased to teach ye."

Dughall smiled nervously. "I would like that."

"Write me." Brother Adam opened the door and spoke softly, "The Abbott is within, sitting by the fire. There is a bottle of my best honey wine and two glasses on a table." The monk bowed slightly. "Forgive me.

I must attend to my duties." He turned and headed for the refectory.

Dughall entered with a sense of foreboding. An apoplexy could destroy a man. What would he find? As his eyes adjusted to the light, he spotted the monk sitting in a chair near the fire. He'd been propped up by pillows. One side of his face drooped and his arm seemed useless. The room smelled slightly of urine.

The Duke pulled up a chair and sat in front of him. The fire was overpowering but he didn't mention it. The monk's lips were tinged with blue and his breathing was rapid and labored. *He's close to death. We don't have much time.* "Brother Lazarus, my friend."

The monk spit into a handkerchief he was clutching. "Ye came." He spit again, bringing up gobs of yellow phlegm. "Forgive me."

Dughall's heart ached. "There's nothing to forgive." He took the monk's hands and noted that they were clammy. "Ye've done so much for my family. But most of all, ye've been a wise and patient teacher. I am grateful."

"Oh…" The monk had tears in his eyes. "But have ye…"

Dughall understood. "I have forgiven my father."

"Then I have not failed."

The Duke smiled. "There is no such thing as failure when counseling others. We are each responsible for our own actions." He squeezed his hands with affection. "Men do not often say such things… But I love ye, Lazarus. It is as if ye were my grandfather."

The old man managed a lopsided smile. "And ye, my grandson. Let us drink together."

Dughall went to the table, poured two glasses of wine, and brought them to the fireside. He sat and handed one to the monk, who took it with his good hand. "Can ye manage it?"

"Aye."

They sipped the wine in silence, like many times before. At last, it was gone. Dughall placed the glasses on the floor.

The Abbott's lips trembled. "Ye once said that there was a place ye went to when ye were dying. Tell me about it."

Dughall took his hands and began to tell the story. The first part was painful. "One night, the Earl tied me to a wall and whipped me until I was senseless. I had been ill, so it brought me close to death. They say that I fainted." He took a breath and smiled. "I found myself at my birthplace, sitting out on the point, watching the North Sea. It was my favorite spot. I spent time watching the gulls and feeling the wind in my hair. There was no pain or fear, just a profound sense of peace."

"Ah."

"I sensed someone sitting next to me, so I turned. It was my Aunt Maggie, who was murdered when I was abducted. She looked so young! Her hair was dark and her skin was smooth. She said that there was no arthritis in that place."

The monk smiled.

"I told her that I was sorry she died for me."

"Did she forgive ye?"

He smiled. "Oh, aye. She said that she would do it all again just to have known me. My heart swelled with love. I asked if I was dead."

"What did she say?"

"She said nay, that I was in a place that was in between. I had a choice to make – to live or die. If I passed, she would guide me to the afterlife."

The Abbott sighed. "Catholics do not believe such things. But I want to believe. Perhaps my father will appear, whole and healed."

Dughall gazed into his rheumy eyes. "I am sure of it."

The monk grunted. "Ye were never a true Catholic."

"No more than I was Protestant. I found God in many places – in a church, the forest, and by the sea. I finally figured out why."

The Abbott's eyes widened. "Why?"

Dughall pointed to his own heart. "Because God is here." He lingered and then touched the monk's chest. "As well as there. We are sparks of Him. He was with me all the time. All I had to do was feel the connection."

"Ah," the monk said. "It reminds me of what my teacher said. We don't pray to worship God. We pray to reveal the God inside us."

Dughall smiled. "Exactly. It's a personal thing. But I believe in religion."

"Ye do?"

"When I worship alone, 'tis like a single musical note. When I join with others, the notes become a verse. Soon, they're an entire song. 'Tis music to God's ears."

"It's so true," he whispered. The monk's head dropped to his chest. "Thank ye, Son. I am ready to die."

Dughall stroked his bald head to ease his passage. "Go, Lazarus. Yer loved ones await ye."

The monk's breathing slowed until it was almost undetectable. But Dughall sensed that he was still alive. At last, his frail body slackened.

Dughall felt the spirit pass out of him. It was like a warm cloak that enveloped him for a moment. His heart swelled with gratitude. "I will miss ye, Lazarus. Save a place for me in heaven."

The Duke stayed with the body for an hour. He cried, remembered, and thanked God that the monk's trials were over. Dughall then left the dwelling to inform the monks and find his servant. The Abbott was his dearest friend. They would need to stay for the funeral.

CHAPTER 9
NEWS

TWO DAYS LATER

CASTLE SKENE, ABERDEENSHIRE, SCOTLAND

Castle Skene lay in a wild glen, a secluded valley with a loch running through it. Many inhabitants spoke Gaelic and their stark features reminded one of ancient Celts. It was a thinly peopled region due to the bare hills, sparse cultivation, and standing stones. The squat dwellings of peasants emitted smoke from fresh peat, the earthy smell mingling with the scent of pine trees.

By the edge of the loch stood Castle Skene, a foreboding granite structure protected by a massive outer wall. Its construction was medieval. Two tall towers stretched to the sky, connected by a main building and catwalks. The thick walls kept the warmth in during winter months, but prevented the summer heat from entering, necessitating hearth fires year round. Hardly any windows were to be seen on the side that faced the valley. The front had some, but they were little more than slits, designed to repel attacks without artillery. None had dared to attack recently. They feared the Lord of the castle.

The weather was overcast and gloomy. It had rained hard that morning and was threatening a repeat performance. Lord Skene stood at a bench in his laboratory, working on an experiment. He was interested in chemistry, an art that involved the preparation of gold and silver. The hypothesis was simple: All metals are compounds. The baser ones contain the same as gold and silver, but are contaminated with impurities. These can be purged away with the application of intense heat and a substance called the philosopher's stone.

"Ah..." Skene held a bottle to his nose and sniffed. "Lapis philosophorum... A powder red in color... It smells strongly... I shall test this tonight."

There was a knock on the door.

Skene placed the bottle on the bench and stared at the oak portal. "Who is it?"

"Fagan, Sir."

His anger flared. "Come!" The massive door opened with a creak, admitting the terrified servant.

The short, spindly legged man lifted a lantern. "My Lord?"

Skene glared. "How dare ye interrupt me in my laboratory?"

Fagan's knees knocked beneath his kilt. He looked down as he spoke, "Forgive me, my Lord. But there is a messenger at the gate. He says that it's important."

Skene growled, "Idiot! They all say that. I should throw ye in the oubliette."

The servant fell to his knees. "Have mercy, my Lord! I am a simple man, unskilled in the ways of the world. I will not do it again."

"Get up!"

The servant scrambled to his feet.

Skene glared. "*Who* is at the gate?"

"Uh…" His voice trembled, "A holy man… A monk in a white robe… He comes with a message from Deer Abbey."

"Hmmphhh!" Normally, Lord Skene answered to no one. But he had an obligation to these monks since they entrusted him with James Gordon. "Escort the monk to my study. Light the fire, straighten my desk, and then provide us with refreshments."

Fagan bowed like a willow in the wind. "As ye wish, my Lord." The servant fled the room.

Skene returned to his bench and placed a stopper in the bottle. He took out an ornate key, unlocked a claw-footed cabinet, and hid the vessel on a shelf. He placed a book beside it, a rare copy of the 'Bibliotheca Chemica Curiosa'.

The experiment would have to wait. He locked the cabinet and scanned his clothes for traces of the rare powder. "These monks are inquisitive. They must not suspect what I'm doing." Pocketing the key, he headed for his study.

*＊＊

THE STUDY

Brother Adam stood by the fire, attempting to dry his clothes. He'd been riding through rain since the crack of dawn. When he reached Castle Skene, it wasn't over. He'd been kept outside for an hour. The monk coughed into his fist. "God help me. I'll catch my death." The study was dry, but not much warmer. The servant who escorted him started a fire in the hearth.

The door opened, admitting the Lord of the castle.

Brother Adam bowed slightly. "Good day, Sir." He waited to be acknowledged.

Lord Skene motioned for him to sit at the desk. They walked to the massive oak piece and sat opposite each other. "Ye are Brother Adam, if I remember correctly."

Adam managed a smile. "I am."

"The bee keeper."

"'Tis true."

Skene folded his hands on the desk. "I apologize for the behavior of my servant. He should have admitted ye right away. I told him to prepare refreshments for us."

The monk smiled. "Bless ye, Sir. Something hot, I hope."

"Aye, toddies and oat cakes. To what do I owe this visit?"

Brother Adam coughed until his face turned red. "Pardon me." He coughed again. "I come bearing sad news. The Abbott suffered an apoplexy. He died a few days ago."

Skene's eyes narrowed. "I am sorry for yer loss. The Abbott was a good man. He will be missed."

"Aye. We plan to hold a service for him the day after tomorrow. Lord Gordon has come. He wants to see his son."

Lord Skene tensed. For a moment, Adam thought that he would deny the request.

Skene seemed to relax. "Of course."

"Then, ye'll follow me back?"

"Aye." The lord took a breath. "Gordon *doesn't* mean to take the boy?"

Brother Adam was getting a bad feeling. "Nay. It's been seven months. He wants to check on his welfare."

Skene's brow wrinkled. "There is no need for him to be concerned. The child is in good health. Surely, ye've told him that."

The monk bristled. "No one means to imply..."

Skene held up a hand. "No offense taken. But I have a question. With the Abbott gone, who will be responsible for the boy's spiritual education?"

"Brother Luke has agreed to teach him."

The room was growing warm at last. The servant arrived with a tray of hot toddies and oat cakes and placed it on the desk. After he left, the two men shared the repast in silence.

Lord Skene stood. "I need an hour to prepare. Stay here, get warm, and dry yer clothes. There is a chamber pot in the corner. I will send my servant with towels and more refreshments."

Brother Adam nodded. "Thank ye for the hospitality. Might I leave to walk the grounds and check on my horse?"

Skene's eyes flashed. "Nay! My servants will attend to yer horse. This castle is dangerous for those unfamiliar with it. Remain here and let us serve ye."

The monk was uneasy. "As ye wish." *The castle was dangerous?* As he watched the man leave the room, he wondered what he meant.

＊＊＊

Lord Skene gritted his teeth as crossed the soggy courtyard. The cooper's wife had been told to sweep the rain off the cobblestones, but hadn't done so. When this affair was done, he would punish her. There was no time to waste because they had to leave for the Abbey. He'd been told that the boy was playing on the far side of the gardens. There was just enough time to retrieve the lad and give him instructions.

They'd had a few bad weeks when the boy arrived here. The lad challenged him several times and tried to run away. A backhand across the face and a night in the root cellar stopped his bad behavior. Since then, they'd settled into a reasonable relationship. Once the child was introduced to the Dark Arts, he'd begun to cooperate.

Skene trudged around the garden and spotted James standing near the stone outer wall. The red-haired boy had his back to him, so he stopped for a moment to observe. It was an eerie scene. Perched on the wall were scores of crows and ravens, stretching their wings and awaiting orders.

James was dressed in leather breeks, a white linen shirt, and a green velvet doublet. He bent over a small wooden cage, lifted the door, and released a rabbit. As the animal bolted, the boy gripped a birch rod and raised it high. "Get him!" he cried.

A dozen crows left their perches and swooped to the ground. There was confusion - a high pitched squeal, a shriek, and the sound of birds squabbling. A large crow flew up to the wall with a rabbit's foot in its mouth.

Skene shook his head in amazement. "James!"

The boy turned and stared. "Aye, Sir."

"I see that ye've learned yer lesson."

James smiled. "I have. There's more." He turned to the flock and raised the rod. "Disperse!" The birds rose in a black cloud, cackling and shrieking. They flew to the surrounding forest.

Skene let out a breath. He'd been holding it since the birds arose, thinking that they might have been sent to attack him. "Excellent!"

James approached and spoke respectfully, "What do ye want, Sir?"

Skene squeezed his shoulder. "I have news. The Abbott died, after suffering an apoplexy."

"The Abbott was my teacher." The boy's face darkened. "What does this mean?"

Skene scowled. Was the lad upset because he cared for the monk? Or because his future was uncertain? For the first time, he couldn't tell. He'd taught James to block the probing thoughts of others. The boy was by far the best pupil he'd ever had. "They shall provide ye with another teacher."

"Good."

"We must leave soon to attend the funeral service."

James began to brush off his clothes. "My clothes are stained. I had better change."

Lord Skene nodded. "First, there is a complication we must discuss. Yer father will be there."

James looked up. "Not my mother?"

"Not as far as I know."

"What does he want from me?"

He cleared his throat. "The monk says that he wants to check on yer welfare."

"Father doesn't care about me!"

Skene had no time for this pettiness. "He obviously has an interest in ye. It doesn't matter. Do ye wish to stay with me?"

"Aye."

"Then here is what ye must do. First and foremost, make no effort to read his mind. Block his thoughts like I taught ye. Don't hurt him. Be courteous, agreeable, and play the part of a loving son. He must think that ye are thriving here."

James frowned. "Father would take me from ye?"

Skene nodded. "He has the right."

The boy reddened. "Then I shall do what ye say."

"Good. There is a monk here to guide us, so be careful what ye say."

"What should I say, Sir?"

They began walking towards the castle. As they approached the door, they talked about what he should and should not say.

***

Lord Skene took James to the wardrobe chamber, where they dressed in riding clothes. They returned to their chambers, packed an overnight bag, and then walked the corridor to the study. By the time they fetched Brother Adam, it was late afternoon. The Abbey was more than a day away under the best of conditions. The roads and paths were soggy. They left the castle, mounted their horses, and followed the monk out of the valley.

Skene planned to attend the service and return to the castle as soon as possible. He was concerned. Lapis philosophorum could be unstable. He was anxious to return to his experiment.

Chapter 10
Requiem

May 24th 1649
Two Days Later

Deer Abbey

DAYBREAK

Dughall was deep in thought as he followed the monks across the flagstone courtyard. They were walking in a queue, one after another, with a designated space between them. The men were headed to the church, to ask for heavenly peace and eternal life for their dear departed brother.

The Duke had accepted an offer from Brother Luke to join them in a Requiem Mass for the Abbott. They were then sequestered in the monks' quarters, and allowed a light supper. The men spent the evening in silent meditation, to the sound of occasional bells and the smell of incense.

Today, Dughall was dressed in the robes of a Cistercian monk, a white flowing garment that draped to the ground. He was naked beneath and barefoot. His long curls had been tied back in a tail.

They reached the steps of the cruciform-shaped church, climbed to the entrance, and opened a wooden door. Inside, there was a vestibule with a font of holy water and a table with a vase of white lilies. One by one, the men dipped their fingers in the font and made the sign of the cross to the words "In the name of the Father, Son, and Holy Ghost." Then they proceeded into the church proper. Chapel bells rang, deep and resonant.

Dughall was among the last to enter. The stone floor felt cold under his bare feet. Following Luke, he walked a long aisle past elaborately carved pews and transepts that housed chapels dedicated to saints. They stopped at the latticework chancel which provided seating for the choir, entered, and sat in a pew. The bells ceased.

The sun was rising in the eastern sky, pouring colored light through the stained glass windows. Tall pillar candles of the finest beeswax burned near the altar and on either side of the casket.

The monks retrieved hymnals from the pews and opened them to a specific page. Luke guided the Duke in this effort. Dughall gave the monk a quizzical look.

Luke whispered, "This is how we pray. The Mass is in Gregorian Chant." He returned to his hymnal.

Dughall was thrilled. He could think of no better way to honor his mentor. There were to be no instruments other than the human voice. He held his breath as they began to chant.

♩♪♩ In paradisum deducant te angeli.
In tuo adventu suscipiant te martyres,
Et perducant te in civitatem sanctam Jerusalem. ♩♪♩

Dughall had studied Latin with Brother Lazarus, so that he could read old books and scrolls. His mind translated as they chanted the melodic phrases.

May angels lead thee into paradise.
May martyrs receive thee at thy coming,
And lead thee into the holy city of Jerusalem.

Dughall smiled. *They are praying that he be taken into paradise. No man deserves it more.* He listened as they sang from a familiar psalm and concluded with:

♩♪♩ Gloria Patri et Filio
Et Spiritu Sancto.
Sicut erat in principio et nunc et semper
et in saecula saeculorum. Amen. ♩♪♩

Glory be to the Father, and to the Son,
And to the Holy Ghost.
As it was in the beginning, is now,
And ever shall be; world without end. Amen.

The monks continued to chant, asking for the intercession of the saints and angels for the salvation of the departed. The rising melody gave Dughall goose bumps. Then they began the Requiem chant.

♩♪♩ Requiem aeternam dona eis, Domine.
Et lux perpetua luceat eis.
Te decet hymnus, Deus, in Sion,
et tibi reddetur votum in Jerusalem.
Exaudi orationem meam, ad te omnis caro veniet. ♩♪♩

Eternal rest grant them, O Lord.

And let perpetual light shine upon them.
A hymn is fittingly sung to Thee in Sion, O God,
And a vow shall be dedicated to Thee in Jerusalem.
Hear my prayer: to Thee all flesh shall come.

♩ ♪ ♩ Kyrie eleison. Christe eleison. Kyrie eleison.
Requiem aeternam dona eis.
Et lux perpetua luceat eis.
In memoria aeterna erit iustus.
Ab auditione mala non timebit. ♩ ♪ ♩

Lord have mercy. Christ have mercy. Lord have mercy.
Eternal rest grant them, O Lord.
And let perpetual light shine upon them.
In eternal memory shall the just man be kept.
He shall not fear a bad hearing.

Tears ran down Dughall's cheeks. He was transfixed by the words and the beauty of the chant. He listened as they continued in perfect harmony, asking God to free the soul of the Abbott from the chains of sin and allow him to escape harsh judgment. The monks sang with all their hearts for the soul of their friend and mentor. Finally, they concluded with:

♩ ♪ ♩ Requiescant in pace. Amen. ♩ ♪ ♩

Rest in peace. Amen.

Dughall felt like he was floating. Like the times when he sat by the sea, he felt a personal connection with God. For the first time, he understood how a man could become a monk. If he didn't have the responsibilities of state and family, he would choose to stay here forever.

There was a slight tug on his sleeve. Brother Luke spoke softly, "Ye felt it."

Dughall smiled. "Oh, aye."

Luke allowed him a moment of reflection. "We must approach the casket."

They stood. Dughall followed Luke out of the pew, and then to a stand in front of the altar. The Abbott was laid out in a simple pine casket with a white wool lining. The other monks had paid their respects. They kneeled.

Dughall looked upon his old friend with affection. *Oh, Lazarus. I am so grateful. I will never forget what ye taught me.*

Brother Luke finished prayers and stood.

Dughall joined him. "May I touch him?"

The monk nodded.

Dughall covered the Abbott's hand with his own. It was cold and stiff. The man was long gone. "Goodbye, my friend. I shall miss ye."

Luke squeezed his shoulder with affection. "Lazarus was fond of ye. His body will remain here for the public ceremony. We must go."

Dughall wiped away a tear. "I am ready."

The monks began to form a line. As they left the church one by one, chapel bells rang, deep and resonant. They chanted once more:

♩♪♩ In paradisum deducant te angeli.
In tuo adventu suscipiant te martyres,
Et perducant te in civitatem sanctam Jerusalem. ♩♪♩

May angels lead thee into paradise.
May martyrs receive thee at thy coming,
And lead thee into the holy city of Jerusalem.

The Duke was the last to leave the church. He followed Brother Luke down the stone steps and across the flagstone courtyard. Dughall felt like he was on a cloud. He was so distracted that he didn't notice a boy on the sidelines, staring at him with a puzzled look. He followed the monks to the refectory for refreshments.

***

9AM

James Gordon *was* puzzled. He expected to see his father, but not in the robes of a Cistercian monk. The man seemed to look right through him and continued on his way. What was going on? He turned to Skene, "Did ye see that?"

Lord Skene grunted. "Aye. What is he up to?" He grasped the boy's arm. "Don't worry. Yer father is an unusual man. It doesn't mean anything."

James frowned. "Would he abandon Mother and become a monk?"

"I doubt it. The man has too much power to give it up. Land, wealth, men to command…" He spotted Brother Luke hurrying towards them. "We will ask the monk."

Luke arrived and bowed slightly. "Forgive us for not stopping. James… Yer father attended a ceremony to ease the passage of the Abbott's soul."

James bristled. "Why was he dressed as a monk?"

Skene's voice was stern, "James… That is none of our business."

The boy stamped his foot. "It *is* my business! He's my father."

Brother Luke stared. "There is no need to be concerned, young one. Yer father will join ye soon." He looked behind him and saw Dughall emerging from the Refectory. "He's coming this way." Luke walked away to meet him.

Lord Skene scowled. "I told ye to behave."

"But…"

"There is no but! Ye will act like the perfect son or suffer the consequences!"

James cringed. He'd spent a night in the root cellar, nursing a split lip. He didn't want to repeat that. He *could* rat on Skene and go back to his family. But then he wouldn't learn the Dark Arts. "I will behave."

"Good. Remember… Ye must block his thoughts."

***

Dughall crossed the courtyard with trepidation. Luke had told him about James' reaction. It had been seven months since he'd seen his son. His attire had to be confusing. He arrived at their location and extended a hand. "Lord Skene. It's good to see ye. I'm sure that we have much to talk about." The two men shook hands.

Dughall turned his attention to his son. The boy looked clean, well-fed, and unafraid. He reached out and tousled his hair. "My son."

James seemed to relax. "Father."

Dughall sighed. "I know that I am dressed strangely. There is an explanation. Since I was the one to help the Abbott pass, I was invited to participate in the Mass for the Dead." He gestured to his clothes. "For this, I had to don the robes of a monk."

James seemed relieved. "Ye're not joining the monastery?"

Dughall shook his head. "Nay, Son. When this is done, I shall return to my wife and children."

The boy smiled. "Good! I am glad to see ye, Father."

Dughall was surprised. This response was more than he could have hoped for. He tried to read the boy's mind, but failed. "I'm glad to see ye, too. Ye look well." He took the child's hand. "Come with me to the Refectory. Lord Skene can follow. The monks are serving refreshments."

They had three hours before the public ceremony. There was much to talk about. With the child's hand in his, they headed for the Refectory.

Chapter 11
Virginia

June 21st 1649
One Month Later

THE BRITISH COLONY OF VIRGINIA

Gilbert Gordon crouched on the shore and let sand sift through his fingers. He was grateful to be alive. Months ago, they'd fled Edinburgh, sailed south around England, and headed for the Indies. The captain explained that they'd been hastily commissioned and needed to acquire provisions.

Their stop in Bermuda was brief, but inspiring. The Gordons explored the island for two days, taking in the sights and sounds of the tropical paradise. Bermuda was populated with cedar trees, colorful plants, and unusual wildlife. They saw sea turtles, wild hogs, and ground-nesting cahows, birds that emitted eerie shrieks like demons. Gilbert was impressed with the island's tobacco. The taste was exquisite, mild yet flavorful. He wondered if it would thrive in the colonies, and acquired several barrels of seeds for the voyage. They returned to the ship with their booty and set sail on the third day.

Bridget and his daughters suffered from varying degrees of seasickness. His son George seemed unaffected, though it might have been from sheer force of will as he tried to impress his father.

Gilbert *was* impressed. The lad was everything he wanted in a son; brave, intelligent, and painfully honest. He reminded him of his brother Dughall. His heart felt a twinge of guilt. *My dear brother. How I wish I knew that ye survived!*

They'd been in Virginia for a few days, staying near Jamestown. The ship's captain had to return to Scotland, so Gilbert was pressed to make a decision. They could make a life here or go on to Maryland or Massachusetts.

Gilbert had few opinions about the colonies. Since the death of his father, he'd been embroiled in Scottish politics. But like most Scotsmen, he'd heard that some of the colonies had been founded on principles of religious freedom. The new world was a place where one could make a fortune. Therefore, his first task was to seek out a local official to educate him on Virginia's advantages.

Virginia had a lot to offer. They welcomed immigrants of all kinds, but especially those who brought skills and wealth. Gilbert was educated, well spoken, and a seasoned negotiator. Thanks to his brother, he was in possession of a box of gold and silver. Bridget was a seamstress and his servant Connor was a former blacksmith by trade. He learned about head rights, a law that granted fifty acres of land to every man, woman, and child who immigrated to the colony. Between Bridget, himself, his son, and his daughters, they were entitled to two hundred and fifty acres, a veritable plantation! Even Connor was entitled to his own small estate.

The only downside was that Virginia was populated primarily by Protestants. State and church were entwined, and a law mandated that Virginians worship in the Anglican Church. The line between religious and civil authority seemed blurred. There was no doubt about it. If he was to become a prominent member of the community, he would have to change religions. There was another option. Through discreet inquiries, he learned that there was a small Catholic settlement in northern Virginia, near Aquia Creek by the Maryland border. Founded by the Giles Brent family, they were also looking for settlers.

Gilbert talked it over with Bridget and Conner and made a private decision. He would ponder the question of religion, but they would stay in Virginia.

"Father?" Young George was approaching.

Gilbert stood and greeted his son by tousling his hair. "Aye, Son."

The boy smiled. "This is a fine place. Mother likes it here."

Gilbert's heart swelled. He would do anything for his son, even change religions. "I like it too. They say that tobacco grows here."

George brightened. "We can plant the seeds we bought!"

"Aye. Run along and tell yer mother we are staying."

Gilbert watched with pride as the boy trudged through sandy soil to the path that led to the inn. When he was out of sight, he started out in the opposite direction, towards the house of the official.

Today he would write a letter to his brother, give it to the captain, and send him on his way. The man intended to sail northeast to lessen the time to get to Scotland.

In the meantime, Gilbert would present himself as one of the lesser sons of a Scottish lord, come to the colonies to make his fortune. There was just one problem. He was still a wanted man in England and this was an English colony. As a precaution, he would assume the name of his deceased cousin George Gordon.

Two hundred and fifty acres! God seemed to be smiling upon him. As he walked the shore, he gazed to the heavens, "Dear Jesus. I hope and pray that ye spared my brother." He would find out soon enough. Today he would write him a letter.

Maggie Gordon

Chapter 12
A Day at Drake

August 17 1649

Eight Weeks Later

Drake Castle

THE STUDY

The Duke stood in his study, gazing out an open window. The day was bright and sultry, with temperatures above eighty. Because of the heat, he was dressed informally - in breeks, a silk shirt, and lattice shoes. "My God, it's hot!" He wiped his brow with a handkerchief and returned to the window. Dughall counted ten children playing in the courtyard, spinning hoops and chasing a terrier. Their joyful shouts and the dog's sharp barks echoed in the air. Seeing the children lifted his spirits.

A gaunt woman in a white apron emerged from the bake house, carrying a basket of bread. She stopped and scolded the wee ones and headed for the castle. As the youngsters dispersed, he spotted Jamison crossing the courtyard with the captain of the Black Swan.

Dughall's heart soared. The Black Swan had been tasked with taking

Gilbert and his family to the colonies. Was there news of his brother? He left the window, arranged two chairs before the desk, and moved his ledgers to the sideboard. There was a knock on the door. He wiped his brow and called out, "Come."

Jamison entered with Captain McGee. The man looked scruffy from the long sea voyage, with a wild beard and dirty clothing.

The servant spoke, "My Lord. The Black Swan is anchored in Moray Firth. Captain McGee has been riding all morning. He has a letter for ye."

Dughall smiled. "Wonderful! From my brother?"

"Himself, my Lord," McGee said.

"How was the return voyage?"

"Uneventful, Sir. We took an alternate route northeast from the Colonies."

"Is my brother well?"

McGee nodded. "Aye." He extracted an envelope from his coat pocket and handed it to the Duke. "Gilbert said to give this to ye."

Dughall wanted to tear it open, but he had business to settle with this man. He set it on the desk. "We are in yer debt, McGee. Jamison, see that he is paid. Give him what we agreed to."

The servant nodded. "As ye wish."

Dughall noted the return address – it was from Jamestown in the Colony of Virginia. "McGee, are there any ships in Moray Firth that are headed west?"

The Captain scratched his head. "Aye. They are provisioning the 'Sea Venture' to leave in two days for the Colonies."

"Can I give ye a letter to post?"

"Aye, Sir."

Dughall rubbed his hands together. "Good. Where is my sense of hospitality? Jamison, take this man to the kitchen and get him a decent meal. Then bring him back to my study for a fine cigar and a whisky."

"As ye wish, my Lord." The two men bowed slightly and left the study.

Dughall sat at the desk and stared at the envelope. It was water stained and grimy from being in a pocket. After noting the address, he opened it. Gilbert's handwriting seemed to jump from the page.

My dear brother. I hope and pray that ye are alive to receive this letter. I have been consumed by guilt for leaving ye in those circumstances. Still, I am grateful for my life and a chance to see my son grow to manhood. We had a long sea voyage aboard the Black Swan, frightening at times, but that can be told in another letter. The captain provisioned at Bermuda, set sail once more, and we arrived in the Colony of Virginia. At first, I thought we would go on to Maryland or Massachusetts, but I soon changed my mind. Though primarily Protestant, Virginia has offered us a reason to stay. My family is entitled to

250 acres of prime land; Connor is entitled to 50. We intend to start a tobacco plantation with seeds we acquired in Bermuda. Imagine me, a farmer! If Father could see me now! Here I am in the New World, come to make my fortune.

How strange… Everywhere I turn, the names of James and Charles are present. Cities, counties, towns, and rivers are named after our beloved Kings. Yet, here I am banished from my homeland for the act of supporting them.

The Black Swan must go, so I shall conclude this letter. Bridget, the children, and Connor are well, and excited at the prospect of living here. As I am a wanted man in England and this is an English colony, I have taken the name of our dead cousin, George Gordon. Please address any letters to that name, in care of the general store in Jamestown. Write me soon, dear brother. Not knowing if ye are alive or dead is torture.

Yer brother always, Gilbert (George from now on)

The Duke was delighted. His brother was alive and well, and thriving in the Colony of Virginia. The poor man didn't know if he was alive or dead. He had to write him immediately. Dughall took out some writing materials and dipped a quill in the inkwell. He poised the pen over the sheet of stationery, and began to write.

Dear Gilbert,

I am starting to believe that I am a cat with nine lives. I survived the situation in Edinburgh with no more than a few breaks and bruises. Of course, that is a story that we will share over a cigar when next I see ye.

Virginia! I have heard much about the place. They say that the weather is almost tropical. I was glad to hear that ye arrived safely with yer family and yer servant. I look forward to visiting yer tobacco plantation, after ye get settled.

My family is well. James is under the care of the monks and Lord Skene. He seems to be thriving. Luc is a strong young man and Maggie at twelve is delightful. It seems that I am to be a father once more, as my wife is pregnant. Pray for us that the child survives, unlike the others.

Drake is prospering, having recently expanded. But brother, I am sorry to report that Huntly and its lands are forfeit to us. I have taken in a few of yer loyal subjects. Lord Balmerino said that they would not pursue ye, but ye are never to set foot in Scotland. Oh, Brother. I know that it must hurt, but take heart! It is a small price for yer life and the safety of yer family.

I suppose that ye want to hear about the state of politics. After the King's death, under the direction of Cromwell, the English parliament abolished the Monarchy, the Privy Council, and the House of Lords. They have established the 'Commonwealth of England'. As near as I can tell, it is a republic. They are currently occupied with an invasion of Ireland, and so far have not bothered Scotland.

Much to my surprise, there are factions in Scotland that wish to restore Charles' son to the throne. Our parliament proclaimed him King of Great Britain and Ireland and offered him a way to return. Of course, there are conditions.

Among other things, he would be required to accept the Covenants of '38 and '43, and subscribe to a Presbyterian agenda. I doubt that he would do this. Personally, I've seen enough of Stuart rule. I suspect, dear brother, that ye have a different opinion.

The English Parliament responded by passing a statute that makes any such proclamation unlawful. So it seems that the Prince is in limbo. What interesting times we live in!

I regret that I cannot write more. The captain of the Black Swan is waiting to take my letter. Stay well, take care of the children, and give my regards to Bridget and Connor. Yer loving brother, Dughall.

Dughall folded the letter and placed it in an envelope. He scribbled the address upon it. *George Gordon, c/o the General Store, Jamestown, Colony of Virginia*

***

THE SEWING CHAMBER

The sewing chamber had a single window that overlooked the castle's flower gardens. It was a small room, utilitarian, with cabinets and cubby holes for sewing materials. It had a work table scattered with rulers and scissors, a ring of chairs, a rocker, and a fireplace.

Today, the curtains were pulled back from the window, giving the room a bright and airy feel. A gentle breeze entered - ripe with the fragrance of summer.

The Duchess sat in a comfortable chair, awaiting the arrival of her daughter Maggie. She was clad in a short-sleeved tartan dress, more generous at the middle. Her slender hands sorted through a basket of material.

Keira hadn't slept well. She had a headache, her face was puffy, and there were circles under her eyes. For the third time since becoming pregnant, she'd been plagued by a frightening dream. It came just before dawn...

She found herself on the bank of a river that wound through a wild glen. The water was so clear that she saw fish swimming near the shore. The weather was balmy, without a cloud in the sky. Song birds warbled in the trees and hummingbirds flitted from flower to flower. "I want to stay here," she said with a sigh.

A large shadow swept over her, blocking the sun and striking terror. As she looked up, trees withered and song birds turned to ravens. They glared at her, making a low throaty rattle. The hummingbirds turned into bats.

A screech drew her attention. Upstream, a red-haired Goddess stood in the river, washing bloody laundry.

Keira flinched as though she'd been struck. This was a prediction of death, a terrible omen! She lifted her skirts, waded frantically to the Morrigan, and fell

*to her knees in supplication. "O, Great One. Have mercy on us!" But it was too
late. The fearsome force opened her mouth and shrieked. A baby cried, and then
another.*

The Duchess stroked her belly. "I won't let her hurt ye. Ever." Keira
was thirty years old and five and a half months pregnant. She wasn't sure
how her husband felt about it. They'd had their share of heartache.
Dughall said that he was happy, but she sensed his fear. She'd lost the
last four wee ones. How could she blame him?

Her mother-in-law said that thirty was late to be pregnant. It
increased the risk of a dangerous delivery. She insisted that Keira rest,
leaving her daily duties to others.

The door opened and Maggie entered. The twelve-year-old girl
smiled like an angel as she took a seat next to the Duchess. She was
wearing a saffron-dyed dress with a white waist ribbon. "Mother... Are
ye feeling better?"

Keira loved Maggie with all her heart. "Aye. Yer grandmother
brought me chamomile tea to calm my nervous stomach."

Maggie smiled knowingly. "It's the best thing." She noted the quilt
on her mother's lap. "We sewed the patches yesterday. It's time for
fancy needlework." The girl picked up the quilt and ran it through her
fingers. "I love this border of stars." She spread a section across her lap.
"I hope ye don't mind. I decided to embroider a spotted woodpecker."

Keira lifted a porcelain cup and took a sip of tea. "It's a fine idea."
It was no secret that her daughter was partial to birds and animals. She
watched Maggie handle the bone needle with skill, drawing scarlet
thread through the fabric. "It's a wonderful color."

Maggie looked up. "'Tis. Beth said that they boiled the thread in
beet juice." The girl finished the bird's rump and the top of the head.
She threaded the needle in black and started on the beak. "I love birds.
They're such pure creatures."

Except for ravens, Keira thought.

Maggie seemed to read her thoughts. "They're *all* creatures of the
Goddess." She worked intently and finished the head of the woodpecker.
"It's for the wee one. I love her already."

Keira felt a twinge of worry. "How do ye know it's a *she?*"

The girl smiled, melting her heart. "I see colors around ye – soft
pinks and violet."

So the child was a girl. "Oh, Maggie. Will ye help me take care of
her?"

"I shall be like a second mother."

The Duchess watched her daughter embroider the body of
the woodpecker. Needlework calmed her, like repetitive prayer or
meditation. As the girl worked, Keira took a moment to think about
her son. James had been gone for nine months. Dughall had seen him

at the monk's funeral and told her that he looked well. The monks' reports were satisfactory. Would her husband allow him to come home for his birthday? She missed her son.

There *was* an upside to him being gone. Dughall's health had improved. They were making love, and she got pregnant. The pregnancy brought her joy, which was accompanied by a fear of losing it.

"Don't lose hope," Maggie said. "Each time is different."

Keira sighed. Like her father, it was impossible to hide anything from her. "Tell me, Daughter. Will I lose this one?"

Maggie wrinkled her nose. "We are all creatures of the Goddess, Mother. Only the Goddess knows."

***

The Duke took long strides towards the wing that housed the sewing room. He had just dispatched the captain with a letter and was anxious to share the news about Gilbert. He took a narrow flight of stairs and walked down a corridor. When he reached the sewing room, he entered quietly.

Dughall was warmed by the sight. Two of the women he loved most in life were sitting side by side, working on a quilt.

Maggie looked up, "Father!"

Keira rose and grasped the quilt. "Let's fold it, daughter. We can finish tomorrow."

Maggie joined her. In a few movements accompanied by laughter, they folded the quilt and placed it on a table.

The Duke could hardly contain himself. "Sit. I have good news." He pulled up a chair and sat opposite them. "I received a letter. Gilbert and Bridget made it to the Colonies."

Keira smiled. "Thank the Goddess."

Maggie clapped her hands. "What about my cousins?"

"The children are well. Connor is well. They have decided to stay in Virginia and grow tobacco."

Maggie beamed. "Can we visit them?"

"Perhaps in a few years when they get settled."

"Can James come, too?"

The topic of his son was a sore subject. "We shall see how he does with his studies."

Maggie looked like she was going to cry. "When can my brother come home?"

"I will decide after I visit him." Dughall opened his arms to comfort her. "Come here." The girl came to him and melted into his embrace. "Be patient, Daughter."

Her voice was anguished, "Do not blame him for what we did. It was my fault."

Dughall stiffened. "Nay, it was not! A young lad must learn to control his urges, especially with his sister." He was protective of Maggie. At twelve, she was developing a womanly figure.

Maggie blushed. "We won't do it again. I promise."

"I shall hold ye to that promise." Dughall was eager to change the subject. "James needs training which only the monks can provide. He can come home when he makes significant progress." He held her apart and gazed at her. "So bonny. No wonder the lads are after ye."

"Father!"

"Go visit yer cousins. I need to talk to yer mother."

Maggie kissed his cheek and left the sewing room.

Dughall stood and offered his wife a hand. As she stood, he sensed that she had something to say. "What is it, wife?"

"The child has good questions."

He reddened. "I answered her truthfully."

"When *can* our son come home?"

He couldn't lie. "Not until a week after the birth of the wee one."

Keira frowned. "Surely ye don't think…"

He sighed. "I don't know what to think. He gave me chest pains and headaches."

"Ye don't believe that."

He held fast to his beliefs, "I do."

She stared. "James wouldn't kill a child. There must be another explanation."

He took her hands. "Just one. The Morrigan has cursed us."

"Dughall!"

He wouldn't let her pull away. "Mother told me about yer dream."

She flushed with anger. "She promised not to tell ye."

Dughall squeezed her hands with affection. "A dream that comes often should be taken seriously. "Tis right that she told me. It's *my* child ye're carrying."

Keira sniffled. "Maggie says it's a lassie."

Dughall drew her closer. "I know. I sensed her long before ye told me."

The lass was close to tears. "I want this child! But my fears are great. How can I face the Morrigan?"

Dughall's heart ached. "Ye don't have to. I'm alive and whole. We're in this together. We will find a way to appease the Morrigan."

"I hope so."

He stroked her cheek. "Remember, lass. We have started anew. Nothing shall come between us."

She nodded. "I love ye."

"I know. Our love will sustain us."

Keira brought a hand to her forehead. "What is wrong with me? I suddenly feel faint."

"Let me take ye to bed. We can't take any chances." Without another word, he picked her up and carried her into the hallway.

***

THE SURGERY

Jessie Hay stood in the surgery, talking to a very pregnant Aileana Hunter. The red-haired lass was carrying her fourth child, after bearing two fine sons and a daughter. Jessie had just examined her. "Everything looks as it should."

Aileana smiled. "I knew it! Cameron says that it's bigger than the others."

"I don't think that it's twins. Perhaps it will be a big healthy son who will grow up to be like Cameron."

The young woman beamed with pride. "My husband would like that." She hugged the midwife with affection. "Oh, Jessie… Ye've been so good to us. I can't wait to recover from the birth so that I can help ye in the surgery."

Jessie was grateful. "That would be most welcome. It will be a long time before Keira can help me."

Aileana frowned. "How is she?"

"I insisted that she give up her duties. The poor lass is terrified that she will lose the baby."

"Keira's had so much heartache. I love her so. She doesn't deserve it."

Jessie stayed silent about the rest. The tiredness… The dreams… Her bargain with the Morrigan… She'd meddled enough by informing her son. "Keira needs the company of young women. Why don't ye visit her tomorrow?"

Aileana nodded. "I will. But I must go. Cameron is watching the children."

"Go, lass. Tell that big strong man to take care of ye."

Jessie watched her leave the surgery and then proceeded to soak her instruments in witch hazel. When they were laid out to dry, she glanced in a mirror. Twenty years ago, *she* looked like Aileana, with smooth skin and flowing red hair. Her heart sank as she studied the image in the mirror. An old woman stared at her. *My hair is white. My face is wrinkled. I wonder how Alex feels about it.*

Of course, her husband's hair was as white as snow. He'd come back from the war with streaks of it. Now, ten years had passed; they were both in their fifties. Life had taken a toll on them.

Still, she was grateful. Alex had partly recovered from his torture, regaining the strength to do simple tasks. He would never handle a scaffie or do a job with lifting. So, he'd made himself useful in other ways, teaching young men to fish and old men to whittle. There was no more talk of returning to their cottage.

Jessie was glad. They belonged here at Drake, with their children and grandchildren. She took a moment to think about the old woman who meant so much to her. She'd always had good advice. *Maggie said that time heals all wounds, or makes them less important. Ye were right, old woman.* They'd even found new ways to make love - less passionate -

more tender.

It had been a busy ten years. Her surgery practice had grown, to encompass surrounding areas. She'd even had cases come in from Fraserburgh. But there was a problem to be solved if she was to remain a healer. She couldn't see as well as she used to. If she held a bottle far away, she could read the label. If she held it close, the marks were blurry. It affected her ability to identify herbs and medicines. Worse yet, she couldn't thread a needle. Dughall was aware of her problem. He'd sent to Inverness for a craftsman who could make her a pair of spectacles.

Jessie smiled at the thought. *Me, a fishwife with spectacles! The old Duke used to wear them.* She tried to use his, but they gave her headaches. *How strange. Dughall says they must be crafted for each person.*

There was a knock at the door.

Beth entered the surgery. "Follow me, my Lady. The Duchess feels faint. She requires yer presence."

Jessie retrieved a bottle of smelling salts and the two women left the chamber.

***

THE LIBRARY

The Duke stood at an oak table, pouring over an old manuscript. Written in Latin, it contained some unfamiliar words. He'd learned a fair amount of the language from Brother Lazarus. Unfortunately, the lessons did not include medical terms. The scroll was brittle, so he had to be careful. Each time it was unrolled, there was a danger of tearing it. Humid weather didn't help. The paper curled on the edges.

He ran a finger down the page, searching for information on newborn mortality. *What causes a child to yellow and die within days of birth? The Greeks said that yellow signified a liver problem. There must be an explanation rooted in medicine.*

There was a knock on the door.

The Duke cried out in frustration, "Come!"

Luc entered and approached him. "Father."

Dughall was always glad to see his son. "What is it, lad?"

The lad smiled. "Murdock is hauling wood for the kitchen. He asked me to escort some visitors to ye."

"Who are they?"

"Donald Grant, the Laird of Clan Grant. He is accompanied by his nephew Philip."

The Duke rolled the scroll carefully and placed it on a shelf. "Show them in."

Luc left the room and returned with the Laird of Grant. He was a stocky man with thick black hair and a heavy beard and moustache. "Father, I present Donald Grant of Clan Grant. He wishes to speak to ye in private."

Dughall offered a hand in friendship. "We met years ago, Sir, during the trouble at Turriff." They shook hands. "Luc, go into the hallway and occupy his nephew."

The lad left the room. The two men pulled out chairs and sat at the rosewood desk.

Dughall spoke first, "What can I do for ye?"

Donald cleared his throat. "I come with a proposal that can unite our clans."

The Duke was always willing to listen. "What would that be?"

The Laird of Grant took a breath. "My brother Angus died on Tower Hill during the rebellion. He left a son who became my responsibility."

Dughall nodded. "Go on."

"Philip has just turned fifteen. He is a fine lad – handsome, brave, and skilled in horsemanship. I propose that he be betrothed to yer daughter Margaret."

Dughall was shocked. "But Maggie is only twelve!"

Donald grunted. "Too young for marriage, but not for betrothal. They could marry when he turns seventeen."

Dughall questioned his motives, "Are ye aware that she is illegitimate? Maggie has no rights to my land or title. She is entitled to only what I grant her in my lifetime."

Donald made a small sound of agreement. "So I have heard. Philip has no claim to mine. Nevertheless, such a match would unite our clans."

The Duke knew that it made sense. "I am willing to consider it. But I believe in love between a man and a woman. I will not force my daughter to marry."

They were quiet for a moment.

Donald spoke first, "I understand. Can we introduce the lad and lassie?"

"First, I'd like to meet yer nephew."

Grant left the room and returned with a lad. They took seats at the desk. "This is my nephew Philip, the only son of Angus and Amelia Grant."

Dughall stared. "Welcome to Drake, Philip." The lad was pleasing to look at, with straight brown hair and sparkling blue eyes. He sensed that the boy was nervous. "I understand that ye are interested in my daughter."

Philip blushed. "I am, Sir."

"Do ye know her?"

"Nay. But..." he stammered. "I saw her at a gathering. She's beautiful."

"That she is. Ye realize that she is only twelve?"

The boy straightened. "Aye, Sir. I'm willing to wait for her."

Dughall nodded. "I will not force my daughter to marry."

The boy looked stricken. "Please, Sir! We belong together. I dreamed of her."

"Philip!" Donald cried. "I told ye not to speak of it."

Dughall was stunned. He walked to the door and opened it. "Luc! Find yer sister and bring her here." Then he returned to his guests and sat opposite them.

The Laird of Grant seemed mortified. "Forgive the lad, Sir."

Dughall ignored him. Instead, he addressed the boy, "I believe in dreams. Tell me about it."

***

THE NURSERY

Maggie sat in the nursery, rocking three-month-old Marcia Hay. The infant was Ian and Mary's seventh child. The girl sang a lullaby to comfort her.

> Hush-a-ba, burdie, croon, croon
> Hush-a-ba, burdie, croon;
> The sheep are gane tae the siller wid,
> An the coos are gane tae the broom,
> broom.
> An it's braw milkin the kye, kye,
> It's braw milkin the kye;
> The birds are singin, the bells are ringin,
> An the wild deer come gallopin by.
> Hush-a-ba burdie, croon, croon,
> Hush-a-ba burdie, croon,
> The gaits are gane tae the mountain hie,
> An they'll no be hame till noon.

Maggie sighed. *Such a bonny child, with hair like yellow silk.* She stroked the infant's head. *When will I find my own true love so that I can have one of these?*

The door opened, admitting Luc. He looked relieved. "Father needs ye right away."

Maggie adored her older brother. "What does he want?"

Luc shrugged. "I don't know. He is entertaining guests in the library."

Maggie stood and placed the child in a cradle. A wet nurse in an apron took over, checking and changing her wet nappie. "Let's not keep Father waiting."

They left the nursery and walked a corridor towards the wing that housed the library. They passed bed chambers, a wall of portraits, and the common privy. A flight of stairs took them to another level, where they walked a hall to the library.

Luc stopped at the door. "Go in. They're waiting for ye."

She smiled like an angel. "Where will ye go?"

"Murdock is hauling firewood. I offered to help him."

"Then I'll see ye at supper." Maggie watched Luc walk away and placed her hand on the doorknob. She heard male voices inside, and entered.

Three men stood as she came into the room – her father, a nobleman, and a handsome young lad. They bowed slightly.

Dughall made introductions, "This is my daughter, Margaret Christal... Maggie, this is the Laird of Grant and his nephew Philip."

Maggie curtsied. "I am pleased to meet ye, Sirs."

"Philip would like to get to know ye."

Maggie sensed her father's apprehension. But she felt something else as well. He approved of the lad. It was no surprise because she'd dreamed of this. She turned to the boy, "Philip, would ye like to see the gardens?"

"Oh, aye, Miss," he stammered.

"Can we, Father?" she asked.

Dughall paled. "Aye."

She reached out a slender hand to Philip, who looked nervously to the Duke for approval.

Dughall gave a slight nod. "Go, lad. Remember what ye promised."

"I will, Sir. I'll be good to her."

Maggie took his hand and led him to the open door. She sensed that her father needed reassurance. "It's all right, Father. I dreamed of him."

Without another word, they left for the gardens.

***

The Duke needed a wee dram. He took out a decanter of whisky and two squat glasses. Dughall poured three fingers worth in each one and placed them on the desk. "Whisky, my friend?"

Donald grinned. "For sure." He lifted a glass and took a sip. "It's excellent. This must be from the Highlands." He made a toast, "Here's to the lad and lassie. Fortune is smiling upon us. They seem to like each other."

Dughall raised his glass in agreement. "Aye. Here is to our new alliance." *Perhaps it will be for the best. With Philip in the picture, Maggie will be less attracted to her younger brother.*

Donald bolted his drink and placed the glass on the desk. "I would like to discuss a fostering arrangement."

The Duke poured another round. It gave him time to think. He wasn't ready to give up his daughter. "Maggie is young. She must stay here with her mother and father."

"Of course. Yer good reputation precedes ye, Sir. I can leave Philip here for a year, under yer expert tutelage."

Dughall took another sip and felt the fiery nectar burn a trail to his belly. "Agreed. By then we should know if there will be a betrothal."

Grant smiled. "I'm glad that's settled. Let's discuss the terms of our alliance. First, we must talk about mutual protection…"

As Dughall listened to the man drone on, his thoughts were with his daughter. *Philip, lad. Be good to her.*

Philip Grant

CHAPTER 13
REUNION

NOVEMBER 17TH 1649

3 MONTHS LATER

THE OUTSKIRTS OF CASTLE GRANT

Castle Grant sat on a hill a few miles north of the river Spey in the county of Moray. It had been the seat of the Grants since the 15th century. The imposing structure had dozens of chambers, one being a massive dining hall. There was a Z-shaped tower house, typical of many built in that period.

Dughall sat upon his stallion, watching his daughter bid goodbye to Philip. They were leaving him with his uncle while they journeyed to visit James. Snow fell lightly as he regarded her. *My daughter grows more beautiful by the day. Her skin glows and her lips are as red as cherries.*

The Duke held his breath as she stroked Philip's cheek. The lad took her hand and brought it to his lips. They lingered for a moment and parted.

Luc sat on a white stallion. "Don't worry, Father. Philip will treat her well. I made sure of it."

Dughall let out his breath slowly. His lungs ached from holding it. "I *have* to worry. I'm her father."

Luc grunted. "It's a good match for her. She says that she likes him."

"I know." He stared. "Ye're nearly twenty. Have ye thought about marrying?"

Luc was painfully shy. "I think about it every day. I need a lass to love me."

Dughall loved his son and wanted to help him. "Ye're a fine young man. Handsome... Brave... Intelligent... I will inquire among my nobles – and ask about their daughters."

Luc blushed. "She doesn't have to be of noble birth. Mother wasn't."

"Agreed. But I will inquire anyway. It's a good place to start."

Dughall saw Maggie put up her hood and walk through the snow towards them. "Yer sister is ready to go."

Luc dismounted and helped her up onto a chestnut mare. Then he walked down the road and whistled for Jamison and Murdock. The servants emerged from the woods where they had been standing guard. The three men had a few words and mounted their horses.

Maggie waved to Philip. "I don't want to leave him."

Dughall teased her, "The lad can live without ye for a week!"

She giggled. "Oh, Father!"

They turned their horses and trotted down the road. Large flakes of snow were falling. They planned to ride twelve miles, stay the night at an inn, and continue on to Castle Skene in the morning. There was no more talk of Philip. They had discussed taking him, but feared James' reaction.

***

DRAKE CASTLE

The Duchess rested in bed, after a busy morning. She'd insisted upon rising at dawn to help her family prepare for the journey. There was clothing to pack, a lunch to prepare, and a flurry of last minute instructions. The roads were snow covered, causing her anxiety.

Keira rolled to her side to get comfortable. She was thin for a pregnant lass, but her belly was large. This morning, the child kicked constantly. She glanced at a clock. *I pray that they made it to Castle Grant. Dear Goddess, protect my family.*

The morning had been bittersweet. She was glad that they were visiting James. They'd received letters from the monks and a few from the boy, but it wasn't like firsthand knowledge. She was disappointed that she couldn't accompany them. Oh, she'd asked to go, but the resistance was great. The trip was too risky for a lass eight months pregnant.

Jessie examined her yesterday and proclaimed that everything was normal. Just four more weeks… It seemed like an eternity… and they would have a precious wee one.

Keira's thoughts turned to young Maggie. Dughall had told her about a possible betrothal. She was glad that he was determined not to force their daughter. The boy *was* winning their hearts. *I like Philip. He is handsome and well-mannered. How tragic about his father.*

Keira was glad that Maggie was going to see James. She wanted the truth about her son. Dughall would gloss over the news to protect her. Luc would do what his father wanted. Maggie was the one she trusted.

***

THE NEXT DAY

It had been an arduous journey. After leaving Castle Grant, the Duke's party rode through a blinding snow storm. Stressed and disoriented, they took a wrong turn. Miles later, Dughall stopped at a cottage and hired a guide. They arrived at the inn after nightfall, where they dried off by a roaring fire. Thankfully, they were able to secure rooms and get a hot meal. The travelers woke at dawn, hoping for a break in the weather. They were lucky. The snow had stopped. The sky was clear. They ate a hearty breakfast and continued on the journey.

Now, they were riding through a wild glen – alongside a loch approaching Castle Skene. Dughall was awed by the sight of it. The castle was a medieval looking granite structure bordered by a massive outer wall. At first glance, it seemed impenetrable. Two tall towers stretched to the sky, connected by a long building and guarded catwalks. The windows were little more than slits. It reminded him of the prison in London.

Maggie brought her mare alongside. "James lives here? It looks creepy."

The Duke grunted. "I was thinking the same thing. Perhaps it's more cheerful inside."

"I have bad feelings, Father."

Dughall coughed. "We've been frozen, thawed, and brought to the brink of exhaustion. We may not be thinking straight. James has been here for a year. He will tell us about it."

Maggie nodded. "I don't see anyone. Are we expected?"

"Aye, Daughter. I sent a letter to them weeks ago."

A sharp whistle went up as they approached the gate. Two guards on the catwalk disappeared to inform their master. Long minutes passed, the gate creaked open, and a spindly legged servant admitted them into the courtyard.

***

James left the laboratory and ran down the corridor. He'd just been informed that his family was at the gate. The terrified servant said that there were four men and a young girl. If that was true, then where was his mother?

A letter arrived a week ago, announcing the visit. It caught him by surprise and caused a flurry of mixed emotions. He'd seen his father six months ago at the funeral of the monk. Their exchange had been cordial, so he didn't fear seeing him. Instead, he looked forward to using his new skills to control him. Luc could drop dead and he wouldn't shed a tear for him. He missed his mother terribly and was looking forward to seeing her. And Maggie.. Oh, sweet Maggie... What a cauldron of emotions!

He turned a corner and bumped into Lord Skene. "Ach!"

Skene scowled. "Watch where ye're going!"

James gritted his teeth. "My family is at the gate."

"I know that. Fagan is showing them to the Great Room."

"We must go to them."

Lord Skene put a firm hand on his shoulder. "First, we must talk about how ye will treat them."

James was impatient. "We've discussed this!"

Skene growled, "Do ye want to stay with me?"

"Aye."

"Then ye will act the perfect son... The perfect brother.... No one must suspect us. Block yer father's thoughts. Did ye say that yer sister has the Sight as well?"

James reddened. "Not exactly...   She feels things."

Skene frowned. "Then ye must block her too."

James didn't want to block Maggie. He enjoyed his connection with her. His master could no longer detect his thoughts, so he lied, "I will, Sir."

Skene released him. "Let's go. They are waiting for us."

***

The Great Room was a windowless chamber with a stone fireplace. The granite walls were plain - no pictures, no murals, or woven tapestries. The floor was bare - no reed mats or scattered heather. It was as though a woman's touch had never been there. Except for a few stuffed chairs, the furniture was ancient. There was a dusty oak curio cabinet and a claw-footed table. The room reeked of burnt wood and pipe tobacco.

Maggie laid her cape over the back of a chair and stood by the fire to get warm. After a moment, she turned to watch her father and brother. *Ah, Luc! Such a steady force in my life.* His winsome smile always made her feel welcome. Just now, he was regarding her with admiration. Her father seemed distressed. The Duke sat in a chair, cradling his head in his hands. *Father has a strange aura about him, as dark as a storm cloud in winter. He's worried about how James will treat us.*

She was anxious as well, but trying her best to hide it. *I must not be outwardly affectionate with James. Father will get angry about it.*

The door opened and her brother entered, accompanied by the Laird of the castle.

Dughall stood to greet them. Luc stayed put.

Maggie ran to him. Her heart was a' flutter. "James!"

Skene held the boy back by placing a hand on his shoulder. "Remember yer manners, lad. First, ye must introduce us. I know yer father and brother. Who is this young lass?"

James bristled. "This is my sister, Margaret Christal. We call her Maggie." He reached up and brushed the man's hand from his shoulder. "Sister, this is Lord Skene."

Maggie curtsied. "I am pleased to meet ye, Sir."

Skene smiled. "I am the one who is pleased." He turned to Dughall. "Ye have a lovely daughter."

The Duke stiffened. "Lovely she is, but I'm afraid that she's spoken for."

The silence in the room spoke volumes. At last Skene spoke, "I meant nothing by it."

Dughall nodded. "Of course. Everyone says that I'm overly protective." He turned to his son. "I'm glad to see ye, James. We have missed ye."

James frowned. "Where is Mother?"

"Mother couldn't come," Maggie said. "It was too harsh a ride. She's pregnant."

The lad glared. "I thought she was done with that."

Dughall blushed. "Sometimes it's not a choice we make. It just happened."

Luc came forth. "It's good to see ye, Brother. I'm going to help Jamison and Murdock with the horses. Can ye show me the castle later?"

"Aye."

Luc smiled and left the chamber.

Lord Skene cleared his throat. "Where is my sense of hospitality? Come with me, Lord Drake. I will show ye to yer rooms. Then ye and I will retire to the study for a smoke and a dram of whisky. We have things to discuss – man to man. James can entertain his sister."

Dughall shot a warning glance at Maggie. "I will see ye both later."

The two men left the chamber.

***

During his year in exile, James day-dreamed about his sister. He obsessed on their last encounter – her love for him… her bonny face… and willing body. Now, they were alone at last. She was even more beautiful than he remembered. He held his breath and embraced her.

Maggie melted into his arms.

He touched her breasts.

She pulled back suddenly. "We must not do this!"

James cupped her head with his hands and tried to kiss her. He received a chaste peck on the cheek. He stood back. "What's wrong?"

Maggie blushed. "Siblings must not do this."

He stamped his foot. "We did it before!"

"I know, dear Brother." She had tears in her eyes. "That was before I knew it was wrong. Father was horrified. Mother was too. She said that it's against the laws of nature."

"We don't have to follow their rules. Ye love me. I know it!"

Maggie took his hands. "Of course, I love ye. Ye're my brother. But brothers and sisters don't make love."

James' heart pounded in his ears. There was a way around it. "We can run away. No one will know that ye're my sister."

Her eyes were soulful. "I can't."

"Why?"

"I don't want to hurt ye." Maggie sighed. "I met the man I intend to marry. My heart belongs to another."

James pulled away. "Nay!" He balled his fists and shook with rage. "I'll kill him!"

"Ye must not!" Maggie cried. The lass was pale. "If ye kill him, I will never speak to ye."

James sank into a chair. He covered his eyes and sobbed like a child whose toy had been stolen. Maggie tried to comfort him, but he pushed her away. "Leave me!"

She spoke softly, "Ye will find a lass to love. I can't be her. I'm sorry."

"Sorry?" James cried in agony. "Ye will suffer for this! I promise." He turned away and refused to look at her. "Leave me, Sister!"

Minutes passed without a sound. He heard the door open and creak shut. How could she leave him like this? His emotions were raw. *Oh, Maggie… Sweet Maggie…* It couldn't end like this. He had to convince her. When he looked up, she was gone.

***

TWO DAYS LATER, AT THE MAIN GATE OF THE CASTLE

The Duke said goodbye to his son. They exchanged a few words, embraced for a long moment, and separated.

James waved to his siblings. "Farewell, Maggie. Goodbye, Luc. Give my regards to Mother."

Dughall mounted his stallion, Black Lightning. Without further ado, he snapped the reins and led his party down a path that wound through the valley. He was satisfied. It had been a pleasant and productive visit.

***

He'd spent time with Skene and found that they had things in common. The man was a connoisseur of tobacco and had a cache of Highland whisky. The castle lacked amenities, but it didn't seem to bother his son. The boy appeared to be healthy and happy. Dughall questioned the lad in private. He had nothing to complain about.

To his surprise, James spent most of his time with Luc. He seemed to have lost interest in Maggie, even shunning her. Now, this was a normal brother-sister relationship! His daughter didn't seem to mind. She stayed with her father when possible and played with the castle's cats and kittens.

Best of all, he no longer feared his son. The lad hadn't probed his mind or inflicted illness upon him. The monks and Lord Skene had done their job. There was one thing that made him curious. He could no longer sense the boy's feelings or read his mind. It was a small price to pay for a good relationship.

***

Maggie brought her mare alongside. "I am glad to be going home, Father."

Dughall agreed, "So am I. But I must say that it's been a good visit. James seems happy here."

Maggie looked down. "I guess so."

The Duke smiled sympathetically. "Take heart, Daughter. James is growing up. It's natural that he prefers to be with his brother."

"Ye don't understand. I'm glad that he spent time with Luc."

"Good." Dughall smiled. "I'm pleased with James. I think that he's changed for the better."

Maggie grasped her reins. "Nay, Father. He hasn't." She guided her horse away, leaving him to contemplate her statement.

Dughall thought that she was jealous. *Maggie will come around. In two days, we'll pick up Philip. The lad has a talent for making her happy.*

He planned to tell his wife that their son had been loving and obedient. After the new baby was a week old, they would bring him home for a visit.

Chapter 14
Gratitude

November 18th 1649
1 Day Later

THE BRITISH COLONY OF VIRGINIA

Five months had passed since Gilbert and his family decided to stay in Virginia. They'd taken advantage of 'head rights', a law that granted fifty acres of land to every man, woman, and child who immigrated to the colony. Pooling their resources, Gilbert, Bridget, their children, and Connor were granted three hundred acres, a small section of which ran along the James River.

Part of their property was a plantation, abandoned five years ago after an Indian massacre that killed five hundred colonists. Fifty acres of corn and tobacco had been planted, but lie fallow. There were several acres of mulberry trees and grapevines. With a bit of work, they could bear fruit to make wine. There were four structures on the property – a barn, a smokehouse, a drying shed, and a crude dwelling.

They hired a carpenter and set about clearing timber to build a proper house for the six of them. Guns, tools, nails, and other materials were acquired in Jamestown and transported to the site by boat on the river. Bridget and the girls kept a garden and made the dwelling comfortable. Young George worked alongside Connor and his father. By early November a new house was built, though it lacked amenities by European standards.

Now, Gilbert and his son George were making their weekly trip into Jamestown. Usually they traveled by boat, but today they took their stallions. The road system was poor and they were armed with pistols. There were few outlaws in Virginia, justice being swift, but the Indians could cause trouble. There was a treaty - Indians were not permitted to enter the peninsula between the James and York rivers. Gilbert didn't trust it.

He guided his stallion around a hole in the road. "Watch out, Son! A horse could break a leg in that one."

George pulled back on the reins. "Whoa!" He clenched his thighs and steered his horse around the dangerous pit.

Gilbert glanced at the boy as he brought his stallion alongside. Like

Gilbert, he was dressed simply - in breeks, a shirt, and a sturdy pair of boots. It was sixty degrees, warm for November, so they didn't need outer garments.

The lad had matured in five months. He had developed the muscles of a laborer and was growing a slight beard and moustache. Gilbert's heart swelled with pride. *I can't believe he's my son!*

They rode three miles, rounded a wide bend, and entered the outskirts of Jamestown. They passed a guard house, a church, and a dozen frame houses.

Their land grant was rich with areas suited for hunting and fishing. They'd sustained themselves on fish, fowl, and a variety of four legged animals. Bridget's garden provided herbs and fresh vegetables. But until their farm could be planted, they relied on the general store for flour, barley, and other staples.

Gilbert and George arrived at the store and tied their horses to a hitching post. They climbed up two stairs onto a porch and hesitated. Gilbert kept his voice low, "Remember. My name is George, just like yers."

The boy smiled. "I know, Father!" The pine floor boards creaked as they entered the store.

Gilbert looked around as they waited. There was a wooden counter with scoops, a scale, and a display of tobacco products. Behind it were shelves of staple items. In front were barrels of corn meal, barley, and flour. In one corner, there were iron pots, tin ware, wooden spoons, rolls of fabric, and a cupboard of sewing notions. In another corner, there were guns and necessary supplies – black powder, balls, flint, and primer.

The man behind the counter concluded with a customer and sent him on his way. He smiled when he spied his new customers. "George Gordon and son. Always glad to see a fellow Scot. Ye're getting brawny, lad."

Young George grinned. "I'm a man now. Father says so."

"Then so it is. I have a daughter looking for a husband."

Gilbert mopped his brow with a handkerchief. "Perhaps in a year. It's good to see ye, Fergus. It certainly is warm for November."

"Aye. I bet they've got snow in northern Scotland. What can I do for ye?"

Gilbert took out a scrap of paper, "Twenty pounds of flour... five pounds of barley... two tins of lard... three sewing needles and a spool of thread... writing paper... pipe tobacco... and a small bag of black powder."

The man retrieved the items and placed them on the counter. "Shall I put it on yer account?"

Gilbert nodded. "I will settle it next time." Thanks to his brother, he had enough gold and silver to last him until after his first harvest.

Fergus scratched his wooly head. "There is one more thing… a letter came for ye… a courier left it… a strange fellow…" He searched in a drawer below the counter.

Gilbert held his breath. *Could it be from Dughall?* It had been five months since he sent his letter. Weeks ago, he'd accepted the possibility that his brother died in his place. It was a terrible stain on his soul.

Fergus held up a stained envelope. "Here it is!" He placed it in Gilbert's open hand.

Gilbert stared at the envelope. It was so dirty that it was hard to read. But, it was addressed to George Gordon of Jamestown.

Fergus smiled. "The courier said that the ship carrying it had trouble. The letter was put on another ship and passed from person to person."

Gilbert's heart pounded. If that was true, the letter could be from Dughall. But it could also be from the Duchess or Jamison informing him of his death. He slipped it into a pocket. "Thank ye, Fergus." Gilbert loaded some of their purchases into George's arms and lifted the bags of meal onto his right shoulder. "See ye in a week."

Father and son left the store and packed the goods into their saddlebags. They unhitched the horses and prepared to mount.

George's eyes widened. "Father! The letter. Is it from Uncle Dughall?"

Gilbert's bowels churned. "I don't know."

"Then open it!" The lad's enthusiasm was contagious.

Gilbert took the envelope from his pocket. With trepidation, he tore it open and extracted a one page letter. To please the boy, he read out loud. *"Dear Gilbert, I am starting to believe that I am a cat with nine lives. I survived the situation in Edinburgh with no more than a few breaks and bruises. Of course, that is a story that we will share over a cigar when next I see ye."*

George hooted. "Uncle Dughall is alive!"

"Aye." Gilbert folded the letter quickly and put it in his pocket. Relief washed over him like an ocean wave. He bowed his head in prayer. "Thank ye, Jesus. Thank ye, Blessed Virgin."

George could barely stand it. "Will ye read the rest?"

" I'll read it when we get home." In truth, the man could read no more. There were too many tears in his eyes.

Chapter 15
A Child is Born

December 13th 1649
25 Days Later

DRAKE CASTLE

They named her Morrigan — Morrigan Rose, in hopes that the Goddess would spare her. She was barely five pounds with delicate features and startling blue eyes. That morning, Dughall had examined her from head to toe, searching for signs of yellowing flesh. He found none. Her skin was pink. Her eyes were clear. It was her fourth day of life. There was hope she would survive.

Now, Dughall stood in his chamber, watching his wife nurse the newborn. Keira positioned the babe at her breast and encouraged her to take her nipple. The tiny infant flexed her hands, opened her mouth, and accepted what was offered.

"She's not shy with the nipple." Keira cooed, "Precious wee one. Momma loves ye."

Dughall sat on the edge of the bed, so as not to disturb them. His wife shifted the child to her other breast, inserting the nipple into her tiny mouth. His thoughts were desperate. *God in heaven. Don't take this wee one from us.*

The child's lips made a slight popping sound. Morrigan took a shallow breath and stopped suckling.

Keira removed the nipple from her mouth and wiped her lips with a soft cloth. "Was that good?" She kissed her tiny forehead. "Oh, Husband. I love her so much. She's perfect."

Dughall forced a smile. "That she is."

Keira looked up. "It's been four days... She lives... Will ye hold her?"

The Duke was ashamed. They'd lost four children in the first three days of life, so he'd avoided holding her. "Of course, my love. Give her to me."

Keira passed the baby to him. "Talk to her. Show her that she has a father."

Her statement stung like a bee, but he supposed that he deserved it. Dughall held his breath as he held the tiny infant. His heart swelled with love as she opened her blue eyes. He remembered holding Maggie and James this way. Would she call him 'Da' like the others? "She's bonny, lass. I love her."

Keira closed her nursing gown and gazed at him with soulful eyes. "Touch her, husband. She needs ye."

Dughall examined a tiny hand. "Such delicate fingers and wee nails. It's a miracle." He was surprised when the child gripped his finger. "She's stronger than we think!" There was a sudden knock on the door. "Who is it?"

A voice spoke, "Maggie."

"Come, Daughter."

Maggie entered the chamber and came to the bedside. The girl was clad in a gray wool dress. "How is my sister?"

Dughall smiled. "Good. I think she's going to make it."

"Oh, Father! How could ye doubt it? I knew it the first time I laid eyes on her."

"Would ye like to hold her?"

"Aye."

Maggie smoothed her dress and sat in a nearby chair. She waited as the wee one was placed in her arms.

Dughall stood over her. "Hold her neck just so, Daughter."

Maggie smiled. "I know how to hold a baby. I care for them in the nursery." She stroked the baby's cheek. "We are going to be great friends, Morrigan." The wee infant gurgled in agreement. "I can't wait to show her to Philip. We hope to have seven of them."

Dughall gave his wife a worried glance. *Keira must speak to her about being a woman. I will pay a visit to Donald Grant. If the lad and lass are determined to marry, it might be time for the betrothal.*

Chapter 16
Hand Fast

December 15th 1649
2 Days Later

CASTLE GRANT, THE HUNTING LODGE

The walls of the hunting lodge were adorned with the heads of animals. Staring down at a ring of comfortable chairs were deer, boars, wildcats, and foxes. It was truly a man's domain. Wolf pelt rugs were scattered on the floor.

Dughall sat across from the Laird of Grant, enjoying a dram of whisky. "Ah… This is excellent."

Donald Grant held up his glass to the light to admire the amber color. "My distillery makes it with the pure waters of the Spey. I will send ye home with a bottle of it."

The Duke was grateful. "Thank ye, friend."

"But ye are not here to discuss my whisky. Why have ye come this day?"

Dughall took another sip. "Maggie and Philip are determined to marry. The time has come for their betrothal."

Donald smiled. "So soon? Excellent!"

Dughall tipped his glass and finished the whisky. "We should hold the betrothal ceremony soon. The lad and lass are strong headed. I don't want them to get into trouble."

Donald cocked an eyebrow. "They are that determined?"

"Aye."

"Then we should plan the wedding as well."

Dughall couldn't imagine his daughter in a marital bed. Yet, the girl claimed she understood. "Such a wedding will take planning. Would next December be to yer liking?"

Donald grunted. "I have no objection. Shall we drink on it?"

The Duke passed his glass and watched him fill both of them. He accepted the offering and held it up. "To Maggie and Philip."

Donald joined him, "May they have a long and happy marriage."

"To the unity of our clans…"

"May we always stand together…"

They drank toast after toast 'til the whisky was gone, content in each other's company.

Dughall felt good. The matter was settled. There was no point in waiting. "Can ye join us this Saturday for the betrothal ceremony? My son James is expected for a visit. The date would be good for us."

The man smiled. "Aye. It's time ye met my wife Anne and daughter Arabella."

✱✱✱

THREE DAYS LATER, DRAKE CASTLE

The Great Hall had been decorated for Maggie and Philip's betrothal. Six guest tables draped with tartan cloth were adorned with pine boughs and dried flowers. Since it was close to Christmas, a pine tree sat in the corner - decorated with ornaments and lit candles. There were two tables for refreshments - one with wine and ale and cider - another with every sweet cake imaginable.

Maggie looked stunning in a tailored tartan dress. She stood with Philip and her parents, welcoming guests into the chamber. Her heart fluttered like the wings of a bird. It was almost time for the betrothal. The lass welcomed her grandparents Alex and Jessie, Uncle Ian, Aunt Mary, and their seven children, her beloved brother Luc, and Philip's family. The only one missing was James. She'd heard that he arrived minutes ago and was being escorted through the gate.

Father John entered, bearing a leather bound note book. The elderly priest smiled. "My dear Maggie. And Philip. Young man, ye must promise to take care of her."

The lad blushed. "Always and forever."

The priest moved on to one of the tables. Dughall and Keira accompanied him.

A commotion in the corridor drew Maggie's attention. James and Lord Skene were approaching the Hall, escorted by Jamison. The servant was telling them about the betrothal.

"What?" James cried. "She's getting married?"

"Nay, lad," the servant said. "It's a betrothal."

Maggie's heart sank. She saw a blazing red aura around James that signified hatred and anger. Would he hurt Philip? She squeezed her beloved's hand and drew him closer.

"What's wrong?" Philip whispered.

"My brother is unhappy with me." She watched Lord Skene scold her brother in a vile and threatening manner. The boy glared at her and stamped his foot. Did he mean to spoil the betrothal? Lord Skene grabbed his arm and shook him. To her surprise, James calmed and proceeded to the reception line. Lord Skene walked off with Jamison.

Maggie loved her brother and didn't want to see him suffer. She embraced him tenderly. "I'm glad that ye came."

James reddened. "So, this is the lad?"

"Aye. This is Philip Grant." Maggie's gut twisted with fear. "Philip, this is James, my brother."

Philip offered his hand. "I'm pleased to meet ye."

Reluctantly, James shook it.

Dughall and Keira approached. She opened her arms and hugged her son. "Oh, James! I've missed ye."

James stood back. "Ye don't look pregnant."

Keira smiled. "I gave birth a week ago to a daughter. Ye have a new sister - her name is Morrigan."

James forced a smile. "I'm happy for ye." Once again, he seemed to have turned from darkness to light. "Mother. Father. Maggie. It's good to see ye." He took a breath. "I'm told that this is a betrothal ceremony."

Dughall seemed tense. "Aye, son."

"Why did no one inform me?"

"It was rather sudden. Philip assures me that he'll take good care of yer sister."

James grunted. "He had better."

Father John approached. "Welcome, young James." He turned to Dughall. "Shall we begin, my Lord? The children are getting restless."

"Aye."

Maggie and Philip followed the priest to the middle of the room. Everyone gathered around them in a large circle. The couple stood together and joined hands.

Father John smiled. "Where are the strips of tartan?"

Dughall came forth with a blue and red strip cut from his best kilt and handed it to the priest. "From my garment, with my blessing."

Donald Grant came forth with a strip representative of his tartan. The two men returned to their wives.

Father John used the strips to tie the couple's hands together. He began the ceremony with an explanation. "Hand fasting is an ancient custom. It is a symbol of betrothal, a commitment to marry. It is neither Christian or pagan - just human."

He turned to the couple and read from his notebook, "These are the hands that will love and cherish ye throughout the years. These hands will wipe the tears from yer eyes: tears of sorrow and tears of joy. These hands will comfort ye in illness and hold ye as ye struggle through difficult times. Lastly, these are the hands that will encourage ye to live yer dreams. Together, dear Maggie and Philip, everything ye wish for can be realized."

Maggie's heart swelled with emotion as she watched the face of her beloved.

The priest continued. "Now, for the vows. Will ye be faithful to one another?"

They answered in unison, "We will."

"Will ye stand by each other in sickness and health, in plenty and want?"

"We will."

"Will ye be open and honest with each other?"

"We will."

"Will ye accept children lovingly from God and bring them up according to the laws of Christ and his Church?"

Maggie knew that this was what Philip wanted. Her beliefs would be respected as well.

They smiled. "We will."

"Then 'tis done." He closed the book. "I declare ye hand fast. Ye will marry in a year and a day."

"Thank ye, Father John." Maggie turned to her parents. "Philip and I wish to take the ancient vows as well." She reached in her pocket and took out a small knife. Then she held his palm, scored it across the lifeline, and offered him her hand.

Philip pressed his lips to her palm and took the knife. She watched as he scored her delicate skin. They joined palms and watched a thin line of blood trickle down her wrist.

Maggie spoke boldly, "Red is the color of courage, strength, and passion."

He replied, "Hand in hand and blood in blood, let this act seal our love. I pledge myself to ye in joy and sadness, wholeness and brokenness, in peace and turmoil, faithfully for all our days. From this moment we are hand fast. We will marry within a year and a day."

She smiled. "We will have children and grow old together."

Philip stroked her check. "I love ye, lass." They sealed their pledge with a tender kiss.

***

There was a collective, "Awww…" – followed by intense clapping. Guests gathered around Maggie and Philip and offered heartfelt congratulations.

James watched as Dughall and Keira embraced the couple. His parents seemed pleased with the match. What a change of events! This visit was supposed to be about *him*. Didn't he matter? He cringed as Philip smiled. *Maggie belongs to me, not this interloper!*

"Will ye congratulate them?" a young girl asked.

James turned to see a lass with fair skin, dark hair, and clear blue eyes. He didn't recognize her. "Who are ye?"

She curtsied, "Arabella Grant. I am Philip's cousin."

"Hmmphhh… How old are ye?"

"Twelve."

James saw a possibility. Perhaps he could make Maggie jealous. He stretched out a hand and smiled. "Ye're a bonny lass, Arabella. Take my hand. We will congratulate them together."

The girl looked surprised, but took his hand. They approached the betrothed couple.

Maggie's eyes widened. "Dear brother."

Philip smiled. "I see that ye met my cousin Arabella."

James' eyes flashed. "Aye. We came to congratulate ye."

"Thank ye. Rest assured. I will take good care of yer sister."

James studied his sister for signs of jealousy. There were none. Instead, she tightened her grip on Philip's hand. He would have to find another way to separate them.

***

The Duke was bursting with emotion. His beloved daughter was hand fast. In a year and a day, she would marry. Their shining faces... The confession of love... The ancient vows... It was overwhelming. He sensed a range of emotions in the room – joy, happiness, and satisfaction. But there was something else as well - someone was profoundly unhappy about it.

Dughall sighed. *I must be getting old. The Sight is failing me. I can't identify the culprit.*

Chapter 17
Kate

December 22nd 1649
4 Days Later

PARIS, FRANCE

Kate Gunn stood in her Paris apartment, admiring herself in a gilded oval mirror. She wore a black velvet dress with lace-trimmed sleeves, broad topped boots, and a mid-length woolen wrap. These items were recently purchased at several upscale tailor, millinery, and cobbler shops. She completed her outfit with a fashionable beaver pelt hat, trimmed with an ostrich feather. Kate adored Paris and had no plans to return to Scotland. Life in the country of her birth seemed crude by comparison. There were interesting men in Paris, as well as high fashion and theatre. A woman could elevate her status. She had. She no longer pined for Lord Dughall Gordon.

It had been more than a decade since her daughter was born. At the time, the child meant nothing to her, except as a bargaining chip with her father. After the birth, Kate waited eight weeks at Huntly, hoping for a word from Dughall. Bitterly disappointed, she'd accepted Gilbert's offer and left for France. No stranger to Paris, she'd taken up residence in a district that she and the late Earl frequented.

The lass liked what she saw in the mirror. The years hadn't spoiled her rare beauty. Her skin was radiant and her breasts were large. Except for a few silvery marks on her belly, it was impossible to tell that she'd carried a child. She was nearly forty, but looked younger.

Kate looked around her apartment with a sense of satisfaction. Years ago, she'd established an account with a barrister to receive Gilbert's stipend. She'd furnished her abode with expensive pieces and spent lavishly on clothing, perfumes, and powders. Every month, Gilbert's silver appeared in her account, reinforcing their bargain.

She wondered how much longer that would continue. The deposits stopped coming from Gilbert Gordon. Her barrister said that the source had changed; they now came from his brother Dughall. At first, she'd interpreted this as a good sign, that he was thinking about her. Yesterday, she'd learned the true reason for it. Parisians were familiar with the trouble between England and Scotland. After the execution of the King, his widow and children sought refuge in France. Gossip told her that Gilbert had been swept up in the civil war, tried as a traitor, and condemned to death. True to his word, Dughall remembered to provide for her.

So, Gilbert Gordon is dead. Poor man. They would have taken his head or disemboweled him. She owed him a debt of gratitude. The man had provided her with letters of introduction, which inflated her worth and status.

***

She thought back to when she first arrived in Paris. The city was exciting. The only thing that bothered her was the loss of Dughall. Each day, she prayed for his marriage to fail and fantasized about their lovemaking. A year passed without word from him. She hardened her heart and explored the seedier side of Paris. On a whim, she tried to locate a brothel that she and the Earl had visited. The place had been well appointed with exotic women and instruments of bondage. Kate had been unable to find the establishment, which was marked with a sign of the phallus. In its place was a stodgy men's club that offered drinking, debating, and fencing competitions. From a neighbor, she learned that a recent edict suppressed prostitution. This had driven the trade underground and made it lucrative. Kate was ambitious. The stakes were high. The pay was excellent. She became a high class prostitute.

***

Now, more than a decade had passed. She was a rich woman and didn't need Gordons' silver. Even so, Kate's curiosity was getting the best of her. "Dughall was close to his brother. I wonder how he is faring." She stared at the image in the mirror. "The young Lord must be thirty. A lot can happen in twelve years. It's time to write him a letter."

Chapter 18
Henrietta

January 30th 1650
38 days later

Paris France

PALAIS DU LOUVRE

The royal palace was situated on the right bank of the river Seine between the Jardin de Tuileries and the Church of Saint-Germain l'Auxerrois. The name 'Louvre' derived from the Frankish word 'loevar', signifying a fortified place. Indeed, it was. The impressive medieval structure was the seat of power.

The day was cold and bleak, a typical January morning. Sunday Mass was over and the chapel was nearly empty. Henrietta Maria knelt at the rail with her daughter Elizabeth, praying for the soul of her husband. It had been one year to the day that Charles had been beheaded. The young girl was crying.

The former Queen was stoic. "Ne pleure pas. Ton père est avec Dieu." She had just told the child that her father was with God, but she seriously doubted that. Henrietta sighed. She wished that she had never taken the girl to the execution. It was a terrible thing to witness.

The marble kneeler was cold beneath her knees. If she didn't rise soon, she would need help to do so. She looked to her daughter, who was praying fervently to the Virgin. It was going to be a while. Henrietta took a moment to contemplate her situation.

* * *

She'd been living in exile for a more than a year. She and her children were safe, well cared for, and revered by the population. The English parliament abolished the monarchy, so they couldn't return to London. It was the opinion of most that it wouldn't last forever. In the meantime, her son Charles, heir apparent, had been exerting his influence in the colonies.

France was being ruled by a regency council since the death of her brother, Louis XIII. This council had been appointed for the duration of his son's minority. Her nephew, Louis XIV, was eleven. Pompous and spoiled, it was a strained situation.

***

Henrietta sighed. It wasn't all bad. She had just completed a year of mourning and was free to take a new husband. She hid a smile. Only one man performed in her deviant fantasies. *What is happening with Lord Gordon? Perhaps I should write him a letter.*

CHAPTER 19
FATHERS BROTHERS AND SONS

MARCH 30TH 1650
2 MONTHS LATER

DRAKE CASTLE

The bath chamber was warm. Apple wood crackled in hearth, emitting a delicate fruity fragrance. An oval wall mirror reflected a washstand laden with soaps and oils. Two copper tubs stood side by side – with steam rising from the water.

The Duke stood naked with his back to the mirror, examining his silvery whip scars. It was thirteen years since the Earl flogged him, but sometimes it seemed like yesterday. He turned and noted other marks – a slash from a sword, a burn from canon fire, and scars from a beating at Edinburgh Castle. It was a testament to what he had been through.

Dughall wondered out loud, "How many more scars will there be, before I stand here as an old man?" There was a knock on the door. He grabbed a towel and wrapped it around his middle. "Come in."

The door opened and his stepfather entered. "Son."

"Father."

Alex began to undress, pulling his shirt over his head. "It's been a while since we've shared a bath."

Dughall smiled. "Aye. I've missed it. 'Tis a good place to discuss things." He watched his father drop his kilt. The man had aged in the last ten years. His hair was white, his skin was wrinkled, and his muscles were practically flaccid. Dughall dropped his towel to the floor. Now, they were both naked. "My manservant said that ye requested a hot bath."

Alex grunted. "Aye. I hope that the hot water will help my arthritis."

They climbed into their respective tubs. Dughall heard him inhale sharply. "Take a deep breath, Father. It won't seem so hot in a minute."

Alex submerged his wrists in the steaming water. "Ahhh... It does help."

"Willow bark should dampen the pain and take down the swelling."

He frowned. "Sometimes it helps. Sometimes, it doesn't. The pain is in my wrists and hands. It's likely from the torture."

Dughall agreed. "I will search my books for another medicine."

Alex rolled a bar of soap between his palms. "Thank ye, Son." He lathered his chest. "What did ye want to talk about?"

"My son."

"What about Luc?"

"It's not about Luc. The lad is helpful and obedient. He is the perfect son."

"Not many men can say that."

"I know," Dughall said with a smile. "Luc has only one fault. He's a bit shy with women. I'm trying to arrange a marriage."

"Luc is a handsome lad. Ye shouldn't have a problem." They were silent for a moment. "So, ye must want to talk about James." There was a tinge of disapproval in his voice.

"Aye." Dughall rinsed his chest. "My wife wants to bring him home for the summer."

"How is the lad?"

"The monks say that he is progressing with his lessons. His behavior is acceptable, though there have been a few outbursts of temper."

"Hmmphhh…"

By God, his father was stubborn! "Try to understand. I can't keep him away forever."

Alex reddened. "He tried to rut with his sister."

Dughall wished that he hadn't told him. "'Tis true."

"Did they do it?"

"I don't know. I was furious when I found them. I beat James and never questioned Maggie. The poor lass cried when she saw what I did." He sighed. "It was a terrible thing to see fear in her eyes."

Alex softened. "It's not her fault. The lad deserved it. A young man must learn to control his impulses."

"Agreed."

"So, what do ye want from me?"

"I need yer help. It would seem that James is no longer obsessed with his sister. When we visited Castle Skene, he shunned her to be with Luc. At the hand fast, he courted young Arabella Grant."

"Ye'll have to keep an eye on that situation."

Dughall bristled. "Agreed. I don't want a problem with our ally." He counted to three to calm himself. "When Ian and I were lads, ye taught us to respect women."

"I did what any father should do."

The Duke was ashamed. "It's no secret that I've failed. That is why I need yer help to set James straight." He added, "Do it for Maggie."

Alex stared. "Is the sweet lass in danger?"

"She thinks so. Maggie knows that what they did was wrong. Now that she is betrothed, she fears her brother's reaction."

The older man grunted. "I will do it."

Dughall was grateful. "Thank ye, Father. We will do it together."

***

VIRGINIA

Gilbert straightened his back and noted the position of the sun. It was time for the midday meal. He unhitched his mare from the wooden plow and grabbed the reins to lead it away. In the distance, he saw George and Connor tilling the soil with hoes. He whistled to them. The men dropped theirs tools and started walking towards him.

Gilbert thought of his son as a man. The lad worked as hard as he did. Previously pampered as an Earl's son, the boy had matured in Virginia.

George and Connor arrived. The former servant wiped sweat from his brow. "Is it time for a meal, my Lord?"

"Aye." Gilbert smiled. "We are equals here, my friend. Ye don't have to call me that."

Connor grinned. "I know. It's habit."

George's stomach growled. "I'm starving! Mother said she would make rabbit stew."

Gilbert tousled his hair. "Thanks to ye, son. Ye've become an excellent hunter."

The boy smiled. "I love that musket."

They led the horse for a mile until they spotted the new house. Nine-year-old Anne and seven-year-old Mary could be seen working in the garden. A scraggly hound dog stood by guarding them. Chickens strutted around the barn yard.

Bridget was hanging out clothes to dry on a line of rope they'd strung for her. George ran on ahead to greet her.

"He's a fine lad," Connor said. They began to take longer strides.

Gilbert's heart swelled. "Aye. He reminds me of my brother."

"Have ye heard from the Duke again?"

"Nay. I posted a letter to him in December. The ship was sailing up the coast to Boston, then going on to England. He may not have received it yet. Sometimes it takes a while."

"Still, he lives. That's a miracle."

Gilbert grinned. "It was the best I could have hoped for."

"The man has more bravery than sense."

"Agreed. But I'm grateful to be alive."

They arrived at the house and saw George at the outdoor cook fire, spooning hot rabbit stew into tin plates. "It looks good, Father."

Bridget approached wearing a plain cotton dress with an apron tied at the waist. Her hair was long and wild and her face was smudged with dirt. "Husband!"

Gilbert found her incredibly attractive. He pulled her close and kissed her.

"Oh, Gilbert."

He nibbled her ear, "Ye must call me George."

She blushed. "I don't care what yer name is. Ye're alive and whole. I still have my husband."

They separated. The girls arrived and hugged their father. The family sat on stumps around the fire, eating rabbit stew and corn bread from tin plates.

Gilbert dipped a piece of bread in the gravy and stuffed it in his mouth. After a morning of toil, the taste was exquisite. A year ago, he would have considered this a crude existence, but he'd come to appreciate it. *How fortunate I am. I have a beautiful wife, two daughters, and a brawny son. But most of all, I have my life.*

***

CASTLE SKENE

James stood in the laboratory, assisting Lord Skene with an experiment. He'd been assigned a task. Skene was working at a charcoal smelter purifying a combination of metals. Upon his signal, James was to measure a pinch of lapis philosophorum and sprinkle the powder into the mixture.

The lad's mind wandered. *I should be with Maggie. Surely, she's tired of Philip by now.* "I want to go home." James held his breath. *Did I say that out loud?*

Skene scoffed, "Ye want to go home to yer family? They don't care about ye."

James flushed with anger. "That's not true! Mother loves me."

"Ha! Are ye blind? She replaced ye with a new baby."

That couldn't be true. "Stop it!"

"Yer sister only has eyes for that lovesick pup! Do ye think she cares what happens to ye?"

James gritted his teeth. "Maggie needs me."

"Ha! Women are fickle. They're all whores."

"How dare ye call my mother and sister whores! Apologize, Sir, or my father will…"

Skene cackled. "Ah… Yer father… I thought that ye hated him. Any fool could tell that he was pleased with yer sister's betrothal. Philip is the son he always wanted."

"Nay!"

"Face it, lad. Ye might as well call *me* Father."

James stamped his foot. "Never! Never! Never!"

Lord Skene scoffed and returned to his experiment.

James was surprised that he hadn't been punished. He'd been pushing the man all week. Defying him in front of servants… Disobeying orders… They bickered constantly. Their relationship was at a boiling point.

Skene dipped an iron rod into the melted ore. "Are ye deaf?

Measure it, ye idiot! "

James stiffened. "I'm the son of a Duke, not yer servant!" His temper flared. *How dare he call me an idiot?* With a quick motion, he hurled the entire contents of the bottle into the open smelter.

Skene screamed like a wounded animal. "My experiment is ruined!" The man beat his breasts and tore at his scraggly hair. "Ye'll pay for this!"

James stepped back. Skene's thoughts and emotions were strong. The man wanted to kill him. He ran for the door, but didn't make it.

Strong hands grabbed his shoulders and pressed his face into the stone wall. "I'll teach ye a lesson ye'll never forget!"

James struggled to get free, but the man's strength was overpowering. He watched him grab a strap from the wall. Fingers grabbed his collar and ripped off his shirt. Blood roared in his ears as he was forced head down over a stool.

Skene's voice was threatening, "Tell anyone, and I'll kill ye."

The man cackled as he struck him, blistering his skin and drawing blood.

James yelped in pain. The strap snapped again and again, making its mark on his back and shoulders. How could this happen to a Duke's son? Would no one save him? "Mercy!"

"There is no mercy here." Skene's breath was rank. "When I'm done, ye'll call me Father."

✳✳✳

DRAKE CASTLE

It was a clear spring day in the forest near Drake Castle. An easterly wind blew across the moor, bringing an early thaw. Snow had melted from higher elevations, swelling streams and rivers. The ground was covered by wild grasses and heather, still brown from the previous season.

Dughall, Ian, and their sons were enjoying an outing – hunting on the moor after a cooped-up winter.

Ian smiled. "What a difference a few days makes." He watched his twelve-year-old son kneel by a pheasant and draw his knife. Red haired Andrew stretched the neck of the flailing bird and slit its throat. It shuddered and kicked for the last time.

"Ye have fine sons," Dughall said.

"Oh, aye." Ian was wistful. "I remember the first time I came here. It was with Jamison just after we rescued ye. He convinced me to stay and serve ye."

"I'm glad that he did."

"Aye. Just look at all we've accomplished."

They watched Andrew's twin place his foot against the bird's body and pull out the arrow. Alexander cleaned the tip, straightened the feathers, and slid it into his quiver. "It's a big male! Father, can the cook prepare this for supper?"

Ian smiled. "We'll ask her when we get back to the castle."

Luc threw a rope to his cousin. "Tie the feet, Alex. We'll throw it over my saddle."

Ian spoke softly, "Luc is a fine lad. Ye're lucky to have him."

Dughall nodded. "Aye. Did I tell ye that James is coming back?"

Ian sensed his apprehension. He couldn't blame him. James was spoiled and selfish and caused trouble with everyone. "Is he coming home for good?"

"Nay. He's not finished with his studies. Keira asked me to bring him home for the summer."

Ian disliked the lad but he tried to make the best of it. "James was respectful at the hand fasting ceremony. I actually had a decent conversation with him."

Dughall brightened. "Good! I think that he's made progress, though there are some who don't agree with me."

"Who?"

"Maggie."

Ian knew about James' attempt to molest his sister. "I guess she has the right to suspect him."

"I share yer concern, Brother. That is why I asked Father to talk to him."

Ian grinned. "There is no better man for the job."

Luc made a loop in the rope and hung the pheasant from his saddle. He took out his knife and stripped off a few iridescent feathers. "For my sister Maggie. She loves pretty feathers."

Ian clapped his hands. "Come on, lads! Let's go back to the castle. My stomach is growling like a hungry beast. It must be time for the midday meal." As the boys mounted, he turned to Dughall. "Take heart, Brother. Next year we will hunt this moor with all of our sons, James included."

Dughall frowned. "I hope so. I have a bad feeling that I can't shake. I wonder if he's in danger."

***

CASTLE SKENE

The dungeon was a medieval chamber located deep in the bowels of the castle. It had no door, just an iron hatch in the ceiling with a platform device to lower prisoners. Skene called it an oubliette, a French word that meant 'a place of forgetting'. The chamber was windowless, so it was impossible to tell day from night. When the hatch was closed, it was quite dark.

James sat on a pile of straw, contemplating his situation. He was thirsty and his body ached from the beating. In the last few hours, his emotions had run a gamut - from anger to outrage to abject fear. He hugged his knees. *Could Skene be right? Oh, Mother. Have ye forgotten me?*

James felt something brush against his leg and jumped to his feet. There were rats in here; he'd seen them. *Daft old Lord! I will never call him Father.* His thoughts grew desperate as the minutes passed. *What if Skene dies and I am left here to rot? Will they find my bones? Will they mourn for me?*

He heard the hatch slide away and gazed at a square of light in the ceiling.

Skene's voice called out, "Have ye learned yer lesson?"

James shouted, "Aye, Sir."

"What's my name?" the angry voice countered.

It irked his being to say it, "Father."

"That's better." The man began to lower the platform into the chamber.

James was having an epiphany. Suddenly, his true father didn't seem so bad. The monks had taught him to pray. For the first time in his life, he did it willingly. *God help me. I have to get back to my family.*

CHAPTER 20
MOTHERS SISTERS AND DAUGHTERS

DRAKE CASTLE, THE NURSERY

Keira stood at the cradle, changing the baby's nappie. *Morrigan is one hundred and eleven days old.* Like a first time mother, she counted the days since birth.

There was a bit of confusion about her name. The priest refused to baptize her 'Morrigan' because it wasn't a Christian name. Instead, he baptized her with her middle name 'Rose'. But she would always be Morrigan to Keira. There was a good side to naming her daughter after the Goddess. A name she once feared, she now loved. There was no more talk of the curse of the Morrigan.

The door creaked open and Maggie entered. The girl was clad in a gray wool dress and had a sprig of dried flowers in her hair. "Mother."

Keira smiled. "Daughter."

"How is my sister?"

Keira fastened the nappie and smoothed the baby's gown. "No colic. No rashes. She's perfect."

Maggie leaned over the cradle and encouraged the child to grip her finger. "She's strong, too. Oh... Father must love her."

"He does." She changed the subject. "Did he tell ye that he agreed to bring James home for the summer?"

The girl's expression darkened. "Nay."

Keira frowned. "What's wrong?"

"Oh, Mother. I can not tell ye."

"What happened between ye and yer brother?"

Maggie reddened. "When we visited Castle Skene, we had a few minutes alone. He tried to take me."

Keira inhaled sharply. "How, daughter?"

Maggie looked down. "I can not say it."

She lifted her daughter's chin. "Ye must."

"He took me in his arms and tried to kiss me."

"Like a brother?"

"Nay! His tongue sought my mouth."

Keira was devastated. She had to be certain. "Could ye be

mistaken?"

"Nay. He touched me like this." She took her mother's slender hands and placed them on her bodice.

Keira's hands dropped. She was overcome with anguish. "Great Goddess! Haven't we suffered enough? Why must our family face this?"

Maggie's eyes filled with tears. "Forgive me, Mother. I shouldn't have mentioned it."

"Does yer father know?"

The girl sounded miserable, "Nay."

"Ye must not tell him."

A single tear slid down her cheek. "Father hates to be lied to. If he asks, I must tell him." Her eyes widened. "Oh, Mother... There is more. James threatened to kill Philip."

Keira loved her son without reservation. But now she understood why Dughall separated them. *What can I do to control my son? Teach him? Scold him? Punish him? He respects no woman, least of all me.*

Maggie sniffled. "I love James. What can we do?"

Just then, a wet nurse entered the room. "My ladies." She bowed her head slightly and began to attend to wee Morrigan.

Keira stiffened. The girl was known to gossip. She guided Maggie to the open door. This was no place to air their problems. Her daughter began to cry. "Hush, child."

"But, Mother..."

"Fear not. We will continue this discussion later."

***

VIRGINIA

Bridget watched the men lead the plough horse to the fields. She had much to do before they returned – clean the dishes, replenish the stew, and bake corn bread in a covered pot. She didn't resent the work. She'd been lucky enough to spend more than a decade as an Earl's wife. Pampered and respected... But she was no stranger to hard work. Before her marriage, she'd been a cook, a seamstress, and a bath chamber attendant.

She knew that the men performed the more difficult tasks - clearing land, building structures, and tilling the fields. They were also responsible for protecting them, though she had taken a hand in that. Every day, she practiced with a pistol and kept it within reach. You never knew when there would be an Indian attack.

Bridget smiled as the men passed from view. She was happy in spite of the hardships. She had three fine children and the man she adored. It was a miracle he had escaped the ax man. *Oh, Gilbert. Ach, I mean George. I love ye so.*

Anne and Mary were approaching. She wiped her hands on her apron. "How are my wee daughters?"

Anne gave her a mock frown. "We're nae so wee anymore."

Mary giggled.

Bridget gathered them to her skirt. "Ye're right. What would I do without my angels? Ye are Momma's second pair of hands."

They gazed up at her, their smiling faces reminding her of Gilbert. "The men will be back before we know it. Come along. I will teach ye how to make bread."

They gathered the soiled dishes and went into the house.

Bridget's mind was troubled. This was the third month that she'd missed her bleeding cycle. There were few women in Virginia. A midwife was a rare commodity. *I'm nearly forty. Perhaps I am done with my cycles. If not, who will deliver a child out here?*

CHAPTER 21
LETTERS

APRIL 7TH 1650
ONE WEEK LATER

DRAKE CASTLE

THE STUDY

The Duke sat at his desk, reviewing the castle's procurement ledgers. Things were simpler now that he didn't have Huntly to consider. The powers that be in Edinburgh had assigned the castle to a son of a Covenanting lord. A few of Gilbert's servants had come to Drake - old Marcia, Tavia, and their immediate families. The rest stayed and took their chances.

Dughall ran his finger down the last ledger, scanning for inconsistencies. There appeared to be none. He scrawled his signature at the bottom. He heard a knock at the door and answered, "Come."

Murdock entered, bearing a tray of tea and scones and what looked like a pack of letters. "My Lord." He placed the tray on a corner of the desk and began to serve the tea. "Marcia asked me to bring this to ye."

Dughall smiled. "Thank ye, friend. Tell her that I appreciate it."

Murdock handed him the package. "A messenger delivered these at the main gate. One is from Virginia and two are from France."

"France?"

"Aye, m'Lord."

Dughall compared the two envelopes. They were written in different hands. "How strange." His curiosity was piqued. *Who would write me from there? Gilbert said that we had relatives.*

Murdock prepared a scone, slathering it golden honey. He placed it on a plate before him. "Do ye need anything else?"

"Nay."

"Then with yer permission, I must go. They need me to haul firewood for the kitchen."

Dughall nodded. "Ye may go."

Murdock retrieved the tray and left the room. The Duke sat for a few minutes sipping his tea and staring at envelopes. He decided to open the one from Virginia. He longed for news of Gilbert.

The envelope looked like it had passed through many hands. It was grimy and sweat stained. He took out a silver letter opener, slit it open, and unfolded the letter. It was dated December 28th. Gilbert's handwriting jumped from the page.

My dear brother. I was elated to receive yer letter. Each night, I thank Jesus and the Blessed Virgin that ye are still alive! The loss of Huntly pales in comparison to the loss of my only brother. Don't worry about me. I sympathize with my former subjects, but that life seems far away. I am now a citizen of Virginia, a farmer, a hunter, and a man who works with my hands. What a surprise. I love it! We were awarded 300 acres of prime land, some of which abuts the James River. It was previously occupied, so some acres were cleared and planted. There were a few crude buildings, enough to get us started. Connor and George and I built a new house, though it is crude by European standards. Aye, I said George. My son has matured into a brawny lad in only a few months. Bridget and my daughters are thriving. They keep house like they were born to it and maintain a vegetable garden. My wife has even learned how to shoot a pistol! What a wonderful woman I married.

Planting season will soon be upon us. We plan to put in ten acres of corn and wheat as well as a crop of tobacco. Yer generous gift of gold and silver sustains us in the meantime. When the major work is done, I intend to integrate into Virginia society and politics. I will let ye know how that goes in a future letter.

Brother, I hope ye had a good Christmas. Rest assured that we are safe, happy, and flourishing in the colony of Virginia. I will never forget that I owe ye my life. And I will never let my children forget. Come visit us. Ye and yer family are always welcome. I must post this, as the ship is leaving. Write me soon. Tell me about yer family and keep me abreast of English and Scottish politics.

Send my love to yer family. Yer brother, Gilbert (George Gordon)

Dughall was delighted. He decided to show the letter to his wife and children and ask them to each craft a short paragraph to him. Perhaps even Marcia would care to write a note. He would write a long letter that would include the state of Scottish politics.

The Duke pushed the paper aside and picked up an envelope that had a return address from Paris. He slit it open and unfolded the letter on the desk. It was dated December 24th. An unfamiliar handwriting jumped from the page.

My dear Dughall (or should I call ye my Lord?),

It's been a long time. Almost thirteen years have passed since I saw ye last. The Gordon brothers have been true to their word, providing me with a monthly stipend.

Dughall stiffened. "Oh, God! It's from Kate." He continued reading.

I have often thought about the time we shared and wondered about the daughter born of our love. Tell me, does she still live? Does she look like me? Is she happy? And how are ye?

I was sorry to hear about yer brother, Gilbert. Last week, I heard that he'd been captured during the war and scheduled to be executed. With King Charles dead, I can only assume that he was killed. Gilbert was a good man and most often fair with me. It hurts to think that he came to such an end. I know that ye two were close. How are ye taking it?

In closing, I appreciate what ye have done for me. But I must tell ye that I am a woman of means and do not need yer money. I release ye from yer obligation from this day forward. I hope that this will repair our stormy relationship.

Please write to acknowledge this letter. I mean ye no harm, truly, and wish ye and our daughter the best. Fondly, Kate Gunn

Dughall was stunned. Kate sounded reasonable. It touched him that she wondered about Maggie and was concerned about his welfare. If that wasn't enough, he was grateful to be released from their contract. There were times when it was a burden. He would answer her letter tomorrow.

The Duke pushed her letter aside and picked up the last envelope. It was also from Paris, France. *Who else could be writing me?* He slit it open and unfolded the letter. It was dated February 3rd. A fancy script jumped from the page as he sipped his tea.

My dear Lord Gordon,
As I write this letter, a year has passed since the death of my husband. I cannot describe what a comfort it was to see you in London on that fateful day.

Dughall choked on his tea. "It's from the Queen!" He continued reading.

Since that time, my children and I have been living at the Palais du Louvre under the protection of my nephew, King Louis XIV. It is a difficult life, quite boring, and I long to return to London. But alas. The rogue Parliament has not yet seen the error of its ways. We must wait until they invite us back. My son Charles is willing and ready to accept his crown. He expects that it will happen eventually and in the meantime is exerting his influence in the Colonies.

I know that you and my husband were at odds. My son tells me that you were first on his list of traitors. But such are the ways of politics. Should my son be restored to the throne, I am willing to come to your defense in these matters and lie to him if necessary. I shall tell him that you were secretly in my service, feeding me information about the rebellion. I will restore you to the Crown's favor.

What I ask in return is simple. A year has passed since Charles died, and I am now free to marry. I would prefer to take you as my husband, but realize that you might still be married. In that case, we could be lovers.

Come back to me, Lord Gordon. Hardly a day passes when I do not think of our intense encounter. I know that you want me. I saw it in your eyes in London.

Do not take this offer lightly. I would hate to see a virile man like you suffer a traitor's death. My son is determined to avenge his father.

It grows late and I must post this letter. Write to me soon and sign it with our secret moniker. (Lord K) I anxiously await your letter.

Jusqu'à ce que nous retrouverons, mon amour. - Henrietta

Dughall rubbed his temples. "How can I answer this letter? I love my wife more than life. I renewed my vow to be faithful."

Yet, he'd learned something important from this letter. His life would be forfeit should Prince Charles come to the throne. Was the Parliament likely to recall him? And what was the Prince doing in the Colonies? He would have to keep abreast of their politics.

The Duke felt trapped. "Should I answer Henrietta?" He felt ashamed as he said it. "Nay! I will never stray again, even if it means my death. It's better not to answer."

Dughall knew that it would anger her. Certainly, there would be consequences. The Queen wouldn't defend him when the time came and could possibly order his demise.

The Duke sipped his tea until he decided upon a course of action. He would show the letter to his protectors and begin to formulate a plan. They would have to monitor politics in England and the Colonies. If Prince Charles assumed the crown, he would need a quick escape route.

CHAPTER 22
REVELATIONS

APRIL 8TH 1650

ONE DAY LATER

DEER ABBEY, THE LIBRARY

Father Ross sat at a long oak table, arguing with James Gordon. His patience was wearing thin. The boy questioned everything. The silver-haired priest had a reputation for working with troubled children. He'd just completed an exorcism on a girl when the new Abbott called upon him. The monk had been less than truthful with him. He described a boy with unnatural abilities, but left out details about his temperament. The lad had the Sight, but could be hostile and manipulative. They'd made significant progress, but for some reason, today was different. The priest sensed that he was wrestling a force of evil.

They'd been reading from the Book of Genesis, about Abraham and Isaac. He marked the page with a ribbon. "Tell me what ye think about it."

James yawned. "It's daft."

Ross was losing patience. "Daft? What do ye mean?"

The boy grimaced. "Abraham loved his son, right?"

"More than anything on earth."

"Yet he agreed to sacrifice him in a horrible manner. He was going to stab him to death."

"'Tis true."

James pounded the table. "That makes no sense!"

Ross sighed. "It makes perfect sense. Abraham had an unshakable faith in God. He was being tested."

The boy stared. "How did he know that God would stop him?"

"He *didn't* know. Abraham had faith in God."

"What is faith?"

It was a deep question, but the priest had a simple explanation. "Faith is being certain of what we do not see."

The boy smiled. "Sounds like the Second Sight."

Father Ross sighed. "Faith is more powerful than the Sight. Abraham surrendered his will to God. He was rewarded. An angel of the LORD stopped the sacrifice."

James frowned. "This angel of the Lord who calls Abraham from heaven... What kind of Lord does he serve? A king? A duke?"

The priest knew he was being taunted. But by what? "Ye know full well we are talking about the LORD GOD." He pushed the Bible towards him. "As punishment, ye will copy Genesis 21 and 22."

The boy pushed the book away. "I will NOT!"

Father Ross gritted his teeth. "Let me show ye what I do to myself when my thoughts become UNHOLY." He withdrew a knotted cord from his pocket, stripped off his shirt, and whipped his back a dozen times. Then he handed it to the boy and commanded, "Try it."

James paled. "Nay!"

Father Ross grabbed the boy's ear and brought him to his feet. They tussled and he tore off his shirt. The priest was shocked. The child's back was bruised and blistered, and bore angry marks from a leather strap. "Who did this to ye?"

James shuddered. "Lord Skene."

Father Ross released him. "Why?"

"I refused to help him with an experiment."

"What experiment?"

"He was trying to teach me alchemy."

A chill run up the priest's spine. "Hmmphhh! Did he teach ye anything else?"

James cowered. "Aye. To control the forces of nature."

"Lord Skene is a warlock?"

"So he says."

The priest was appalled. *The boy is being influenced by an evil presence. It explains his unholy behavior.*

"I wasn't supposed to tell. He'll kill me!" James wrung his hands. "Don't send me back to him."

Ross placed a hand on his shoulder. "Wait here. No one will punish ye. I must talk to the Abbott." He left the library in a hurry with the hem of his black robe flying.

✳✳✳

James breathed a sigh of relief. "I'm safe. They can't send me back to a warlock." The morning had been contentious, but it accomplished what he wanted. He'd ratted on Skene, sealed his fate, and emerged as the innocent victim.

The boy walked to the open window and gazed at the courtyard. Apple and cherry trees were blossoming. It wasn't like Skene Castle, where everything was gloomy and lifeless. His spirits lifted.

James knew that he was at a crossroads and had to make a decision. "From now on, I shall be pious and obedient - the perfect student and the perfect son. I'm finished with Skene and his Dark Arts. I must return to my true father."

✳✳✳

THE ABBOTT'S QUARTERS

Brother Luke sat at his desk, pouring over a scroll. He was in charge of the Gregorian chant for the upcoming Easter liturgy. Luke had assumed Lazarus' role until a new Abbott could be appointed. The Vatican hadn't made much progress in the matter. There was a frantic knock on the door. "Come."

Father Ross entered. "Abbott. Could we speak?"

Luke looked up from his work. "Aye."

The priest reddened. "I've come about James Gordon."

Luke rolled up the scroll, and motioned for the priest to take a seat opposite him. "Go on."

Father Ross sat. "I'm afraid that I have bad news. A mistake has been made. The Abbey placed this boy with a warlock."

Luke frowned. "Are ye referring to Lord Skene?"

"Aye."

"We've had dealings with this man for years. He's a respected Christian."

Ross scowled. "He is a wolf in sheep's clothing."

"This is a serious charge. What is the evidence?"

The priest leaned forward. "James said that he was teaching him alchemy."

"Hmmphhh…"

"That's not all. He was showing him how to control the forces of nature."

The monk was shocked. "Can that be done?"

"Aye. I've seen it before. Skene told him that he was a warlock."

Luke's heart sank. This was a disaster. "Could the boy be lying?"

"I don't think so. James fears the man, and rightfully so. Skene has been beating him."

"Was it simple discipline?"

"Nay. The boy's back is covered with welts. I'm glad that I saw it. It explains his unholy behavior."

"How did he react when ye questioned him?"

"He begged me not to send him back."

Luke took a calming breath. He wasn't used to handling ugly matters. He'd much rather work with his hands or meditate. What would the Abbott have done? The child was their responsibility. "Lord Skene is waiting in the Refectory. Tell him that we intend to keep the lad until after Easter."

"Will ye confront him?"

"Not today. I need to question the boy."

"And when ye're satisfied?"

"We will write the Vatican."

"What about the lad?"

Luke sighed. "We must counsel him."

The priest nodded. "Good. What about his father?"

"In any case, we will need to involve Lord Gordon."

Luc Gordon

CHAPTER 23
EASTER SUNDAY

APRIL 17TH 1650

NINE DAYS LATER

DEER ABBEY

It was just after midnight. The monks stood in the dark around an open fire, waiting to ascend the steps of the cruciform-shaped church. They were dressed in ceremonial garb, white flowing garments that draped to the ground, and were barefoot.

James Gordon was with them. He'd been given a choice - to attend a later ceremony with the servants or to join the monks as a guest. His choice had been the latter, and so far he wasn't disappointed. The boy was dressed in a white robe and was naked underneath.

***

James reflected on the last eight days. Lord Skene had been ordered to leave without him. It hadn't gone well. The man demanded an audience with the Abbott and threatened to tell Lord Gordon. Brother Luke stood firm and told the man what he suspected. This threw Skene into a fit of rage, where upon he was escorted off the premises.

James had been gently questioned. He had to admit that the monks had been kind to him. They'd given him a few days to rest, and then proceeded to counsel him. One by one, they relayed stories of their personal trials and assured him of God's love. The Abbott promised to summon his father.

***

Now, the Abbott lit the Christ candle and traced a cross upon it. He held it up and began the liturgy. "Christ, yesterday and today, the beginning and the ending. To Christ belongs all time and all the ages. To Christ belongs glory and dominion now and forever. Amen."

The monks responded, "Amen."

James whispered, "Amen."

The Abbott held up the candle with reverence. "Behold the light of Christ, rising in Glory, as it dispels the darkness of our hearts and minds." He led the procession up the steps of the church and opened the wooden door. As he entered the vestibule, he lifted the candle and repeated, "Behold the light of Christ."

The monks murmured, "Thanks be to God." One by one, they dipped their fingers in the font of holy water and made the sign of the cross. Then they proceeded into the church proper.

***

James was the last to enter. The flagstone floor felt cold under his bare feet. Following Brother Adam, he walked past carved pews until they stopped at a latticework chancel. He looked around. The church was illuminated by a few pillar candles. They entered and sat in a pew.

The Abbott stood at the altar and raised the Christ candle high, "Behold the light of Christ."

James heard the monks respond, "Thanks be to God." He took a breath and repeated, "Thanks be to God."

The Abbott blessed the candle and placed it on the altar. Brother Adam retrieved a hymnal from the pew and opened it to a specific page. He handed it to the boy.

James scanned the page. There was a musical score with accompanying words - in Latin and English. He kept his voice low, "What is this?"

Adam whispered, "We pray in Gregorian Chant."

James held his breath as the monks began to chant. His eyes searched for the translation.

♩♪♩ Victimae paschali laudes
immolent Christiani.
Agnus redemit oves: ♩♪♩

"May you praise the Paschal Victim,
immolated for Christians.
The Lamb redeemed the sheep:"

Christus innocens Patri
reconciliavit peccatores.
Mors et vita duello
conflixere mirando:
dux vitae mortuus,
regnat vivus.

"Christ, the innocent one,
has reconciled sinners to the Father.
A wonderful duel to behold,
as death and life struggle:
The Prince of life dead,
now reigns alive."

Dic nobis Maria,
quid vidisti in via?
Sepulcrum Christi viventis,
et gloriam vidi resurgentis:

"Tell us, Mary Magdalen,
what did you see in the way?
I saw the sepulchre of the living Christ,
and I saw the glory of the Resurrected one:"

Angelicos testes,
sudarium, et vestes.
Surrexit Christus spes mea:
praecedet suos in Galilaeam.

"The Angelic witnesses,
the winding cloth, and His garments.
The risen Christ is my hope:
He will go before His own into Galilee."

Scimus Christum surrexisse
a mortuis vere:
tu nobis, victor Rex,
miserere.

"We know Christ to have risen
truly from the dead:

*And thou, victorious King,
have mercy on us. "*

♩ ♪ ♩   Amen. Alleluia.   ♩ ♪ ♩

The chanting stopped and the church was quiet. Brother Adam whispered, "That hymn was written in 1048. It expresses the simple, living and childlike faith that the Saints were known to have."

James felt a chill run up his spine. "Oh."

"We must have this faith." The monk smiled. "Faith sustains us through times of joy and times of terrible troubles. Each life is made up of these."

James whispered, "Yer life, too?"

"Aye. I will tell ye about it tomorrow." He faced forward and bowed his head in prayer.

James listened as the monks began to chant. They sang in perfect harmony, celebrating the light of Christ. The boy felt like he was floating on a cloud. He was shocked to find tears on his cheeks, and wiped them away. *Oh! What is happening to me?*

Just then, a white light emerged from the Christ candle. It crossed the chapel and descended upon him.

The monks concluded the chant with "Amen. Alleluia."

James responded with conviction, "Amen. Alleluia."

For the first time in his life, he knew peace and redemption.

COLONY OF VIRGINIA, JAMESTOWN, EASTER MORNING

Gilbert stood on the steps of the church, greeting passing members of the congregation. "Fergus... Thomas... Robert... Miss Jane..."

He'd been attending church regularly. At first, the services seemed strange, because at heart he was a Catholic. But he'd persisted and gotten a surprise. God was here. Perhaps his brother was right. It didn't matter *where* you worshipped, as long as you felt close to God.

Gilbert descended the steps and joined his family. They were clad in their best clothes – the ones they wore when they fled Scotland.

A distinguished gentleman approached, who looked to be in his forties. The man wore a rust-colored waistcoat and trousers with a frilled shirt. A shoulder length wig complemented his outfit. He offered his hand in friendship, "I don't believe we've met. I am Sir William Berkeley, Governor of this colony."

Gilbert shook his hand. "Pleased to meet ye, Sir Berkeley. I am George Gordon." He introduced his family, "This is my wife Bridget, my daughters Anne and Mary, and my son George."

As was the custom, Bridget offered her hand.

Berkeley took it and kissed it lightly. "Madame, you are a sight for sore eyes. My wife will be pleased to meet you. There are few women in the colonies." He turned to Gilbert. "You have a handsome family, George. Can we walk and talk?"

Gilbert smiled. "Aye."

"Good! In the meantime, my wife will entertain your family." He snapped his fingers. "Elizabeth! Come here."

A yellow haired beauty half his age came to his side. "Yes, William?" She was wearing a white dress with a royal blue sash and a wide brimmed hat.

Berkeley smiled. "This is Mrs. Gordon. Show Bridget and her children the flower gardens. Tell them about the parties we hold at Green Spring."

Elizabeth smiled. "I'm glad to meet you." She escorted Bridget and the children to the church yard.

The two men started walking. Berkeley began the conversation. "Where do you hail from, George Gordon?"

"Scotland. I am a lesser son of a Scottish lord, come to make my fortune."

Berkeley frowned. "Ah, Scotland. That rebellion was nasty business. How did you fare in the troubles with England?"

Gilbert knew he was being tested. It was no secret that the Governor was a Royalist. "My family supported the King in his efforts. I'm afraid that we suffered for it."

"We all did." Berkeley slapped him on the back. "Charles was my King and a dear friend as well. As a young man, I was part of his household."

Gilbert was solemn. "I offer my sympathies, Sir. I was appalled to hear that he was executed."

Berkeley nodded. "It was a terrible shock. I shall miss him." He sighed. "Rest assured that Virginia remains loyal to the Stuarts. England cannot survive for long solely under Parliamentary rule. It's only a matter of time until Charles' son is restored to the throne."

Gilbert made a small sound of agreement. "That will be a good day."

Berkeley smiled. "Where were you educated, Gordon?"

"I was schooled in France. Later, I spent a year at Oxford."

The man's eyes widened. "Do you speak French?"

"Reasonably well."

They stopped walking.

"I could use a man like you. There is a place for you in my administration as a commissioner. There is compensation."

Gilbert was flattered. "I shall consider it."

Berkeley smiled. "Good! Come to my plantation, Green Spring, on Saturday. Bring the wife and children. We will provide supper. My wife will be thrilled. She recently came from England and finds life in the colonies boring.

Gilbert shook his hand. "We will be there."

They began walking back to the church. When they arrived, Bridget and the children greeted them.

Berkeley bowed gracefully. "I will see you all next Saturday." Then he left them to discuss their experiences.

Bridget smiled. "I like his wife."

Gilbert grinned. "Good! It looks like we will be seeing more of them. He invited us to his plantation for supper."

"When?"

"Next Saturday."

The girls squealed with delight.

Young George asked, "What did he want, Father?"

"He offered me a job as a commissioner. We plan to talk about it."

Bridget took his arm. "Today we met the Governor of Virginia! What was he like?"

Gilbert smiled. "We're home at last. He's a Royalist."

✳✳✳

DRAKE CASTLE, THE HIGHLANDS, EASTER MORNING

The Duke stood outside the chapel, holding his four month old daughter. Wee Morrigan was a darling child with dark curly hair and a broad nose. She reached up and grabbed his beard.

Dughall laughed. "Hey! What are ye doing to Da?"

The baby made a wet razzing sound with her mouth, splattering him with spittle.

Keira giggled. "She got it on yer shirt." The lass took a cloth out of her pocket and wiped them. "Oh, Husband. I love her."

Dughall smiled. "I know, lass. So do I."

Maggie emerged from the chapel with Philip and Luc. The youngsters were clad in their Sunday clothes – she in a yellow saffron-dyed dress and the lads in formal kilts and jackets. Maggie approached. "Father... Mother... It was a wonderful Easter service."

Dughall nodded. "Aye. That it was. Ye should tell Father John."

"I did." She looked at Philip. "We must check the preparations in the Great Hall. Yer family is coming today for a visit."

Philip bowed slightly. "We must take our leave." The couple turned and headed for the castle.

Luc stroked the baby's shoulder. "Such a bonny wee lassie. Shall I take her inside? Old Marcia made colored eggs. They are hiding them in the castle."

Keira seemed nervous. "She's too young to join the hunt."

"Aye. But we can watch."

Dughall passed the infant to Luc. "Take her, Son. We will follow in a few minutes." They watched him take the child into the castle. "Don't worry, lass. Luc is a good lad. He will make a fine father some day."

She managed a smile. "I know. Have ye found him a lass?"

"Not yet. I will talk to the Laird of Grant today."

Murdock approached with an envelope. "My Lord. My Lady. Forgive the interruption." He handed the letter to Dughall. "A messenger left this at the main gate. He says that it's important."

The Duke frowned. "Thank ye, Murdock. Ye may go."

The servant turned and walked to the bake house.

Dughall turned over the envelope and recognized the Abbey's wax seal. "It's from the monks."

Keira squeezed his arm. "Open it."

The Duke took out a dirk, slit the envelope, and removed a one page letter. He read aloud, *"Dear Lord Gordon, We require a meeting with ye in regards to yer son, James. Please make arrangements to arrive after Easter, as we are occupied with preparations for our Vigil. Rest assured that the boy is alive and remains under our care and protection. – Brother Luke, acting Abbott, Deer Abbey"*

Keira frowned. "Is something wrong with our son?"

"I don't know, lass." In truth, the Duke expected trouble. He'd been having disturbing dreams. His son living in fear... Crying out... Begging to come home... Was it the truth or guilt for his failure as a father? Could he trust the dreams?

Dughall closed his eyes and reached out to his son. His Sight told him that the boy was alive and looking forward to his visit. It warmed his heart. He opened his eyes. "Don't fret, Wife. I will ride to the Abbey tomorrow."

Her eyes filled with tears. "And if something is wrong?"

"James is our son. We will face it together."

.

Chapter 24
Confrontation

April 18th 1650

One Day Later

DEER ABBEY

It was a fine spring day at the Abbey. The skies were clear and the weather was warm. It was a good day for planting. Monks scurried about, tending the gardens and performing their duties. The day was bright but the mood was tense. Lord Gordon was with the Abbott, discussing his son's predicament.

The Duke sat in a stuffed chair across from Brother Luke, the acting Abbott. They'd just finished a glass of wine and were ready to get down to business. Dughall leaned forward and clasped his hands. "Ye summoned me from Drake. What about my son?"

Brother Luke reddened. "James is alive and under our protection. He..."

Dughall interrupted, "Does this mean that he's no longer with Skene?"

"Aye. But let me finish." The monk sighed. "The Abbey made a terrible mistake. We placed yer son with a warlock."

Dughall thought that his ears were fooling him. Surely, the monk didn't say that. "With a *what?*"

The Abbott stared. "A warlock. Do ye know what that is?"

The Duke did know. He'd been falsely accused of being one. "I know what it is. Are ye sure?"

"We are quite sure. When he arrived for his last lesson, James asked for our protection." Luke hesitated. "We questioned him extensively. Lord Skene involved yer son in the Dark Arts. When the boy objected, he whipped him."

Dughall flinched. "How badly?"

"His backside is covered with bruises and welts. Worse yet, he was locked in a dungeon. Lord Gordon, I am deeply sorry for our mistake. The Abbey never meant to..." The monk droned on with the apology.

Dughall barely heard him. His dreams were true! Why did he ignore them? At last, he found his voice, "Where is my son?"

The Abbott was solemn. "He has been living with us for the last ten days, under the supervision of Brother Adam. We need ye to take him home. Lord Skene has threatened us."

"How so?"

"He says that he will attack the Abbey if we do not return the child to him."

Dughall was angry that his son had been placed with this man. But he was grateful that the monks saved him. "I will take my son home and send soldiers to protect ye. Then I will tell Lord Skene that I have the boy. He had better not come near me!"

The monk nodded. "We are grateful for yer protection." He stood and smoothed his robe. "I shall take ye to the boy. But be gentle with him. He's been through quite an ordeal." They left the Abbott's quarters.

They ran into the Duke's protectors in the courtyard. Dughall took a moment to explain and then ordered Gilroy and Suttie back to Drake Castle. They were to return with forty armed soldiers – twenty to guard the Abbey – the other twenty to guard his son. They would not attempt a trip home without protection.

Dughall and the monk headed for the library. As they walked, they discussed the boy's emotional state.

The Duke was tense. "Can I show him the book the Abbey has on our family?"

Luke was silent for a moment. "He is very young. It would be irregular."

Dughall persisted, "I think it would help him heal."

"Then I will allow it. Visit with him. Then I will take ye to the secret passage."

***

The Duke entered the library quietly and saw his son gazing out the window. He summoned his gentlest voice, "My son."

The lad turned. "Father!"

Dughall was relieved. His Sight told him that the boy wanted to see him. He held out his hands. "Come to me."

James came to him and melted into his embrace. "I am so glad to see ye."

The Duke was choked with emotion. "I'm here to take ye home."

The boy looked up. "Oh, good!"

Dughall hugged him. "James… I'm sorry."

The child stiffened. "Do ye know what happened to me?" They separated.

The Duke sighed. "Not all of it. I'd like ye to tell me." He took his hand and led him to a couch, where they sat together. "Tell me what happened with Lord Skene."

James sniffled. "I defied him."

"And?"

The boy took a ragged breath. "He forced me over a stool and beat me with a strap. He demanded that I call him Father."

The Duke was stunned. It reminded him of his first encounter with the Earl. "What else?"

"Then he lowered me into the oubliette."

"An old style dungeon... They call it a place of forgetting. How long were ye down there?"

The boy shuddered. "I don't know. A day... Maybe two... It was dark. I was cold and thirsty." He sniffled. "My back burned. Rats crawled over me. I wondered if he would come back for me."

The Duke's heart was breaking. "Ye cried out for me."

"Aye."

"Oh, lad. I know what it's like."

The boy straightened. "Nay, ye don't!"

Dughall sighed. "There is something that ye don't know." Slowly, he stripped off his shirt and put it aside. Then he twisted to show the boy. Moments passed before he felt it - a small finger on his back, tracing the silvery whip marks.

"Who did this to ye?"

The memory was painful. "My father."

"*Grandfather* did this?"

Dughall shook his head. "Not the grandfather ye know. Alex Hay raised me. The man who beat me was my birth father, the Earl of Huntly. The last time he whipped me, he left me to die in a stable."

"Why did ye never tell me?"

Dughall sighed. "It's complicated. 'Tis a long story and not too pleasant."

"Oh... Will ye tell me later?"

"Aye. When we get home."

The child's finger moved lower. "What is this mark from?"

"I was beaten by guards in Edinburgh Castle. They whipped me with an iron chain. They cracked my ribs. Ye haven't seen the half of it." The Duke put on his shirt. "Let me see yer back."

James stripped off his shirt and displayed his wounds like a badge of honor. It seemed they had something in common.

Dughall traced a welt with his finger. "Ah... He got ye good."

The boy turned to face him. "Father, why did ye send me away?"

Dughall knew that the truth was best. "Because of that incident with Maggie."

James reddened. "It was wrong. I won't do it again."

He hesitated. "There was something else. I thought ye were trying to kill me."

James hung his head in shame. "I was."

"Oh. Ye must not do that."

"I'm sorry, Father."

The Duke tipped his chin and gazed into his eyes. "I accept yer apology. A father and son must stand together – no matter what happens. Promise me that ye will try."

"I will."

Dughall hugged him. "I haven't been the best father to ye. But that will change. I want us to start over."

James sniffled. "I'd like that."

"Good! Put on yer shirt. I have something to show ye."

***

The Abbott escorted them down a hallway until they came to the scriptorium. They entered and saw monks studying at long oak tables. A few looked up and greeted them.

Brother Luke acknowledged them, "Ye may go back to yer work."

"Why are we here?" James asked.

Dughall smiled. "The Abbey keeps a book on our family. It's in a secret place."

The Abbott led them across the room to a wall that was covered with a massive bookcase. He removed a leather bound volume and touched something behind it. The bookcase rolled to the right, exposing a wall with a doorway that led to a staircase.

James stared. "That's amazing!"

The Abbott smiled. "There have been times when we needed to hide someone. This must be kept secret. Can we trust ye?"

"Oh, aye!"

They went down a stone staircase and arrived at an oak door. Its metal knocker plate was covered with runic seals, which played a part in tripping the lock.

The Duke touched a seal, "May I?"

The Abbott's eyes widened. "Ye know the sequence?"

"Aye. I sensed it when I was here with Lazarus."

"Go ahead."

Dughall named the seals as he turned them, "These are Teiwaz, Uruz, and Kenaz - the symbols for Duty, Energy, and Wisdom." The door creaked open.

"There are so many seals. Do ye know what they mean?" James asked.

"Aye. When we get back to Drake, I will teach ye."

They entered the chamber. The room was filled with rows of tables and a wall of glass-faced bookcases.

The Abbott opened one and retrieved a leather-bound volume with the Drake seal on its spine. He brought it to a table and left it there while he lit candles on nearby tables. "We never light a candle on a table we're working on," he explained. "One spark could damage the manuscript we are viewing." They stood at the table and opened the book.

The Abbott stood back. "Take care with the pages that are stuck together. I shall leave so that ye can have a private conversation." He left the room.

Dughall had dreamed of the day when he could share this with his son. They looked at the first page. "The monks inscribe the books in old script with brilliant colors and gold and silver paint. The first word on a page is larger than the rest and is adorned with images befitting the subject."

James whispered, "It's beautiful."

"'Tis. See how it starts with a 'C' for Callum? It's decorated with a silver sword and our red and blue tartan."

"It *is* our tartan!"

"Lazarus told me that the Abbey began recording our history one hundred and fifty years ago. Callum Drake was yer great, great, great-grandfather. As ye can see, there is a notation here that says he had a son." He turned the page to reveal the name Tcharloch, beautifully scripted and adorned with a fire-breathing dragon. "Hmmm... Let me see if I can remember the story. Callum visited the monastery with his son Tcharloch, demanding that they drive the devil out of him."

James frowned. "Did he have a devil in him?"

"Nay. He was a boy about your age who drove his elders daft with his antics. They claimed that he knew what they were thinking and feeling."

"Sounds like he had the Sight."

Dughall nodded. "He did. They separated the boy from his family and tested his abilities. He was able to read thoughts, feelings, and intentions. The monks told Callum it had nothing to do with the devil. It was a rare gift that needed training. The boy had to be convinced to use it for good instead of mischief."

James grunted. "Sounds like me."

Dughall grinned. "Lazarus said that those were dangerous times. The chances of the boy surviving in society were close to nil. The monastery took him in, educated him, and sent him home when he turned twenty-one."

James touched the page with reverence. "Tcharloch had a child, or we wouldn't be here."

"'Tis true. The monks arranged a marriage to a girl from another family they were watching. The Sight also ran in her blood. She gave birth to twin boys, but one died within a year. The other, a lad named Ferraghuss, had the gift."

James looked up. "So it passes from father to son?"

"Aye. To daughters as well."

"I want to see Ferraghuss' page."

Dughall frowned. "He doesn't have one. The lad turned to the Dark Gate at the age of sixteen. The monks couldn't save him. The boy was identified as a warlock and burned at the stake."

James shivered. "Burned alive?"

"Aye. It's a terrible death."

"Oh. What is the Dark Gate?"

"It's another name for evil, but not in the traditional sense. It means that ye consider all else beneath ye and act accordingly. Ye fail to see God in all things."

The boy was pale. "If a person goes down that path, will God let them come back?"

Dughall sensed his fear. "Aye. It's never too late."

"Good. So if Ferraghuss died, how did we get here?"

"Tcharloch's wife died of a broken heart. He remarried and they had a child." Dughall turned the page. "The child of their union was named James." The letter 'J' was adorned with silver thread, heather, and a golden lion's head.

"Who was he?"

"Yer great-Grandfather. He didn't have the Sight, so they thought the line was finished. Tcharloch died in peace, convinced that the gift was trouble."

"Ha! It wasn't finished."

"Nay. James married and had children. He discovered that his daughter had the gift." He turned the page with great reverence. "Her name was Christal." The 'C' in her name was drawn with symbols that resembled flowers. "She was my birth mother."

"Did ye know her?"

"Nay, she died giving birth to me. They say that she was determined to use her gift for good." The Duke gave him a moment and turned the page. "That's me." The 'D' in his name was scripted with blue and gold thread. It was adorned with flowing symbols and mythical creatures. There was another name below it in ornate script that looked like 'Doo-ull'.

"What is that word?"

"That is the old Gaelic for Dughall." There was text below it describing his gifts and healing abilities and notations about the birth of his three children – Maggie, James, and Morrigan Rose.

The boy's eyes widened. "Do I have a page?"

Dughall turned the page but the next one was blank. "Yer page is to be written. It is why I have been bringing ye here."

"Maggie, too."

"Aye. Our family is special. The Sight is in our blood. In some, it's strong. In others, it's weak." He placed a hand on the boy's shoulder. "We must use it for good, my son. We must not use it to control others."

James looked up. "Or we'll end up like Ferraghuss."

"Aye."

The boy smiled. "Thank ye, Father."

Thank God, Dughall thought. *This was just what the child needed.*

"Will we go home now?"

"Not for a few days. I sent to Drake for soldiers to protect us."

James closed his eyes. "I hope they hurry. Lord Skene is coming."

Dughall inhaled sharply. "When?"

The boy opened his eyes. "He's approaching the Abbey with his forces."

There was a frantic pounding on the door. The lock turned and the portal opened. Brother Adam appeared. "Come quickly! We are under siege."

***

Lord Skene stood at the gates of the Abbey, barking commands at his soldiers. "Fire the trebuchet!"

Three men struggled with a medieval catapult. One placed a projectile in a pouch in the sling and set it on fire. The others used their combined strength to trip the trigger mechanism. The sling and the beam swung around and the sling released. The pouch opened and hurled the projectile. A fifty pound rock wrapped in a flaming rag catapulted over the wall. There were shouts and screams from within the Abbey.

The Abbott appeared at the top of the wall. "Cease and desist, Sir! Ye are attacking Church property."

Skene didn't care. He had to get the boy back or face terrible consequences. He raised his sword. "Send the lad out or I'll fire the nine-pounders!"

The Abbott's eyes widened. "We will never give up the boy. Desist, Sir! Ye invite eternal damnation." He disappeared from the top of the wall.

Skene sneered. "Idiot! He just told me that the lad is still here. We will break in and take him." He knew that he was late to the game. It had taken him a week to assemble his forces. Now, he would have to take the child to a secret location to avoid the wrath of his father. He gave an order, "Fire the trebuchet! Load the cannons!"

***

Dughall raced across the courtyard with his son at his heels. He'd thought about leaving him in the secret room but decided otherwise. They'd promised to stand together as father and son. He didn't want the boy to feel abandoned. He found Jamison near the rear of the Church.

"My Lord!" The servant was armed with a sword. "Skene is outside, demanding that they release yer son to him."

James cringed. "Don't let him take me!"

Dughall squeezed his shoulder. "As long as there is breath in this body, he will not take ye. But we must protect the Abbey. How many men does he have?"

Jamison scowled. "I peered over the wall. It looks like twenty. He has a trebuchet and a pair of cannons. They've been catapulting flaming rocks into the Abbey. One grazed Brother Simon."

"How big are the cannons?"

"They look to be nine-pounders."

Dughall's heart sank. "A volley of shots could breach the door."

They heard a whoosh. A flaming projectile cleared the wall and dropped into the courtyard. Monks rushed to put out the fire with blankets and buckets of water.

"What about Gilroy and Suttie?"

"If they got past them, they won't be back until the day after tomorrow."

They heard the roar of a cannon and the crack of wood. They were attempting to breach the door.

Dughall grasped his son's shoulders and gazed into his eyes. "Stay with Jamison. He will protect ye."

James paled. "What about ye?"

"I must face Skene and fight for ye."

"Nay, Father! He has powers."

Jamison frowned. "My Lord. I can not let ye do this."

The Duke held fast. "Ye can and ye will. Give me yer sword." He accepted the weapon and pushed the boy towards the servant. "Defend my son to the death; for he will succeed me." He spotted the Abbott and ran to him. The monk was attending to Brother Simon.

The Abbott stood. "What will we do? They have nearly breached the door."

The Duke was tense. "I will face him. How do I get to the top of the wall?"

The monk led him around the side of the church. A ladder lay on the ground beside the wall. "Use this. Ye can talk to him up there."

The Duke picked up the ladder and set it against the wall. He climbed to the top and looked down on the ragtag soldiers. They were about to fire a cannon. "Stop!"

Lord Skene looked up. "Lord Gordon! This surely is a complication."

Dughall glared. "Leave my son alone."

The man's eyes narrowed. "I'm afraid I can't do that. He belongs with me and others like him. I'm his true father."

"Nay, ye are not! Ye will have to fight me for him."

Skene raised a hand to stop the cannon. "Wait." He was grinning like a madman. "Then come down here. I accept yer offer. We will settle this with swords."

The Duke climbed down the ladder and picked up his sword. He saw James running towards him with the servant on his heels. The boy arrived and hugged him fiercely. "I don't want to lose ye."

Dughall swallowed hard. "Ye won't." He stroked the lad's hair. "Be brave, my son. I must go." They separated and he ran to the door.

***

James sniffled. "Skene will kill him!"

Jamison grunted. "Ye must let him fight. It's a matter of honor. Brother Adam is on his way. He will take ye to the secret room."

"I won't go!"

Jamison grabbed him. "Ye must! Don't let yer father die in vain."

James threw off his grip. "Let me climb the ladder. I can save him."

The servant seemed torn. "Are ye sure?"

"Aye."

"Then do it."

James scrambled up the ladder. When he got to the top, he saw a fearful sight. Skene and his father were circling one another, getting ready to fight. The boy knew that Skene had the power to paralyze a man's intentions. His father was at a disadvantage. He got an idea. "I can use my gifts to fight evil." James closed his eyes and went within. He connected to the forces of nature and summoned the crows and ravens. When he opened his eyes, he spotted hundreds of birds in surrounding yew trees, stretching their wings and awaiting orders. More were arriving each minute. Some lighted on the wall of the Abbey.

The boy watched as his father raised his sword and lashed out in a thrust, slash and overhead cut. Skene warded off the blow with his weapon, sending sparks into the air. Swords clanged. Men shouted.

Skene uttered an ancient curse.

The Duke lowered his weapon and looked around in confusion. "Ach!"

Skene began to circle him. "Ye can't lift it."

The Duke tried to lift his sword and failed. It clattered to the ground. He made an effort to retreat. "I can't lift my feet! What is happening to me?"

"I glued ye to this spot. Now, drop to yer knees."

James cried out, "Nay! Don't kill him."

Dughall looked up, "Run, James!"

"I said, drop to yer knees!"

The Duke was growing weaker. He fell to his knees and hung his head. "Kill me, but don't take my son."

The man cackled. "I'll take yer head and yer son." He raised his sword and prepared to strike.

James raised a hand, "Get them!"

Hundreds of crows and ravens left their perches and swooped down on the men. They shrieked as they attacked, scattering the soldiers. Forty or more landed on Skene and pecked his head and shoulders. A few began to attack his father.

James scrambled down the ladder. "We must rescue him!" He ran to the door and left the Abbey. His servant was close behind.

Outside, it was almost as if day had turned to night. The air was thick with crows and ravens. There had to be thousands of them. Jamison waved his arms, "Ach! They're as thick as rain. Watch yer head, lad!"

James was untouched. "They won't hurt me!" He ran to his father.

The Duke lay face down on the ground, shielding his head with bloody hands. He appeared to be convulsing.

The boy shook him. "Father! What's wrong?" The man twitched, but he was unresponsive.

Jamison stood over them. "This has happened before. He's suffering a fit. Soon, he'll be senseless."

Lord Skene was enveloped in a cloud of angry birds. He staggered blindly and fell to the ground. His eyes were gone, picked to the sockets.

James hovered over his father to keep the birds away. "He stopped twitching. Shall we carry him?"

The servant lifted the Duke to his feet. With the boy's help, he dragged his lord and master through the damaged door of the Abbey.

***

THE NEXT DAY

The Duke woke in a narrow bed in the guest quarters of the Abbey. He felt weak and had a headache. The first thing he focused on was a wall crucifix. "Am I dead?"

James sat in a chair at his bedside. "Nay, Father. We stood together and defeated Skene."

Dughall's heart swelled with gratitude. His son was safe and it was all that mattered. He stared at his bandaged hands. "How did this happen?"

"Ye were attacked by crows and ravens."

The memory was foggy. "I vaguely remember. Where is Lord Skene?"

"He's dead. The birds pecked his eyes out. They stripped his flesh to the bone."

Dughall shuddered. It was a terrible death, even for an enemy. "Where did the birds come from?"

James spoke in a small voice. "I summoned them."

Dughall understood. "Ah. Ye did it to save yer father."

The boy brightened. "I did."

"What happened to Skene's men?"

"One is dead. The rest fled with their horses."

"So, the Abbey is safe?"

"Aye. Jamison is helping them repair the door." The boy stood and hugged his father. "Will God forgive me for what I've done? I couldn't

DARK DESTINY – *JEANNE TREAT*

let him kill ye."

Dughall smiled. At last, the child had a conscience. "Ye did it to protect yer father and these holy monks as well. I think that God will forgive ye."

"Oh, good."

The door opened and Jamison entered. "Ye're awake!"

The Duke nodded. "How long was I asleep?"

"A day. Ye suffered a fit."

Dughall nodded. "No wonder I feel so weak! What's going on?"

"Our soldiers have arrived. We can return to Drake when ye're ready. Did the young master tell ye about Skene?"

"Aye. I should thank ye."

Jamison interrupted, "Don't thank *me*. Yer son saved ye."

James blushed. "Oh, Father. I'm sorry about yer hands."

The Duke examined a hand. "It's hard to tell. Are my fingers all there?"

"Aye."

Dughall grinned. "What are a few more scars for a Gordon?"

The boy laughed.

The Duke's stomach growled. "I'm starving! Can I get a meal? We'll leave for Drake tomorrow."

Chapter 25
Green Spring

April 22nd 1650

Three Days Later

THE BRITISH COLONY OF VIRGINIA

Gilbert felt the warmth of the sun as he rode alongside Sir William Berkeley. They had spent the morning touring a section of his plantation, which abutted the James River. He liked this man. They had a lot in common. "How many acres do ye have?"

William grinned. "When I assumed the governorship, they granted me 984 acres. Since then, I've acquired a few neighboring farms. Green Spring has grown to almost 2,000 acres. I also have the use of a 3,000-acre tract bordering the western boundary of the plantation."

Gilbert guided his stallion around a fallen log. "Impressive. Why do ye call it Green Spring?"

"There is a mossy spring on the property. The water is so cold that you must let it warm before drinking it."

"Ah. It sounds wonderful."

"I understand that you've been granted the rights to the Smith plantation. It's a fertile tract of land with abundant fishing and hunting. Have you named it?"

Gilbert hadn't thought about it. "Nay. I shall have to think of a name."

William glanced at him. "Are there special features that would inspire a name?"

"Nay."

"Well then, what does the place mean to you?"

"For us, it is a place to start over – we feel like the first man and woman."

"Then ye must call it 'Eden'."

Gilbert smiled. "I like it. Eden Plantation it shall be. What was it named before?"

William grasped the reins and guided his horse through a stand of trees. "Be careful of these branches." He returned to the question, "The Smiths didn't name it. They abandoned it after the Indian attack."

Gilbert's expression darkened. "I heard about that. Are we in danger?"

"No, though it's best to be armed. I am. We punished the offending tribes and executed their leader. After that, a treaty was signed. Indians are not permitted to enter the peninsula between the James and York rivers. No doubt, you've seen the forts we built at the falls of the major rivers."

"Just from a distance."

"Someday I will show you them."

"Thank ye. It seems that we're secure. Nevertheless, I've taught my wife how to shoot a pistol."

William grinned. "Ah. She's quite a woman."

Gilbert reddened. "Aye." It was the third time Sir Berkeley had mentioned it. This was a harsh environment for women. Too many were lost to childbirth. A man always had his eye out for a replacement wife.

The men were only a few miles from the mansion. They emerged from the woods and rode side by side.

"George. Today, I showed you my tobacco fields. It's a profitable crop, but it has drawbacks. The plants quickly deplete the soil of nutrients. Rotation is necessary. And the labor involved is intensive."

"We are finding that out through experience."

"Sometimes, there is an overabundance of the crop, which cheapens it."

"Hmmphhh…"

"Raise tobacco, but it's best to complement it with other crops. When you come again, I will show you my experimental farm where I grow cotton, flax, and hemp."

"Remarkable. This climate supports that?"

"Yes. We grow corn as well. It's a staple in the colony. I also have vast orchards of apricots, peaches, quinces, and pears. And we grow grapes for wine."

Gilbert smiled. "I look forward to seeing it."

"Good! Think about planting a variety of crops. I will provide you with trees and cuttings to get started."

"Thank ye. But there are only six of us. How will we manage it?"

Sir William slapped his horse to pick up the pace. "I employ indentured servants and seasonal workers. When we get back to the house, we will discuss it."

They were on the road now, approaching the mansion. Green Spring was a massive dwelling seated on a high natural terrace, facing Jamestown. The brick house was almost one hundred feet wide and twenty-five feet deep. There was a second story and dozens of large windows, a rarity in the colony. Porches ran the width of the building and there was a raised entrance.

"Astonishing," Gilbert murmured. Sir William was a valuable ally. Fortune was smiling upon him.

***

Bridget sat in a rocking chair on the porch, cooling herself with a folding fan. She stared at the work of art. One side sported well painted leaves, while the other had elaborately drawn flowers. The ivory sticks were inlaid with exquisite silver pique work. She held it out. "Such a beautiful thing!" Sir Berkeley's wife had given it to her, along with a fashionable pair of shoes from her extensive wardrobe.

The yellow-haired lass had gone into the mansion to fetch them another drink.

Bridget sipped the last of her cocktail from a fancy glass. It made her want to dance. Perhaps they would. They'd spotted the men on horseback in the distance.

Elizabeth stepped onto the porch with a tray of drinks. There were six – two for the men and four for the women. She placed the tray on a table between their chairs. "I made something different this time – from rum, sugar cane, and bruised mint. It's a favorite here."

Bridget lifted the glass to her nose. The drink was garnished with a fresh mint sprig. "Ah! It smells lovely."

Elizabeth sat down. "I'm so glad that you're here! It can be quite boring in the colonies."

Bridget didn't find it boring because there were so many chores to do. But she appreciated the friendship. "I like it here." She looked out into the courtyard, where her children were playing tag with a border collie. "So do the children." There was something she wanted to ask before the men arrived. "I have a question. Are there any physicians or midwives in the colony?"

The lass raised an eyebrow. "No physicians. William is trying to lure one here. But there is a midwife. She also acts as a bonesetter. Do you need a midwife?"

"Nay. I thought that I might because I missed my bleeding cycle. But it's back now, though it's spotty. It must be the change. I'm nearly forty."

Elizabeth's eyes widened. "You don't look that old! Oh... Forgive me. I meant nothing by it."

Bridget smiled. "It's all right, lass. I'm fortunate to be mistaken for a younger woman." She sipped the drink and felt it burn a warm path to her belly. "I can see why this is a favorite."

They laughed.

Elizabeth took a long sip. "William and I recently married. I've often wondered who would birth my baby if I got pregnant. We should visit this midwife together. I hear that she's good with herbs and poultices."

"I would like that. My sister-in-law and her mother are healers. But they're both in Scotland."

Elizabeth smiled. "Perhaps we can tempt them to come here. Do you have other family?"

Bridget nodded. "A sister, Juliana. She's married and will never leave Scotland. Our parents are long dead."

"Oh, look! The men are coming. Let's bolt our drinks and hide the glasses."

***

Gilbert watched as Sir William dismounted and opened the gate to the plantation. He took his horse through and waited as his new friend joined him. The children could be seen in the courtyard, playing with a dog. They left their sport and ran to him.

"Father!" George cried.

Gilbert had wanted to take George with them as they toured the plantation. But he knew that they had private business to discuss. He would make it up to him later. He dismounted. "My son."

The lad smiled. "Lady Berkeley offered us a dog!"

Gilbert's eyes widened. "This one?"

"Nay, one of her pups."

The girls squealed. "Oh please, Father? Can we have one?"

Gilbert relented, "It's a fine dog. We would be honored to have one of the pups."

Sir William grinned. "They are excellent dogs for herding livestock."

Gilbert heard the sound of women laughing. It was coming from the porch. To him, it sounded musical.

William shook his head. "I see that my wife has gotten into the rum, and corrupted your wife as well."

Young George asked, "What is rum?"

"Ah. Being men of Scotland, you're acquainted with whisky."

Gilbert smiled. "Aye."

"Whisky is distilled from barley. Rum is distilled from sugar cane. We import it from the Caribbean islands. It has a delightful taste and is known for removing inhibitions."

George piped up, "Can I try some, Father?"

Gilbert frowned. "Perhaps, a wee dram." He spotted the ladies on the porch. They were waving their fans.

William chuckled. "Just as I thought. Why don't we join them?"

They led the horses to a hitching post and tied them off, then proceeded up the stairs to the porch.

Bridget met Gilbert with a big hug. "Oh, Husband."

Gilbert smiled. "I think ye're tipsy."

"Does it matter?"

"Nay. We've had a hard life. I'm glad to see ye enjoying it."

They sat on the porch sipping drinks. A servant brought another round and apple cider for the children. They could smell a pig roasting and bread baking.

The cook appeared. "Supper is served in the dining room."

Young George exclaimed, "I'm starved."

As they stood to follow, William spoke to Gilbert, "Gordon... After the meal, you and I will retire to my study to talk about you serving as my commissioner."

Gilbert made a small sound of agreement. Things were progressing just fine. He'd been in Virginia for less than a year, yet he'd inserted himself into local politics. He would have to write his brother.

Charles Stuart

CHAPTER 26
PRINCE CHARLES HEIR APPARENT

MAY 1ST 1650
9 DAYS LATER

BREDA, THE NETHERLANDS

Charles Stuart stood in his quarters, studying his reflection in a mirror. He was a few weeks short of his twentieth birthday. Slightly over six feet tall, he had wavy hair, bushy brows, and dark eyes like his mother. The Prince was nearly twenty, but looked older. There was good reason. The weight of the world was on his shoulders.

***

As a lad, Charles accompanied his father as he fought Parliamentary and Puritan forces in the civil war. He participated in battles and at fourteen was made a commander. By the spring of 1646, with his father losing the war, young Charles was sent to France to his mother. He later moved to The Hague to live with his sister Mary and brother-in-law William, Prince of Orange. When he heard that his father was to be executed, he made diplomatic efforts to save him. These failed miserably and remained a terrible stain on his soul. After England executed his father and abolished the monarchy, Scotland offered to crown him King of all Britain. But there were onerous conditions. He had to formally agree to the Covenant, authorize Presbyterian Church governance across Britain, and renounce his mother's Catholic religion.

***

Charles pinched the bridge of his nose with his thumb and forefinger to curb a frightening headache. Points of light danced before his eyes. "Breathe, Charles! Imagine a shining pool of water. Breathe!" He took several breaths and his headache began to subside.

It had been a disastrous month. He'd sent an army of mercenaries into northern Scotland to weaken the grip of the Covenanters. Led by General Montrose, they were to prepare the way for his homecoming. That morning, he'd received word that his army was defeated and his general captured. Gone was the hope of forcing an agreement with the Scots that would be more to his liking. Resigned, he'd called upon the Scottish ambassador.

Charles sighed. "The things I must do to gain my throne!" Today, he would be expected to sign a treaty and formally agree to the Covenant. With a single stroke of his pen, he would authorize Presbyterian Church governance across Britain. His father would never have agreed to this. Oh, how he despised these Covenanters! His headache flared. "Forgive me, Father. This is a minor setback. I will avenge your death when I am crowned."

Charles recalled what his father told him in the spring of 1646. The war was going badly and he was being sent abroad out of fears for his safety. He'd received a cryptic mandate from his father of what he must do when he became King. He was to execute a traitor, Lord Dughall Gordon, in a most unspeakable manner. There had been no time to discuss it. He had to flee.

Charles had located this traitor. Lord Gordon was a duke of a Highland estate and a staunch Covenanter. He'd asked Montrose to bring him in, but that hadn't happened. As soon as he claimed his crown, he would make Gordon's death a priority.

There was a knock at the door.

Charles took a deep breath. "Come in." What was a Prince to do? It was time for hypocrisy and humiliation. His thoughts were dark. *I will use the Scots to regain my English throne and repudiate my pledge later.*

CHAPTER 27
BELIEVERS SKEPTICS AND SKIRMISHES

MAY 6TH 1650
5 DAYS LATER

DRAKE CASTLE, THE STUDY

It was a warm spring day. The windows in the study were wide open. Birds chattered in the trees and children laughed in the courtyard. Inside, it was more contentious. The Duke sat at his rosewood desk, arguing with his stepfather. He was trying to convince him that his son had turned a corner. "I tell ye. James has changed for the better."

Alex frowned. "Are ye sure he's not playing with ye?"

Dughall summoned his patience. "Nay, Father. The lad and I are getting along. He saved my life at the Abbey. Ye can ask Jamison."

"I will. Have ye talked to him about his sister?"

"I did. James knows that he did wrong. He promised not to do it."

Alex's eyes widened. "So, ye don't want me to talk to him?"

Dughall sensed that he was offended. "Of course, I do. Just don't be specific."

"How am I going to do that?"

"Teach him to respect lasses, but don't mention Maggie."

"Hmmphhh!"

The Duke longed for a whisky, but couldn't drink it in front of his father. "James is my flesh and blood. The boy deserves another chance. Promise me that ye will try." He watched his father turn red. For a moment, he thought he would refuse him.

At last, Alex grunted. "For the lassie's sake, I will try."

Dughall sighed. "Thank ye, Father. Ye won't regret it." There was a sudden knock at the door. "Come in."

Jamison entered with an envelope. "My Lord. A messenger left this at the front gate. He says it's important."

Alex stood. "I shall leave ye to yer correspondence." He bowed slightly and left the chamber.

Dughall accepted the envelope and saw that it was from the Laird of Grant. He motioned for the servant to take a seat. "Stay. We will read it together." He took out an opener, slit the envelope, and extracted a one page letter. Donald Grant's thick handwriting crowded the page.

He read out loud.

Lord Gordon,

Our old nemesis, James Graham, Marquess of Montrose, has been up to his tricks again. Evidently, he was appointed Lieutenant-Governor of Scotland by the exiled Prince Charles. Graham recently entered Scotland through the Orkneys with a thousand foreign mercenaries, mostly Danes and Germans. They say he was sent ahead of the King to cow the Covenanters in northern Scotland. His troops crossed to the mainland and halted at Carbisdale on the southern side of the Kyle of Sutherland.

I sent word to Drake for yer assistance, but they said that ye were gone to the Abbey. So I raised 200 men and joined Colonel Archibald Strachan. To be short, we soundly defeated Montrose's troops – 400 killed and 450 taken prisoner – but Graham initially avoided capture. Thereupon, he made his final mistake. He sought refuge in Ardvreck Castle, where Lady Christine lured him into a vaulted dungeon. The man was imprisoned and turned over to our forces. It violated the tradition of Highland hospitality, but it was worth it. As this time, Montrose is being transported to Edinburgh to be tried and executed for treason. I hope they hang him!

It seems that we have defeated the snake, at least for the time being. But we must be vigilant, because the Prince has set his sights on Scotland. Should we crown him King just because he is a Stuart? He attacks us to avoid taking the Covenants.

We must talk soon, about this event and our mutual agreement.

Stay safe, my friend. - Donald Grant

Jamison let out a low whistle. "So James Graham is about to fall."

Dughall grunted. "I'm not sorry about it. He caused my family hardship."

The servant made a small sound of agreement. "I have a contact in Edinburgh. I will write him about Montrose."

"Why?"

Jamison shrugged. "Morbid curiosity. What will they do to a fellow Lord?"

Dughall frowned. "They would have taken Gilbert's head. They almost took mine."

"True. The Prince seems determined to regain his crown. The men to convince are in Edinburgh. Why would he come to the Highlands?"

The Duke had a sick feeling. "His first act will be to avenge his father."

They were silent for a moment. Jamison frowned. "He knows something."

"Henrietta thought so."

"Do ye think he knows the truth?"

"Nay. She wouldn't have pressed me to marry her. But he could have been told to kill me."

"What should we do?"

"Stay at Drake, but prepare an escape route." The Duke sighed. "If the Prince comes here first, I'm a dead man." He opened the desk, took out a decanter and two glasses, and poured a dram. "I need a whisky."

Jamison accepted a glass. "I'm for that."

Dughall took a long swallow. "Ah. That's just what I needed. Our plans can wait 'til tomorrow."

✻✻✻

THE COURTYARD GARDENS

Maggie sat on a warm stone bench, waiting for her brother James. She'd agreed to meet him alone to talk about their relationship. The lass took in familiar fragrances - wood smoke, pine, and flowering apple trees. Birds twittered in the canopy, soothing her soul and lifting her spirits.

Maggie was anxious. Her brother had been home for almost two weeks. He'd been respectful to her with words and actions, but his aura displayed a cauldron of emotions. She gripped the bench and offered a prayer, "Great Goddess, mother of us all. Help us to get past this." The young lass smoothed her skirt and waited. Minutes later, footsteps sounded on a path to her left.

James appeared, neatly dressed in a shirt, kilt and leather sporran. He was carrying a nosegay of yellow daisies. The lad sat on the bench and handed it to her. "For my dear sister."

Maggie sniffed them. "They're my favorite. Ye remembered."

"Aye." He smiled. "I offer them as an apology for my behavior at Castle Skene."

Great Goddess! This is too good to be true. Her eyes misted. "Oh, James. Of course, I forgive ye. Can we go forth as brother and sister?"

"Aye." He swallowed visibly. "I will never touch ye that way again."

Maggie heard the words, but saw that his aura was dark. She sensed his agony. "Ye're hurt. I'm sorry."

He sniffled. "Me, too. It could have been different."

Maggie gave his hand an affectionate squeeze. "Ye will find a lass to love. I know it."

He looked down. "Can we talk about something else?"

"All right." She was more than willing to change the subject. "I hear that ye're getting along with Father. I'm glad."

James looked up and smiled. "Aye. We discovered that we have things in common."

She was surprised. "What things?"

"Men things. I cannot tell ye."

"Ah. They say that ye saved his life."

"Skene was going to kill him. We stood together and defeated him."

Maggie smiled. "Ye're a brave lad."

They heard footsteps. Philip was approaching on a path to their right.

Maggie felt fear in the pit of her stomach. Her brother had vowed to kill him.

James reddened. "Don't worry. I won't hurt him." He stood and greeted the lad like a gentleman. "Philip. 'Tis a bonny day to sit in nature. I shall leave ye to my sister."

Maggie felt guilty. "Stay with us a while."

His face was grim. "I don't think so." Before they could utter another word, he bowed respectfully and fled the garden.

***

THE RETIRING ROOM

It was early evening. The lace curtains in the retiring room were drawn for privacy. Apple wood crackled in the hearth, emitting a pleasant odor. Four overstuffed chairs were arranged in a circle to accommodate the ladies of the castle.

Keira relaxed in a brocade chair, nursing her infant daughter. Wee Morrigan was five months old and growing stronger every day. She no longer counted the days since the birth or worried that she might not survive.

To her right was her mother-in-law, Jessie. The older woman was fast asleep. She sat with her eyes closed and an unfinished piece of needlework in her lap.

Maggie sat to her left, embroidering a silk pillowcase.

Morrigan released the nipple with a pop. The infant's eyes were half-closed.

Keira closed her nursing blouse and fastened the buttons. She laid a cloth on her shoulder, lifted the baby to it, and patted her back. "There... give Momma a big burp."

Maggie looked up from her needlework. "She's a sweet baby."

Keira smiled. "That she is." The child belched. She shifted the infant to her other shoulder. "I hear that ye talked to James today."

The girl managed a smile. "It was a good visit, but a bit strained. He apologized for what he did to me."

Keira was grateful. It was more than she could have hoped for. "Thank the Goddess."

"He assured me that he would not harm Philip." Maggie sighed. "Oh, Mother. James is hurting. I can feel it. I hope that we can forget the bad things and love each other as brother and sister."

"Ye will. We shall ask the Goddess to heal ye."

Maggie placed her needlework on a side table. "Thank ye, Mother. I must go. I promised to play the harp for Philip." She stood and left the retiring room.

The baby farted. It sounded like she made a mess in her nappie. Keira laid her across her lap and checked the diaper. "Wet *and* dirty.

Let's get ye to the nursery." She stood with the baby in her arms and tapped her mother-in-law on the shoulder. "Wake up, Mother. It's getting late."

The older woman opened her eyes. "I'm sorry. I fell asleep."

"It's all right. Ye had a long day in the surgery."

Jessie nodded. "Go on, lass. I'll be along."

Keira's heart was light as she left the retiring room. *Dughall and James are the best of friends. The lad has lost his obsession with his sister. We're a family again. Bless the Virgin and thank the Goddess!*

Chapter 28
Sounding the Alarm

June 5th 1650
4 weeks later

LONDON, ENGLAND

Oliver Cromwell was feeling grim. The dour-faced Puritan had just come from an emergency session of the Commonwealth Council of State. There he'd been informed that a treaty had been signed between the Scots and Charles Stuart that would restore him to the Scottish throne . It would also authorize Presbyterian Church governance across Britain. They hadn't expected this. The Prince had been busy. Their spies said that he was planning to enter Scotland this month. It was the first step towards claiming his English throne.

Cromwell couldn't let that happen. Britain was a republic now and didn't need a King, especially one with a chip on his shoulder. What would the Prince do to those who executed his father? It went without saying that Presbyterian rule would be unacceptable.

The Council of State had acted fast. They resolved to mount an immediate invasion of Scotland to forestall the possibility of a Scottish attack on England. The commander of the Commonwealth Army, Sir Thomas Fairfax, protested at the meeting. Reluctant to lead an offensive against the Scots, he resigned his commission. Oliver Cromwell was appointed commander-in-chief in his place.

Cromwell had to muster his army. The first step was to choose his commander. "I shall appoint Charles Fleetwood as my lieutenant-general." He wasn't worried. His New Model Army was in top form from their recent conflict with Ireland. He had seven regiments of horse soldiers, nine of foot, and six companies of dragoons, numbering 15,000 men in total. The army would be supported by a naval supply fleet commanded by General-at-sea Richard Deane.

Cromwell sighed. He'd hoped for a sabbatical after the Irish crusade. Perhaps this would be a short campaign. He mused, "I don't blame the Scots or their Kirk run parliament. They have been deceived by the Prince, our true enemy. Perhaps we can persuade them and establish a pro-English government in Scotland." He had to try. "I will send messengers ahead into Scotland to proclaim the righteousness of the Commonwealth cause."

CHAPTER 29
TOO CLOSE FOR COMFORT

JUNE 23RD 1650
18 DAYS LATER

GARMOUTH, MORAY, SCOTLAND

It was a grey windy day in the tiny fishing village of Garmouth. North Sea gales buffeted the sails of the ships in the harbor. Charles Stuart disembarked from the 'Skidam', a ship that had carried him here from the Netherlands. The voyage across the channel had taken nearly two weeks due to bad weather. During that time, the Scottish commissioner attempted to indoctrinate him on the Covenant and his role in upholding it now that he was to take the throne.

Charles felt a knot in the pit of his stomach. He knew that he would be required to sign the hated Covenant. For this purpose, he was being escorted by his protectors and the Scottish commissioner to a local inn. His thoughts were bleak. *What a desolate country! This is the smallest harbor I've ever seen. And I shall be King of this?*

The silver-haired commissioner cleared his throat. "Garmouth lies at the mouth of the River Spey. Beautiful, is it not?"

The Prince forced himself to smile. "Yes. I expected a welcoming party. Where are my royalist allies?"

"I'm told that they are waiting at the inn, my Lord."

Charles stiffened. He surmised that they would not call him 'my King' until he was properly crowned. They walked down a steep path and arrived at the inn, a one-story granite building primitive by his standards, and entered through a weathered oak door.

More than twenty people greeted him. The introductions began. "John Hay, son of Lady Margaret Kerr." "Duncan and Malcolm Innes." "Lord Keith." And so they continued...

Charles took off his outer jacket and gave it to one of his protectors. He was escorted to a long oak table, where he was provided with a glass of ale and modest meal. When he was done eating, the dishes were cleared and a copy of the Covenant was presented.

The commissioner inked a quill and handed it to him. "This is a historic moment, my Lord. It is time to sign the Covenant."

Uttering a silent apology to his father, Charles scrawled his signature on the document. His future subjects beamed with approval. He was anxious to claim his throne. "The deed is done. When shall I be crowned?"

A soldier came forth and bowed slightly. "There is no time for a proper coronation, Sire. I come from our southern border. The English army is about to invade us."

The Prince was stunned. "Who commands them?"

The soldier reddened. "Sir Oliver Cromwell."

Charles' anger flared. This man above all others was responsible for his father's death. "Have I an army?"

"Aye. We were only 6,000 strong a week ago. But we are mobilizing the militia to raise regiments."

The Prince's head throbbed. *We have six thousand trained men? How on earth can we fight Cromwell?* "Who commands my army?"

The soldier snapped to attention. "Sir David Leslie, the 1st Lord of Newark."

The Prince recognized the name. "Any relation to Alexander Leslie?"

The soldier nodded. "His nephew."

Charles stood. "There is no time to waste. Take me to my commander."

"A carriage awaits, Sire."

The Prince fumed as he put on his coat. *Will I not get a moment's peace?* Soldiers formed a protective circle and escorted him out of the inn. As he approached his carriage, he gazed to the heavens and offered a silent apology. *Forgive me, Father. Lord Gordon's execution will have to wait.*

***

SIX DAYS LATER, NEAR THE ENGLISH-SCOTTISH BORDER

Oliver Cromwell surveyed his troops as they marched northward. From atop his magnificent steed, he could see regiments stretching for miles in both directions. He knew that the Scots were expecting him. He'd sent messengers ahead with a declaration stating that the English army had no intention of harming the people of Scotland. Only those persons who by their conduct sought the restoration of the Stuart monarchy would be in danger.

Cromwell frowned. Diplomacy had failed. The Scots were raising an army of soldiers and cavalry. If it were not to make war upon England, then what could it be for?

Worse yet, he'd been informed by his spies that the Prince had entered Scotland and signed the Covenant. The young man was crafty. It wouldn't be long before they crowned him.

He yelled to his lieutenant-general, "Move them along, Fleetwood! We have a long way to go before we make camp for the night." He sighed. *There's no rest for the righteous. It's going to be a long campaign.*

Chapter 30
Letters

June 29th 1650
Same Day

DRAKE CASTLE

The Duke stood in his study, gazing out the open window. The day was oppressively hot, with temperatures above ninety. Because of the weather, he was informally dressed - in breeks, a shirt, and no shoes or socks. "Whew, it's hot!" He mopped his brow with a handkerchief.

Dughall spotted Jamison crossing the courtyard with a pack of letters in his hand. His spirits lifted. "Perhaps it's from Gilbert." He left the window and moved his ledgers to the sideboard. There was a knock on the door. "Come in."

Jamison entered. "My Lord." The servant was sweaty from the heat. "A courier dropped these letters at the gate." He placed them on the desk.

"How many are there?"

"Three."

Dughall motioned for him to take a seat. He picked up one of the envelopes and saw that it was addressed to Jamison. "This one is for ye."

The servant grinned. "I know. I want to read it together. It's from my contact in Edinburgh. He's a member of Parliament. I asked about Montrose."

Dughall frowned. "Ah... The trial."

"And execution."

"We shall see." The Duke sliced open the envelope and extracted the letter. "Shall I read out loud?"

"Aye."

The author had some schooling. It was written in fancy handwriting.

Jamison my friend,

You inquired about the Marquess of Montrose. There is quite a story to tell. The Parliament condemned him to death in absentia before he arrived here. James Graham was brought as a prisoner to Edinburgh and without trial was sentenced to death on May 20th. Archibald Johnston read his fate out loud for all to hear. He was to be hanged at the Market Cross with a copy of De Rebus hung 'round his neck. This book you may remember was Bishop Wishart's favorable biography of Graham's life. But there was more to his humiliation! He was to swing on the scaffold for three hours, after which time, his head was to be severed and his body quartered. Unless he repented, he was to be buried in unhallowed ground.

Graham did not repent. He insisted that he was a real Covenanter and a loyal subject. This was met with jeers and shameful gestures of mockery.

I watched the sentence carried out on May 21st at the town market cross. I must say that Graham accepted his fate with grace and courage. When allowed final words, he prayed to heaven, "Scatter my ashes! Strew them in the air, Lord, since thou knowest where all these atoms are."

The hanging was then carried out. As prescribed, his body hung for three hours, was decapitated, and quartered. The head was displayed on a pike at the Tollbooth Prison, while the parts were dispersed for display in Glasgow, Perth, Stirling, and Aberdeen.

I suspect that you will approve of this action, given your experience with the man. But it was a disgraceful end for a Lord of the realm. I fear that we have set a bad precedent. After his death, some of us convinced Parliament to bury his body parts in hallowed ground. They were going to dump them in a common grave on Burgh Muir.

In closing, we must be careful what we wish for! Someday, it could apply to us. I hope that this satisfies your curiosity. Stay safe, my friend. Give my regards to Lord Drake and the Lady of the castle.

Sincerely - John H.

The Duke shuddered. "He's right. That was a disgraceful way for a lord to die."

Jamison grunted. "Agreed."

"Does he have a family?"

"A wife and son."

Dughall's heart sank. "I will write them and send our condolences." He picked up the second letter and saw that it was from the Laird of Grant. "This one is from Donald." He opened it and began to read.

Lord Gordon,

I write to inform ye of a serious situation. Perhaps ye have already heard. Prince Charles entered Scotland at Garmouth on June 23rd. I was told that he was accompanied by one of our commissioners. He was met by a small party of Royalists, the Hays and Keiths among them.

Jamison stiffened and drew his knife. "Garmouth? That's less than a day's ride from here."

Dughall's heart was pounding. "Let me continue."

The Prince signed the Covenant and asked to be crowned immediately, but was called away to a serious situation. It seems that the English army is about to invade our southern border. From what I understand, Sir David Leslie is raising an army to fight the English, but trained men are hard to come by. I have not yet decided if I will join them. The Prince signed the Covenant, but I do not trust him. Let's see if he renounces his mother's religion.

Come to me, my friend. We will discuss this over a glass of whisky. - Donald Grant

Jamison scowled. "Yer life is in grave danger. What should we do?"

Dughall was pale. "I must leave Scotland before he is crowned." He wiped sweat from his brow. "It's so hot, I can't think!"

"Will ye see the Laird of Grant?"

"I will go there tomorrow. I need to raise some gold and silver. Perhaps I can sell him something."

Jamison thought for a moment. "He has always admired Seaford Shores."

It hurt to think about selling Grandfather's retreat, but it had to be done. It would do no one good if he was executed as a traitor. "We will have to name a price for it."

"Aye. Or he might make an offer."

Dughall picked up the third letter and saw that it was from Virginia. "This one is from Gilbert. I hope it's not bad news." He opened it and read out loud.

My dear Brother,

We have made remarkable progress on our plantation, which we have boldly named 'Eden'. With hired help, we planted forty acres of tobacco, twelve of corn, and five experimental acres of cotton and flax. I am amazed at what grows in this warm climate! We also planted an orchard with apricots, quinces, and pears.

Our success has been in part due to a fortunate turn of events. At church, I became acquainted with the Governor of Virginia, Sir William Berkeley, who provided me with plants and valuable advice. Bridget has befriended his young wife Elizabeth and seems quite content with life in the colonies.

There is further good news. Sir Berkeley intends to make me a commissioner for James City County. This compensated post involves taking depositions, issuing warrants, and resolving minor disputes. My title will be 'Justice of the Peace'. I must attend monthly meetings to settle civil and lesser criminal cases. Me, a Justice!

Sir Berkeley is an interesting man. As a royalist, he is of the opinion that the King's son will be restored to the throne. Berkeley was previously a member of the royal court and Charles the younger has been in contact with him. When ye come to visit, be advised. Ye will have to hide the fact that ye supported the Covenant.

In closing, I am in good health and growing stronger by the day. Connor is well. Bridget is well. My daughters are thriving and George has grown into a brawny young man. We would love to have ye visit our 'Eden'.

I miss our talks as brother to brother! Come to us when ye can. Whisky is scarce, but we can sit on the porch and drink rum, a potent spirit distilled from sugar cane. Even the ladies like it with a touch of bruised mint.

Give my regards to yer wife and children. Write me and tell me how ye are faring. I will never forget what ye did for me. - Yer brother always, Gilbert (George)

Dughall was silent for a moment. "The Prince is raising support in the colonies."

Jamison nodded. "Aye. Gilbert made some important connections. Ye could ask him to keep ye informed."

Dughall opened a drawer and took out a quill and paper. "I will write him today." He managed a smile. "I'm pleased that he's doing well."

Jamison grinned. "How can he not? They live in 'Eden'."

"Ha!"

"My Lord. Gilbert invited ye to Virginia. It might be the answer to yer problem."

Dughall nodded. "I was thinking the same thing. We could arrange a visit."

"Agreed."

"Besides, I'm looking forward to drinking that rum."

Chapter 31
Negotiations

June 30th 1650

NEXT DAY

CASTLE GRANT

Dughall sat in the main room of the hunting lodge, admiring the preserved heads of animals. There was no doubt that Donald Grant was a skilled hunter. He complimented him, "I am amazed at yer hunting prowess."

The stocky man smiled as he scratched his heavy beard. "Hunting is my greatest pleasure. A man who hunts will never go hungry. The beasts of the earth are there for our taking."

Dughall grinned. "Agreed."

Donald lifted his glass, "Drink with me, my friend."

The Duke joined him, "Here's to our friendship, in good times and bad." He took a swallow and savored the peaty taste. "Ah... This is excellent as usual."

Donald bolted his whisky and put down the glass. "We have much to discuss. It seems that our colleagues in Edinburgh wish to restore the monarchy."

Dughall took another sip. It was too good to bolt. "Aye. I got a shock when I learned that the Prince entered at Garmouth."

Donald scowled. "First he uses Montrose to attack us. Of course, he denies that. Then he expects us to kiss his ring when he signs the Covenant. The man is a snake like his father! He is using us to regain his English throne."

"I agree."

The Laird of Grant seemed surprised. He signaled for Dughall to put down his glass and poured them another dram. "It seems that we are of the same mind."

"Aye." Dughall accepted the glass gratefully. "Thank ye, my friend." He took a swallow and sighed. "I'm afraid that I have bad news. Can we speak in confidence?"

He cocked an eyebrow. "Of course."

"The Prince's return puts my life in danger."

"How so?"

Dughall leaned forward and clasped his hands. "I have been informed by someone close to the Prince. One of his first acts as King will be to execute me as a traitor."

Donald frowned. "Who said this?"

Dughall blushed. "I can not reveal my source. But it is reliable."

"Why would the Prince do such a thing?"

He told a partial truth. "The King was displeased that I rescued two men from the Tower. He put me high on his list of traitors."

"By God! My brother was executed on Tower Hill in a most unspeakable manner. I wish that ye could have saved him as well. This is yer crime?"

Dughall bolted his whisky. "Aye. I must leave Scotland before he is crowned."

Donald refilled their glasses. "How can I help?"

Dughall was encouraged. "I am provisioning a ship to take us to a secret location. We will weather the storm there and return when it's wise. I will need ye to keep me abreast of politics in Scotland."

"I will do it."

"Our location must be kept secret."

"Of course."

"I also need a place to send mail to that won't be conspicuous."

"Send it here and I will deliver it. Is there anything else?"

"Aye. I need to sell some property to raise gold and silver for a few years abroad. Would ye be interested in Seaford Shores?"

A smile spread across his bearded face. "Perhaps. I have long admired the place. What do ye want for it?"

Dughall extracted a piece of paper from his pocket upon which the price was written. He passed it to the man.

Donald stared at it. "I will pay this on one condition. The furnishings and the Arabians go with it."

"Can the staff stay?"

"Aye. I will honor the arrangements ye have made with them."

Dughall took a long swallow and felt the whisky burn a trail to his belly. Twelve Arabian horses were worth a small fortune, but he was in no position to bargain. He had to finance his trip abroad. "Ye drive a hard bargain, but I agree. There is only one thing I want from Seaford Shores. I have hidden a sword there."

Donald raised his eyebrows. "The sword of Red Conan?"

"Aye."

"It's cursed. I don't want it on the property." He cleared his throat. "Ye seem to have a way with it."

Dughall nodded. "Aye. I will remove it in the next few days and inform the staff of the transfer."

"Good. Then the deal is done."

Dughall knew that if Grant's nephew accompanied him, he would never reveal their location. "There is one more thing. I wish to take Philip and Maggie abroad with me."

The man's brow furrowed. "Will he be safe?"

"Of course, my friend. The Prince wants my head, no one else's. The youngsters will travel with us. But for this purpose, they should be married."

"I have no objection."

"When I return from Seaford Shores, they shall be married. I will send a courier to fetch ye for the ceremony."

Donald bolted his whisky and poured them another. "Let us drink on it."

They sat among the heads of wild animals, finishing the bottle of fine whisky.

At last, Donald Grant stood. "Let us go to my treasury and get yer gold and silver."

Dughall joined him. "On the way, I will tell ye about the Marquess of Montrose."

CHAPTER 32
SEAFORD SHORES

JULY 2ND 1650
2 DAYS LATER

SEAFORD SHORES

It was a perfect summer day on Findhorn Bay. Waves lapped the shore in the protected harbor. Dughall stood at the water, surveying miles of rocky beach that belonged to his estate. A light wind lifted his hair and blew it around his shoulders. This was one of God's sacred places. It did his heart good.

Seaford Shores was a magnificent estate. A favorite of the late Duke, it was comprised of a sprawling stone house, a large barn with stables, several outbuildings, and miles of beachfront property. Over the years, Dughall used it for a retreat. He'd brought his family here after the war to heal and reconnect with each other. He'd come alone many times to ride the horses and meditate. He understood why his grandfather loved the place. The staff was always friendly and regaled him with stories of his family. The Arabian horses were magnificent.

Now, he and Jamison were there for the last time before transferring it to the Laird of Grant. Donald had been gracious about it to be sure. He'd told Dughall that he would always be welcome to visit.

The day had been bittersweet. They'd taken out two Arabians for a long ride along the shore. They'd enjoyed a wonderful midday meal of salmon and sea trout. Then they informed the staff of the impending transfer. There were tearful goodbyes and fervent promises.

Dughall glanced behind him. Jamison was standing with their stallions, Black Lightning and Celtic Thunder. They were packed and ready for the return trip but they had one task left to do. "I'm ready, my friend."

Jamison frowned. "Are ye sure ye want to do this, my Lord?"

Dughall approached him. "Aye. I promised Donald I would remove the sword from this property. He is aware of its history."

"I can't blame him for wanting it gone. What will we do with it?"

Dughall sighed. "I haven't decided yet."

The servant scowled. "One thing is sure... Ye must not touch it!"

"We shall see. Where is it hidden?"

Jamison sulked. "I'll take ye there."

They led the horses down the beach until they came to a small sea cave. The tide was out so the water was shallow.

Jamison handed over the reins. "Stay with the horses. I will fetch it."

Dughall watched the servant wade into the water and disappear into the dark cave. He waited for a while and was about to follow when the man emerged carrying the scabbard. It was wrapped in a ream of hemp cloth.

Jamison was short of breath. "It was just where I left it. There is a high natural shelf in that cave that never gets flooded."

The Duke handed him the reins. "Take the horses. I want to see it."

The servant handed it over reluctantly. "My Lord, please! Aren't we in enough trouble?"

Dughall managed a smile. "Aye, we are. I just want to see it for old time's sake." He kneeled on the beach and proceeded to unwrap the cloth. At last, the sword lay before him, a bit green from exposure but still intact. It was beautiful and it vibrated, calling to him. Perhaps he could hold it just one more time.

"Don't touch it, my Lord! Think of yer family."

Dughall shuddered. Once again, he'd almost been seduced by the sword. His servant was right. He stood and took the reins. "Cover it up and take it with us."

Jamison sprang into action, wrapping the sword and mounting it on the back of his own horse.

The men mounted and began the journey home. They rode along side the Findhorn River, passed the town of Forres, and followed a gorge with spectacular red sandstone outcrops.

Dughall's heart was in his throat. The entire time they'd been riding, the sword had been calling to him. He knew what he had to do. "Let's go to the edge of the gorge."

Jamison stared. "Why?"

"Ye shall see. Take the sword." They dismounted, tied their horses to a tree, and walked to the edge. "Unwrap it, my friend."

Jamison removed the rough cloth from the scabbard. "What now?"

Dughall heard the sword singing. The high vibration was intoxicating. But he couldn't let it control him. He resisted touching it, and whispered, "Goodbye, Conan." He signaled to his friend. "Throw it in the gorge before I change my mind!"

Jamison wasted no time. He hurled the weapon and watched it sail into the gorge below. It entered the clear water and sank like a stone. "Ye did it!"

Dughall had tears in his eyes. "Aye. I hope it's the right thing." Deep in his heart, he knew that it was.

They continued on their journey.

CHAPTER 33
STRATEGY

JULY 7TH 1650
5 DAYS LATER

FIFTEEN MILES SOUTH OF EDINBURGH, SCOTLAND

Sir David Leslie sat atop his faithful steed, surveying the handiwork of his troops. In the distance, he could see great billowing clouds of smoke where crops and food supplies were being burned.

Leslie could say that he was unhappy with the progress of the army, but in truth he was downright disturbed. They'd started out with 6,000 regulars, among them a number of seasoned commanders. They recently added 20,000 men by raising the militia, but these soldiers were poorly equipped and commanded.

When the Prince arrived in Edinburgh, he'd refused to publicly condemn his mother's 'Popery' and his father's 'bad counsel'. This infuriated the Kirk Party, causing them to dismiss 80 veteran cavalier officers and 3,000 soldiers who were less than enthusiastic about the Covenant. Leslie had a few encounters with the Prince. Young and arrogant, he'd tried to control the process. This child-man was definitely a thorn in his side. But he would soon be King.

He sighed. An experienced colonel had just told him that their army had been left with nothing but useless clerks and ministers' sons who had never seen a sword, no less used one. *This is a disaster! What would Uncle Alex say?*

David Leslie was a professional soldier. He'd fought with the Swedish army, led the Scottish cavalry attack at Marsdon Moor, and recently destroyed Montrose's army. He knew a bad situation when he saw it. This was why he was burning all the crops and supplies between Edinburgh and the English border.

"Let Cromwell's army cross! I shall avoid open battle and wage a war of attrition through hunger and disease. When they weaken, I will harass them with guerilla tactics."

This sort of campaign would take some time. He wondered if the Prince would approve. The young man made it plain that he wished to be crowned and viewed the invasion as a minor setback.

Leslie turned his horse and headed for Edinburgh. He was expected to meet with the Tables and later with Prince Charles. His thoughts were bleak as he approached the granite city. *Shall I tell them that we are 40 depleted regiments cobbled together as an army?*

CHAPTER 34
WEDDING DAY

JULY 13TH 1650
6 DAYS LATER

DRAKE CASTLE, THE SEWING ROOM

It was a perfect summer day. Trees and wildflowers were in bloom and heather covered the hills. Temperatures hovered around seventy, making it comfortable.

Maggie Gordon stood on a stool, enduring the final adjustments to her wedding gown. A silver-haired tailor knelt at her feet, with six pins in his mouth. He was tacking the hem of the gown to shorten it.

"How much longer will ye be?" she asked.

The man tried to speak but only managed to mumble.

"I'm sorry!" she cried. "Ye have pins in yer mouth."

He finished placing the final pin. "There, young Miss. We are done at last."

"Oh, good."

"Yer maid will help ye change. Then I will sew the hem so it's ready for the ceremony." He stood stiffly and left the room.

Maggie's heart soared as her maid entered the chamber. "Marjorie! I'm so happy. Today is my wedding day."

The elderly woman smiled. "'Tis. I prayed that I would live to see this day." She began to unfasten the buttons in the back. "It's a lovely dress, lass. There must be a thousand tiny pearls on the fabric. They say that yer Aunt Bridget wore it at her wedding."

"I know." Maggie smiled. "We didn't have time to make a new one. Father wants us to marry now."

Marjorie helped her out of the dress and laid the precious garment on a table. "I wonder why?"

"It's a surprise. He won't tell us until after the wedding." She was curious, too. Father seemed preoccupied, like something serious was on his mind. His aura was an unusual shade of blue, reflecting sadness and possibilities.

The servant helped her into a simple yellow dress with a lace collar. "I'm sure that everything will be all right. Ye haven't seen Philip today, have ye?"

Maggie giggled. "Nay! I'm not supposed to see him until the wedding. It's bad luck."

"Where will ye go now?"

"Father wants to talk to me in the study."

"I will accompany ye there and wait outside."

The young lass stepped down from the stool. She slipped on a pair of comfortable shoes and they left the sewing room.

***

THE STUDY

The Duke sat at his desk, affixing his signature to a deed. The day had come to turn Seaford Shores over to the Laird of Grant. He dated the document and then placed it on the sideboard. Signing the deed was easy because he was resigned to the property transfer. What would not be easy was talking to his daughter.

Dughall's nerves were raw. *Maggie is barely thirteen years old, yet I'm allowing her to take a husband. How can I send her to a marital bed?* He'd asked Keira to talk to her about the duties of a wife towards her husband. He'd also asked his mother to have a conversation with her.

There was a knock on the door. "Come."

Maggie entered the room and closed the door behind her. She took a seat at the desk opposite him. "I've come, Father."

Dughall had a lump in his throat. She was beautiful. No wonder the lad was stricken with her. "My beloved daughter. The day has come for yer wedding."

She beamed with joy. "Aye."

"Are ye happy about it?"

"Of course, Father! Philip and I are meant to be together. I dreamed of him."

Dughall had tears in his eyes. "So young. So innocent." He reddened. "Did yer mother... ah... talk to ye about..."

The lass seemed amused with his discomfort. "About the marital bed? Aye! Ye don't have to worry. I look forward to it. I love him."

It was more than he could ask for. His voice cracked with emotion, "He'd better be good to you."

Maggie rose from her chair. She came to him and melted into his arms. "Philip loves me. Try not to worry."

"I'll try." He suppressed a sob. "Oh, Maggie. Ye mean so much to me. I love ye more than life."

She hugged him tightly. "I love ye, too."

***

THE GREAT HALL

James stood in the entrance to the Great Hall, watching the preparations for the wedding. On one side of the room, four tables were set with linen table cloths, fine china, and polished silver tableware. The tables were adorned with candles and crystal bowls of daisies, his sister's favorite. Servants scurried about, dusting and arranging serving tables. On the other side of the room, there was a stage for minstrels and a long red carpet. It led to an oak lectern where the priest would stand when he married the young couple.

James was a cauldron of emotions. *It's Maggie's wedding day.* He loved his sister and wanted her to be happy. Yet he knew that she was the only woman for him. He knew it was wrong to feel this way – wrong according to the Church, his family, and his newly found morals. He must do the right thing and support her in her marriage.

His heart was broken. *Oh, Maggie. I will never love anyone else.* He swallowed a sob. *God, help me. I'm on the verge of tears. How will I make it through this day?*

James had a few hours to compose himself. He had to wash, dress, and think about what to say. The lad was expected to give a toast to the newly married couple. He left the Great Hall and headed for his bed chamber.

***

THE NURSERY

The Duchess had just finished her personal preparations for the wedding – styling her hair, applying a touch of rouge, and donning a green silk dress. Now, she stood at the crib in the nursery, dressing wee Morrigan for the ceremony. Her heart was light as she selected a flowing white gown for the infant. "We should change her nappy."

Tarrah stood at her side. "Would ye like me to do it, my Lady? It would be a shame to get powder on yer fine dress."

Keira smiled. "Thank ye, lass." She took a step back and watched the nursemaid change the child's diaper. "I'm so exited about the wedding!"

The servant placed the last pin. "I passed by the Great Hall. It looks wonderful."

The two women worked together, dressing the child in the flowing gown. They completed her outfit with a lacey cap tied under her chin.

"She looks bonny." Tarrah searched through a drawer and extracted several neatly folded cloths. "For yer shoulder, if she rests there, or if she decides to whoops." She handed them to her mistress. "Shall I carry her to the Hall?"

Keira stroked the child's cheek. "What do ye say, sweet pea? Shall Tarrah carry ye?" The baby cooed. "It's a good idea, lass. We'd better go. The ceremony will start soon."

Tarrah lifted the child to her shoulder. "I shall remain on duty should the wee one need a nap after the ceremony."

Keira was grateful. The celebration could last into the night. "Bless ye, lass. It would be nice to spend time with the wedding guests and partake in a glass of wine. I will need yer help." With further ado, they left the nursery and headed for the ceremony.

***

THE GREAT HALL

The tables were set, candles were lit, and the guests had arrived. On stage, a white-haired woman played the dulcimer, while her daughter played a flute. Father John and Philip had just arrived and were standing at the oak lectern. The lad looked handsome in a fine jacket and ceremonial kilt that reflected his Grant ancestry.

Dughall stood with his wife and infant daughter, awaiting the entrance of his daughter Maggie. He was a bundle of nerves. He whispered, "Are we doing the right thing?"

Keira smiled. "Of course. They're young but they love each other."

He took a deep breath to calm himself. There was a commotion in the hallway, a sign that she was approaching. All eyes were on the open door.

Maggie walked through gracefully, wearing a silk wedding dress embroidered with tiny pearls. She had a sprig of heather in her hair, a sign of good luck and fertility. The young lass came to Dughall and offered her right hand. "Father. Will ye give me away?"

The Duke swallowed hard. "I will, Daughter."

The music got softer and stopped.

The priest spoke, "Who gives this woman to be married to this man?"

Dughall took her hand and led her slowly down the red carpet to her future husband.

Philip turned to them. The lad was beaming with joy.

Father John continued, "Marriage is a serious commitment, not to be taken lightly. If any man can show just cause why they may not be lawfully joined, let him now speak, or else hereafter forever hold his peace."

The Duke heard no objections, save the one in his own mind, *She's too young! How can I give my daughter to this man?* There were tears in his eyes. He gripped her hand tightly.

"There are no objections," the priest said. "We may continue."

"Ye can let go now, Father", Maggie whispered. "Ye're supposed to give me to him."

"Forgive me," he said in low tones. Trembling, he took her hand and placed it in Philip's. "I give ye my beloved daughter. Be good to her."

Philip smiled. "Forever and always, Sir."

The young couple separated and turned to face the priest.

Dughall returned to his wife and wee daughter. His heart was beating like a drum. He knew that Maggie and Philip had decided to change the ceremony. He hoped that Donald Grant would approve.

Father John began, "Dear friends. I am honored to preside over this joining. I have known this young lass for most of her life and am acquainted with the young master." He opened his book. "Dearly beloved, ye have come together in this place so that the Lord may seal and strengthen yer love in the presence of the Church's minister. Christ and the Blessed Virgin sanctify this love. They enrich and strengthen ye by special sacrament so that ye may assume the duties of marriage in mutual and lasting fidelity."

The audience was solemn.

"And so, in the presence of Christ, the Church, and the Blessed Virgin, I ask ye to state yer intentions." He turned a page. "Have ye come here freely and without reservation to give yerself to each other in marriage?"

Philip gazed at her. "Aye."

Maggie smiled. "Oh, aye!"

"Will ye love and honor each other as man and wife for the rest of yer lives?"

They answered together. "Aye."

"Will ye accept children lovingly from God and bring them up according to the laws of Christ and his Church?"

They practically beamed with joy. "Aye."

"Now, ye must declare yer consent before God and his Church. Philip Grant, will ye take Margaret Christal Gordon here present, for yer lawful wife according to the rite of our Holy Mother, the Church?"

He smiled. "I will."

Father John turned. " Margaret Gordon, will ye take Philip Grant here present, for yer lawful husband according to the rite of our Holy Mother, the Church?"

She smiled like an angel. "I will."

"Then it is time to recite the promise."

They young couple faced each other and joined hands. "I, Philip Grant, take ye Margaret, for my wife, to have and to hold, from this day forward, for better, for worse, for richer, for poorer, in sickness and in health, until death do us part."

It was her turn. "I, Margaret Gordon, take ye Philip, for my husband, to have and to hold, from this day forward, for better, for worse, for richer, for poorer, in sickness and in health, until death do us part."

The priest nodded. "Bring forth the rings."

Ian's six-year-old daughter Marsaili came forward bearing a silk pillow with two gold rings. She presented it to the couple.

Philip accepted it gratefully. "Thank ye, child."

The girl ran back to her parents.

The groom unpinned the rings and slipped one onto Maggie's ring finger. The other he gave to her. With great ceremony, she slipped it on his finger.

The priest smiled. "I now pronounce ye man and wife. Ye may kiss the bride."

Philip embraced her and kissed her tenderly.

Dughall tensed. He wasn't the only one. He sensed another in the room who was miserable about the match. But, who could it be?

The young couple thanked the priest. They left the lectern and approached the guests amidst a storm of clapping.

***

James Gordon was devastated. The woman he loved was married to another man. Worse yet, he was expected to congratulate them. He'd rehearsed it for hours this afternoon. James approached the couple and offered his hand in friendship to Philip. They shook vigorously. He swallowed his agony. "This makes us brothers-in-law. I trust that ye will take good care of my sister."

Philip smiled. "I will. She is very special to me."

Maggie hugged him. "I love ye, Brother. Bless ye for supporting me."

James swallowed the lump in his throat. "I love ye too. I always will." There were tears in his eyes.

They were being called to the head table. Philip and Maggie sat in the place of honor, while James took his place next to his parents.

Wine was poured and the toasts began. "To a love that's true." "To a long and prosperous life." "To many healthy children."

At last, it was James' turn. "To the man who won my sister's heart. May he always love and protect her."

The guests clinked their glasses with their silverware. "Hear! Hear!"

The servants entered and a wonderful meal was served, of lamb and fowl and vegetables and potatoes. Wine and whisky flowed freely.

James barely poked at his meal. His stomach was doing flip-flops. At last, he turned to the Duke. "Father. I am ill."

Dughall frowned. "What's wrong?"

"My stomach is in knots. It must have been that glass of wine. With yer permission, I will go to my bed chamber."

The Duke nodded. "Perhaps it's best. Shall I send a servant with some chamomile tea?"

James forced a smile. "Aye, I would appreciate it." He saw Philip and Maggie in the center of the room, dancing. "Give my regards to my sister."

"Go, my son."

James stood and brushed off his kilt. The music was ending and he didn't want to face the newly wed couple. With a slight bow, he offered his apologies and left the Great Hall.

***

TWO HOURS LATER, JAMES' BED CHAMBER

James lay on his back in bed with a wet compress over his eyes. He was suffering from a frightful headache. He didn't have it when he left the party. It started when he went to his room and cried for an hour. He tried to think of something else – the monastery, his stallion, anything but Philip and Maggie. But his thoughts always returned to another man ravaging his sister. *Soon they will be in their marital bed. He will touch her as I did and take her cherry. Oh, Maggie!*

The pain flared until points of light danced in front of his eyes. He couldn't go on like this. He recalled Brother Adam's instructions and took a series of measured breaths. The pain eased and before long, a pervasive cold sent chills through his body. He opened his eyes and saw his breath. *How strange.*

"Hello, Grandson."

Grandson? The voice was unfamiliar. He sat up in bed and saw a Lord sitting in his side chair, pouring a glass of whisky from a crystal decanter. He was dressed in the Gordon kilt, a blue doublet, and a cream silk shirt. The lad felt violated. "How dare ye enter my bed chamber! Who are ye?"

"Ha! I'm yer grandfather." The man lifted the glass to his lips and belted the contents. "I stole this from the wedding. It's been a long time since I had the good stuff."

James stiffened. "Yer *not* my grandfather."

His eyes narrowed in mock anger. "I am. My blood runs through yer veins."

"My grandfather is at the wedding."

The man smirked. "That ignorant fisherman? I suppose ye think he's yer grandfather. But he's not. He caused yer father far more trouble than I did. Almost got him killed in London. But I'll let him tell ye about that."

James was beginning to think that this was a bad dream. "Who are ye?"

"I'm yer father's birth father. The original Blackheart."

The lad reddened. "Prove it."

"Tsk... Tsk..." The man clicked his tongue. "Think, lad. Remember the portrait in the Great Hall at Huntly? Look at me."

James' skin crawled. "Ye do look like him."

"That's because I am him." The man bolted his whisky and poured another. "Join me?"

"I'm only twelve years old!"

"Not too young to start. I started when I was ten." He poured a dram and handed it to him.

James was astonished. The glass was solid. He took a sip and felt it burn a trail to his belly. He gagged and almost vomited. "Ach! How can ye drink this stuff?"

Blackheart grinned. "Take another swallow. It *grows* on ye."

James complied. The whisky went straight to his head this time and emboldened him. "Ye beat my father with a leather strap. I saw the scars."

"'Tis true. Have ye never been beaten?"

"Aye, but..."

"Well, get over it! If it's the worst thing that ever happens, ye'll be lucky. Sure, I beat yer father. It made him the man he is today."

The lad was stunned. *Could that be true? Can a man benefit from a beating? I will have to ask my father.*

"Sure, go ahead and ask him."

James stiffened. Was the man reading his mind? "What do ye want from me?"

"Ah." Blackheart held up his glass and admired the amber color. "I've been listening to ye lament about yer sister. So ye wanted to burst her cherry? Do ye not know that it's forbidden fruit?"

James reddened. The man *was* reading his thoughts. "How do ye know this?"

"I'm dead. We can read minds and discern intentions. Ye desire yer sister. The question is 'What will ye do about it?'"

The boy shrugged. "Nothing. It's against the laws of God and man." He took another sip of whisky. This time, he didn't gag. "It *does* grow on ye."

"Ha!" The man slapped his leg. "Ye are a Gordon. I must say that ye turned out better than I thought given the circumstances of yer conception."

That grabbed his attention. "Which were?"

Blackheart smiled. "Better take another sip. Ye won't like it."

James bolted the whisky. "Well?"

"Let's see. Yer mother was barren. She was desperate to conceive." He took a sip. "Ye do know that Maggie is not her child?"

"I heard that."

"She is yer father's child. He was banging my mistress."

James frowned. *It doesn't sound like something that Father would do.* "Never mind that. What about my conception?"

The man's eyes narrowed. "Yer father was obsessed with that cursed sword. It was killing him. He was convinced that the Goddess Morrigan was after him. Yer mother used pagan magic to save him."

James' head was starting to spin. "How?" He put down his empty glass.

Blackheart poured them another drink. "The lass called it 'drawing down the moon'. She stood naked in the forest under a full moon and called the Goddess Morrigan into herself. She's a shape shifter, the red-haired goddess of battle and sex."

"I don't believe it!" He accepted the drink and took a sip.

"That's right. Drink. Life always looks better through a glass of whisky." He took a swallow. "Ah! Where was I? Sorry, lad. There's just no good way to say this. Yer mother was not herself when she conceived ye. It was her body but the Morrigan was in control."

"Ye're lying!"

"I'm not. Did ye ever wonder where yer red hair came from?"

"Uncle Ian has red hair."

"Think, lad! He's the son of that ignorant fisherman. He's not yer blood uncle."

James was skeptical. "Why should I believe ye?"

"Don't. Ask yer mother. Ask yer father. Why do ye think ye have such unholy thoughts? And powers beyond the normal? How many lads can sic crows and ravens on an enemy? Neat trick, by the way."

James cringed. *How can he know about that?*

"Like I said, I'm yer grandfather. I've followed ye all yer life."

The boy's headache flared. He took another swallow to blunt the pain. "Why are ye here?"

"To give ye some grandfatherly advice."

"Advice?" The lad leaned forward. "What is it?"

Blackheart was solemn. "With yer history, it would irresponsible to conceive a child."

James knew the truth when he heard it. It didn't leave him many options. His shoulders sagged. "I know what to do."

The man sipped his whisky and smiled. "Good! Ah. I would give anything to be in the flesh again and enjoy its pleasures." His image was fading. "Ach! It's time to go."

James didn't want to be alone. "Don't go, Grandfather!"

His voice was faint. "It seems that I must."

"Nay!" James rubbed his eyes. The room was spinning from all that whisky. The lad cradled his head in his hands and groaned. He heard a window open and slam shut. The room grew warmer. When at last he looked up, the spirit of his grandfather was gone. Was it a bad dream?

The truth was hard to deny. On the table next to him sat a glass of whisky.

Chapter 35
Revelations

July 14th 1650

Next Day

DRAKE CASTLE, JAMES'S BED CHAMBER

Morning light filtered into the bed chamber. James woke with a start, wondering if Blackheart was sitting next to him. He rolled over and saw that he was gone. "Thank God! I've heard enough from him."

Last night, he lay awake for hours, pondering the man's words. What if they were true? How could he confirm them? Was Maggie's mother a common mistress? Did his father gain from Blackheart's beatings? And worst of all... *Was* he conceived with pagan magic? His mind reeled with possibilities. To fall asleep, he'd finished the whisky.

Now, he sat up in bed and brought a hand to his temple. His head throbbed and his mouth was dry. And what was that disgusting taste? "Ach! It must be the whisky."

There was a knock on the door and Murdock entered. The servant had recently been assigned to him. He came to the bedside and held out a goblet. "Drink this, my Lord."

James stared at the vessel through bloodshot eyes. "What is it?"

"Water with a pinch of willow bark. They said that ye drank a bit of wine last night."

"I did." James accepted the cup and drank it down, wincing at the bitter taste. It was indeed willow bark. "Thank ye."

The servant spotted an empty glass on the side table. He picked it up and sniffed it. "My Lord. I don't mean to criticize. But was this whisky?"

James nodded. "Aye. It's awful stuff. That's the last time I drink it."

The servant smiled. "That's what yer father said after the first time."

The lad took a long gulp of water. It occurred to him that this man could be a resource. "Murdock. How long have ye been with my father?"

The servant beamed with pride. "Fourteen years. I was assigned to him when he came to Huntly."

"What was he like then?"

He grinned. "Innocent and principled. He turned the place upside down with his ideas."

"Did he get along with his father?"

Murdock frowned. "Blackheart was a cruel and powerful man. Everyone feared him for good reason. I advised yer father to obey him."

"Did he?"

"Most of the time. They got along until Kate got between them."

James perked up. "Who was Kate?"

Murdock reddened. "I shouldn't be discussing such things with ye."

"Are ye not my manservant?"

"Aye, but..."

"There is no BUT... As my manservant, ye must answer my questions. Was Kate Maggie's mother?"

"Aye." The servant was clearly uncomfortable. "She was Blackheart's mistress as well. Kate was a rare beauty. But she was a conniving sort who trapped men and threw them to the wolves."

Now, this was interesting. "Did she do that to my father?"

"She tried to."

James wanted more. "But she didn't succeed?"

"Nay, lad. Yer father couldn't lie to save his life. He told his father the truth and suffered for it."

"Did Blackheart whip him?"

"Aye. But it wasn't simple discipline." The servant sighed. "He tied him to a wall and scourged him until blood soaked his breeks. It was an awful sight. I tried to stop it but failed."

James was shocked. How could a man do this to his son? "Poor Father. Did it change him?"

"In some ways. It haunted him. But it gave him the courage to claim his birthright."

The boy was stunned. *The spirit was telling the truth. I wonder if the rest is true.* "So, Kate was Maggie's mother. The lass didn't want her own child?"

Murdock grunted. "Nay, my Lord. But yer father wanted it. That's why yer sister came to Drake."

"How fortunate for Maggie. Mother accepted her?"

"Aye. She was conceived before they were married."

"I see." James guessed that a servant wouldn't know about the circumstances of his conception. He would have to ask his parents. But first, he had to do some research. Nature was calling. "I need to use the chamber pot."

The servant helped him to his feet and guided him to the pot. He turned his back to give him privacy as he relieved himself.

James shook off the last few drops. "Help me to get dressed. I want to visit the library."

"As ye wish, my Lord." The servant began to pull clothes from a drawer. "What sort of book are ye looking for? Poetry? Medicine? Perhaps astronomy?"

James' expression was serious. "Nay. A book on Celtic mythology. I want to read about the Goddess Morrigan."

He was so self-absorbed that he didn't notice that the servant had gone pale.

***

ONE HOUR LATER, THE BREAKFAST ROOM

The breakfast room was practically empty. Most guests stayed up into the wee hours of the morning, celebrating the wedding of Maggie and Philip. Many were still in bed, sleeping off the effects of wine and whisky.

The Duke was a notable exception. It was true that he'd stayed up late, conducting business with the Laird of Grant. When that concluded, he hijacked his son-in-law from the party to join him for a cigar in the study. There he extracted a solemn promise that the lad would be gentle with his daughter. With that matter resolved, he went to his chamber, crawled into bed, and proceeded to fall asleep.

Now, he sat alone at the table, eating breakfast and planning his next move. With Maggie married and the property transferred, it was time to leave Scotland. Prince Charles was occupied with the invasion to the south. But once he was crowned, there was a good chance that he would order Dughall's execution.

The Duke didn't want to leave, but it seemed that he had to. *Cromwell says that the Scots are not England's enemy, only the son of Charles. Man should be allowed to rule himself. Why do we need the monarchy? With courage and determination we could remain a republic.* He sighed. *'Tis a battle I cannot fight. The safety of my family lies in the Colonies.*

Jamison had just updated him about the preparations. Captain McGee was done provisioning the Black Swan for a sea voyage. The vessel was rigged and ready to sail. The only things that remained were to inform his family and take them to the harbor.

Dughall intended to take his immediate family – Keira, the baby, Luc, James, Maggie, and Philip. He'd considered taking Jamison, but the servant was needed to run the castle. Ian would help Jamison. He knew that his father would never leave Scotland and his mother was needed in the surgery. The rest were needed to maintain the castle. He sighed. *I will miss every one of them.*

The Duke hated to lie to his subjects, but in this case it was necessary. He would announce that he was going to France to conduct business with Gordon relatives. Only his inner circle would know the truth – Jamison, Ian, Murdock, and his father and mother. They would also be informed about the death threat against him.

Dughall was satisfied with the plan. The official story would be that he was in France on business. That is what people would say if the

Prince inquired about him. His family would be told that they were sailing to France and then told about Virginia when they reached the harbor. This would prevent any loose gossip.

The door opened. Murdock escorted James into the room. The servant's face was ashen. "My Lord. The young master wishes to join ye for breakfast."

Dughall smiled. "Thank ye, Murdock. Ye may go." He sensed the servant's uneasiness as he left the room. *How strange.* "How is my son this morning?"

James took a seat opposite him and placed a napkin on his lap. "My stomach is settled. I'm feeling better." He began to load his plate with breakfast items.

"Good. Ye're the only one to come so far. They're all sleeping in after the wedding."

The lad bit into a scone and chewed it. He chased it down with a swallow of tea. "Maggie is married. I guess it's for the best."

Dughall detected a profound sadness in his voice. "Aye. Take heart, my son. Ye will find a lass to love. I promise."

James sighed. "I don't think so. God has other plans for me."

The Duke felt a chill. "What do ye mean?"

The boy wiped his mouth on a napkin. "I will tell ye, but first, I have a question. I need to know about the circumstances of my conception."

Dughall felt his heart drop. It was a dark secret that he'd hoped to never reveal. Now, his son was asking about it. He couldn't lie. The lad could read his soul.

James' eyes widened. "So, it is true. Tell me everything."

Dughall clasped his hands and bowed his head in silent prayer. *God, help me!* The answer was clear. He had to tell the truth. He looked into his son's eyes and began with the story of the sword of Red Conan.

When he was done, James frowned. "So, ye claimed a sword that had a curse on it."

Dughall sighed. "Aye. It was foolish. I thought that it wouldn't harm me."

"But, it did."

"Aye. It caused madness. I thought that everyone was against me. I believed that the Morrigan wanted to mate with me. If I didn't comply, she'd kill me."

"Was it true?"

"I thought so."

James took a sharp breath. "Tell me about the Morrigan."

Dughall's skin crawled. "She's the pagan Goddess of Battle and Sex; a fearful force to be reckoned with. Legend says she was obsessed with bedding Red Conan. As the owner of the sword, I was Conan."

The lad was riveted to his words. "What happened next?"

"I refused her demands in a dream, earning her anger. The next morning, the high fevers came. I broke out in hives and my mind wandered. This went on for days and I grew weak. They say that I suffered a grand fit and fell senseless."

The boy stared. "I've seen ye suffer a fit. How did ye survive it?"

Dughall sighed. "Two things happened. Jamison and Ian absconded with the cursed blade. After they left the castle, I woke, but was still dying. That's when yer mother did something to save me."

"What?"

His voice was tight, "Do not make me tell ye."

James reddened. "Someone has already told me. I must know if it's true."

"Who told ye?"

"My grandfather, Blackheart."

Dughall's heart dropped. "He appeared to ye?"

"Last night. So far, he told the truth."

The Duke was stricken. Once again, his father had wounded him from beyond the grave. The boy needed to hear it from his own sire. "Yer mother went into the forest and used the moon to call upon the Morrigan. The Goddess appeared and they made a pact. The Morrigan could use her body for the night and mate with me. In return, I would live. Yer mother would conceive a child, something she was desperate for." He paused for a long moment. "Oh, James! I know it was wrong. My wife drew the Morrigan down into her. She returned to the castle and we mated."

They were quiet for a few minutes, each trying to read the other's feelings.

The lad spoke first, "Blackheart was right. I was conceived with pagan magic."

"I admit it." Dughall's heart ached. "But it doesn't matter. We wanted a son desperately. We love ye more than life."

"I know, Father." To his surprise, the lad was calm. "Nevertheless, I can not marry. Knowing this, it would irresponsible for me to conceive a child."

The Duke swallowed hard. The boy was right. "Ye said that God has other plans for ye."

"Aye. With yer permission, I shall return to the Abbey and study to be a monk."

Dughall felt like he'd been kicked. He'd just lost his only heir. "Is that what ye want?"

"Aye."

"Perhaps, when ye're older."

The boy held his ground. "Nay! I must go now. I cannot be near my sister. I have unholy thoughts about her."

"I see." Dughall was devastated. "There is something ye must know. I'm taking our family abroad the day after tomorrow to avoid a dangerous situation. A family should stay together."

The boy frowned. "I cannot go with ye, Father. I must go to the Abbey." He took a sharp breath. "I have one last question. Why did ye name my sister Morrigan?"

Dughall sighed. "We lost four children soon after birth. We thought that the Morrigan had cursed us. I didn't think she'd kill her namesake."

James nodded. "Oh. I'm glad that Mother had another child. It makes up for my being a disappointment."

Dughall felt like crying. "Oh, James. It's not yer fault. I'm so sorry."

"I forgive ye."

"Do not hate us."

The lad managed a smile. "I could never hate ye. Brother Adam says that hate is a destructive emotion."

Dughall agreed. "Indeed. And forgiveness is worth it's weight in gold. Will ye question yer mother?"

"Nay. I know the truth. She's suffered enough."

There was nothing more to say. They finished their breakfast in silence.

***

LATER THAT DAY, AT THE SUPPER TABLE

The day progressed without further conflict. One by one, the guests awoke and wandered to the breakfast table. Some walked in the gardens or visited the horse stables.

By then, Dughall was busy with preparations. He'd met with Jamison and Ian to talk about maintaining the castle in his absence. He spent time with Alex and Jessie, explaining his dire situation. Then he summoned his immediate family to supper, with the intent of announcing the voyage.

Now, he sat at the head of the table, finishing an exquisite meal. The kitchen had cooked a feast of roasted pheasant, root vegetables, and a variety of plain and sweet breads. He suspected that it would be months before they ate this well again.

Dughall laid down his fork and pushed his plate away. "Ah! This was excellent."

There were murmurs of agreement.

The Duke looked around the table. His wife Keira sat to his right, holding wee Morrigan on her lap. The infant had smeared squash on her face. Beyond them sat James and Luc, topping off their meals with sweet breads and butter. To his left were Maggie and Philip. They were smiling and holding hands.

He cleared his throat. "My beloved family. I've brought ye together to make an announcement." All eyes were upon him. "The day after tomorrow, we will leave Drake Castle to take a trip by sea to France."

Keira's eyes widened. "Why must we leave so soon?"

"I have business to conduct of a sensitive nature."

Maggie spoke, "How long will we be gone?"

"It could be for a year, so pack clothes accordingly."

Philip squeezed her hand. "It sounds exciting!"

Luc grinned. "Can I take Artus?" Of course, this was Artus III. 'Wee' Artus died of natural causes a year ago and was succeeded by a new puppy.

Dughall nodded. "I have no objections. But ye must remember to take a tether for him."

Luc could barely contain himself. "I will, Father. Are we all going?"

"Nay." Dughall knew that James was uncomfortable. But the lad owed his family an explanation. "Yer brother has an announcement. James, will ye tell them?"

James took a breath and looked around the table. "I will not be going with ye."

"Why not?" Keira cried.

The lad was nervous. "I shall return to the Abbey where I will study to be a monk. God has called me."

There was stunned silence. Finally, Maggie spoke, "Are ye sure about this, Brother?"

James blushed. "I've never been so sure in my life."

Luc nodded. "Then, ye must do it."

Keira frowned. "Nay! Ye're too young to make that decision."

Dughall intervened, "We already discussed it, Wife. James knows what he wants. He experienced a calling."

She held the baby close. "How do ye know that the Abbey will take him?"

The Duke had concerns as well. "I will accompany him to the Abbey tomorrow and talk to the Abbott. We will offer them compensation to provide for his needs." He was eager to conclude this conversation. "Well! I'm glad that it's settled. We have a lot of packing to do. Sea trunks have been placed in yer chambers. Go there and get started."

The family stood and began to leave the dining room. Keira tried to stay behind to question James, but Dughall got between them. "Take the baby to the nursery, lass. Ye must pack for the three of us. I'll catch up with ye in our chamber."

She gave him a desperate look and left the room. In the end, all that was left was James and Dughall.

The boy hugged him. "Thank ye, Father. I didn't want to answer her questions."

Dughall's heart swelled. "It's the least I could do." He held him apart and gazed into his eyes. "My son, one of God's holy monks! I'm proud of ye."

Chapter 36
Voyage

July 16th 1650
2 Days Later

MORAY FIRTH, THE HARBOR

The last few days had been a whirlwind. There was a considerable amount of packing to do. The Gordon family expected to be abroad for a year and had to bring clothes and outerwear for four seasons. Several horse drawn carts were loaded to capacity with sea trunks and other baggage.

The Duke took a trip to the Abbey to place his son under their supervision. Grateful for his intervention when Skene attacked, the Abbott accepted the boy and promised to care for him. But there was a caveat. Brother Luke explained that becoming a monk was a gradual process that gives one time to be sure that it is God's will. James was told that he would enter a period of postulancy, where he would share in the work of the community and get used to the rhythm of monastic life. In a year, if he wished to carry on, he would become a novitiate and deepen his studies of the Church and the liturgy. Later, James would take simple vows before God, the monks, and his family. When he turned sixteen, he would take solemn vows promising stability, obedience, and chastity. The boy indicated that he understood and agreed to become a postulant. Dughall returned to Drake and informed his family of the outcome.

***

Early that morning, they'd left Drake Castle in a procession of horse drawn carts and headed for Moray Firth. Now, they were at the harbor, staring up at the Duke's magnificent sailing ship. The Black Swan was a large merchant vessel normally employed to provision the castle. It would go to sea six times a year with cargo to trade and came back with goods from foreign ports. Wine, china, jewelry, fine cloth, and exotic foods were among the many things that were acquired.

The Black Swan wasn't built for passengers, though it had a few small cabins. These had been recently improved in expectation of the Duke's trip. The ninety foot ship was powered by the wind. The square-rigged boat had three masts and six sails. To adjust them, the crew had to work fifty five different lines, like flying a kite. To do this, they took orders from the boatswain. Sails were drawn in during a storm, to keep the ship from being blown off course.

Now, the Gordon family watched in awe as the white sails were unfurled. They flapped in the wind, adding to their excitement. Captain McGee and several crew members stood on deck, waving. They lowered a dinghy to retrieve their passengers.

Dughall addressed the servants who would return to Drake with the carts and horses. "Please wait over there for my signal. Then return to Drake." He paused until they were out of earshot, handed the baby to his wife, and turned to face his family. It was time to tell the truth. He looked around at their faces, so trusting. "My dear family. I have something to confess. I have not told ye the entire truth. We are going on a voyage, but we are not going to France." He watched their eyes widen. "We are going to Virginia to visit Gilbert."

The lads seemed pleased.

Keira frowned. "Why did ye not tell us?"

Dughall sighed. "I had to lie. My life is in danger. It is likely that the Prince will order my execution once he is crowned King."

Maggie gasped. "Why, Father?"

"Because I saved two men from the Tower Prison."

The girl's eyes widened. "Grandfather and Great-Uncle Robert."

"Aye."

Luc spoke, "Why did ye not tell us?"

The Duke was solemn, "I could not. It was important that everyone thought we were going to France. That way, if the Prince inquires, he will look for me in Paris."

Keira shifted the baby to her hip. There was fear in her eyes. "We left James here!"

"I know, lass. I told him that my life was in danger. He did not want to come with us. He wanted to go to the monastery."

She frowned. "When will we return to Scotland?"

Dughall tried to cast it in the best light. "I don't know. The Prince is a snake of a man. I hope that our government in Edinburgh will realize that before it's too late."

"And if not, Husband?"

The Duke sighed. "Then they will crown him King."

She was almost in tears. "And?"

"We will lose Drake and send for James. The Hays will have a choice – to come to the colonies or go to Peterhead." He saw their shocked faces. "But take heart! We don't know what will happen." He signaled to the captain that they were ready to board. "Let's go! The Black Swan is waiting."

The dinghy arrived at the shore. Dughall signaled to his servants, directing them to return to Drake with the carts.

The Gordon family got in the small boat. Two men rowed vigorously and it made its way to the Black Swan. The captain lowered a wooden ladder for them.

Luc was the first one up the ladder. "This is the biggest ship I've ever seen!" The dog was handed up to him. "I'm glad that I brought my best friend, Artus."

Maggie and Philip climbed the ladder and gazed down at her parents. "Hand us wee Morrigan."

Dughall passed the baby up. "Thank ye, Daughter." Then he turned and kissed his wife tenderly. "Don't worry, lass."

She sniffled. "How can I not?"

"The Prince will never find me in the colonies."

"And if he does?"

"We will cross that bridge when we come to it. We must go."

They climbed the ladder and boarded the ship. Several crew members scrambled into the dinghy to retrieve the trunks and luggage. Dughall stood on deck with his family as the trip was made and the last of it was loaded. Maggie came to her parents and took wee Morrigan.

Dughall embraced his wife. He sensed that she was a bundle of emotions. "I love ye."

She sighed. "I know." The anchor was pulled up and the Black Swan began to slowly drift out to sea. Keira was shaking, not from the cold, but from nervousness.

Dughall drew her close. He couldn't blame her. A voyage to the Colonies was a frightening prospect. Their eyes never left the shore until they were out to sea. His heart was heavy as the landmarks disappeared. *Farewell, Scotland.*

CHAPTER 37
AN EASY INVASION

JULY 22ND 1650

6 DAYS LATER

THE BORDER BETWEEN ENGLAND AND SCOTLAND

It was an unusually cold and wet summer in southern Scotland. The skies were gray and the land was plagued with endless drizzle. The New Model Army crossed the border at Berwick and entered Scotland unchallenged. To their surprise, there was no opposing army, no cannon or gunfire, or resistance from the Scottish people.

Oliver Cromwell had fought in enough campaigns to be suspicious. He knew that they were expected. He'd sent couriers into Scotland with a declaration stating that the English army did not intend to harm the Scots. In that posting, he reminded them that the same army had come to Scotland a few years ago at the bidding of the Scottish Parliament and done no harm. Only those who by their conduct encouraged the restoration of the Stuart monarchy would be in danger.

Still, the lack of resistance was suspicious. Cromwell sat atop his white steed, surveying the fields before them. In the distance, he spotted a rider coming towards him. It was one of his loyal couriers. The grim-faced Puritan spoke his thoughts, "Perhaps he can shed light on this pitiful showing."

The man arrived and quickly dismounted.

Cromwell joined him. He always made an effort to be on the same level as his men. "Well?"

The soldier's uniform was soiled and sweat stained. He snapped to attention. "Sir!"

Cromwell waved his hand. "At ease. What did you find?"

"I posted the declaration at the Market Cross in Edinburgh. Some read the document as I nailed it. They allowed me to leave unmolested."

"Good."

"As I left town a man approached me. By the looks of it, he was gentry. He asked who sent me and then invited me for a drink in a tavern. The conversation was enlightening. The Scots are divided, Sir. Some wish to see the Prince restored to the throne, and some do not. This gentleman was of the latter persuasion. He provided me with valuable information. The Scots Army is still being mustered."

Cromwell smiled. "Go on."

"They number less than 20,000. Most of them are poorly equipped and commanded. Six thousand were well trained, and among them were a number of seasoned commanders. But that was before the Prince interfered. I was told that he infuriated the Kirk Party by refusing to publicly condemn his mother's Popery and his father's bad counsel. They responded by dismissing eighty veteran cavalier officers and 3,000 soldiers who were royalist leaning." The man stopped to take a breath.

Cromwell grunted. "It didn't take the Prince long to turn on them. The apple didn't fall far from the tree. He's just like his father."

The soldier nodded. "That seems to be the sentiment."

"This might be a short campaign after all. Who heads their army?"

"The Earl of Leven, but only in name. The man is seventy and exhausted from years of campaigning. He tried to resign, but they wouldn't let him. The acting commander is Sir David Leslie."

"I've heard of him. What else did you learn?"

"The generals are being overseen by a commission representing the Kirk Party. They have forbidden any military operations on the Sabbath."

"Fools!"

"Agreed. We do have a problem, however. Their army is constructing a line of earthworks between Edinburgh and Leith to take up a defensive position. Some claim that it's impregnable."

Cromwell reddened. "Nothing is impregnable."

The soldier snapped to attention. "Yes, Sir! One more thing, as I rode south from Edinburgh, I noticed that the crops were being burned and the livestock transported."

The commander frowned. "So, that's their strategy! They will force us to get our supplies from England." He was silent for a moment and then barked a command, "Summon my lieutenants!"

"Yes, Sir!" The man mounted quickly and rode away.

Cromwell paced back and forth, deep in thought. His posture was tense as he considered the valuable information. At last, he came up with a plan. "We will move swiftly and occupy the sheltered harbor at Dunbar. It will secure a sea route for our supplies. Then we will advance on Edinburgh."

Chapter 38
A Day in the Life of a Monk

July 24th 1650
2 days later

DEER ABBEY

It was a hot summer day in northern Scotland. The skies were clear and the air was balmy. James Gordon stood in the forest, helping Brother Adam capture a bee swarm. The monk and postulant were dressed in usual garb – long white robes with a crucifix around the neck. But because of the task at hand, they wore brimmed hats with attached netting.

The lad's job as he understood it was to hold the ladder steady against the large oak tree.

Brother Adam picked up a smoker - a crude metal pot filled with smoldering twine. He blew on the fuel to fan the fire and closed the top. Smoke billowed from a narrow opening.

"What are ye doing?" James asked.

Adam smiled. "We smoke the bees to make them docile. It confuses them. It gives me a chance to catch the swarm. Hold the ladder steady. Then get ready to pass me the stick and bucket."

James nodded. "I will." He steadied the ladder and watched the monk climb up to the branch that held the swarm. He heard an angry buzz. *The man is fearless. There has to be thousands of bees up there.*

Adam waved his smoker back and forth, releasing the smoke and calming the bees. A number of bees broke away and flew around frantically.

James looked down at his robe. There were scores of them on his garment and they were beginning to cling to his face net. His first reaction was panic, but that seemed to anger the insects. He lowered his energy and watched them calm. "Ah!"

The monk was coming down the ladder. When he got to the bottom, James accepted the smoker and handed him the stick and bucket. Adam climbed up to the branch and fastened the bucket to it. He positioned it under the swarm and then used the stick to tap the branch. Large clumps of bees fell into the bucket.

"Amazing!" James shouted.

The monk unfastened the bucket and hurried down the ladder. He placed the bucket on the ground and covered it with a wooden top. He grinned. "We did it! With luck, we captured the queen as well. These bees will provide us with honey for a season."

James gathered their equipment.

Adam picked up the bucket. They brushed back their nets and started walking towards the Abbey. "Ye did good."

The lad smiled. "Thank ye. Does it always go this well?"

The man snorted. "Nay. Sometimes they swarm to another tree and sometimes they sting ye. I've had as many as twenty bites."

"Ouch! From the same bee?"

"Nay. Once a bee stings ye, it dies. It rips their innards out."

"Interesting. Ye said they have a queen."

"Aye. It's a large female, the mother of the hive. She lays eggs constantly to produce worker bees and drones. The bees make honey to feed the colony."

They reached the Abbey and entered through the weathered oak door.

James was curious. "What do we do now?"

They began walking towards the bee yard. "We put them in a skep. That's the tricky part."

James thought that they'd done the tricky part. There was more to this than met the eye. "I guess I have a lot to learn."

They reached the bee yard and positioned their face nets.

Brother Adam put down the bucket and began to work with a skep he'd prepared.

James had seen the monks making skeps, which were conical baskets woven with coils of straw. They were placed open side down on a flat surface. There was a single entrance at the bottom of the skep for bees to enter.

The monk showed him the inside of the basket. "See this? I smeared some old comb and a wee bit of honey on the inside to give them the idea. Now, we will transfer the bees and hope that they stay here." He removed the top of the bucket, placed the skep over it, and shook it so the bees would go in the basket. Then he dropped the bucket and slid the skep onto a flat stone surface.

James inhaled sharply. Not all of the bees entered the skep. Some flew around angrily, buzzing them. "Ach!"

"Don't let them see ye flinch, lad!"

James took several measured breaths and the bees left his body. One by one, the insects found their way to the hive entrance. "Amazing!"

Adam beamed with pride. "Aye. I never tire of seeing it." They removed their face nets and began walking to the Refectory. "Yer father is interested in bee keeping."

"He is?"

"Aye. He mentioned it to me more than once."

James felt a pang of homesickness. "What do ye know about my father?"

Brother Adam smiled. "Lord Drake is a good man. It's a rare man who is called to the Abbott's death bed."

The boy thought about his conception. "Yet, he has faults."

The monk was solemn. "No man is perfect. All have sinned. Even in yer short life there have been transgressions. The miracle is that we can be forgiven. All we have to do is ask."

"Ah." It was a comforting thought.

"Yer father confided in me once. It was just after he attended the Requiem Mass for the Abbott. Lord Drake said that he felt the Holy Ghost descend upon him. He said that if he wasn't beholden to family, he would forsake everything and become a monk."

James was surprised. "My father said that?"

"Aye."

"That explains why he let me become a monk."

Brother Adam nodded. "It had to be a difficult decision. Ye're his only natural son. Now, he has no heir."

"I didn't think of that."

They reached the Refectory and entered. James watched intently as Brother Adam poured them each a glass of water. He accepted the vessel and drank deeply. Since arriving at the Abbey, he'd learned that water was one of life's simple pleasures.

His heart ached for the loss of his parents, but he was grateful for this wise man and his new family, the monks of Deer Abbey.

CHAPTER 39
ROUND ONE

AUGUST 6TH 1650
2 WEEKS LATER

A FEW MILES SOUTHEAST OF EDINBURGH, SCOTLAND

Oliver Cromwell sat upon his steed in the pouring rain, watching his troops withdraw from Musselburgh. Water literally dripped from his helmet as he regarded the retreat.

It had been a disappointing two weeks. At first, they'd been successful. He occupied the harbor at Dunbar to secure a sea route for supplies. Leaving several regiments behind, he advanced his army to within a few miles of Edinburgh. There he quickly realized that the Scottish lines of defense were too strong to risk a direct assault.

While English warships bombarded Leith, Cromwell attempted to draw the Scottish army out into the open. But the Scots stayed put behind their defenses. To make things worse, a heavy rain began to fall on July 30th, forcing the English army to fall back to Musselburgh. Even this position proved untenable as rough weather prevented supplies from being landed there. Provisions were short. Hunger and sickness were rampant.

Cromwell grumbled under his breath. "Damn rain!" He galloped ahead and led his army back to Dunbar.

***

Miles away behind the Scottish lines, Sir David Leslie was encouraged by news of the retreat. Their plan had worked. Though poorly trained, they'd avoided open battle and waged a war of attrition through hunger and disease. Lord Leven's strategy was vindicated. The Covenanter committee was pleased and so was the future King.

Sir Leslie was solemn. "We won the first round."

His junior commander agreed. "God was on our side."

"Because of the rain?"

"Aye."

Leslie frowned. "I think we got lucky. If God had anything to do with it, let's hope that He stays on our side."

Chapter 40
Out to Sea

August 13th 1650
1 week later

THE NORTH ATLANTIC OCEAN

The Gordons had been at sea for a month. Leaving Moray Firth, they sailed northeast and rounded the tip of Scotland. Then heading southwest, they passed Scotland and Ireland and sailed west towards the Colonies.

During the first week, Dughall explored the ship. He visited the Hold, where food and supplies were stored. The provisions consisted of food that could be stored for long periods at sea – like oatmeal, peas, beans, cheese, and salted fish and pork. It wasn't what they were accustomed to. He watched the cook in the galley and inquired about his use of lemon juice. The man swore that it prevented scurvy.

Dughall inspected the Great Cabin where the captain and crew lived, slept, and ate. Despite its name, it wasn't very big. The thing he found most fascinating was the Steerage, a room below deck where the helmsman moved a large lever called a whipstaff, which in turn moved the ship's rudder. Dughall was amazed. The helmsman couldn't see outside. His 'eyes' were provided by a crewman called the 'connor' who shouted instructions to him from the deck above. The helmsman steered the ninety foot ship without sight of the horizon!

***

Today was a rough day on the North Atlantic. The wind whipped up the sea and the swells were large. The sound of sails flapping was almost deafening.

The Duke climbed the steps that led out of his cabin and emerged on the deck of the Black Swan. He'd just left his wife and infant daughter, who were suffering from seasickness. Dughall had tried to tell her that it was best to be above deck in such weather, to fix your eyes on a point on the horizon. It was also good to keep food in your stomach. But she would not listen. In any case, the baby needed her.

Of the group, Dughall and Luc were least affected by the rolling seas. Dughall, because he'd sailed. Luc, because of sheer will to please his father. In his quest to learn to sail, the lad was the captain's shadow.

The Duke tread carefully to keep his balance. Because of the waves, the ship was tilted five degrees. *Thank God I was a sailor!* He proceeded to the Round House, where the ship's course was charted. He opened the door and entered.

Captain McGee sat on the floor, teaching two cabin boys his trade. Luc sat at his side, paying rapt attention. They were learning the thirty-two points on a compass.

McGee completed the lesson and looked up. "Good day, my Lord."

The Duke managed a grim smile. "'Tis a bit rough, though."

The captain grinned. "Is the Duchess in trouble again?"

"I'm afraid so. She never got her sea legs."

Luc frowned. "Poor Mother. Will she be all right?"

"I think so."

The lad smiled. "Good! Ye don't have to worry about me. I love to sail! I've learned so much."

"What have ye learned?"

"How to read a compass. How to tell time with a sun dial. And how to check the speed of travel with the log-line and half-minute glass!"

The captain grinned. "He's a quick study."

Luc beamed with pride. "I'm glad that I studied mathematics."

"With yer permission, my Lord, I will teach him to use the astrolabe and the nocturnal."

Dughall was pleased. "Of course. Where is Artus?"

The lad smiled. "He's with Maggie and Philip in their cabin."

"Good!" Maggie had been bored since the Black Swan entered the open ocean. He was glad that she had a husband to attend to her.

The captain stood and dismissed the cabin boys.

Dughall waited until they left the quarters. "I'd like to give my wife some news. How much longer to Virginia?"

The captain scratched his wooly beard. "Five or six weeks. Soon we will pass a frozen land mass at the tip of the Labrador Sea. No point in stopping there. Then we will sail on to the northern Colonies. We could stop in Boston."

Dughall was surprised. "Massachusetts?"

"Aye, my Lord. We will be low on food and water at that point. We could stop to take on provisions."

"I have no objections."

"Good. Then it's a plan! We shall rest a few days in Boston. Longer, if the ladies need it. Then we will sail south to Virginia. That won't be such a bad trip. We'll be in sight of land most of the time."

Luc could barely contain himself. "The Gordon clan in Massachusetts! I've read about the place. It will be a grand adventure."

Dughall grinned. "I can't wait. Come on. Let's go tell yer mother."

They left the Round House and staggered onto the deck. The sea was getting rougher.

***

Maggie stood on deck bending over a wooden bucket. She struggled to stay upright as she washed the baby's nappies.

Keira gripped the railing until her knuckles were white. She was waiting for her daughter to pass her a washed nappie so she could rinse it in another pail.

The Black Swan rose and fell with a large wave. Maggie stepped back and tossed the diaper into the rinse bucket. "Great Goddess! I can barely stand." She watched Keira lean over the side and vomit into the ocean. "Poor Mother."

Her father and brother emerged from the Round House and staggered onto the deck. She cried out to them, "Mother needs help!"

Dughall hurried to his wife and grabbed her shoulders. He held her tight as she puked over the rail. "That's right. Get it all out."

Luc came to Maggie's side. The lad was as steady as a rock. "Can I help, Sister?"

Maggie nodded. "Aye. Stand at that bucket and rinse the nappies when I pass them to ye. There's one in there already." She was grateful for his help. "Thank ye, Brother."

Dughall picked up Keira. The lass was as limp as a rag doll. "I'll take her below." His eyes widened. "Where is the wee one?"

Maggie looked up. "Philip has her in our cabin. We fetched her to visit with Artus." She glanced at Keira. "Mother insisted on washing nappies. I didn't want her on deck alone."

Dughall's face was ashen. "Thank ye, lass. She's so weak, she could have fallen over." He steadied himself and carried her towards their cabin.

Maggie scrubbed two nappies and twisted the fabric to remove the soap and water. She tossed them into Luc's pail. "That's the last of them for today." She gripped the handrail as the sea swelled. Bile rose in her throat. Would she vomit? "Oh, dear."

Luc rinsed them. "Are ye all right, Sister?"

She didn't want to worry him. "Aye. Wring them out. We'll take them below and hang them to dry."

He did as she asked. They tossed the wash water into the sea and stowed the buckets in a locker. Then they began to walk carefully towards their parents' cabin.

Luc frowned. "Will Mother be all right? She's getting thin."

The young lass was worried. Her mother's aura was weak. "I hope so."

When they reached the cabin, Luc grinned. "We got some good news today. The Captain says we will reach the Colonies in five or six weeks!"

Maggie tried to hide her disappointment. "Oh." She'd hoped that they were no more than two weeks away. "Let's go inside and hang these nappies."

They opened the door and went below. The small cabin was illuminated by a hanging lantern that cast shadows as it swung back and forth. There were pitiful signs of distress – the smell of vomit and a ripe chamber pot. It was the same in all the cabins. Heavily salted food and bad water caused gas, stomach upsets, and diarrhea.

Her mother lay on the bunk with a wet cloth over her eyes. Her father sat at the bedside attending her.

Maggie sensed his anxiety. "Will she be all right?"

Dughall turned. There was worry etched on his face. "She's very weak. We must pray for her."

"I shall." She took a breath. "Stay with her, Father. Insist that she drinks and eats every hour. Don't take no for an answer. I will assume responsibility for the baby."

"Thank ye, Daughter. I don't know what I'd do without ye."

She watched him take the cloth from her mother's face, freshen it, and place it over her eyes. Then he bent over and whispered into her ear.

Keira tried to sit and failed. "Six weeks!" She began sobbing. "Great Goddess! I can't do this!"

Maggie touched Luc's shoulder. It was time to leave their parents alone to work through their problems. Without a word, they took the stairs and left the cabin.

On deck, the wind was strong and the swells were large. Waves washed over the deck, scattering mops and buckets. The boat was now tilted almost ten degrees. Luc took his sister's arm to steady her.

Maggie sighed. It was going to be a long six weeks.

Chapter 41
Royal Outrage

August 16th 1650
3 days later

EDINBURGH CASTLE

Prince Charles sat at a gilded meeting table, preparing to sign the Kirk's declaration of fidelity to the Covenant. The idea of signing such a document irked his being. He'd refused to sign a declaration disavowing his parents' religions. But signing this one was a necessary evil.

After his retreat to Dunbar, Cromwell appealed to the Scottish clergy, asking them to consider whether Charles was a fitting king for a godly people. His words spread far and wide, "I beseech you, in the bowels of Christ, to think it possible you may be mistaken." The resulting debate caused doubt among some Covenanter leaders and army officers.

Charles had been furious. He knew that he was popular with the Scottish troops, so much so that Covenanter leaders had insisted that he end his tour. As the debate over Charles' personal integrity continued, Cromwell had advanced from Dunbar and occupied the Braid Hills to the south of Edinburgh. There he tried to open negotiations for a peaceful settlement with Scottish officers who mistrusted the Prince. There was only one thing they could do to stop the defections. The Covenanter leaders insisted that he publicly sign a declaration of fidelity to the Covenant.

The Prince's head pounded as he inked the quill. *How dare they make me do this! When I am crowned King, they will suffer for this. And I will have Cromwell's head on a stake!*

Charles forced himself to smile as he looked around the table. They were watching him closely. One by one, he memorized their faces. So dour and self righteous... They would suffer for this! He swallowed hard and signed the document.

***

TWO DAYS LATER
SOUTH OF EDINBURGH
AT THE ENGLISH ARMY'S ENCAMPMENT

Oliver Cromwell sat in his tent with his head bowed, praying to the Almighty. He was disappointed. He'd just met with several devout

Scottish officers who told him that Charles signed the Kirk's declaration of fidelity to the Covenant. Worse yet, it was accepted by the clergy as a sign of his devotion. These officers doubted Charles' sincerity, but none were prepared to change sides.

Cromwell didn't want to fight the Covenanters, with whom he shared similar religious convictions. But it seemed that he had to. His heart was heavy as he concluded his prayer, "God help us. Amen." With no hope of a peaceful settlement and supplies running low, he withdrew his army to Musselburgh.

Chapter 42
The Battle of Dunbar

September 2nd 1650
2 weeks later

Dunbar Scotland

DOON HILL, THE SCOTTISH ENCAMPMENT, MORNING

Sir David Leslie was exhausted. As lieutenant-general of the Scottish forces, he'd been busy. The English army stormed and captured a fortified manor house commanding the crossing of the Water of Leith on August 24th and advanced to a few miles west of Edinburgh four days later. Following Lord Leven's advice, Sir Leslie maintained a strong defensive position and prevented the English from breaking through to Queensferry. That's when they'd heard that the English army was low on supplies and sickness was rife in its ranks. It was more than a rumor. Cromwell withdrew his troops to Musselburgh once again on August 28th.

Sir Leslie advanced with the Army of the Covenant to shadow Cromwell's movements and watch for an opportunity to attack. His army took up a commanding position on Doon Hill overlooking the English encampment at Dunbar, and with that action he blocked Cromwell's route back to England. The English army was trapped between the sea, the Covenanter army, and a blockaded road. All the Scots had to do was wait. This was the war of attrition they'd hoped for! They would starve the English until they died of disease. But it was not to be.

Sir Leslie felt like he was between a rock and a hard place. A 'godly' committee had accompanied his army, consisting of important members of the Kirk Party. He'd managed to keep them at bay, considering their advice only when it pleased him. But this time, they'd brought the Prince to his tent.

Charles was livid. "You will attack them now!"

Leslie felt his heart pounding. It was a terrible idea. "My Lord. Their defeat is inevitable if we do nothing. By all accounts, they are starving and sickness is rife in their ranks."

The Prince frowned. "How long would we have to wait?"

"Two weeks, maybe three."

The young man appeared to consider this. Then he sneered. "I want this to be over with so that I can be crowned King! Attack now!"

Leslie bowed slightly. "We will do as ye wish, my Lord." He felt like he'd been punched in the stomach. "It may prove to be dangerous. Perhaps ye should move to a safer location."

Prince Charles grunted. "I shall." Without a word of thanks or encouragement, he grabbed his coat and followed the committeemen out of the tent.

Alone, David Leslie poured himself a whisky. He wasn't a man who drank to excess, but this attack was pure insanity. He bolted the drink, savored the taste, and summoned his junior commanders.

***

THE ENGLISH ENCAMPMENT, AFTERNOON

Oliver Cromwell was suffering from a bowel complaint. Like his men, he'd existed on meager food rations and drank contaminated water. But this wasn't his biggest problem. Intelligence told him they were trapped – between the sea, the Scots, and a blockaded road. They were doomed unless the enemy made a mistake.

He drank a cup of water to stave off dehydration. *Has God abandoned us?*

The flap of his tent opened, admitting one of his commanders. Lieutenant Empson snapped to attention. "Sir!"

"As you were." Cromwell winced as he experienced a painful cramp. "What is it?"

"The Scots are marching down from the heights of Doon Hill."

This was too good to be true. "Are you sure?"

"Yes! They are drawing up a battle line to prepare for an attack."

Cromwell was amazed. The Scots intended to attack his army at ground level. They'd been trying to draw them into the open for weeks. It gave them a chance at victory. "Show me their line of battle."

He followed Lieutenant Empson out of the tent to a position where they could monitor their progress. They stayed there for hours until they could see that the new Scottish line stretched in an arc aligned with a stream called the Broxburn. On the left of the Scottish position, the Broxburn passed through a deep ravine. On the right, towards the coast, the ground leveled out and the stream was crossed by the road from Dunbar to Berwick.

Cromwell identified a major tactical flaw in their position. "Praise God!"

"What is it, Sir?"

"Their centre and left flank have little room for maneuver. I see a way to defeat them! We will attack at dawn."

***

SUNRISE NEXT MORNING

The Covenanter army spent the night in rain-soaked fields. Many officers left their units during the night to seek shelter from the driving wind and rain. It left them at a disadvantage.

The English attacked the Scottish right flank at dawn with three regiments of horse soldiers commanded by Lambert, Fleetwood, and Whalley. They advanced along Berwick road to secure the crossing of the Broxburn. Lambert's soldiers were disrupted by an attack from a brigade of Scottish lancers. An infantry brigade joined the fray to support the English cavalry. They were met with fierce resistance from Scottish infantry.

As Cromwell anticipated, the cramped position prevented the Scots from maneuvering. The Scottish right wing collapsed when Cromwell committed his reserve brigade. As the Scots began to break and flee, the sun emerged from behind the clouds. Cromwell was inspired, "Let God arise and his enemies be scattered!"

***

The battle lasted two hours. More than a thousand Scots were killed in the fray and six thousand were taken prisoner. The English army lost less than five hundred. It was a severe defeat for the Covenanters. Wounded Scottish prisoners were released, but 5,000 men were forced on an eight day march 118 miles south to Durham.

***

The day after the battle, Sir David Leslie fell back to the easily defended Stirling with four thousand survivors of the battle. There he set about strengthening the city's defenses, rearming the survivors, and raising fresh troops.

No longer defended, Leith and Edinburgh fell to the English army. The Prince fled to a safe location. He blamed his army for reckless decisions and demanded to be crowned the King of Scotland. He was more determined than ever to regain his English throne.

CHAPTER 43
BOSTON HARBOR

MONDAY OCTOBER 3RD 1650
4 WEEKS LATER

BOSTON MASSACHUSETTS, THE HARBOR

The Duke stood on the deck of the Black Swan, gazing upon Boston. It was a small city by European standards, with a population of 3,000. It wasn't London, but after months on the open seas, it was heaven. He watched the swaying salt marshes as they navigated the harbor. Tide and wind driven waves pounded the peninsula. There weren't many trees, but there were hundreds of buildings.

They dropped anchor near Bendell's Cove, an inlet halfway between Gallop's Point and Fort Point. The cove was filled with sailing ships of varying sizes and construction. Sails flapped in the wind like the wings of great butterflies.

The Captain barked orders at the crew, "Secure the anchor!" "Stow the sails!" "Ready the dinghy!"

The Duke had sent Philip below to fetch Maggie and the baby and Luc to fetch his mother. Dughall's heart swelled with gratitude. By God's grace, they'd survived the voyage.

The salt marshes reminded him of the mouth of the Ythan, where he'd played as a wee lad. It inspired him to sing a seafaring song.

The letter came late yesterday
The ship must sail the morn
'Alas', then cried my own true love
'That ever I was born.'

And it's braw sailing on the sea
When wind and weather is fair
It's better being in my love's arms
And oh that I were there

The moon rose full o'er the deep
Where sea and sky do meet
But naught I heard but a murmuring wave

That broke upon my feet

And it's braw sailing on the sea
When wind and weather is fair
It's better being in my love's arms
And oh that I were there

Distant shores be fair and wild
And friends in ports be dear
But in every song and every glass
I wish my love were near

And it's braw sailing on the sea
When wind and weather is fair
It's better being in my love's arms
And oh that I were there ♩♪♩

Keira appeared at his side. She took his arm and snuggled against him. "Ye're singing."

He grinned. "Aye, lass. I'm happy. We made it to the Colonies."

"'Tis a sad song, though."

"A bit. But a true song for a sailor." He kissed her. "I'm glad that I still have my one true love." She'd been desperately ill during the voyage, but they'd nursed her back to health. Except for feedings, Maggie assumed responsibility for the baby, allowing Keira to rest. Dughall stayed at his wife's side, coaxing her to take morsels of food and sips of water. He apologized a thousand times and begged the Goddess to heal her.

She squeezed his arm. "Don't worry. I'm not dead yet."

Dughall smiled. "My father likes to say that."

"Aye. It will be a blessing to walk on solid ground. How long will we stay here?"

He sensed her apprehension. "A few days. Then we will sail to Virginia."

She frowned.

"Don't fret, lass. No more open ocean. No rolling seas. We'll be in sight of land the whole time."

"Oh, good."

He smiled. "This is Boston! We will take rooms at an inn and get a proper bath. There will be wine and ale and decent meals. I can hardly wait."

She made a small sound of agreement. "We need to wash clothes and I'd like to purchase a bolt of linen. Morrigan needs new nappies."

"Then ye shall have it. Only the best for my wee daughter."

Keira sighed. "Maggie has been a big help. She will make a good mother."

"Aye. Philip is lucky to have her." He gazed at the wharf. "McGee says that there are several inns in town. Will ye help me to choose one?"

She smiled. "Aye. But let's all choose. Here come the young ones."

Emerging on deck were Luc, Philip, and Maggie, holding the infant on her hip. They approached the Duke and Duchess. Maggie grinned. "We made it, Mother!" The baby in her arms giggled.

Keira nodded. "That we did. I couldn't have done it without ye." She reached out and accepted her infant daughter. "Come to me, darling."

The baby snuggled against her. "Momma!"

Keira smiled. "Ah."

Gazing at their faces, Dughall realized what it meant to be touched by God's grace. They had survived the voyage. He gathered them into a circle and spoke words of gratitude, "My dear family. Many a night did we huddle in our cabins praying for deliverance. Now, gazing upon this city on a hill, we see that our prayers were answered. We thank God and the Goddess for guiding us safely to the Colonies. Amen."

They responded in unison, "Amen."

The crew was putting a ladder down to the dinghy. They could disembark at any time. Dughall smiled. "Let's leave the crew to their tasks and find a comfortable inn for the night."

CHAPTER 44
BOSTON

MONDAY OCTOBER 3RD 1650
LATER THAT DAY

The Gordon clan wandered into Boston and took three rooms at the 'Sign of the Anchor'. The two story brick and wood establishment was known for moderately priced lodgings, good food, and ale. They sent Luc back to the ship to tell the crew to bring their bags. The lad returned with a cart of luggage and his beloved deerhound Artus.

The family supped on beef, potatoes, squash, corn bread, and apple pie; and drank a fair amount of ale and cider. After months of bad food, it felt like heaven. Dughall arranged for the same meal to be sent to the crew and captain.

That evening, they heated water for baths, and one by one cleansed their ripe and battered bodies. The innkeeper introduced them to a laundress, who took most of their clothes to wash them. Just before midnight, they crawled into bed, sleepy but satisfied.

NEXT DAY, TUESDAY

The Duke slept past dawn. He woke in the unfamiliar chamber to the sound of his daughter cooing. There was one bed in the room, so they'd slept with the child between them. He rolled over and saw that she was awake.

Morrigan kicked her feet. "Dada!"

Dughall grinned. "Shhhh.. Mama is asleep." There was a sharp smell in the room, so he checked her nappy. "Ach! Ye're soaked." He got out of bed, picked up the child, and looked for something to change her with. His wife had planned ahead. A rough towel lay over the back of a chair. He grabbed it and laid the baby at the foot of the bed.

She gurgled. "Da!"

The job was normally done by his wife. But he was willing to give it a try. "Hmmm..." Dughall unpinned the garment on both sides, removed it, and used a dry section to wipe her. He noted an angry rash on her bum. Then he lifted her feet, placed the towel under her, and fastened the pins.

Keira opened her eyes. She giggled when she saw what was going on. "Ye changed her?"

Dughall reddened. "Aye. The wee lassie has a rash on her arse."

"I know. There was no way to stay clean on the boat; and we washed her nappies in sea water. Perhaps we can find an apothecary. They might have some ointment." She sat up and rolled down her nightshirt. "Let me nurse her."

Dughall passed the child to her and watched as the infant took her nipple. He never tired of seeing this. "Maggie got her to eat oatmeal and mashed peas. We should try to feed her more solid food."

Keira frowned slightly. "I guess it's time. I will miss the day when I no longer nurse her."

He smiled sheepishly. "Perhaps we will have another child. A son or a daughter..."

Keira smiled. "Perhaps." There was a pop as the baby finished. She pulled up her nightshirt and passed him the infant. "Let's dress and go to the dining room. I'm hungry."

Dughall entertained the baby as his wife dressed. He took her to the window and looked out. "See the carriages and horses? And there is yer brother, Luc." He rapped on the window and saw the lad look up.

Morrigan flailed her wee arms. "Doggie!"

Dughall smiled. "Aye, the doggie is with him."

"I'll take her, Husband."

The Duke passed her the baby and pulled on his dusty breeks. "I spotted Luc below. He just entered the inn. It's likely that they're all waiting for us." He sat down and slipped on his socks and boots. "Let's join them."

"All right."

They left their chamber, walked a narrow hallway, and took a flight of stairs down to the dining room.

***

Maggie sat at a table in the dining room, next to her husband, Philip. The couple had been the first to wake, to the sound of the town bell ringer. After dressing quickly and going downstairs, they'd been treated to a tray of tea and scones. Luc checked in, but left the inn with his dog to allow the animal to relieve himself. Patrons had come and gone, partaking in a hasty breakfast. But Dughall and Keira were no where in sight. She turned to Philip. "Where are my parents?"

Philip smiled. "They were exhausted. I'm sure they will be down soon."

The front door opened, admitting Luc and Artus. The lad was grinning. "I saw Father in a window! He signaled that they would be coming down."

Maggie was relieved. "Good!" She'd been worried – about Mother's health and Father's predicament. She hoped that the Colonies would be good for them.

Luc took a seat opposite Maggie. "I'm starving!" He poured himself a cup of tea and stuffed a cranberry scone in his mouth. As he chewed, he passed a piece to Artus under the table. "I wandered for a block or two. The city is not as big as Aberdeen, mind ye. But it rivals Peterhead."

Philip nodded. "Maggie and I took a walk last night. There are hundreds of buildings. But the roads are dirt, not cobblestone. And they don't have sewers. Still, they manage to keep it clean. I saw a town official removing refuse."

Maggie smiled. "There are shops! They were closed last night, but they should be open now. I could use a brimmed hat."

Philip placed his hand over hers. "Then ye shall have it, Wife."

Luc made a small sound of agreement. "Only the best for my sister."

The innkeeper approached the table. Robert Turner was a lanky man with grey hair and spectacles. He wore leather breeks and a linen shirt, with an apron tied around his middle. "How are my Scottish friends this morning?"

Philip smiled. "Good. We plan to explore the city today."

Turner frowned slightly. "Be careful, lads. These Puritans are strict folk. Don't stare at their young women. I'd hate to see you in the stocks."

Luc's eyes widened. "Thank ye for the advice."

"There's more. Don't enter their churches. You must be a member."

Philip nodded. "We will respect their wishes." He placed his hand over Maggie's. "As for staring, I am a newly married man. I have eyes only for my wife."

Turner collected the teapot and tray. "Congratulations on your wedding. I will refresh this and bring it back. Would you like breakfast?"

Maggie smiled. "Aye. Bring breakfast for five. I see my mother and father."

Dughall and Keira had just entered the room. He was carrying wee Morrigan against his shoulder.

Maggie made a final request, "Bring some oatmeal for the baby."

Turner nodded. "As you wish." He left the table.

***

The Gordon clan enjoyed a hearty breakfast of eggs, ham, poached pears, and bread. There was butter, rhubarb jelly, and raspberry jam. Morrigan ate a few spoonfuls of oatmeal before throwing up on the table.

The baby slapped her hands in the vomit. "Ha!"

Luc tried to hide a smile. "She's all right." He passed a chunk of ham to the dog.

His father made a small sound of disapproval.

"I have to feed him, Father. There are no woods to hunt in."

Dughall frowned. "All right."

Keira wiped the baby's hands with a napkin. "All clean."

Luc was anxious to get started. "I took a walk. There are shops on the main street. They should be open. Can we explore the city?"

"Aye, Son."

They finished their breakfast, settled with the innkeeper, and left the establishment by the front door.

Luc smiled as they stepped into the sunlight. It was a beautiful fall morning with the temperature upwards of fifty. The few trees along the street were covered with burnished leaves. He reached down and put Artus on a tether. "It's just for a while, boy." He walked ahead of his family, leading them to a shop they'd talked about. Luc at twenty was a happy young man. The abuse he suffered at the hand of his stepfather was only a bad memory. Now, he belonged to a good family that loved and respected him. This was the model he intended to emulate when he got married. His father had failed to find him a lass. That was fine with Luc. He wanted to find his own wife. He wanted to fall in love like Maggie.

They arrived at the shop. The one story wood and brick structure had three small signs that said, "Mercer", "Milliner", and "Haberdasher." The door was open.

Luc announced, "This is it, Father."

Maggie beamed. "A milliner! I can get a hat."

Keira shifted the baby to her hip. "A mercer should have a bolt of cloth for nappies. A haberdasher has notions. We can buy scissors and some pins, too."

Luc tied the dog to a hitching post and they entered the shop. It was small, about twenty feet by thirty, but it was packed with goods. On the back wall, there were oak drawers from ceiling to floor, with a sliding ladder that serviced it. There was a wooden counter with a silver haired man standing behind it. He was wearing a brown leather apron.

The man grinned. "Ah, customers! What can I do for you folks?"

Dughall spoke, "Please forgive the state of our clothes. We arrived yesterday after months at sea."

"Where did you come from?"

"Scotland."

"Ah. Where the troubles are."

Dughall sighed. "'Tis true. Have ye heard any news?"

The man scratched his wooly beard. "I saw a London paper yesterday. It was several months old. Cromwell was about to invade Scotland."

"When I left, his troops were gathering on our southern border."

The shopkeeper frowned. "So, it may already have happened. Why did you come to the Colonies?"

"Our fortunes have been affected by recent conflicts. My brother has a plantation in Virginia. We intend to join him."

Luc's curiosity was piqued. *Does my father mean to stay here?*

"Excellent!" the man said. "We can use good men in the Colonies." He smiled. "Women, too. They're a scarce commodity. Enough talk! What can I sell ye?"

Keira handed the baby to her husband. "I'd like a bolt of cloth to make nappies for the wee one. And scissors and pins. The sign said ye have notions."

The man turned and slid his ladder to a location. He climbed it, opened a drawer, and extracted a bolt of cream colored cloth. He climbed down and laid it on the counter. "Will this do?"

Keira ran her hand across the fabric. "Aye. It's softer than what she has now."

"Good." He turned and opened a lower drawer, extracted a tray of notions, and set it on the counter. "This is what I have."

Keira sorted through the items. She selected a pack of pins, a card of bone buttons, several needles, a spool of thread, and a pair of scissors.

The man smiled. "Can I get you anything else?"

Luc spoke up, "My sister would like a hat."

The man stared. "We sell two types of hats. The Puritan lasses wear white caps that conceal their head and hair. I don't suppose you want one of those."

Maggie smiled. "Nay. I'd like a wide brimmed hat, either fabric or straw, to keep the sun off my face."

"Hmmm...." The shopkeeper looked thoughtful. He moved his ladder to a different section, climbed it, opened a deep drawer, and took out a stack of women's hats. This he brought to the counter. "These just arrived on a ship from London." He gave her an oval hand mirror. "Try one on."

Maggie sorted through the stack until she came to a straw hat with yellow daisies embroidered on it. "My favorite flower." She placed it on her head and gazed in the mirror. "It's a wee bit too big, though."

The man smiled. "I'm a milliner, lass. I can adjust it." He ran his fingers along the band to determine what to do. "This will take a few minutes. Do you want it?"

"Aye."

The milliner lifted the hat from her head and took it to a work table in the corner. He began to work a strip of fabric into the band.

While they waited, a severe looking woman and her three daughters entered the shop. The woman was clad in a long black dress with a white waist apron and a broad lace collar. She wore the typical white cap on her head. Her daughters were similarly dressed, but yellow hair peeked from the caps.

Luc recalled the innkeeper's words and averted his eyes. It was too late. The young lasses were staring at him.

"Prudence!" "Patience!" "Faith!" the woman cried. She cuffed one of the girls on the ear. "How many times have I told you? You must not look upon an unmarried man." Two of the girls looked down.

Luc blushed. What did it matter if he was unmarried? He didn't mean to cause trouble.

"But, Mother. He's handsome."

This elicited a smack to the back of the speaker's head. "How dare you!"

"Ow!"

The woman hissed, "I should have named you Chastity."

Luc's heart pounded. He wasn't handsome. They couldn't be talking about him. The girl obviously needed spectacles. He turned to his parents. "Forgive, me Father. I must check on Artus."

Dughall nodded. "Go, Son. We will be along in a few minutes."

Luc practically fled the shop. Outside, he untied his dog from the hitching post and took him for a run. When the animal relieved himself, he turned and headed back to the milliner's shop.

His family was emerging from the door, carrying their purchases.

Maggie was wearing her new hat. "The lass was right. Ye are handsome."

The lad stared desperately. "I am not!"

She smirked. "Oh, aye. Ye are."

Luc reddened. *They all need spectacles!* He would have to be careful in Boston.

***

They spent the next few hours going from shop to shop, purchasing things they might need in Virginia. The shops were well stocked with goods, busy, and noisy. They bought three pairs of goat skin gloves from a glover and two pairs of boots from an old shoemaker. A kindly butcher named John Shaw sold them a crate of tallow candles and a packet of meat scraps for Artus. They found ointment for the baby at the Apothecary.

They observed people going about their daily duties. Some were dressed like they were - the men in breeks and shirts and the women in modest dresses of color. Others were dressed in the severe garb of the Puritans. They took care not to stare at the women.

The Gordon clan wandered into another part of town and marveled at the majesty of the governor's mansion. They avoided churches, but got a peek at the public Meeting House. Dughall spoke to several men about their system of government. They seemed happy that England was a commonwealth. While officially under English rule, the colony governed themselves with elected magistrates and legislators. It was an idea worth considering.

They also saw a public school. Here, there was no distinction between the gentry and commoners. Most of the children were educated.

Finally, the baby was getting restless. They returned to the inn to attend to her. Keira and Maggie made nappies from the bolt of cloth and retrieved their clean clothes from the laundress.

The men went to the harbor to check on the provisioning. They returned to the inn with sobering news. The Black Swan was fully provisioned. It would be ready to sail on the morrow.

THE NEXT MORNING, WEDNESDAY

The Duke accepted the baby from his wife and held her against his shoulder. They were ready to leave Boston. The cart had arrived early that morning and transported their belongings to the ship. They'd lingered for a while at the inn, enjoying a breakfast of eggs, ham, and apple pastries. After the meal, the youngsters had gone on ahead – Philip, Maggie, and Luc, accompanied by his faithful deerhound. They were eager to continue the voyage.

Dughall sensed his wife's apprehension. She was reluctant to sail and he couldn't blame her. "Are ye ready?"

She frowned slightly. "I suppose so."

He smiled sympathetically. "I promise that it won't be bad this time. The captain says that we'll be in sight of land for the whole voyage. That means no big waves."

She managed a smile. "Good."

They left the inn and stepped out into the bright sunlight. It was a beautiful day with a light breeze coming from the harbor. He pulled up the baby's hood. You could never be too careful with an infant.

The wee lassie snuggled against him. "Da!"

His heart was light as they walked to the harbor. "The young ones must be on the ship. I don't see them."

Keira took his free arm. "Aye." She smiled. "It was nice to see a young lass interested in Luc. He doesn't know how handsome he is."

"Aye. The lad turned red when Maggie teased him."

"Those Puritan lasses had strange names – Prudence, Patience, and Faith."

"They're old names – Biblical in origin." He grinned. "There was purpose in their naming. The Puritans think that by the act of naming the child, it will assume that attribute or quality."

She was silent for a moment. "The mother said that should have named one of them Chastity."

He smirked. "Aye."

"That's a strange wish for a daughter. In any case, we have no right to criticize. We named our child after the Morrigan."

"Ha! Ye're right."

They arrived at the dock and walked along it, following a fisherman and his two sons.

Dughall was warmed by the sight. The long haired man appeared to be in his thirties. He wore a rough sweater, wool breeks, and scuffed sea boots. Two young boys trailed behind him, imitating his walk. They were twins, no older than seven. "Ah."

"What is it, Husband?"

"They remind me of my father and brother. Ian and I walked behind our father just like that." The memory tugged at his heartstrings.

She squeezed his arm. "Ye will see them again."

"I hope so, lass." The fisherman and his sons boarded a boat and rowed along the shore.

The crew of the Black Swan spotted Dughall and Keira and began to lower a dinghy into the water. Maggie, Philip, and Luc waved to them from the deck. They looked excited.

Dughall shifted the baby to his other shoulder. "It's time to go, precious." He addressed the child, but in truth he was telling his wife.

She managed a grim smile. "I'm ready."

The dinghy arrived at the dock and they boarded. It was time to leave Boston Harbor.

Chapter 45
Disturbing News

October 12th 1650
1 week later

DRAKE CASTLE

Jamison and Ian sat in the Duke's private study, reviewing the financial ledger. It was a grueling process that neither looked forward to. Now that the Duke was gone, all expenses had to be justified. They were almost finished.

Jamison signed the document and slid it across the desk. "Everything looks right. Sign it."

Ian scanned the ledger one last time. "We spent less this month. That's a good thing."

Jamison sighed. "We spent less because there are two hundred less men to support at the Range. Few returned from the battle at Dunbar."

Ian signed it with a scrawl. "I wish we could have told them about my brother's predicament. They would have been less likely to join the Covenanter army."

"Agreed. But even so it served a purpose. By sending men, it appears that the Duke is loyal to the Covenanters and the Prince. It's like hedging yer bets. Even the Laird of Grant sent one hundred and forty men. We know what he thinks of the Prince."

Ian frowned. "Why keep up appearances? I doubt it will work in my brother's favor. This was too high of a price to pay. Most of our men were slaughtered."

Jamison grunted. "At least they're dead. I feel bad for Fang and Gilroy. They were captured and forced to march to Durham. Who knows what awaits them there? They'd be better off dead." The servant reached back and brought forth a decanter of whisky and two squat glasses. "I need more than a dram." He poured three fingers in each. "Let's drink to them."

Ian raised his glass. "To Fang and Gilroy."

Jamison joined him. "Two of the bravest men I've ever known."

They bolted the whisky and poured another.

The servant sipped his drink. "We must inform yer brother."

"Where do we send the letter?"

"To George Gordon in Jamestown, Virginia. He should arrive there soon."

Ian's eyes widened. "What will we tell Dughall?"

"The truth." Jamison sighed. "That the battle was lost and his men were killed. That Edinburgh is occupied by English troops. Scotland is in dire trouble."

"My brother will be devastated. I wish we had better news about the Prince."

"Aye. The Prince emerged from the battle unscathed. The snake blamed everyone but himself for the failure. Our leaders are blind. He will soon be crowned King of Scotland."

Ian took a large swallow of whisky. "Are we safe at Drake?"

The servant's nostrils flared. "For the moment. But our master must not return. There was an inquiry this morning about his whereabouts."

Ian stiffened. "Dear Jesus! Who asked?"

"An envoy from the Prince. I told him the Duke was in France on business."

"Did he accept that?"

"I doubt it. He asked about what region he was visiting. I told him Paris."

"Did that satisfy him?"

"Nay. I was told that he questioned a few of our subjects."

"Hmmphhh! It's a good thing they don't know about his true whereabouts." Ian bolted his drink and set the glass on the desk. "Father might not be safe here. I will insist that he return to Whinnyfold."

Jamison nodded. "It's a wise move. The Prince could use Alex to lure the Duke back." He opened a drawer, took out a piece of stationery, and passed it to Ian. "One of our ships leaves for the Colonies this week to acquire timber. Let's write yer brother."

Ian sighed. "We should send a package and include the letter that arrived from young James."

"Agreed. Yer brother could use some good news."

Ian inked a quill and poised it over the paper. To protect everyone involved, it would bear no return address or reference to Drake Castle. He scrawled the date at the top of the page and wrote, *"Dear Brother."*

Fang Adams

CHAPTER 46
FANG

OCTOBER 12TH 1650
SAME DAY

DURHAM, ENGLAND

Fang Adams was lucky to be alive. The prisoners had been forced to march one hundred and eighteen miles without food or water. Men dropped like flies from dehydration, starvation, and sickness. One night, as they rested in a farmer's field, Fang knew that his body was on the verge of collapse. He dug into the soil with his bare hands and ate worm infested cabbages. It saved his life. Less than three thousand survivors staggered into Durham on September 10th - Fang was one of them. Tragically, Gilroy had succumbed to sickness.

Once in Durham, they had another cross to bear. The Cathedral had been converted to a prison, but food intended for the prisoners had been stolen and sold by their guards. For thirty days, their rations consisted of gruel made from oatmeal and cabbage, a few quarts a day for each prisoner. They had coals to warm them and straw to lie upon. But no one tended their wounds or removed sewage. Death from disease was rampant. Nine hundred prisoners died in the first month.

Even so, Fang held out hope for survival. That day, he'd heard that able bodied prisoners would be sent to the Colonies. He was determined to be one of them. He would be sold as an indentured servant, work for 6 years to pay for his passage, and then be granted his freedom.

Fang bristled. "I don't want to be a slave! But I will survive this." The light from the coals was fading fast. "I must conserve my strength. The first ship leaves in a few weeks. I intend to be on it." Stomach aching from lack of food, he rolled over and went to sleep.

Chapter 47
Reunion

October 28th 1650
16 days later

JAMESTOWN, VIRGINIA

Gilbert Gordon left the chamber where he'd been sitting for the last seven hours. As a Justice, he attended monthly meetings to settle civil matters and minor criminal cases. This month the docket had been full. With other justices, he'd considered the case of a thief who robbed shops in the city. Witnesses were called and testimony taken. In the end, the man was pronounced guilty and sentenced to a long period of indenture. They'd also settled the adoption of three children and apprenticed a lad to the blacksmith. There was a property dispute to settle as well, and a matter considering trade with the Indians.

Gilbert had served a Justice for four months and found the work challenging. It was a welcome change from working the plantation and provided his family with income. His brother's gold was dwindling. He entered the cloak room and removed his robe, hanging it on a peg. Then he took off his white wig and placed it on a stand for next time.

Justice John Smith entered and disrobed. "It's been a long day."

Gilbert nodded. "Aye, but satisfying." He slipped on a cotton shirt, buttoned it, and tucked the tails into his breeks.

"I'm glad that you're with us, George. You have thoughtful opinions."

"Thank ye, John."

"I won't keep you. You'd best run along. A messenger caught me in the hall. Your brother and his family have arrived from Scotland."

Gilbert could hardly believe it. "My brother?"

"That's what he said. They are staying at the inn on the water."

"Did the messenger wait?"

"No."

"Thank ye, John! I will go there."

***

Gilbert left the meeting house and took long strides until he came to a sandy path that would take him to the harbor. There was only one inn on the water. He'd stayed in it when he first landed. *Could it be*

Dughall? he wondered. *Why would he come unannounced?*.

Gilbert arrived at the inn. The brick and wood structure bore a weathered sign that proclaimed it the 'Jamestown Tavern'. There was no one on the porch, but plenty of light within. He entered and approached the innkeeper.

The middle aged man was wiping a table. "What can I do for you, Sir?"

Gilbert glanced around. "My name is George Gordon. I am looking for my brother."

"Ah," the innkeeper said with a smile. "You must mean Duncan Gordon. He and his family are eating supper in the next room."

Gilbert froze. *Duncan?* Was the innkeeper wrong or had his brother assumed a name? "Thank ye. I can find them."

Gilbert walked into the dining room and saw dozens of people sitting at tables. His nostrils flared. The smell of roasted beef made his stomach grumble. He spotted them at a table and crossed the room. "Brother!"

Dughall stood to greet him. With a look of joy, he embraced him. "I'm glad to see ye!" Then softer in his ear, "I'm in trouble. Ye must call me Duncan."

They separated.

"I will." Gilbert's heart swelled with gratitude. This man had gone to the chopping block in his place. By God's grace, he'd survived it. "Likewise... Ye must call me George." He took a seat at the table.

Dughall sat and acknowledged the others. "My wife Keira, of course, and our infant daughter. Ye remember Luc and Maggie. And this is Philip Grant, Maggie's husband. They are newly wedded."

Gilbert was surprised. The lass was barely thirteen. He wondered if she was pregnant. "Welcome to the family, Philip. Where is James?"

Keira sighed. "We left him at Deer Abbey. He decided to become a monk."

Dughall nodded. "We have much to tell ye."

A serving lass came to the table. They ordered supper for Gilbert and a round of ale for the men. She returned within minutes with their order.

Gilbert picked up a fork and dug into the roasted beef. He hadn't eaten a bite since breakfast. "It tastes good. How long have ye been here?"

Dughall sipped his ale. "Five days. We had a long sea voyage and stopped in Boston. From there, it took us weeks to get here. The ship had to stop in Maryland for repairs. A official said that ye'd be at the meeting house today. So, we decided to wait."

Gilbert continued eating, spearing a piece of squash. "Why did ye not write ahead?"

Dughall sighed. "I had to leave Scotland in a hurry. We can talk about it tomorrow."

Gilbert's eyes widened. He changed the subject, focusing on the children. "Maggie and Luc have certainly grown up! And what is the name of the wee lassie?"

Keira stroked the baby's hair. "Morrigan."

Gilbert frowned. "That's not a proper Christian name. It will cause trouble in the Colonies. Does she have a middle name?"

"Rose."

"Then Rose it must be."

They were silent for a moment.

Keira reddened. "I suppose so."

Dughall squeezed her arm with affection. "It will be all right, lass."

Gilbert finished his meal and ordered another round of ale. "I must return to Eden this evening."

Maggie smiled. "Tell us, Uncle. What is Eden?"

"Eden is the name of our plantation. We have three hundred acres. About a third of that is farm land. Ye are welcome to join us." He turned to his brother. "Tomorrow, I will send a horse drawn cart to retrieve ye. The lads will have to walk, but the women can ride. How much luggage do ye have?"

Luc spoke up, "A small cartload. There are bags and trunks and things for a homestead. Philip and I can carry bags. Oh, and there is Artus."

"Yer dog?"

"Aye. The dog will earn his keep. He's a skilled hunter."

"Good."

Keira smiled. "How is my sister-in-law? And the children?"

Gilbert sipped his ale. "Bridget is well. She likes it here in spite of the hardships. George has grown into a brawny young man. Ye should see him handle a musket! My daughters are learning to cook and preserve food. They are big help to their mother. Ye will see them tomorrow." He stood to leave. "Bridget expects me. I must return to Eden."

Dughall stood and they embraced. "I've dreamed of this day, Brother."

"Aye." Gilbert choked up, "I will always remember what ye did for me."

They separated.

"I will send a wagon in the morning." Gilbert left the inn and began to walk to the stables. *We have plenty of room. The main house is full, but the second house is empty. We can always use extra hands with planting, harvesting, fishing, and hunting. Bridget needs help with the garden and preserving.*

He reached the stables and retrieved his stallion. The beast knew the way home, so it gave him time to contemplate. *I wonder what kind of trouble he's in? What does it matter? I owe this man my life.*

CHAPTER 48
EDEN

OCTOBER 29TH 1650
NEXT DAY

It was a sultry day in Virginia. Young George arrived at the inn after breakfast, driving a horse drawn wagon. The men loaded the cart, helped the women board, and began the ride to Eden. At first it was slow going, guiding the heavy wagon over dirt roads. It soon became evident that it was overloaded. To lighten the load, Maggie got out and walked and the men carried more packages. They arrived at Eden midday, to a warm reception from Gilbert and Bridget. They'd taken a rare day off from the fields to welcome their relations from Scotland.

Now, Dughall sat on the porch enjoying a delightful concoction. He held up his glass and admired the golden color. "What is this?"

Gilbert took a sip. "Rum, sugar cane, and bruised mint."

Dughall grinned. "It's not whisky, but I like it."

"Ye won't find much whisky in Virginia. It's considered a waste of barley. Rum is plentiful though. We import it from the islands."

He took another swallow. "It's sweet like honey."

Gilbert nodded. "That's the sugar cane. The children suck on the stalks and Bridget uses it in baking."

They were smoking cigars as well. "Did ye grow this tobacco?"

"It's from our first batch. We used hickory smoke to speed up the curing process."

Dughall blew out a ring and watched it float away. "It's good. Smooth and flavorful."

Gilbert smiled. "When we left Scotland, the ship stopped in Bermuda to take on supplies. I liked their tobacco, so I acquired a few barrels of seeds. It grows well here."

"I'm not surprised. Is it always so warm?"

"It freezes in winter, but not for long. It's not like Scotland."

They watched Anne and Mary chasing a young border collie. A scraggly hound with a notched ear loped behind them. In the distance, they saw George and Luc coming in from the fields, carrying muskets and the spoils of their hunting. Artus was toting a duck carcass.

Dughall crushed out his cigar in a tin. "Ye seem happy here."

Gilbert did the same. "Aye. It surprised me. I don't have servants or the amenities of the castle. Except for Sunday, we work from sun up to sun down. But it's mine. Here, I am free to define myself. Even Connor has done it. He's like family."

Dughall liked what he was hearing. "Ah..."

Gilbert raised his glass. "To the man who made it possible. Stay as long as ye like, Brother."

"We plan to earn our keep."

"The help will be appreciated." He took a sip and put the glass down. "Tell me about yer trouble."

Dughall bolted his drink and placed the glass on the table. "Did ye know that the Prince entered Scotland?"

"I heard that."

"Our government offered him the crown if he would abide by certain conditions. The Prince agreed and was taken to our southern border. Cromwell's army was about to invade us. I don't know if it happened."

Gilbert sighed. "It did. A ship arrived a few days ago with news. The Scottish army was defeated at Dunbar. Thousands of our countrymen were killed and more taken prisoner. They intend to transport hundreds of prisoners to Virginia. The men will be sold."

Dughall's heart sank. "As slaves?"

Gilbert shook his head. "Nay, as indentured servants. Plantation owners will pay the ship's captain 20£ per man for their transport. In return, the man must serve the owner for six years."

"That's hardly better than a slave."

"Aye. But it's better than dying in prison. We must provide them with food, clothing, and shelter."

"Is there a lot of interest?"

"Oh, aye. They expect to place all these men on plantations. I was trying to raise funds to buy the contracts of a dozen men. This year, we struggled with temporary help. We need more workers on the plantation."

Dughall knew that Eden's men would be fairly treated. "I can provide the funds for twenty."

Gilbert's eyes widened. "Ye can?"

"Aye. I sold Seaford Shores to the Laird of Grant. I brought half the gold with me. It's a small fortune."

He poured them another drink. "With more men, we can till more acres. That means profit. We will have to build cottages to shelter them." He passed Dughall a glass. "Now, back to yer trouble. What is it?"

Dughall was nervous and rightfully so. He was about to bare his soul. "Promise me ye'll tell no one."

"I promise."

"I will start with a question. Did the ship bring news of the Prince?"

"Aye." Gilbert sipped his drink. "He survived the battle. They say that he will soon be crowned King of Scotland."

Dughall sighed. "Then I can not return to Drake. One of his first acts as King will be to execute me as a traitor."

"God in heaven! Who said this?"

Dughall couldn't lie to his brother. "Queen Henrietta. It's a long story."

"Then ye'd best tell it."

"When we visited the King, she and I were sent to the Observatory. That's where she propositioned me to be her lover. The woman left me with a standing offer."

Gilbert was riveted to his words. "Go on."

"Months later, I agreed to her terms to gain my father's release from the Tower. The risk was great. I went to the Queen's House and served her in her bed chamber. True to her word, she released him. We barely escaped London."

Gilbert was pale. "Did she keep quiet?"

"She kept it secret for a long time. But eventually, the King found out about our tryst. By that time, he was engaged in a civil war. I was the least of his problems. He was imprisoned and executed."

"A dead man can't hurt ye."

Dughall sighed. "His son can. The Queen told me that that I was first on his list of traitors. He intends to execute me in a most unpleasant manner."

Gilbert blew his breath out slowly. "No wonder ye took a new name. Ye have more bravery than sense, Brother! First ye rescue Alex, then me..."

Dughall smiled. "It was worth it."

They were distracted by the sound of women laughing. Bridget and Keira were approaching the porch, engaged in a lively conversation.

Dughall whispered, "My family knows nothing of this."

Gilbert nodded. "We will talk more later."

The women arrived on the porch and sat in straight backed chairs. Keira smiled. "Maggie and Philip have wee 'Rose'. I don't know what I'd do without them."

Bridget kicked off her shoes. "I told her about my favorite drink. Can we have one?"

Gilbert pointed to a pitcher and two empty glasses. "Aye, my Lady." He poured fresh drinks and passed them around. "Brother, tomorrow we will take a ride. I will show ye the plantation." He lifted his glass. "To Eden."

They joined him, "To Eden!"

Dughall's heart was light as he listened to their conversation. They were together again at last and that was all that mattered. *I'm alive and whole and out of danger. At least for a while, I will not think of Scotland.*

CHAPTER 49
OUT TO SEA

NOVEMBER 19TH 1650
3 WEEKS LATER

THE NORTH ATLANTIC OCEAN

It was a frigid day on the North Atlantic. The deck of the 'Unity' was coated with snow and icicles hung from the rigging. They'd lowered the sails because a storm was coming.

The grizzled captain barked orders to a crew member. "Idiot! Tie off to the masthead!"

Fang Adams stood on deck. He'd signed on as a deck hand for a coat, boots, and extra rations. He'd befriended the man on the masthead. The lad reminded him of Ian Hay.

Bevis Johnson tied off to the mast.

"Ye did it!" The ship rose and fell with a wave. Fang watched in horror as the lad slipped and dangled by a rope over water. "Shit! Shit! Shit!" He staggered across deck and tied himself to an iron ring. Swallowing his fear, he reached way over the side, grabbed the rope, and pulled him in. They collapsed on the deck.

Captain Walker stood over them. "God damn idiots! I almost lost both of you."

Fang got to his feet. "But, Sir! He would have drowned."

"Get below! I'll deal with ye later."

Lightning streaked across the sky, accompanied by a fearsome crackle. The heavens opened and it began to pour. Adams stared at a bank of dark clouds. They were drifting into it. "Jesus Christ!"

"Last chance to get below!"

Fang lifted Bevis and threw him over his shoulder. He followed the captain through an open hatch and down a staircase to the crew's quarters. He brought his friend to a bunk, and dropped and covered him.

The lad's eyes opened. "Thank ye."

Adams grunted. "Get warm. I'll bring ye supper."

The ship pitched as he walked to the galley. He wondered if they would survive this. "I was safer in prison." He reached the galley and entered.

The old cook was stirring a pot of stew. The man was as pale as his straggly white hair. "Have ye been on deck?"

He coughed. "Aye."

"How is it?"

"Bad. There's a storm coming."

The ship pitched and the cook staggered. "God help us. Did ye want yer rations?"

Fang held out two bowls. "Johnson's as well. I will take it to him. He nearly fell into the water. I rescued him."

The man ladled stew into the bowls and added two pieces of corn bread. "Ye're a good man, Fang. The captain likes ye. Stay on with us as a crew member."

Adams felt bile rise in his throat. The ship had risen and was falling again. "I'd rather be a slave in Virginia!"

Fang returned to Johnson's bed and coaxed him to eat. The stew was three days old. He couldn't identify the meat or vegetables, but it was welcome nourishment. When they were done, he stowed the bowls in a locker and crawled into an empty bunk. The captain would call if he needed him.

Fang Adams didn't dare to complain. He was better off than his fellow prisoners. Ninety-one men were locked in the ship's hold without bunks, blankets, or adequate food and water. He'd been there. The stench of piss and vomit was overpowering.

Fang covered himself with a lice-ridden blanket. *The cook says I'm a good man. Ha! If that's true, then God help me. God help US!* He rolled over, farted, and went to sleep.

Chapter 50
A Day in Eden

December 23rd 1650
1 Month Later

Dughall stood in the drying barn, packing cured tobacco into hogsheads. The drums were five feet wide and five feet tall. They were made of straight staves and hooped with split saplings. The Duke and his sons were clad like colonists, in shirts, knee britches, and long stockings. They'd save their good clothes for church.

Dughall packed six bundles of tobacco into the drum. He inserted a handled iron tool with a flat end and stood back. "It's ready."

Luc grasped the tool and thumped the tobacco, compacting it to half its height. "Whew!"

Philip climbed down a ladder with six more bundles of tobacco that had been hanging from a rafter. He packed them in the drum. "It's amazing how much we can get in a barrel."

Dughall nodded. "This is the last hogshead. I want to finish today."

Luc frowned. "How do we get these drums to the harbor?"

"Gilbert says that each cask weighs 500 pounds. We will tip it on its side and roll it to the James River. The raft can transport two or three of these."

Philip frowned. "How did Uncle Gilbert manage this last year?"

"He didn't. This is the first harvest."

"Hmmm." Philip returned to the ladder to gather more bundles.

Luc thumped the tobacco until it was flat. He'd served as thumper for the last two hours. "There has to be a better way of doing this."

The Duke nodded. "I once saw a screw press in a book about ancient Rome. They used it for pressing oil from olives. The concept is the same. When things settle down, we'll invent one."

"I'm for that! My hands are blistered."

Dughall accepted the tool. "Let me thump for a while. Help Philip gather the tobacco." He rolled up his sleeves. They were six inches from the top. With luck, they would finish the job before supper.

***

The women stood in the outdoor cookhouse, preparing supper. They were clad in plain cotton dresses with bibbed aprons that extended below the knee. Clothing was hard to come by. They didn't dare to ruin it.

Bridget was making batter for corn bread. She started by combining dry ingredients in a wooden bowl – corn meal, flour, salt, and baking soda. "Ye must not forget the soda. Or it won't rise."

Keira asked, "Where does soda come from?"

"We import it from England." Bridget put it aside and broke three eggs into a second bowl. She beat them gently and added a small pitcher of milk.

Keira was cutting up sweet potatoes. "Ye're lucky to have a cow and chickens."

Bridget nodded. " We didn't at first. Gilbert had to buy everything in Jamestown. We had the funds, thanks to yer husband."

Maggie stood by, cutting up carrots. "Corn bread is perfect for babies. The wee one loves it."

The infant was crawling on the floor, playing with Anne and Mary. They'd finally become accustomed to calling her 'Rose'.

Bridget combined the wet and dry ingredients and drizzled in a cup of melted lard. She poured the batter into an iron skillet, covered it with a lid, and placed it on coals in the fireplace. Then she used a small shovel to place coals on top of it. "Done."

"The carrots are cut," Maggie said, as she wiped her hands on her apron. "I will watch it."

"Thank ye, Niece. Turn the pot every so often. Check that it isn't burning." Bridget was grateful for their help. It was a challenge to prepare daily meals and preserve food for the winter. Last month, they'd pickled purple cabbage, green walnuts, radish pods, elder buds, parsley, mushrooms, and asparagus. They hung up ropes of persimmons to dry and salted crocks of herring. They made vinegar from apple peels and cores, storing them in cloth-covered buckets for weeks and extracting the liquid below the slime.

Keira put down her knife. "The potatoes are done. Shall we add the vegetables to the stew?"

Bridget smiled. "Aye. Thank ye, Sister."

The women went to the hearth. They used a tool to swing out the iron crane and another to lift the lid of the iron pot. The rich aroma of stewed rabbit filled the room.

Bridget stirred it. "It smells good. George and Luc are excellent hunters. This is more rabbit meat than we've seen in a long time."

Keira nodded. "Artus is a big help. He flushes rabbits from the underbrush." She added the potatoes, carrots, and a head of purple cabbage. The lass reached into her pocket and took out a handful of wild onions, parsley, and mushrooms. "I gathered these yesterday." They went in the pot as well.

They replaced the lid and swung the iron crane back into the fireplace.

Bridget smiled. "We have plenty of time. Let's clean up and make fruit pies for Christmas."

The baby clapped her hands. "Kissmas!"

Keira laughed. "The wee one agrees. We can celebrate her birthday as well. She turned one a few weeks ago."

The women smiled knowingly. Too many children died in the first year of life. Turning one was an accomplishment.

***

Gilbert and George were working on a cottage for indentured servants. They'd spent a month framing the sixteen by twenty structure and adding a fireplace and chimney. There was room in one wall for a door and two glassless windows with shutters.

Today, they were making clapboards to cover the roof and walls. George was nailing clapboards to the roof. It was Gilbert's turn to split logs for shingles.

The log he chose was four feet long and ten inches thick. Gilbert stood it on end against a prop and held a handled iron wedge against its center. His other hand wielded a mallet against the wedge, splitting the log in two. He took one of the halves and repeated the process, splitting it into two thinner pieces. He did this over and over again until he had a respectable pile of clapboards. Gilbert wiped the sweat from his brow. "Whew!" He laid down the mallet and yelled, "I finished another pile!"

George climbed down the ladder and stared at the pile of clapboards. His eyes widened. "We plan to buy twenty contracts. The ship will arrive soon. Will the cottage be finished?"

"Aye. Even if it kills me."

"We will house twenty men in one cottage?"

Gilbert wiped his brow. "At first. It won't be worse than their ship's quarters. Their first job will be to help us raise another cottage."

"Makes sense. The lads can help us with the walls tomorrow. Uncle Dughall says they're loading the last hogshead."

Gilbert frowned. "Call him Uncle Duncan."

"I know. Does it matter what we say in private?"

"Aye. The man is in dire trouble. We must be consistent. If we slip, it could mean his death. "

The lad nodded. "I will do as ye wish, Father."

They watched the women emerge from the cookhouse, carrying pots and bowls with the evening's supper.

Gilbert's stomach growled. "Time to quit. Go to the drying barn and inform my brother." He watched George turn and run in that direction. "Thank God that Dughall is here! His gold will sustain us for another year. The indentured servants will make us prosperous."

Chapter 51
Dry Land

December 31st 1650
8 Days Later

JAMESTOWN

Fang Adams stood on the deck of the 'Unity', surveying the harbor. Jamestown was a small port by Scottish standards. He'd heard that Virginia was a primitive place inhabited by hunters, planters, and wild savages. "I wonder what sort of man lives here."

Fang was lucky to be alive. They'd survived the storm. After the tempest, the sickness came - fever, diarrhea, and green vomit. The smell from the hold was revolting. Every morning, his first task was to throw dead prisoners overboard.

Ninety-two prisoners sailed from England. Only seventy-one survived. Most of the survivors suffered from scurvy. Their gums were tender. Noses bled. Skin was pale and eyes were sunken.

Fang Adams was a notable exception. The extra rations made a difference. The captain was impressed with him and offered to buy his contract. But Fang would not hear of it. He'd been dreaming of planting his feet on dry land. Now, he was staring at it. *Why should I be a slave? I wonder if I could run for it?*

"Yer master is here," the captain said.

Fang bristled. *I will be no man's slave.* He'd been in the hold when the planters arrived, counting the survivors.

"Did ye hear what I said? Go below and sign the indenture papers."

He followed the captain down a narrow staircase to the ship's cabin. They entered and saw two men leaning over a table, signing contracts.

Fang stood still. He couldn't see one man's face, but the other was unmistakable. "My Lord?"

Dughall turned to face him. "Fang! What are ye doing here?"

The captain's eyes narrowed. "He's a prisoner. Ye just signed his contract."

Fang stared. "I'm to go with him?"

"Aye."

"Good. He's the one man I will serve willingly."

Gilbert gave him a warning look. "We purchased the contracts of twenty men, including yerself. Can this man fetch them?"

"Aye."

The captain brought him to the table. "First, ye must sign yer contract."

Fang scribbled his mark on the bottom of the document. He knew that these men would treat him fairly. "Done."

The captain handed him a list. "Bring these men up to sign their contracts."

"Aye, Sir," Fang said with a smile. Fortune was smiling upon him. With a spring in his step, he left the cabin.

***

Dughall signed the last contract. "That makes twenty." He laid down the quill.

The captain nodded. "Ye owe me 20£ per man for their transport." He paused to make a calculation. "That's 400£. Will ye pay in goods or gold and silver?"

Dughall picked up a leather bag. "I brought gold and silver."

The man grinned. "That's rare in these Colonies."

He opened the bag and counted out coins to pay for his purchase. When he finished, there was a stack on the table. "Will ye count it?"

"No need. I watched ye." The captain signed a document of receipt and passed it to Gilbert. "It was a pleasure doing business with ye." He swept the coins from the table into a wooden chest.

Gilbert slipped the receipt into a pocket. "Were there other ships carrying prisoners from Dunbar?"

"Aye. Two should arrive in Virginia next month. Three headed to the northern colonies. Massachusetts agreed to take three hundred men. Pennsylvania two hundred. Four ships sailed south. Those poor bastards were sold to the islands."

Dughall frowned. "How many men survived the battle?"

"I don't know. But nine hundred were sent to the Colonies."

There was a knock on the door. Fang entered and snapped to attention. "The men are on deck, Sir!"

The captain nodded. "Good. Take these gentlemen up top. Send the prisoners down five at a time to sign their contracts."

The brothers followed Fang up a flight of stairs and onto the deck of the 'Unity'. There they inspected their new servants. The men looked like they'd had the life sucked out of them.

Dughall suspected that they had scurvy. His mind searched for a remedy. *The cook on the Black Swan said that lemon juice prevented scurvy. Perhaps a diet rich in fruit would heal their bodies. The women preserved apples, pears, and persimmons. Ah, and cranberries!*

Gilbert addressed the men, "My brother and I are from Scotland. We will treat ye fairly."

Soon, they were joined by the last of their men. They walked down the plank to the wharf, where they'd left their horse drawn wagon. Flasks of water and a bag of bread were passed around. Five men rode while the rest walked. They took turns as they traveled to Eden. When they arrived, they were given a meal and shown to their sleeping quarters.

Dughall stood on the porch, talking to Fang Adams. "What happened at Dunbar?"

"We fought bravely, my Lord. But it was a slaughter."

"How many of my men were lost?"

"Two hundred."

He swallowed hard. "Did my brother fight?"

"Nay, Sir. But good men were lost. Some in battle and some afterwards. Gilroy died on the march to Durham."

Dughall's heart ached. "Gilroy was a brave man. I shall miss him."

"He was one of hundreds who died from lack of water. It was worse in prison. The conditions were deplorable. I begged to be sent to the Colonies."

He was afraid to ask, "What about Murdock?"

"He stayed with the castle." Fang hesitated. "My Lord. What are ye doing here? Ye were the last man I expected to find in Virginia."

Dughall owed him an explanation - and he needed his silence. "I had to flee Scotland."

Fang's eyes widened. "Why?"

Dughall sighed. "The Prince plans to execute me as a traitor."

"A traitor! Why?"

"For freeing my father from the Tower. Now, I go by a different name, Duncan Gordon. Gilbert goes by George Gordon. The Prince thinks I'm in France. He must not learn that we are in the Colonies."

"Yer secret is safe with me." Fang frowned. "Why then did we follow the Prince? We fought and died for nothing!"

Dughall sensed his agony. "I wish I could have stopped ye. I had only a few hours to flee Scotland."

The servant grunted.

Dughall needed to move on. "These men... Do ye know them?"

"Nay. They came from other regiments. But we share one thing. We survived the battle."

The Duke nodded. "Ye look good. But they look terrible."

"Aye. I signed on as a deck hand to get extra rations."

"Ah." Dughall thought for a moment. "I suspect that they're suffering from scurvy. With good food and fresh air, we can restore them to health."

"Good."

It was time to make his pitch. "We made a new life here, growing tobacco. This plantation needs men to till the fields and help with the harvest. Ye're a good man, Fang. I'd like ye to be my foreman."

Fang folded his arms across his chest. "I will, my Lord."

"Ye must not call me that here."

"Aye, Sir." He stared into the distance. "How big is this plantation?"

Dughall smiled. "Three hundred acres. The forests are ripe with game. The fish practically jump out of the water. We have fertile fields, a natural spring, and access to the James River."

Fang grinned. "Sounds like a good place to start over."

"That's why we call it Eden." Dughall looked into his eyes. "Serve me well. I'll release ye early."

CHAPTER 52
CORONATION

JANUARY 1ST 1651
NEXT DAY

SCONE, PERTH, SCOTLAND

The village of Scone had a long history of crowning Scottish kings. Ancient Gaelic poetry referred to it as *Scoine sciath-airde* or 'Scone of the high shields.' The Abbey at Scone had two important functions. It housed the coronation stone and served as a royal residence.

Prince Charles had been received by the Abbey with all outward respect imaginable. Chaplains previously hostile to him approached on bended knees, in the humblest of postures. The Marquis of Argyle was gracious, entertaining him with pleasant discourses. But all was not as expected. Upon arrival, the Prince had been separated from his English servants. Attempts to restore them to his company were futile. All else, he'd been allowed – fine meals, a good horse to ride, a walk in the night air. At public appearances, he received the respect due a great king. Why then, did he feel like a prisoner?

That morning, the Prince dressed in a royal coronation robe. He was conducted from his bed chamber by the constable and the marshal to the Chamber of Presence. There, he was placed in a comfortable chair by the Lord of Angus. After a short repose, the commissioners of barons and boroughs entered the hall and presented themselves before him.

Charles was growing impatient. "Get on with it."

The Lord Chancellor's eyes widened. "Sir, yer good subjects desire ye may be crowned, as the righteous and lawful heir of the crown of this kingdom. But there are conditions - That ye maintain religion as it is presently professed and established. That ye conform to the National Covenant. That according to yer declaration of August last; that ye receive them under yer highness' protection, to govern them by the laws of the kingdom, and to defend them in their rights and liberties..." The man droned on and on.

Charles stifled a yawn. He cleared his ears and caught the last of it.

"...For the maintenance of religion, for the safety of yer Majesty's sacred person, and maintenance of yer crown, which they entreat yer

Majesty to accept, and pray Almighty God that for years ye may happily enjoy the same."

The Prince gave a rehearsed answer, "I do esteem the affections of my good people more than the crowns of many kingdoms, and shall be ready, by God's assistance, to bestow my life in their defense, wishing to live no longer than I may see religion and this kingdom flourish in all happiness." Charles gazed at the faces in the audience. They seemed satisfied. He stood.

The commissioners and noblemen began the walk to the Kirk of Scone, two by two in order according to their rank. The sword was carried by the Earle of Rothes, the scepter by the Earle of Craufurd, and the crown by the Marquis of Argyle. Then came the soon to be king, with the constable on his right hand and the great marshal on his left, his long train being carried by chosen lords and their sons.

The procession entered the Kirk, which had been prepared for the solemn ceremony. There was a table upon which the honors were laid, and a stage. Upon this stage was a chair where his majesty would hear the sermon, and another chair where he would sit to receive the crown. Under this chair was the Stone of Scone. The commissioners and noblemen took seats on benches. The Prince sat in the chair meant for the hearing of the sermon.

Charles pinched the bridge of his nose. He was getting a frightful headache.

The Marquis of Argyle inquired, "Are ye ill, yer Majesty?"

"Nay!" Charles snapped. "You may proceed." He stopped pinching his nose and composed himself.

The minister arrived and began the sermon.

Charles suffered through his boring words. *The things one must endure to regain their throne!* At last, the sermon was done. They escorted him to the chair that sat over the Stone of Scone.

The Marquis of Argyle placed the crown on his head. With great ceremony, he uttered the words that would make him king. The man concluded, "And now, yer Majesty, yer subjects shall approach." They came on bended knees, bearing exquisite gifts – a pistol, a harp, an ancient gold coin... the list was endless. Did they expect him to remember?

King Charles cared nothing for these gifts or the men who gave them. His thoughts were with his murdered father. *I accomplished the first step, Father. With the Scottish army, I will regain my English throne and punish the men who ordered your death. Then all that shall remain will be to kill Lord Gordon.*

Chapter 53
Letters

January 8th 1651

One Week Later

JAMESTOWN

A weathered flag flapped at the general store, indicating that it was open. Dughall and Luc arrived in a horse drawn cart and tied the animals to a hitching post. They climbed up two stairs onto the porch and entered. The pine floor boards creaked.

Dughall spoke softly, "Remember. My name is Duncan."

Luc smiled. "I know, Father!" He picked up a reed shopping basket.

The man behind the counter was attending to a customer, so they looked around as they waited. Being men, they were drawn to a corner where there was a display of guns and firearm supplies.

Dughall gathered up a supply of black powder, flint, and primer and placed them in Luc's basket. "We will need this for extra hunting parties. It's best to get the meat while it's plentiful."

Luc nodded. "What else do we need?"

"Yer mother needs a bolt of sturdy fabric to make breeches for the servants. Their clothes are threadbare." He selected a roll of cloth and set it on the counter. Then he added two spools of thread and a card of needles to the basket. "What else did she say? Ah... Buttons!"

Luc picked out several cards of buttons and tossed them into his basket. "I feel sorry for some of these the men. They're far from home and miss their families."

"Aye. But they're fortunate they came to us. Some prisoners were sold to the islands. They don't live long on those big plantations. The foreman are brutal. I've heard that they whip them."

The shopkeeper concluded with his customer and sent her on her way. Dughall helped her out the door and returned to the counter.

"Duncan and Luc Gordon!" Fergus said. "Always glad to see fellow Scots. Ye're getting stronger, lad. Just look at those muscles!"

Luc grinned. "It comes from hard work. We've been clearing and plowing fields."

"A lad like ye should have a wife. My oldest daughter is looking for a husband."

The young man blushed and looked to his father.

Dughall smiled. "It's all right, Luc. Perhaps ye should meet her."

Fergus slapped the counter. "Good! I'll introduce ye at Church on Sunday. Now, what can I do for ye?"

They placed their purchases on the counter. "The bolt of cloth, everything in the basket, and three tins of baking soda. Oh... and some writing paper if ye have it."

"I do. It's crude paper, though. The carpenter makes it." He retrieved the baking soda and paper, tallied up their purchases, and placed them in a wooden crate. "No charge for the box. Ye're good customers." He passed Dughall a scrap of paper across the counter. "That's the total. Shall I put it on yer account or will ye pay in silver?"

Dughall took out several silver coins and laid them on the counter. "This should cover it."

Fergus picked them up and examined them. "Always glad to get silver." He stashed them in a drawer and appeared to notice something. "There is a package here for yer brother. Will ye take it to him?"

"Aye." Dughall's heart raced as the box was brought forth. The top bore a gilded etching of the head of a lion. It had to be from Drake Castle. The package was sealed with heavy twine, so he tucked it under his arm. "See ye next week."

"Or at Church. Remember?"

Father and son left the store and loaded their purchases into the cart. They untied their horses and climbed up onto the bench seat.

Dughall was clutching the etched box. "Can ye drive for a while?"

"Aye!" Luc grabbed the reins and snaked them across the horses' rumps. "Git!" The wagon lurched forward, shaking the occupants.

"Hey!"

"Sorry, Father. I'll be more careful." The lad skillfully turned the team and wagon. It straightened out and they began the trip back to Eden. "Will ye open it?"

Dughall frowned. "It says it's for Gilbert."

"But it's not! That's one of our boxes."

The lad was right. The Duke had sent a letter to Jamison, shortly after they landed. It was likely he hadn't received it yet. Their agreement was that he should write George Gordon until told otherwise. He set the box on his lap and sliced off the twine. *It could be bad news. Should I open it?*

"Open it!"

Dughall opened the box and extracted two letters. One was written on castle stationery and the other was from the Abbey. He opened the one from Drake. "It's from Ian. It was mailed before we arrived here." He read out loud.

Dear Brother,

I hope that this letter finds ye safe in the Colonies. We've been maintaining the castle and have managed to keep it in good condition. There have been minor disputes among yer subjects, but we've been able to settle them.

The rest I tell ye with a heavy heart. Two hundred of our men perished in the battle with the English. Of those who returned, one said that Fang and Gilroy were captured. The prisoners were taken on a death march. There is little hope of their survival. Edinburgh is occupied by English troops. Scotland is in dire trouble.

There is more to tell. The Prince will soon be crowned King of Scotland. He sent an envoy to the castle to inquire about yer whereabouts. The story relayed by all was that ye were doing business in Paris. I'm not sure he believed it.

I convinced Mother and Father to move to Whinnyfold. I thought there was a chance that the Prince would abduct them to attract ye. My own family is prepared to move to Peterhead at the first sign of trouble.

I must close now. Don't try to return, Brother! Yer life is in mortal danger. Write us when ye can, in care of the party we agreed upon. I have included a letter from yer son. I hope he has better news for ye.

Yer devoted brother, Ian

Luc snapped the reins. "It's a good thing we left Scotland. Will ye tell Mother?"

Dughall was in shock. "Uh... Not now. Can ye keep this secret?"

"Aye."

"I will have to tell Gilbert." He fingered the second letter. "This is from James."

Luc guided the horses around a hole. "Read it, Father."

Dughall unfolded the letter. "The date was October 14th - a few weeks after his birthday." He read out loud.

Dear Father and Mother,

As I write this, I have been at the Abbey for three months. It is hard work being a postulant, but I like it. Brother Adam befriended me and taught me many things about monastic life. The most interesting thing is working with the bees! We captured swarms, tended the scaps, and collected crocks of marvelous honey. Next month, I will learn to make mead, a honey wine fit for royalty. I will save some for my favorite Duke and Duchess.

Father... Yesterday I went to the secret room and read the book about our family. The trials of young Ferraghuss touched my heart. They are an affirmation that I made the right decision.

I miss ye both, as well as my brother and sisters. Tell them that I love them. Perhaps ye can all visit me next August, at the ceremony where I will become a novitiate. How I long to deepen my studies of the liturgy!

Please know I am at peace with my decision. I mean to stay here forever.

May God be with ye and keep ye safe. Yer loving son, James

Luc grinned. "We can show this one to Mother."

"Agreed."

"Will we attend his ceremony?"

"It depends upon what happens with the Prince." His fear blossomed. Would the Prince use James as bait to lure him back to Scotland? "Yer brother's whereabouts must be kept secret. I will write the Abbott tomorrow."

Luc frowned. "I'm yer son too. Am I in danger?"

Dughall sighed. "Not bodily. Neither is James. The Prince will be satisfied when my head is on a spike."

They continued the journey to Eden in silence.

Chapter 54
Visitation

January 15th 1651

One Week Later

DRAKE CASTLE, THE LIBRARY

Donald Grant stood at a window, gazing at the storm in the courtyard below. It was a raw day, with brisk winds and blowing snow. Donald usually stayed home in such weather. The stocky man wasn't getting any younger. His arthritis was kicking up and he had a lung ailment. He shivered and pulled his fur around his shoulders.

The door opened and two familiar men entered.

Jamison and Ian greeted him. "Sir Grant." "My Lord." "How are ye?"

Donald coughed. "My lungs are ailing."

Jamison grunted. "Many are sick at the castle as well. It's the curse of the winter season."

They took seats at a rosewood table, with Grant facing Ian and Jamison.

Jamison looked hopeful. "We haven't seen ye in a while. Do ye have something for us?"

"Aye." Donald handed him a small bundle of letters. "These were delivered to Castle Grant. They are meant for ye." He sniffled. "Several arrived for us as well - one from Lord Drake and one from my nephew Philip. They made it safely to Virginia."

Ian smiled. "Thank God!"

"Yer brother is being careful. He has taken the name Duncan Gordon."

"When were the letters written?"

"Sometime in November."

Jamison eyed the package. "Thank ye for bringing them. 'Tis crucial that we use ye as an agent. Our master is in trouble. The Prince has been inquiring about him."

Donald's stomach twisted with fear. "The Prince was here?"

"Nay, Sir. He sent an envoy. We told him that Lord Drake was in Paris. I doubt that he believed us."

The Laird of Grant took a breath and coughed uncontrollably. He covered his mouth with a handkerchief. "Forgive me."

"Of course. Can we get ye something to drink?"

"Nay." Donald struggled to regain his composure. "I have other news that affects us. Prince Charles has been crowned King."

Jamison clenched his fists. "So, it has happened."

"Aye. They crowned him at Scone on the first of January. He has taken control of our army."

"How do ye know this?"

"They asked me to contribute men and supplies. The commander they sent had loose lips. The King plans to invade England."

Ian stared in disbelief. "Invade England? We lost two hundred men in the last skirmish. How many more will be slaughtered?"

Jamison grunted. "It's strange that the army hasn't approached us. They must not consider us allies."

"We should write my brother about the coronation. He must not return to Scotland."

Donald felt weak. He was suffering from a slight fever. "I must go. Send me yer letters for delivery. Do not trust the usual channels. The King has devious methods." He stood to leave and offered his hand in friendship.

The men joined him. Jamison shook his offered hand. "Thank ye, Sir. We appreciate yer efforts."

"I will act as yer agent as long as I can, for a man I admire and my nephew Philip." He stifled a cough. "Keep me informed about the King. I must know his true intentions."

"We will."

Donald followed the men into the corridor. They went down several flights of stairs, passed the Great Hall, and left the castle. By this time, he was quite winded. They seemed to sense his distress and escorted him to his waiting carriage.

A servant helped him up into the coach and settled his furs around him. As the coach lurched forward, he waved at the men from the window. "Goodbye, my friends," he whispered. "These are dangerous times. May God go with all of us."

Chapter 55
A Time to Sow

February 5th 1651

Three Weeks Later

EDEN, THE COLONY OF VIRGINIA

A day in the life of 'Eden' was characterized by endless activity. The growing plantation supported thirty-two men, women, and children.

The men built cabins, gathered wood, and toted water from the James River. This was done at ebb tide, when it had less salt content. They used water barrels as well, to catch rain from the rooftops. George and Luc hunted and fished, to acquire meat and fish for the supper table.

The women tended the livestock – a cow, pigs, and scores of chickens. They cooked, preserved, washed and sewed clothes, and maintained the homestead. They also taught the children.

Mary and Anne tended the garden and took turns watching the baby.

There were seasonal tasks as well – such as clearing land, planting crops, weeding, and harvesting. This month was the beginning of the planting season.

***

EARLY MORNING

Fang wielded an axe on a tree, showing his men how to 'girdle'. Girdling killed a tree by stripping a ring of bark from its trunk. He'd learned the process from Gilbert, who claimed it came from the Indians. He stripped off the last of the bark with his fingernails. "Arghhhh!"

Today, they were girdling a section of forest to clear the land for food crops. Planting usually waited until the trees died. But girdling had an advantage. Girdled trees lost foliage quickly, allowing the sun to shine through. You could plant corn, beans, and squash between them. The Indians called these crops 'the three sisters'.

Fang handed his axe to a lad. "That's how ye do it!"

Four of his men began to strip the bark. They only had four axes.

The foreman turned his attention to planting. They had three bags of seed, a basket of fish, and a bundle of pointed planting sticks. He'd chosen three men for this duty because they were sons of farmers. "We will plant crops between the girdled trees. The beauty is, we don't have to plow." Fang grabbed a planting stick and drove it into a hill of soil. He opened the seed bags, sank to his knees, and demonstrated. "Put two kernels of corn in the hole and cover it."

A man frowned. "Nothing grows in the shade."

Fang looked up. "These trees will be dead in a week. Soon, there will be plenty of sunshine." He made a deeper hole and buried a fish. "Stinks but makes the soil fertile." Then he made six holes around it and planted bean and squash seeds. Fang stood and brushed off his hands. "Any questions?"

The man scratched his head. "We plant three crops together?"

"Aye. Our master says it will work. The bean vines climb the corn stalks."

"Seems like a waste of trees..."

Fang grunted. "There are plenty of trees in Virginia. After the harvest, we'll chop them down for timber."

The men seemed satisfied with his explanation.

Fang handed them each a planting stick. "Get to work. We have much to do before supper." He walked back to the axe men and grabbed a lad who was faltering. "Give me that axe! Go help the planters. I'd rather girdle."

***

LATE MORNING

Dughall wiped the sweat from his brow as he surveyed the woodland seed beds. They'd been cultivating them all morning with primitive hoes and shovels. Today, there were no masters and servants. He worked alongside them. "Come on, lads! Let's get some water."

Eight Scots walked to a hand-pulled cart and waited for him to dispense the water.

Dughall opened a covered crock and ladled water into a row of tin cups. He observed each man as he handed them out. Gone were the sunken eyes and pasty skin. He was right. A diet with fruit erased the symptoms of scurvy.

A young man sank down and sat on the ground. "Can we rest for a bit?"

Dughall noted the position of the sun in the sky. "For a bit."

The lad's name was Greer. "Thank ye, Sir. I've never seen a master work with his servants."

Dughall smiled. "I like working the soil. It feels good."

"Tell me about growing tobacco, Sir."

He relayed what his brother had taught him, "We sow tobacco seeds in woodland seed beds in February. The forest provides them with just the right amount of sun, shade, and moisture. They grow into seedling plants, which we set in field rows in May."

"Ah."

The lad seemed interested, so he continued, "By July, we have five foot tall stalks with flower buds. Behind each flower is a bulge, the seed pod. When that turns brown, we pop it off and remove the flower. Each pod contains hundreds of tiny seeds, which we save for the next season. By August, the plants are ready to harvest. We cut them close to the ground and impale the leaves on slender sticks."

Greer took a swallow of water, "What are the sticks for?"

"They hold the plants as they hang head down, to wilt and cure until winter."

The young man grinned. "Not much of a winter here."

Dughall laughed. "Ha! Where are ye from, lad?"

"I was born near Edinburgh to a family of cabbage farmers."

"So, ye know something about farming. That's a valuable skill in the Colonies."

The lad stood and placed his cup on the wagon. "Thank ye, Sir, for talking to me. Ye remind me of my father."

Dughall was touched by the tears in his eyes. "Does he still live?"

"Aye."

"We should let him know that ye're safe. I acquired some writing paper at the general store. Would ye like to write him?"

The lad reddened. "I don't know how to write."

Dughall smiled. "I'll help ye."

***

THAT EVENING

The Gordon clan sat on the porch, enjoying a hearty supper. In the distance, the servants gathered around a fire, eating their meal and talking. Connor had decided to join them.

Keira was exhausted. It was hard work cooking for thirty-two people. She was also responsible for sewing clothes and treating wounds and illnesses. The lass smiled. In some ways it reminded her of her former life, in the tiny woodland village. She finished the last bite of sweet potato and placed the tin plate on the floor. "It was good."

Dughall smiled. "That it was, lass."

Maggie was feeding the baby. "She loves squash. But she hates potatoes."

Keira sighed. "I will nurse her later." She was hot and sweaty and a bit upset. She was always more emotional when she had her cycle.

Gilbert set down his plate and addressed his brother. "Sir Berkeley has been pressing me. He wants to know when ye will apply for head rights. There is a three hundred acre tract of prime land available. It's near Eden."

Dughall stiffened. "We should discuss this in private."

This meant 'not in front of the women'. Keira was determined to be part of it. "What are head rights?"

A strained look passed between the brothers.

Gilbert cleared his throat. "Every man, woman, and child who immigrates to Virginia is entitled to fifty acres of land. There are six of ye. That means ye are entitled to three hundred acres. All ye must do is agree to stay here."

Keira frowned. "Stay?" She had prepared herself for one last sea voyage, that would take them home to Scotland.

Bridget spoke softly, "I thought ye liked it here."

"I do. But our son is in Scotland." She'd read his letter a hundred times and longed to attend his ceremony.

Luc put down his plate. "We have to stay here. It's dangerous for Father to return to Scotland."

She suspected they were keeping things from her. "What has happened?"

Dughall reddened. "I don't want to worry ye."

"I deserve to know. Tell me."

Dughall hesitated. "The Prince has been searching for me. It isn't likely to end well. He will soon be crowned King of Scotland."

Keira swallowed hard. "Does he mean to kill ye?"

"In a most unspeakable manner."

Her fear blossomed. "Will he find ye here?"

"I don't think so. He's been told that I'm in France."

"What about our son? Will we send for him?"

Luc spoke, "James found his vocation, Mother. We can't ask him to leave the Abbey."

Her heart sank. "I guess so."

Dughall leaned forward and clasped his hands, "James is safe. Few know of his location. The others might not be so safe. Mother and Father moved to Whinnyfold to avoid abduction. Ian may send his family to Peterhead."

"Is Drake lost, Husband?"

"The Prince hasn't seized it yet." Dughall sighed. "He's waiting for me to return from Paris."

"What will we do?"

His answer shook her world. "I think we should apply for head rights."

She was speechless.

Maggie settled the baby on her knee. "Why did no one tell the women?" She looked to her husband. "Philip?"

The lad reddened. "We tried to protect ye."

"Ye must not! We need to know so we can help Father."

Philip was embarrassed. This was the closest thing they'd had to an argument. "Forgive me, lass."

Keira was close to tears. She loved her husband and wanted him to survive. But they'd left their son in Scotland. When would they see him? Never? "Maggie is right. From now on, I want ye to tell me everything."

Dughall frowned. "Ye may not like it."

They finished the meal in silence.

Keira was on the verge of tears. Without a word, she gathered the plates and took them to the outdoor washtub. As she scrubbed a plate, she sobbed, "My son! My son! Goddess help me."

Chapter 56
Oliver

February 19th 1651
Two Weeks Later

EDINBURGH CASTLE

It had been a difficult autumn for Oliver Cromwell. After the battle of Dunbar, he'd fought to gain control of Edinburgh. The city fell quickly, with the exception of the castle. They finally prevailed in December, when Sir Walter Dundas surrendered it.

Cromwell established a command post in the castle and used it as a residence. At first, he tried to persuade the Scots of the righteousness of his cause. He declared that the English army had no intention of harming the Scottish people. Only those persons who sought the restoration of the Stuart monarchy would be in danger. He tried to convince them that Prince Charles was not a fitting king for a godly people. These efforts failed miserably.

Cromwell's army controlled southern Scotland, but he was unable to dislodge Sir David Leslie from his protected stronghold at Stirling. Leslie commanded the lowest crossing of the River Forth and the landward route into Fife and northeast Scotland.

Cromwell suffered from persistent bowel complaints. Unable to lead, he adopted a strategy of watchful waiting. Then, something happened that changed his game plan. Word arrived that the Prince had been crowned at Scone. The time for negotiation was over. He put Major-General Lambert in charge of his army and commanded him to take Stirling. Desperately ill, he took to his bed.

***

Oliver Cromwell was suffering from a seriously high fever. His muscles ached, his head hurt, and he was having hallucinations. The pious man couldn't get out of bed to sink to his knees to pray. He wondered if he was being poisoned.

Cromwell folded his hands in prayer, "Lord, though I am a miserable and wretched creature, I am in covenant with Thee through grace. Thou hast made me, though unworthy, an instrument to do some good. Many have set too high a value upon me, while others wish me dead. Lord, no matter how thou dispose of me, continue to do them good.

Forgive their sins and do not forsake them, but love and bless them."
Prayer always comforted him. He lay back and tried to sleep.

∗∗∗

There was a knock on the door that startled him. "Come."

A soldier entered. He came to the bedside and snapped to attention.
"Sir!"

Cromwell struggled to sit up. "At ease. What is it?"

"I have a message from Major-General Lambert."

He shivered and drew his blanket higher. "Go on."

"Sir Monck and Sir Deane led a bloody offensive. They stormed
and captured the Scottish strongholds at Blackness." He grinned. "We
secured the south bank of the Firth of Forth."

Cromwell's prayers had been answered. "Thank God! Is there
more?"

"Victory is within reach. He respectfully asks that you join him."

Cromwell smiled in spite of his weakness. "Help me out of this bed!"

CHAPTER 57
ROYAL DETERMINATION

MARCH 12TH 1651

THREE WEEKS LATER

STIRLING

King Charles was disappointed. Days ago, he'd arrived at Stirling to check on the progress of his army. Things were not as expected.

He had to admit that David Leslie had established an impregnable defensive position. The city could not be taken unless he allowed himself to be drawn into the open. Leslie had strengthened defenses, acquired weapons, and recruited thousands of fresh soldiers.

Charles frowned. "It would suffice if my only goal was to keep the Commonwealth army in Edinburgh. We need to retake our capitol, as well as my throne in England." He'd asked for a headcount of troops and was told that there were nine thousand. His head ached at the thought of it. "Four thousand survived the battle of Dunbar. Have we only raised five thousand? How will I invade England?"

The tent flap opened, admitting Sir David Leslie and Major-General Holbourne.

Leslie bowed slightly. "Ye sent for us, Yer Majesty?"

The King nodded. "I did. We have much to discuss."

The three took a seat at a small round table.

Charles began, "I received a disturbing piece of information. One of your officers told me that we have nine thousand troops in total."

A disturbed look passed between the men. Leslie spoke, "That was true at last count."

"When was that taken?"

"A week ago."

Charles took a deep breath. "How many men have arrived in the meantime?"

Leslie paled. "A few hundred."

"This is hard to believe. My agents have been scouring the countryside to raise support for the army. Most of the lords pledged men and supplies."

Major-General Holbourne spoke, "There have been few arrivals in the last month."

"What about Lord Argyll's men? He promised three thousand."

"We haven't seen them."

Charles pinched the bridge of his nose. He was getting a headache. "I was told that Cromwell's army captured our strongholds at Blackness. Do they control the south bank of the Firth of Forth?"

Leslie nodded. "Aye. They are affecting our supply lines."

Charles felt his temper rise. Was he dealing with idiots? "Why was I not told this sooner?"

The excuses began. "We thought we could retake it." "We sent a messenger." "The messenger's horse returned without a rider."

"Enough!" Charles cried. "I wish to be perfectly clear. We are not simply defending Stirling or planning to retake the capitol. We are raising an army to invade England."

Leslie swallowed hard. "When will this happen?"

"Sometime this year. I must move quickly to regain my English throne. We need far more troops than have gathered here." He stared at them until they blinked. "I shall continue to do my part, raising commitments for the army. But I need a monthly accounting of troops. I must know where they came from. How else shall I know who is evading me?"

"We shall keep ye informed."

"Good." The King stood and put on his wrap. "I must go. I will expect my first report in a week. Send it to me care of Drum Castle. I have business to attend to in Aberdeenshire ."

The men stood and bowed slightly. "As ye wish, Yer Majesty."

Charles left the tent and headed for the royal carriage. *Where else have my agents failed me? It's time to make some personal inquiries about Lord Dughall Gordon.*

CHAPTER 58
LONG AWAITED NEWS

JUNE 11TH 1651

THREE MONTHS LATER

EDEN

The sun rose over the sprawling plantation called 'Eden'. A rooster crowed, signaling the start of another long work day.

Dughall lay in bed, admiring the form of his sleeping wife. There wasn't much left to the imagination. They'd slept naked for most of the night because it was hot and sticky. The rooster crowed a second time. Keira stirred, but didn't wake. Her shapely backside faced him. *So bonny. My wife, my companion, my very life.*

Four months had passed since their last argument. It happened after he proposed to stay in Virginia. She'd confronted him and reminded him of his promise – to send for James if they couldn't return to Scotland. The couple argued, but in the end came to a compromise. Their son should make the decision. They wrote James, telling him that they couldn't attend his ceremony. Dughall relayed the truth about his plight and invited the lad to join them.

The letter was sent to the Laird of Grant, who had agreed to act as an intermediary. It was dangerous to send letters to the castle or the monastery. The newly crowned King was searching for the Duke.

Dughall got out of bed and dressed - in yesterday's breeks, a linen shirt, socks, and his sturdiest boots. *I will take her to the general store. Perhaps there will be a letter.*

Keira rolled over and opened her eyes. "Oh. It's morning." She sat up and smiled. "Ye're dressed." Her hair needed a combing.

Dughall found this attractive. "Aye, lass. We have a busy day ahead of us. I thought we'd drive the wagon to town." He grinned. "Gilbert said that a ship arrived. There might be a letter for us."

She looked hopeful. "From James?"

"Four months have passed. It's possible." He welcomed a letter from their son, but part of him dreaded it. She expected the lad to join them. His Sight told him otherwise.

Keira got out of bed and stretched. Her breasts were small but pendulous. "It's so warm here!" She walked to him and snuggled against him.

Dughall's loins swelled. It had been weeks since they made love. He was tempted to strip and take her. "We will finish this tonight, wench." He slapped her bottom. "Get dressed." They separated.

Keira smiled coyly. "I'm done nursing. Perhaps I'll get pregnant." She began to dress in a plain cotton shift. "I'll cook breakfast."

He sniffed. "I smell ham. Maggie has already started it."

"Good." She began to comb her long dark hair.

"Put on sturdy shoes, lass. The roads are rough."

***

George and Luc sat around a camp fire, smoking meat to preserve it. They'd killed and gutted a deer, taken the leanest muscle meat, and cut it into thin strips. These they hung from a rack made of thin branches that traversed the smoky fire. The object was to dry the meat, not cook it. The smoke kept away the blowflies and other egg-laying insects.

George poked the fire with a stick. "Do we need more firewood?" He checked one of the meat strips. "Nay. These are dry."

Luc grunted. "What do we do with them?"

"We take them off the rack and store them in a box."

"How long do they last?"

"Months... But we eat them before then."

Luc used a stick to lift a strip off a branch. It was black on the outside. "They look done." He grinned. "Good thing. Tomorrow, I'm riding with Father to survey our new acreage."

George began to take strips off the branches, putting them in a wooden box. "I'm glad that ye decided to stay."

Luc nodded. "Me, too. This is better than being a Duke's son. Here, I can be a man in my own right."

"Ye're a landowner now. Will ye marry soon?"

"Who?"

"Fergus' daughter Fiona."

Luc reddened. "I've seen her in church and at a few socials."

"The lass has big breasts and dark hair. She's bonny enough."

"Oh, aye." Luc began to kick dirt on the fire. "But there are three men to every woman. I don't know if she likes me."

George was astonished. "Maggie says ye're the only one she talks about!"

"That's not true!"

"I swear it. Why don't ye ask her to dinner?"

Luc blushed. "I think I will."

***

JAMESTOWN

Dughall and Keira arrived at the general store. He helped her down from the wagon and tied the horses to a hitching post. It was a sultry day with temperatures near ninety and nary a breeze to be found. Their cotton clothes were damp with sweat. They climbed several steps onto the hot porch and entered the establishment. Fergus was attending to several customers, so they looked around.

Keira was delighted with the new items – bolts of fine cloth, baskets of notions, quills, writing paper, and books! "Can we afford to buy something?"

"Get what ye want," Dughall said with a smile. "Fergus will put it on our account."

She took a basket and began to fill it. "There are so many things that would make things better. Oh! The children will love this. It's a story book." She handed it to him.

Dughall scanned the first page. "It's a tale that begins in a dark forest." He placed it in her basket. "I hope it's not too scary." He thumbed through two more books and added them. "One is about ancient Greece. We might learn something from it."

Fergus concluded with a customer, who left the store. He spoke to them as he serviced the other. "I'll be right with ye, Duncan and Missus."

Keira selected a packet of writing paper tied with a red ribbon, a quill, a well, and a bottle of ink. "Will ye help me write James and yer Father and Mother?"

"Aye."

Fergus concluded with his customer, a woman they both knew.

Abigail Johnson turned to leave. "Mister and Missus Gordon."

Dughall bowed his head slightly. "Aye. It's good to see ye, Missus Johnson. How is the family?"

Her brow knitted. "The wee one is suffering from a bowel complaint."

Keira frowned, "Poor baby. Have ye tried chamomile tea?"

"Nay. What do ye know of such things?"

"I healed with herbs when we lived in Scotland."

"I shall try it, then." Abigail smiled. "I must go. John must be at his wits' end. He is watching the wee one." She left the store.

Dughall placed their basket on the counter. "This is it."

Fergus tallied up the items. "I just got those books in from England." He scratched a number on a scrap of paper and passed it to Dughall. "That's the total. Shall I put it on yer account?"

"Aye. Thank ye, Fergus."

The storekeeper packed their purchases into a wooden crate. "The box is free. Ye're one of my best customers."

"Thank ye." Dughall cleared his throat. "My brother said that a ship arrived. We were wondering if there was a letter for us."

Fergus looked thoughtful. "I almost forgot! There is a letter." He searched a shallow drawer and found it. "Here it is." He handed it to Dughall.

Keira saw that the envelope bore the seal of Lord Grant. "It could be from our son."

Dughall handed her the envelope. "Thank ye, Fergus." He picked up the crate and grinned. "We will see ye in church on Sunday."

Church attendance was mandatory in Virginia.

Fergus smiled. "Tell Luc that Fiona will be there. She'd like to talk to him."

"We will tell him."

They left the store and loaded the crate into the wagon. Dughall helped Keira up onto the bench seat, unhitched the horses, and joined her.

Keira was a bundle of nerves. At last, they would have their answer. She handed him the envelope. "Can we read it now?"

"Aye." He opened it and took out a one page letter. "It must be from James. It's written on Abbey stationery."

She'd been holding her breath. "Read it, Husband."

He read out loud.

Dearest Mother and Father,

I am grateful to receive yer letter. The Laird of Grant brought it to me personally and is waiting for my reply. Please forgive the haste in which this is written as the man needs to return to his castle.

I was not aware of Father's dire predicament, though in truth, I have sensed it. Our connection is strong in spite of the miles between us. I will miss ye both at the ceremony where I will become a novitiate. But I understand yer absence. I would not risk Father's life for such a selfish purpose. As to yer offer, I appreciate that ye want us to be together. But I have chosen a path to serve God, and that requires me to stay at the Abbey.

Oh, Mother. I understand the fierce love that ye have for me. We were so close, perhaps too close, and now it is time to let me go. Just as Father gave Maggie to Philip, ye must allow me to serve God. Father, please know that I am at peace and sure of my decision. I will someday take solemn vows promising stability, obedience, and chastity. Forgive me, because as such I cannot be yer heir. Ye alone know that this is a wise decision.

I must go now, as Donald Grant is waiting. I love ye both with all my heart and know that we will meet again. God is merciful and God is great! He will not keep us apart. Give my love to my siblings, especially my sister Maggie. May God bless ye and keep ye safe. - Yer loving son, James

Keira let out a strangled sob. "Nay! I can't bear it!" She'd expected the lad to join them.

Dughall's voice was soft. "He loves us, Wife."

Tears ran down her cheeks. "I know."

"We must let him go."

She took the letter and held it to her heart. "Will we ever see him again?"

Dughall snapped the reins and moved the wagon forward. "Aye. I promise." They traveled in silence until they passed the boundary of Jamestown.

Keira sniffled. "Can we write him tonight?"

"Of course."

"I want to tell him that I'm proud of him. And that I will always love him."

CHAPTER 59
TURNING POINT

JULY 20TH 1651

SIX WEEKS LATER

INVERKEITHING, SCOTLAND

It had been a disastrous week for the King's army. Cromwell mounted an amphibious invasion of Fife and drew them from their impregnable position.

Sixteen hundred English crossed the Firth of Forth in flat-bottom boats and established a bridgehead on the northern bank. They were soon joined by 2,500 more troops, under the command of Major-General Lambert. His men hunkered down in hills to the south, where they constructed earthworks and a gun battery.

The King's army was cut off from its supply lines. General Leslie sent Major-General Holbourne and Sir John Browne with 4,000 troops and the MacLean Highlanders to challenge the English bridgehead. Holbourne deployed his troops on high ground near Inverkeithing. Facing fierce English opposition, he withdrew his forces using an attack by Browne's cavalry to disguise the maneuver. They attacked the English flanks, but were soon driven from the field by Lambert's cavalry and infantry. The foot soldiers fled, leaving the MacLean Highlanders to fight alone.

***

Sir Hector MacLean, chieftain of the Maclean Highlanders, knew that he was in a fight to the death. They'd made several failed attempts to break through enemy lines. When they tried to withdraw, they were surrounded by English soldiers.

Warlike, chivalrous, brave, and generous, "Red Hector" was prepared to die a noble death. Several hundred of his clansmen stood with him. Three hundred were already dead.

Red Hector surveyed the ring of English soldiers. They were armed with pikes, swords, and muskets. There would be no escaping this. He stepped forward and raised his sword, "Fight! Fight to the death!"

Enemy soldiers rushed him. Seven brothers came to his defense. As one brother fell, another came forward to cover him, crying "Another for Hector." The fierce fighting continued until the brothers were dead.

Kneeling at the side of the last, Red Hector was killed by a musket shot to the head. He was in good company. Five hundred MacLean Highlanders perished in the battle.

***

Oliver Cromwell was satisfied. His army lost less than two hundred men. A quick body count told him that the King lost two thousand. He ferried the bulk of his troops across the Forth, leaving eight regiments to guard Edinburgh. As his commanders stormed Scottish strongholds, he took a large force north to the city of Perth, which surrendered to him on August 2nd.

Now, Cromwell was getting ready to leave Perth. Pointing at a map, he relayed his concerns to Major-General Lambert, "My advance north left the road to England open. Charles may decide to invade."

Lambert frowned. "We can't let that happen."

Cromwell coughed. "On the contrary, the Scots-Royalist army will garner little support in England. I could defeat him there more decisively."

Lambert nodded. "How do we get him to invade?"

"I left Sir Monck with six thousand troops and half of the artillery train to attack Stirling. He promised to put on a good show. The Prince is barely wet behind the ears. He may assume that we've left England unprotected. We will take the bulk of our forces south, recruit, resupply, and establish a position."

"Do you think he'll fall for it?"

Cromwell coughed. "I'd bet my life on it." He rolled up the map. "Let's move out."

Chapter 60
A Rash Decision

August 3rd 1651
One Day Later

STIRLING

King Charles was in a terrible mood. He'd just learned that Perth surrendered to Cromwell. "How dare they surrender? They should fight to the death!"

Sir David Leslie stood next to him. "We cannot blame them, my King. The city of Perth was undefended."

Charles reddened. "How can we defend every city when my army is under siege?" It was true. Stirling had been under siege since he arrived here a week ago. He pinched the bridge of his nose to stave off a headache. "Must I do everything myself?"

Leslie stared. "Nay, yer Majesty."

Charles took a deep breath. He was starting to see stars in his field of vision. *What would Father have done? Analyze... Strategize...* "The bulk of the English army is in Perth. Is that correct?"

"Aye."

"The rest is here in Fife, attacking Stirling and Dundee."

"Aye."

He was beginning to formulate a plan. "Cromwell left England unprotected! How many men do we have?"

"Fourteen thousand."

The King was sweating. *Breathe, Charles...* He took a series of measured breaths.

"Yer Majesty?" There was fear in his face. "Fourteen thousand is a fraction of the English army."

The King paced the room. "Nevertheless, we must invade England and take London. I will raise troops as we march through Lancashire and along the Welsh border. Royalists and Presbyterians will join us by the thousands."

David Leslie frowned. "When would we do this?"

Charles was irritated. "Why, tomorrow of course."

He looked shocked. "We would leave Stirling and Dundee undefended?"

The King took a deep breath. He was developing an intense dislike for this man. "Yes. What does it matter? Edinburgh is occupied. Perth has fallen. When I conquer London, it's all mine."

"As yer commander, I cannot recommend this."

There was dead silence.

Charles seethed with anger. "I see. Then, I assert my authority as commander-in-chief of this army. We shall begin an advance into England tomorrow."

David Leslie paled. "As ye wish, yer Majesty."

"Ready the troops!" He raised his hand in disgust. "Leave me now."

Leslie bowed and left the room.
***

Charles paced in front of the windows. "Idiot! What kind of commander is this? He does not understand strategy." The King fumed until his headache worsened. He lay down on a couch and pinched the bridge of his nose. *Breathe, Charles... Breathe... Think of something pleasant... Ah, yes... My search for Lord Dughall Gordon...*

His search in Paris had netted him nothing. He was convinced that the man was hiding out in Scotland. But he'd been clever. Everyone they interviewed said that he'd gone to France. He certainly covered his tracks well. There was one detail that intrigued him. They'd talked to a peasant who worked for the late Lord Skene. The sniveling man said that Lord Gordon's son was staying at a nearby Abbey. His sources verified this.

Charles smiled. His headache was almost gone. "After I regain my English throne, I will seize his son and imprison him in the Tower. That should flush out Lord Dughall Gordon."

Chapter 61
Shocking News

August 4th 1651

One Day Later

VIRGINIA

Dughall sat on the porch, enjoying a hearty supper with his family. On each plate, there was a generous portion of rabbit stew, a dollop of sweet potatoes, and a piece of corn bread. When they were done, Bridget passed around a plate of cranberry scones.

Dughall wondered what the women were up to. It wasn't anyone's birthday. He washed down the sweet cake with a swallow of water. "These are good."

Keira smiled. "We added some scrapings of sugar cane. It's almost as sweet as honey."

He sensed that they had something to tell him. "What's going on?"

A strange look passed between the women.

Maggie took the plate from her lap and placed it on the floor. She grasped Philip's hand and squeezed it. They gazed at each other as couples had done since the beginning of time. "We have an announcement. I'm with child."

Dughall wondered if he heard her right. *How can she be pregnant? She's fourteen years old! We've been working so hard. When would they have had the strength to do it?* Then, he remembered what he was like at Philip's age. Nothing would have stopped him.

"Father?"

They were staring at him. He had to say something. "Are ye sure?"

Maggie smiled like an angel. "Aye, Father. I've missed three cycles. Ye're going to be a grandfather."

Philip grinned. "I hope that ye're pleased, Sir."

Dughall hid his true emotions. "Of course. We are about to have our first addition to the Gordon-Grant clan."

Philip was delighted by the mention of his name. "Thank ye, Sir."

Keira passed the plate. "Take the last scone, Husband. It's small."

Dughall put it in his mouth and chewed. As he swallowed, he got a strange feeling. They weren't done telling him things. "What else, Wife?"

Keira blushed. "I... uh... didn't want to spoil Maggie's announcement." She wiped her hands on her apron. "I thought ye knew. Ye always did before."

Dughall stared. It couldn't be. "Ye're pregnant?"

"Aye."

He felt like he'd been hit with a ton of bricks. How could he not have sensed it? They'd been so damned tired when they fell into bed at the end of each day. "How long?"

"Two cycles."

"We're getting old. Could it be that..."

She reddened. "Nay. I have morning sickness."

Dughall sensed that she was about to cry. He stood and embraced her. "Don't fret, lass. I'm happy about it. It's a shock to learn that I'm to be a father and grandfather in the same day."

She relaxed in his arms and they separated.

Gilbert smiled. "Congratulations, Brother! Perhaps it will be a son." The rest went unspoken. There was a chance that he would return to Drake. As a monk, James could not succeed him. Neither could Luc.

Dughall said the right thing, "Lad or lassie. Either will be fine."

Gilbert smiled knowingly. "Of course." He brought forth a bottle of rum. "Perhaps the men will join me for a smoke and a drink in the barn."

***

They left the women to clean up and retired to the barn, taking their pewter mugs with them – Gilbert, Dughall, George, Luc, and Philip.

Gilbert poured them a generous round and raised his mug in a toast. "Here's to the Gordon-Grant clan of Virginia. May we grow in numbers."

Philip joined him. "And prosper."

"Aye." Dughall took a long swallow and felt it burn to his belly. He was feeling better. "But I'm getting too old to father any more. The young men must do their part."

Luc blushed. "Father!"

"Fiona is lovely girl, son. Perhaps, ye'll have an announcement soon."

George grinned. "Ye've been seeing her for two months! It's no secret. Fiona is determined to marry ye."

Luc bolted his rum. "I like her. I just don't want to force her to do anything."

Dughall suspected that this stemmed from the abuse he suffered. They'd never discussed the act. He made a mental note to speak to him. "We'll talk later, Son."

They retrieved their pipes from the top of a barrel and proceeded to light them. It was a nightly ritual. Dughall inhaled deeply. Their tobacco was mild and flavorful. He blew it out in a ring and watched it dissipate. "Ah… Life is good."'

They nodded their heads in agreement.

***

It was a typical Virginia evening – so hot and humid that it was almost unbearable. Dughall invited Luc to join him on a walk to inspect the chicken coop. They'd built the crude structure to protect their flock. But it had been recently harassed by varmints.

Dughall lit an oil lantern and tossed the taper into the campfire. "We lost another hen yesterday. Anne found feathers behind the coop, alongside a severed foot. The wee lassie was hysterical."

Luc carried a flintlock pistol. "Anne is too attached to those chickens. She shouldn't name them." He called Artus to his side. "Do ye think it's a fox?"

"Aye, or a raccoon."

"In either case, we can use the pelt."

They began walking towards the coop. Biting insects were out in full force.

Dughall swatted a mosquito. "Ach!"

Luc held a hand out in a silent signal. "Shhhh...." Artus had run ahead and was standing still, pointing at something behind the coop. They heard growling. "It must be a 'coon!"

They ran to the coop. Now, Artus was barking, running circles around the trapped animal.

Dughall raised the lantern. "That's the biggest raccoon I've ever seen!" Grayish brown with black markings, it had to go thirty pounds. "Look! It got another hen."

The animal was snarling, guarding its catch.

Luc cocked the hammer until it set and aimed carefully. "Get back, Artus!" The dog obeyed instantly and Luc pulled the trigger.

Dughall watched the animal drop. "Ye got him!"

Luc grunted. "I always do." He poked the body with the butt of his gun. "Dead. Let's take it back to barn. I'll skin it tomorrow." He stroked the dog's head. "Good boy, Artus. Raccoon meat is nasty. I'll give it to the dogs."

Dughall took a rope and bent over the carcass. He tied the legs together, leaving a length of rope on each side to carry it. Each man took an end and they headed for the shack where they slaughtered animals.

Once inside, Luc placed the raccoon on a table. "This can wait until tomorrow."

Dughall put the lantern on the table and gazed at his son. The lad's skin was tanned from the sun. He was more handsome than ever. "Ye're a fine hunter."

Luc grinned. "Thank ye, Father."

"I'm glad that we did this together. It gives me a chance to talk to ye."

The lad reddened. "About Fiona?"

"Aye. She's a fine, lass. But only ye can decide if she's right for ye. Marriage is a serious commitment."

Luc nodded. "I know. I like her. We've held hands and kissed. But I don't want to force her to do anything." This was what he'd said before.

"Ye're referring to the act of love."

"Aye, Father."

Dughall saw an opening. "We don't force women to make love. They do it because they want to. There are things ye can do to make them ready."

His eyes widened. "There are?"

"Aye. I can tell ye about them. There's just one condition."

"What?"

"Ye must reserve them for marriage."

Luc smiled. "I will."

"And ye must never repeat what I tell ye."

"All right."

Dughall tapped the oil lantern. They had fuel for a half hour. He spoke in low tones, "Let me tell ye how to please a woman. Then ye must tell her what ye want."

The lad was riveted to his words.

Dughall sighed. "There once was a woman who taught me everything."

"Mother?"

"Nay. The woman was my father's mistress. Her name was Kate Gunn..."

They talked until the lantern burned out.

CHAPTER 62
BATTLE OF WORCESTER

SEPTEMBER 3RD 1651
ONE MONTH LATER

WORCESTER ENGLAND

THE NEW MODEL ARMY'S ENCAMPMENT, DAWN

Oliver Cromwell was feeling confident. The royalist army was surrounded. All of the King's potential routes to London were cut off and English forces blockaded the road back to Scotland. It hadn't been an easy task.

***

The Council of State in Westminster had done their part, calling out the militia. Lieutenant-General Fleetwood drew together the midland contingents. The London trained bands reported for service at more than 14,000 strong. Suspected Royalists were watched and stockpiles of arms in the gentry's houses were removed to guarded places.

Cromwell left his least efficient regiments to carry on the war in Scotland and began the march southward. Upon hearing that Charles entered England, he dispatched Lieutenant-General Lambert with the cavalry to harass the invaders. Major-General Harrison arrived at Newcastle and picked the best county mounted troops to add to his regulars.

The King's army arrived at Kendal on August 9th. But Lambert's forces hovered in their rear and Harrison's forces barred their way forward. They joined forces on August 15th and fell back, to avoid a fight along the London road.

Cromwell's army marched twenty miles a day in extreme heat, with country people carrying their arms and equipment. Along the way, they soundly defeated the Lancashire royalists lead by the Earl of Derby. The New Model army reached Ferrybridge on August 19th. It seemed probable that a great battle would take place in that vicinity, and that Cromwell, Harrison, Lambert, and Fleetwood would take part in it. But the enemy's movements changed the venue.

In a surprise move, the King abandoned his march on London and headed for the Severn Valley, where his father found support in the first war. He was joined by Sir Edward Massey and his men, who tried to raise support among fellow Presbyterians. Charles arrived in Worcester on August 22nd and spent five days resting his troops and gathering new recruits.

The bulk of Cromwell's troops gathered on the west bank of the Severn, preparing to attack the city from the south. His artillery and the rest of the army stayed on the hills to the east of the city. With the bridges damaged, they needed something to connect the two wings. Cromwell knew just how to do it. On August 30th, he delayed the start of the battle so that two pontoon bridges could be constructed, one to go over the River Severn and the other over the River Teme near their confluence. He picked a time to install them.

***

For the first time in his career, Cromwell had a two-to-one advantage. The royalist army was barely 16,000. His army was well over 32,000. He delayed the launch of the attack until the 3rd of September, one year to the day since his victory at Dunbar. The date was a good omen. God was smiling upon them.

***

THE KING'S ENCAMPMENT, OFFICER'S TENT, EARLY MORNING

Sir David Leslie was in a terrible state. He'd just been informed that they were vastly outnumbered. He suspected as much on the march south. When English royalists did not rise up to support the King, he became increasingly morose and pessimistic. Worse yet, Sir Massey was badly wounded in a skirmish. The Earl of Derby lived, but his forces had been defeated.

Leslie turned his eyes to heaven. "God help us!"

"What was that, Sir?" a lieutenant asked.

Leslie reddened. "Nothing. Go about yer business." He composed himself and headed for the King's quarters.

***

THE KING'S ENCAMPMENT, THE KING'S TENT,
EARLY AFTERNOON

King Charles paced his tent. The emotion he felt was close to rage. Earlier, he'd been informed by his general that they were vastly outnumbered.

The campaign had been a disappointment. He'd expected support from English royalists and Presbyterians, but came up empty handed. His army was almost purely Scottish. They'd fortified their position at Worcester by making repairs to existing earthworks and destroying bridges to hamper the English advance. He'd issued a proclamation summoning all loyal subjects to rally to his standard, but few Englishmen or Welshmen responded.

Charles had a fierce headache. "They ignored me! When I am crowned, they will suffer for this."

David Leslie entered the tent. He bowed slightly. "Come quickly, yer Majesty. We are under attack."

Charles felt the anger rise in him. He had an intense dislike for this man. "What is it?"

Leslie flinched. "A fleet of great boats is advancing up the west bank of the Severn. They look like pontoons."

"Pontoons? How far away are they?"

"Almost to the River Teme."

"God damn them! They intend to use them as a bridge. How did they get past our scouts?"

The officer shrugged. "They must have killed them."

Charles scowled. "If they're not dead, I'll kill them myself!" He threw on his wrap. "Who commands the men at the Teme?"

"Major-General Montgomery is camped in Powick Meadows on the north bank. Colonel Keith and Colonel Pitscottie are with him."

"Hmmphhh! I must see what is going on. Take me to the tower of Worcester Cathedral so that I can watch the battle." He threw back the flap and they left the tent. His head was pounding so hard that he was nauseous. "We must not allow them to construct the floating bridges."

✳✳✳

Lieutenant-General Fleetwood's pontoon boats arrived at the rivers' confluence and began to construct the bridges. His forces disembarked and advanced in two columns. Major-General Deane led an attack on Powick Bridge to the west to divert attention from the second column, which was responsible for securing the bridges of boats across the Severn and the Teme. A contingent of musketeers crossed the Teme in boats to cover the construction of the floating bridges.

The fighting along the Teme was bitter. The King's men fought fiercely. Colonel Keith held Powick Bridge against Deane's attempt to force a crossing, while Colonel Piscottie's Highlanders drove back Fleetwood's forces as they crossed a pontoon over the Teme.

Noting the difficulties on his left wing, Cromwell led three brigades across the pontoon over the Severn and attacked Piscottie's flank. The Highlanders fell back, demoralized. Colonel Keith was captured as Deane crossed the bridge. The Scottish position collapsed as Cromwell gained control of the north bank of the Teme.

When General Montgomery was badly wounded, the Scots fled backward towards Worcester pursued by English soldiers. So many followed that the English position on Red Hill and Perry Wood was weakened.

✳✳✳

Watching the desperate battle from the tower, the King saw an opening. Charles rushed down the stairs and rallied his troops to attack the English east of the river. The attack was two pronged. The King commanded the thrust against Red Hill, while the Duke of Hamilton attacked Perry Wood. They were supported by cavalry.

The King rode on a magnificent white steed. "Advance! Advance!" he cried, brandishing a sword. Anger ran through his blood like a current of fire.

His forces advanced through Sidbury Gate covered by their artillery and charged the English forces uphill. Fierce fighting ensued.

Charles yelled, "Don't protect me. Fight! Fight!" The men about him scattered. Galloping to a skirmish, his horse was killed beneath him. He quickly commandeered another.

David Leslie approached on horseback. "My King! The Duke of Hamilton is dead. They blew his head off."

The young man grimaced. "Dear God! Where is Cromwell?"

"He has returned to the Severn pontoon bridge with three brigades."

"He must mean to reinforce it."

Shots rang out and the horse began to drop. Charles slid off just before it fell. "Pass the word! We shall retreat back to Worcester."

Leslie gave him his horse and ran on foot to inform the others.

Arriving back in the city, Charles found his troops laying down their arms. He admonished them, "I command you – upon your honor and loyalty – charge!"

They refused to advance on the enemy.

The King pointed out a man who protested. "Kill this man!"

But no one would do it.

Charles gritted his teeth. *I will deal with them later.* He ran to the Cathedral and climbed stairs to the tower to get a bird's eye view of the battle. What he saw horrified him. There was a hill to the south-east of Worcester called Fort Royal. Charles had fortified this area with his heavy artillery. It was an important part of his defenses. From his perch in the tower, he saw the English storming it.

Charles watched in horror as the English turned the guns on Worcester. His remaining troops were scattering. "Have we lost?"

The Duke of Buckingham joined him and yelled over the sound of the big guns. "You must flee, Your Majesty!"

The King felt like vomiting. "I cannot."

The Duke was a friend. He squeezed his shoulder with affection. "There isn't much time. They are preparing to storm what is left of our defenses."

Charles was stunned. "Must I run away like a coward?"

"Don't think of it that way. You will live to fight another day."

"But my crown!"

The Duke stared. "I do not wish to see you lose your head like your father. Cromwell *will* take it."

Charles felt his heart drop. The man was right. "I will flee. But God's will shall prevail. Someday, I will be King of England."

Night was beginning to fall. Shots rang out and men screamed in agony. Cromwell's forces were beginning to breach the city. They descended the stairs with trepidation and joined Lord Wilmot and the Earl of Derby.

As his soldiers died by the thousands, Charles left Worcester by the northern gate with three loyal companions. He never suspected that he would spend six desperate weeks as a fugitive in his beloved England.

CHAPTER 63
AFTERMATH OF THE BATTLE

OCTOBER 31ST 1651

TWO MONTHS LATER

PARIS, FRANCE, PALAIS DU LOUVRE

King Charles was depressed. He'd just presented his case to the Regency Council and his twelve-year-old cousin, Louis XIV. Not only had they refused to help him regain his crown, the boy king ridiculed him. That left him only one option – exile. *Oh, Father! How did it come to this?*

Henrietta Maria entered his chamber, wearing a modest black dress and a lace head piece. She looked regal even though she was no longer Queen. Her expression was solemn. "My son."

Charles rose to greet her. "Mother." He immediately poured out his problems. "My cousin will not help me regain my crown. He laughed at me!"

Henrietta clicked her tongue. "Such are the conditions I have lived under since the death of your father." She embraced him. "At least you are alive. I worried that they might capture you."

Charles frowned. "They almost did." He motioned to a brocade couch and they sat down together. She arranged her skirts around her. He began his harrowing tale. "The road to London was blocked, so we settled at Worcester and fortified our position. Cromwell's forces outnumbered us two-to-one. They attacked first. It was a terrible bloody battle. I fought alongside my men and had two horses killed beneath me. The Duke of Buckingham convinced me to flee."

Her eyes were wide. "I am grateful to him."

"As am I. We escaped through the northern gate of the city and rode to Breewood Forest, where I stayed at the Boscobel estate."

"The home of the Giffards," she remarked.

"Aye. There I exchanged my clothes for the garb of a peasant – a crude shirt, leather breeches, and a floppy felt hat. Imagine! They cut my hair short and I imitated a country accent." He took a breath. "Even so, Cromwell's search parties nearly captured me. I hid in a hollow oak tree for an entire day with a companion. We ate bread and cheese and drank beer, while soldiers scoured the area. I heard them talking."

Henrietta Maria made the sign of the cross. "Mon Dieu!"

Charles continued, "The Boscobel estate had secret places – a priest hole, a chapel, an a sheltered arbor. I slept in a loft and left the next morning, dressed as a peasant. This time, we took refuge at Moseley Hall. Soldiers stopped at this house and almost searched it. By this time, Cromwell had offered 1,000£ for information leading to my capture." He was feeling tired and discouraged. "Oh, Mother. There is more to tell. I spent six weeks as a fugitive in my own country! I moved from house to house, praying that they were true royalists."

"By God's grace, they were."

"If not for their help, I would be captured or beheaded. Finally, I boarded a ship at Shoreham and sailed for France."

She smiled. "You sought out your mother."

Charles stared. Was she serious? "NO. I sought out my cousin, the King of France. I thought he might help me regain my throne."

Henrietta looked like she'd been slapped. "Oh. But Louis refused you."

Charles rubbed his temples. Why must she state the obvious? "Enough! I *will* regain my crown someday. Those who opposed me will suffer."

Henrietta squeezed his arm and stood to leave. "Have faith, my son. Pray to God for guidance. He is the only one who can help you." She smoothed her skirts. "I must go now and see your sister." She left the room.

Charles lay back on the couch and took a deep breath. He loved his mother, but she drove him to distraction. No wonder his father was unfaithful to her. "Forget her! Breathe, Charles. Breathe! Imagine a perfect garden." He was getting a fierce headache. "Women! I wish I could talk to Father."

***

AYLESBURY, BUCKINGHAMSHIRE, ENGLAND

Oliver Cromwell sat in the King's Head Inn, writing a return letter to William Lenthall, the Speaker of the House of Commons. He'd just received the sincere thanks of Parliament for his final defeat of the Royalists.

It had been a hectic two months. Cromwell pursued Charles throughout England in an attempt to capture or kill him. Though unsuccessful, he chased the King out of England and Scotland. His spies said that he was in France, living in exile. Cromwell dispensed the prisoners by sending them abroad as indentured servants. He dismissed his militia after giving them praise and honors. Lastly, he negotiated with the powers in Edinburgh, to bring the Scots people into the Commonwealth.

Oliver inked a quill and poised it over a sheet of paper. He began to write.

Dear William,

I humbly accept your praise and thanks for our final defeat of the Royalists. Please know that I did not do this alone. I owe much to the men of the New Model Army, their brave commanders, and the militia, who performed beyond my expectations. But most of all, I owe God my gratitude. This victory was the greatest of all the favors or mercies given to me by God. The dimensions of this mercy are above my thoughts. It is, for aught I know, a crowning mercy.

I shall return soon to London. Hopefully, we can spend some time together to discuss the matter further.

Your humble servant,
Oliver Cromwell

***

JAMESTOWN, VIRGINIA

Gilbert finished his business at the courthouse. He was pleased with the outcome. His stature in Virginia was growing by leaps and bounds. Having served as Justice of the Peace, he was being asked to take a turn as Sheriff. It was a lucrative position with perks and compensation. Usually, a Justice would serve three years before being offered the position of Sheriff. But Governor Berkeley had requested him.

Gilbert smiled. "Such an honor! I will give him my answer at Church on Sunday."

By contrast, his brother had taken pains to stay out of politics. Gilbert didn't blame him. Virginia was a royalist colony. They might fall out of favor if the Governor discerned his position. It was best that he stay in the background.

Gilbert retrieved his stallion and rode to the general store. He'd promised Bridget that he would purchase some tea, a rare commodity in the colonies. She wanted to serve it for his brother's birthday. He stopped at the store, dismounted, and tethered his horse to a hitching post. The flag was down but the store looked open. He climbed several stairs to the porch and entered.

Fergus was storing the tobacco products under the counter. He raised an eyebrow. "George Gordon!"

"Am I too late?"

"Nay. I'm closing up. Ye can be my last customer."

Gilbert smiled. "I won't be long. I'd like three pounds of tea for my wife."

Fergus stared. "Three pounds? That will be expensive."

"I can afford it. I've just been offered the job of Sheriff."

Fergus grinned. "A fellow Scot as the Sheriff! I never thought I'd see it." He reached below the counter and took out a bottle and two small glasses. "We should celebrate. Will ye join me in a dram of whisky?"

Whisky was as rare as tea in the colonies. Gilbert watched him pour the amber liquid. He accepted the glass and took a long swallow. "It's good."

Fergus took a sip. "Aye. Have ye heard the news about the King?"

"Nay."

"A ship arrived from London an hour ago. I spoke to the captain. In September, the King invaded England with the Scottish army. Cromwell's forces outnumbered them two-to-one. The canny Puritan defeated them."

Gilbert was shocked. "What about the King?"

"King Charles escaped capture. They think that he's gone into exile."

"He didn't go back to Scotland?"

"Nay. They're not sure where he is."

"What happened to our army?"

Fergus sighed. "Three thousand of our countrymen were killed. Ten thousand were taken prisoner. Several officers were executed. The captain said that thousands of Scots are on the way to the colonies to be sold as indentured servants."

Gilbert bolted his whisky. It burned a trail to his belly. "We can take some of them."

Fergus grunted. "Good. The Gordons will be fair with them." He opened a barrel and began to scoop tea leaves into a sack. After several weighing attempts, he closed it. "There. Just a bit over three pounds."

Gilbert accepted the sack. "Thank ye for the dram, friend. I must get home. It's my brother's birthday."

"Ah. Do ye need a gift? I have a bottle of whisky for sale."

He hesitated. "Put it on my account."

The storekeeper retrieved the bottle and gave it to him. "Looks like ye have things to discuss tonight - good and bad. One thing for sure... Everything looks better through a glass of whisky."

Gilbert smiled. "Ha! My father used to say that. See ye at Church on Sunday." He left the store, stuffed his purchases in the saddlebag, untied the horse and mounted. After a quick glance at the sky, he began the ride to Eden. He urged the horse into a trot. "It's later than I thought. They must be wondering about me." He left the outskirts of the city.

Gilbert looked forward to the evening. They had two things to celebrate – Dughall's birthday and his promotion to Sheriff. After that, the men would retire to the smoking barn and discuss the trouble with the King. There was no point bothering the women. Two of them were in a delicate condition.

***

THE HUNTING LODGE, CASTLE GRANT, SCOTLAND

Donald Grant sat in a comfortable chair, opposite Lord Drake's manservant. The men were warmed by a crackling fire and surrounded by the heads of stuffed animals. He filled two glasses with whisky and handed one to his guest. "Let's toast." He held up his, "To freedom from Kings!"

Jamison joined him. "Aye! The snake has abandoned Scotland. "

Grant had just received news that the King surfaced in France and intended to stay in exile. Their own parliament was negotiating with Cromwell and was expected to revoke the King's title. The rumor was that they would now be part of the Commonwealth.

Jamison took a sip. "This whisky is excellent."

"'Tis made by my own distillery, with the pure waters of the Spey."

"Ah."

Donald sighed. "Too bad that it took a bloodbath to get rid of the King. I lost two hundred men, one of them a favorite nephew."

Jamison grunted. "Did he die in battle?"

"I suspect so. There has been no word from him."

"Perhaps he is among the prisoners who were sent to the islands or the colonies. I can ask my master to look out for him. What's his name?"

"Peter Grant."

They were quiet for a moment. At last, Jamison spoke, "Do ye think it's safe for me to write Lord Drake?"

Donald nodded. "Aye. Yer master is safe. Charles will wish to keep his head. He won't set foot in Scotland." He took a sip. "Where is Ian Hay?"

The servant frowned. "Ian moved to Peterhead. The King's men were questioning our subjects, asking about extended family. As my master's stepbrother, we feared that he would be taken into custody."

"I see. Will ye inform Ian about the King?"

"Aye. I hope he comes back to the castle."

"What about the lad in the monastery? Young James?"

"I will visit him personally and tell him the news."

Grant finished his drink. "The war is over. Lord Drake can return when he wants to. Shall we write him together?"

The servant smiled. "I'd like that."

Donald refilled their glasses. "Ye're a good man, Jamison. It's not easy running a castle in yer master's absence. If ye ever need a new assignment, I'd be interested."

Jamison accepted his glass. "I'll keep that in mind, Sir."

"Good." He smiled. "Let's write that letter. There's a ship leaving for the colonies tomorrow."

Chapter 64
A Blessed Event

January 15th 1652

Two and a Half Months Later

EDEN PLANTATION, VIRGINIA

Luc ran stealthily through the woods with Artus at his side. He'd been waiting for George when he spotted the rump of a deer upwind fifty yards away.

The deerhound panted as he ran.

"Easy, Artus," the lad whispered. We'll get him."

It was crucial that he take down a deer or two in the next few days. Their meat supply was getting low. More people lived at the plantation now, his wife Fiona and twenty new indentured men. That made a total of fifty-three mouths to feed. Soon, there would be more. Maggie's baby was due any day. Keira's was due next month.

Luc stopped to look at some tracks. They were heavy and sank into the wet ground. It was a buck, and a big one at that. It looked like he'd dragged his feet when he came out of a step. "We spooked him, Artus." He followed the tracks, carrying his musket, and came upon a cluster of oaks. There were bushes nearby and the twigs were bent. *He came through here.*

The deerhound's athletic body quivered with anticipation. He let out a low throaty growl.

"I see him, Artus. Get him!"

The dog sprang through the trees. Luc followed with his heart pounding. They emerged in a clearing and saw a giant buck. "My God!"

The buck tried to escape, but the dog was on him. The canine jumped on the hind quarters of the deer and dug his teeth in. The buck reared and tried to kick him.

Luc admired the dog's courage. He stepped back to prepare his musket. He'd previously loaded it. Now, he had to prime it. He opened a bag and poured ten grains of powder into the priming pan. Pulling back on the steel with the small finger of his right hand, he closed the pan.

The buck was thrashing. Artus was in mortal danger.

"Hang on, boy!" Luc wrapped his left hand wrapped around the stock and used his right hand to cock it. He aimed carefully and fired. The sound was deafening and smoke billowed from the weapon. The lad saw that he hit the deer to the rear of the shoulder. This was the best place to fell a deer with one shot as it hit the vital organs. The animal squealed and began to fall. "Jump off, Artus!"

The dog obeyed instantly and came to his side. He was splattered with blood and sinew.

Luc stroked his head. "Good boy." He approached the fallen animal. The buck kicked feebly and then stopped dead. The lad was lucky. There was no need to waste another shot.

"Luc!" George entered the clearing and let out a low whistle. "It's a monster. We'll never be able to drag it."

"I'm glad to see ye," Luc said. He noted that the lad carried a pistol. "Stay here and guard the carcass. I'll fetch our tools so we can dress it."

George grinned. "Father will be pleased. Bring a few men and a pole to carry it."

Luc nodded. "I will." He called the dog to his side and sprinted towards the farm house.

***

Dughall stood outside, supervising a group of men putting up a cottage. Their plantation was growing by leaps and bounds. They desperately needed more housing. He and Philip had been running the plantation because Gilbert was gone so much. As Sheriff, he collected taxes, responded to sticky situations, and administered justice. The compensation was good, but it required a lot of time.

Dughall walked to where they had erected a pit saw, a device used to cut crude planks from a log. Weeks ago, they dug a pit that was six feet deep and three feet wide. The men had joked that it looked like a hole for a coffin.

A pit saw was a remarkable device. It was manned by two men with a long two-handled saw. The timber to be cut was stripped of bark and set over a pit, sometimes on a scaffold. The top sawyer stood on the log and guided the saw up along a line marked by charcoal. The pitman stood in the pit under the log, time after time pulling the saw down on its cutting stroke. Sawing a good-sized tree into planks was a grueling task that could take as long as a week.

Dughall watched the men as they wielded the saw. Fang stood shirtless on top of the log, using his great strength to pull the blade up. Another man, a former blacksmith, stood in the pit ready to draw it back down.

Fang grunted. "Ach! Yer turn." The cut was made and the pitman began to pull it down.

Dughall grimaced. "Good work, Fang! Pull it straight, Robertson." This was back breaking work. He resolved to build a water powered sawmill, like the one he saw in Boston. He heard someone yell and turned to see Luc running towards him. The dog was at his side.

Luc stopped when he got to the saw and held his knees to catch his breath. "We killed a giant buck! It must be three hundred pounds. Too big to drag back. I will get my tools to dress him, but I need help bringing him back."

Dughall grinned. "Thank God! We are low on meat." He assigned two men to help him. "Smith. Bell. Bring a long pole and some ropes. After he guts him, the four of ye can carry him back."

Luc ran off to the slaughtering shed with the two men. They retrieved his tools and a pole and three ropes. Then, they ran into the woods with the dog at their heels.

Dughall smiled. His son had blossomed since his marriage a month ago. Luc was happy and self confident. Fiona had been a welcome addition to their family. The lass was no stranger to hard work, and helped the women with cooking, washing, and sewing. It was especially important now that Maggie was close to giving birth. His beloved daughter would soon be a mother.

Dughall wondered how he would leave this place. After Christmas, he'd received a letter from Donald Grant and Jamison, informing him that it was safe to return. The King was in exile with a price on his head. He would not dare to set foot to Scotland.

Dughall frowned. *How can I leave? Luc has made a life here. Philip says that he intends to stay. Maggie and Keira are pregnant.* He'd told them the news to relieve their worry. His life was no longer in danger. But an unspoken question hung in the air – would he return to Scotland? One thing was sure, Keira would not be ready for a sea voyage until the new baby was done with nursing. He sighed. *I will have to go by myself to check on my estate and my subjects.* It wasn't all bad. *I will see James and visit Ian and Mother and Father. It will be good to see Jamison and Murdock.* From now on, he would live between two places – Virginia and Scotland.

Fiona emerged from the main house and approached him. The big breasted lass with dark hair had a worried look on her face. "Sir!"

Dughall smiled. "Ye may call me Father if ye wish."

She wiped her hands on her apron. "Father... They sent me to tell ye... Maggie is in labor."

Dughall felt a rush of fear. "When did it start?"

Fiona reddened. "Four hours ago. We wanted to be sure that it wasn't false labor. Will ye tell Philip?"

"I will. Thank ye, lass. Ye may go." He watched as she turned to walk back to the house. "Fiona?"

She turned again. "Aye."

"Luc just took down a giant buck."

Her face lit up with joy. "He's a good husband!"

"That he is."

"I must go." The lass picked up her skirts and ran to the house.

Dughall's thoughts turned to his daughter. Maggie was only fourteen. The delivery could be dangerous. He prayed for an easy birth and the survival of his daughter and grandson. He'd sensed that it was a laddie months ago but hadn't told anyone.

Philip was supervising a work party miles away. They were cutting down trees to clear land for more cornfields. Night temperatures were dropping to the freezing point. The trees would be used for firewood.

Dughall left to find him.

***

Maggie woke that morning with a strange feeling, but didn't tell Philip. Her husband was needed in the fields and she was needed in the kitchen. She patted her swollen belly. The child had dropped over the last few days. So what was happening? It felt like waves of gentle contractions. Philip went to work and she to the kitchen. She assisted Bridget in cooking breakfast for their ever expanding family. As she cleared the plates, Maggie had her first real pain. She hid them until the dishes were done. That was when Keira noticed. The women excused her and put her to bed.

***

Four hours had passed. Maggie got out of bed and straightened the sheets for the tenth time. They'd added extra ones to absorb the mess when her water broke. She wore a loose nightgown and nothing else to make it easier for Keira to examine her.

Maggie climbed into bed and pulled the covers up to her midsection. The house was chilly if you weren't moving. She felt a contraction coming and grasped the sheets. "Oh!"

Fiona came into the room. "Yer father is fetching Philip."

Maggie grimaced. "Good! I think that they're coming closer."

"Shall I get Keira?"

Maggie took a few shallow breaths. "Nay. The women have too much work to do."

Fiona frowned. "The work can wait. This is important."

Maggie gasped. "Here comes another one!" She felt a tightening at the base of her vagina that continued to the top of her belly. "It hurts!"

Fiona stared. "I'm getting Keira."

"Nay!" But the lass was already gone. Maggie had helped her mother with a few deliveries, so she wasn't a stranger to childbirth. She knew that a first child could take many hours. "Come on, wee one."

Keira rushed into the room with her birthing kit. She laid it down on a side table and wiped her hands on a towel. "I just washed my hands. Let me examine ye."

"All right, Mother." Maggie lay back against some propped up pillows and raised her knees. "Wait!" A painful contraction washed over her. She panted through it. "Go ahead."

Keira slipped a hand into her opening. "Try to relax, Daughter." She reached in and felt the cervix. "It's opening up. Ye're a lucky lass. The child is coming." She withdrew her hand and covered her.

"Thank the Goddess!" Maggie clawed the sheets as a fierce contraction seized her. "Ohhh… It's tearing me apart."

Dughall and Philip rushed into the room. Keira and Dughall stood back as Philip came to her side.

The young man was sweaty and disheveled. He sat on the bed and clutched her hand. "My dear wife."

Maggie smiled through the pain. "It's all right, Husband." She inhaled sharply. "Don't leave me!"

Philip glanced at Keira. "Can I stay?"

She nodded. "Aye. Dughall, ask the women to boil water. Then bring me some swaddling. The child is coming."

The nervous grandfather-to-be left the room.

Philip stroked her hair. "Yer father says it's a laddie."

She perked up. "A son?"

"Aye."

The contractions were coming faster. Sweat beaded on Maggie's forehead. She was trying to be brave for her husband. Her water broke suddenly. "Oh! My water broke."

Keira came forth. "That's supposed to happen. I need to check ye again."

"That one was strong. I thought I was dying." Maggie laid back and spread her knees apart.

Keira slipped a hand into her opening. "I won't let ye die." Her eyes widened. "It's not breech. I feel a head."

Maggie's heart pounded. "Good."

"We can make it come faster if ye kneel."

Maggie was confused. "Ye want me to get on my knees?"

"Aye. My mother used to say that it's best to use the force of the earth to deliver the child. Can ye get out of bed and sink to yer knees?"

Philip frowned. "Are ye sure about this?"

Keira stared. "I'm a midwife."

Maggie cried out. "Ohhh… Wait… There's another one coming." She grasped Philip hand and squeezed until it was white.

"Breathe, Wife!"

Maggie was exhausted. The pain stopped, but another was building.

Keira helped her out of bed to her knees. "Help me, Philip!" They kneeled on either side of her and supported her. "Push, lass!"

Maggie held them tight. She panted as her body adjusted and spread her legs apart. "It feels like it dropped."

Keira laid a towel under her and reached between her legs. "The head has crowned." Indeed, a wet hairy mass was peeking out. She slipped her hands around the neck, slightly rotating the infant. The head appeared and a shoulder popped out.

Maggie shrieked. "It hurts!"

"It's almost over." The child glided into Keira's hands and was placed on the floor. "Yer father was right. It's a laddie." The newborn cried lustily.

Philip whooped. "I have a son!"

Keira opened her kit. She cleared the infant's nose and throat and wiped the mucous from his face and head. She tied the cord with deer sinew, cut it, and swaddled the infant in a towel. "Take him, Philip."

The new father took the wee infant.

Maggie was breathless. "Is it over?"

"Nay." Keira massaged Maggie's belly. "We must deliver the afterbirth." After several minutes of massage, it was expelled. She changed the sheets and helped Maggie into bed. The new mother's eyes were heavy with exhaustion. "Give her the child."

Philip placed the baby in his wife's arms. "Thank ye, lass. He's a fine son."

Keira smiled. "What will ye name him?"

"Donald, after my grandfather and uncle."

"It's a fine name."

Maggie opened her gown. She offered her breast to the baby, who took it readily. "Oh... It feels wonderful."

Keira gathered the soiled sheets and towels. "I must wash up. I'll be right back." She left the room.

Dughall entered with an armful of swaddling. "I just passed yer mother. I see I'm too late."

Maggie grinned. "Oh, Father. It's a laddie, like ye predicted. We named him Donald."

"The Laird of Grant will be pleased."

Maggie's heart swelled with love for the wee infant. She played with his tiny fingers. "He's beautiful. So perfect... When we have the next one..."

Philip raised his eyebrows. "After all the pain, ye want another?"

She smiled. "Remember our agreement. We planned to have seven."

The expression on Philip's face was priceless.

They got a chuckle out of that.

Chapter 65
Trouble in Paradise

March 4th 1652
Seven Weeks Later

EDEN PLANTATION, VIRGINIA, EARLY MORNING

Dughall propped his musket against a wall and entered his bedroom. There was trouble in Jamestown. He and his men were going into town to assist Gilbert and Governor Berkeley. His wife was sitting up in bed, nursing their two week old son, Duncan. Wee Rosie sat at her side, snuggled against her mother and new brother.

I will never tire of seeing this, he thought. He sat on the bed and watched them.

Keira looked up. "Are ye leaving?"

"Aye. I must help Gilbert."

She frowned. "Tell me again what is happening. I don't understand it."

Dughall sighed. "I received a message from Gilbert. Governor Berkeley got word that the English Parliament means to exert control over the colonists. The English fleet is on the way with troops and commissioners."

"But are we not an English colony?"

"Aye, Wife. But our sworn allegiances are to the King of England. Rumor is that they will force us to take an oath of allegiance to the new government."

Keira switched the baby to her other breast. "I would think that ye would want that. Ye said that the King meant to kill ye."

He took her hand and squeezed it. "'Tis true. For my own sake, I wish that England would stay a Commonwealth. But Gilbert needs my help."

Rosie smiled like an angel. "Dada!"

Dughall's heart melted. "My precious daughter. Dada loves ye."

Keira wouldn't let it go. "What will the Governor do?"

"I don't know. But he has called for able bodied men to take up arms and join him."

There was a pop as the baby released the nipple. Wee Duncan was done nursing.

Dughall kissed his wife on the cheek. He stroked his daughter's hair and played with his son's tiny fingers. "I may be gone a while. Don't worry."

"Are any of the men staying?"

"Aye. Philip and twenty servants. We can't ignore the plantation." Dughall stood and gazed at them. *I am the luckiest man in the world.* He swallowed hard. "Take care of the children."

He left the room, retrieved his musket, and joined his men by the outdoor fire. Luc, George, and Fang were armed with guns. The rest carried knives and sharp farm implements. Some carried pouches of food that the women prepared – they contained corn bread and cheese and strips of dried meat. No one knew how long they'd be gone.

Dughall read them Gilbert's note and they began to march to Jamestown.

***

JAMESTOWN, LATER THAT MORNING

Gilbert Gordon was running on his nerves. He hadn't slept a wink last night. The Governor had called a meeting to inform everyone of the danger. Gilbert had attended it with the Justices, as well as members of the Assembly and the House of Burgesses. It had been a contentious meeting. Governor Berkeley declared that Virginia would remain faithful to King Charles II, even if it meant a fight. He was a popular man. Few dared to oppose him. Those who did put forth a strong argument for swearing allegiance to the Commonwealth. In the end, Sir Berkeley prevailed. They would meet the commissioners with a show of force when they landed. They were asked to call out the militia and muster additional men. That was when he'd sent a message to Dughall.

Gilbert swallowed hard. They had advance notice from a small ship that the English fleet was approaching Jamestown. Militiamen and colonists were arriving by the hundreds to do Governor Berkeley's bidding. *God in heaven! Will we come to blows?*

"George!"

Gilbert turned to see a group of men approaching - his brother Dughall, his son George, Luc, Fang, and twenty of his servants. "Brother!" He hurried to them.

Dughall seemed anxious. "Tell me what's going on."

The men gathered around.

Gilbert frowned. "The English fleet will arrive soon."

"How do we know that?"

"A small ship spotted them."

"Ah. How many ships do they have?"

"Three. The captain saw quite a few soldiers on deck, dressed in red British uniforms."

Young George spoke up, "Father. What does Sir Berkeley intend to do?"

Gilbert sighed. "He intends to declare that Virginia will remain faithful to the King."

Dughall let out a low whistle. "The King is in exile. Why would he do this?"

"The Governor was a personal friend of the King's father. He lived in his court for years. He will never swear allegiance to the Commonwealth."

Dughall frowned. "Did no one oppose him?"

Gilbert nodded. "A few. They made convincing arguments. No one wants to lose what they've worked for."

"Then, we must garner support for this opinion. Otherwise, we will have to fight."

Gilbert glanced at his son. What if they came to bloody blows? He couldn't imagine losing George. "All right. But we must do it in secret. I have to be careful. Sir Berkeley is a friend."

Dughall stared. "Blood is thicker than water. We are brothers. Like before, we will present opposing arguments. Don't fret, we will use diplomacy."

The town crier came down the street ringing a bell. "The ships are approaching! The Governor says to bring your arms to the harbor."

A thrill of excitement rushed through the men. For Gilbert, it was tinged with fear. "Try to stay together!" he shouted.

They joined hundreds of men marching towards the harbor.

***

Governor William Berkeley stood in front of his men, watching the English ships drop anchor in the harbor. The gentleman was clad in his Sunday clothes - a rust colored waistcoat and trousers and a frilled linen shirt. A shoulder length white wig complemented his outfit. Virginia had an unfair reputation as a place inhabited by planters, hunters, and wild savages. He had to look civilized for the commissioners.

Sir Berkeley had prepared for this possibility since the death of King Charles I. He knew that the Parliament would get to them eventually. He thought it might be avoided when the Prince made efforts to claim his crown, but now that was over. Berkeley had developed a deep affection for Virginia and tirelessly championed the colony. He believed that prosperity was linked to a diversified economy, free trade, a close-knit society, and autonomy from London. He turned to look at the men gathered behind him. Most of them were armed, but the English army had superior weapons.

Gilbert Gordon approached. "We did a count of the men as ye asked. There are nearly a thousand."

This pleased him. "How many are armed with guns?"

"Seven in ten. The rest have knives and sharp farm implements."

That was distressing. "Keep those without guns in the back. We must let them think that we can match them man to man."

"I will. Can we not try to negotiate this?"

Sir Berkeley ranted, "Negotiate? Charles is my King! I will not swear allegiance to the new government! Who knows what they will want? They might decide to dissolve our Assembly and House of Burgesses. And what about our religion? Will we have the freedom to worship?"

Gilbert said, "All good questions. Perhaps we should hear them out."

Berkeley reddened. He wasn't used to being challenged. "We will. But I know these men. Chances are we will have to fight."

Gilbert paled. "I will go move the unarmed men." He left his presence.

The Governor watched intently as a small boat was lowered from the largest ship. Three well dressed men and fifteen soldiers climbed down a ladder into the boat and began rowing towards the shore. *I cannot let them destroy this colony!* There was scarcely a word from the men behind him. They were awaiting his orders. Even his Sheriff was silent, and for that he was grateful.

The large rowboat arrived at the dock and tied off. Twelve of the fifteen soldiers disembarked first, displaying their weapons. There were two musketeers for each pike man. The three commissioners were helped off next.

The Governor was surprised to see that two of them – Richard Bennett and William Claiborne – were former citizens of Virginia.

Claiborne had long wavy locks of hair and a neatly trimmed goatee and moustache. He approached Sir Berkeley and offered his hand in friendship.

The Governor hesitated, then shook his hand reluctantly. "It's been a long time, William." His voice was harsh. "What business do ye have in Virginia?"

Claiborne's eyes narrowed. "In good time. Let me introduce my fellow commissioners – Richard Bennett and Edmund Curtis. We were five originally, but a ship was lost at sea."

Sir Berkeley squinted. "Richard and I are acquainted."

William Claiborne continued, "We are here by the decree of Parliament. As you must know, England no longer answers to a king. We are a Commonwealth."

The Governor glared. "Go on."

"William. Your sympathies with the former King are well known. But the King is dead. His son is in exile."

"The Prince will be restored to his crown! It's only a matter of time."

"I'm afraid not." Richard Bennett was a distinguished looking man in his early forties. "We are here, Sir, to ask that Virginians take an oath of allegiance to the new government."

Murmurs shot through the crowd. The Governor puffed up like a cock about to fight. "There are some here who will not swear allegiance. I am one of them! What will you do? Dismantle our government?

Outlaw our religion?"

The militia responded by displaying their weapons. The red soldiers watched nervously and poised to protect the commissioners.

William Claiborne frowned. "We come in peace with a fair offer. But we are prepared to match arms with arms!"

***

Gilbert was sick to his stomach. They were about to come to blows. His own son was eager to get into the fray. What would he tell Bridget if the lad was injured or killed? He swallowed hard and stepped forward. "Can we not listen to what they have to say?"

Sir Berkeley glared at him. But there were murmurs of agreement.

Richard Bennett spoke, "Who are you, Sir?"

He gave his pseudonym. "George Gordon, Sheriff of this county."

Bennett nodded. "Pleased to meet you, George." He addressed the crowd. "No one here desires a clash. From what I see, we each have a thousand men. The results could be deadly."

The Governor relented. "We will hear you out in the courthouse. But there are terms. My militia stays here, and no one else disembarks until the meeting is over."

Claiborne hesitated. "Agreed."

Sir Berkeley gave orders, "Members of the Assembly and the House of Burgesses will go to the courthouse immediately. I also want three citizen representatives."

Three men stepped forward. One of them was Dughall. He identified himself to the commissioners, "I am Duncan Gordon."

They headed for the courthouse.

***

Seven days of negotiations ensued. Dughall spoke eloquently on a variety of issues. Gilbert appeared to sympathize with Sir Berkeley until it seemed that the colony was in danger. Careful bargaining between the two sides, both of which valued Virginia, resulted in a remarkably even handed agreement.

It was called a voluntary act and culminated in two treaties. The first treaty forgave all persons for any word or act against Parliament, allowed a year before requiring them to take an oath of allegiance to the new government, confirmed the Assembly's position in the government as well as existing land policies and titles, and allowed the use of the Book of Common Prayer. The second treaty accommodated Governor Berkeley. He was excused from swearing allegiance to the new government and was allowed to speak well of the King in private. He could keep his land and possessions or sell them and leave the colony. He could communicate with the King in exile. Upon acceptance of these terms, he yielded up command to the commissioners.

The commissioners had been ordered by the English Council of State to hold a new election of the House of Burgesses by all freemen who signed the oath of allegiance. The Burgesses would elect a new Governor.

***

Dughall was eager to return to the plantation. He'd sent Luc home to inform the women, but he knew that Keira would be worried about him. He left the courthouse in search of his men.

Richard Bennett caught up with him. "Duncan Gordon!"

Dughall nodded. "Aye."

"I'd like to talk to you."

They kept walking. "Go on."

"The commissioners were impressed with your thoughtful arguments. We'd like you to run for the House of Burgesses."

Dughall stopped walking. "Me? I'm a common man."

The man smiled. "With uncommon opinions. You are just what we need in colonial government."

"Sir Berkeley wasn't pleased with me."

"That's because he favors the monarchy. You seem to be of the opinion we can do without it."

"Aye. I've studied old cultures – Greece, Rome, and the ancient Jews. There was something to be learned from each of them. I believe that with God's guidance and a strong moral compass, man can rule himself."

Bennett was excited. "Exactly! What is your background, Sir?"

Dughall stuck to their storyline. "My brother and I are lesser sons of a Scottish lord, come to make our fortune in the Colonies."

"That you shall! I assume that you will take the oath of allegiance."

"Aye."

He offered his hand in friendship. "Good. Promise me that you will think about running for the House of Burgesses."

Dughall shook his hand. "I promise."

The election will be next week. Then the Burgesses must elect a new governor."

"I see."

Bennett frowned slightly. "Will your brother take the oath? We would like to keep him as Sheriff."

"I will try to convince him." Dughall smiled. "Please excuse me, Sir. I must gather my men and go home. My wife gave birth to a son three weeks ago."

"Congratulations!" Bennett said. "We will talk later." He walked back towards the courthouse.

Dughall was flattered, but he had to be practical. "How can I run for the House of Burgesses? I have to return to Scotland." He ran off to find his men.

Chapter 66
Homecoming

June 17th 1652

3 Months Later

PETERHEAD, SCOTLAND

The Duke stood on deck as the captain of the "Mercy" steered the ship into the harbor. Dughall had sailed into this port hundreds of times and had to resist the urge to advise him. He winced as the boat scraped the dock and came to a halting stop. Several crew members jumped out to secure it.

It was a perfect summer day by the North Sea. The sun was strong, the breeze was light, and waves sparkled in the harbor. Dughall smiled. "It's just like I remembered it." He lifted his sea bag onto his shoulder and said goodbye to the captain. Walking down the plank to the dock, he spotted a familiar face - Ian's son, Alexander.

"Alexander Hay!" he cried.

The red-haired lad turned. "Uncle Dughall!" He ran to him. "What are ye doing here?"

The Duke grinned. "I'm here for a visit."

Alexander looked around. "Where is Luc and the rest of the family?"

"They had to stay behind. We'll talk about it later."

"All right, Sir. Does Father expect ye?"

"Nay. This is a grand surprise."

Alexander was excited. "I just finished unloading a boat. Shall I take ye to him?"

"Aye."

They left the dock and walked along King's Common Gate, passing a row of stone cottages and tenements. The lad pointed out one of the newer cottages. "That's our house. Andrew and I helped Father build it."

"It looks sturdy. Is yer Father inside?"

"Nay, Sir. Mother is there, cooking a meal with my sister Morag. Father is at 'The Crack' with Grandfather Andrew."

Dughall longed for a dram of whisky. "How is yer Grandfather?"

Alexander frowned. "He says that he's feeling his age."

"I know the feeling."

They continued on past the fish-house tenement and Walker's place until they came to the road that led to Keith Inch. There stood a two-storied tavern built of timber, with a covered veranda. A weathered sign proclaimed, 'The Crack. She wrecked on Keith Inch in 1588.'

Dughall didn't see the figurehead from the bow of the ill-fated ship. "Where is the mermaid?"

The lad blushed. "Ummm... They're painting it."

"Ha! What part?" The statue had red hair, a green dress, and bare breasts with nipples. He and Ian used to stare at it. "Never mind."

Alexander seemed relieved.

They climbed the wooden steps to the upper story. Dughall opened the heavy door and ushered the boy inside. Faces regarded them warily as they walked past the long bar.

Klaas Van Dyck greeted him, "Dughall Gordon!"

Dughall smiled. "Good to see ye, Klaas. Is my brother here?"

The innkeeper nodded. "He's in the back with Andrew McFarlein."

"Bring us a round of yer best whisky."

"For the lad, too?"

"That will be up to his father." They pulled aside a leather flap and entered the back room. The light was dim and it smelled of tobacco. Dughall recognized the back of his brother's head – long red hair that fell below his shoulders. He was talking to old man McFarlein. "Ye must be losing yer touch, Ian. Ye didn't even sense me."

Ian turned quickly. With a shocked look, he stood and embraced his brother. "Dughall!"

The Duke looked him over. His brother wore breeks, a sweater, and bright blue socks – usual garb for a Peterhead fisherman. "I've missed ye."

Andrew McFarlein stood and shook his hand. "It's good to see ye, my Lord."

Dughall was taken aback. It had been almost two years since anyone called him that. He supposed that he'd better get used to it. "Thank ye." He studied the old man. Time had marched on. His hair was thinning and his brows were white.

They took seats around the table with young Alexander joining them.

Klaas approached with a tray and set a glass of whisky in front of each of them. He went back to the bar.

"May I, Father?" Alexander begged.

Ian frowned. "Just this once. After all, it's a special occasion."

"That's a lot of whisky for a young lad," Dughall remarked.

Ian nodded. He took a swig of his own whisky and then poured some from the lad's glass into his. "That should do it."

They sipped their whisky, savoring the peaty flavor.

"Ah. We don't have whisky like this in Virginia."

"Where is yer family, Brother?"

Dughall sighed. "I had to leave them behind." It was safe to talk about it now that the King was in exile. "The plantation has grown by leaps and bounds. It's six hundred acres. Gilbert needs all the help he can get. We took on forty indentured servants."

"Ah..."

Dughall smiled. "Join me in a toast." The men raised their glasses. "Our clan has increased in numbers. Luc married a buxom lass. Maggie and Keira recently gave birth to sons."

Ian grinned. "To the clan! So ye have another son."

"Aye. We named him Duncan. That's the name I use in the colonies."

"Congratulations! Ye have an heir."

Dughall took a long swallow. "Aye."

Ian's eyes widened. "Did I hear ye right? Ye're a grandfather?"

"Aye. It makes me feel old."

Andrew McFarlein grunted. "Ye're a youngster."

Dughall smiled. "I guess. What about ye, Brother?"

"Mary and I just had our ninth, a wee lassie named Isla." Ian laughed. "We're running out of names. I think I'm done. I'm exhausted."

Dughall chuckled. "Ha!"

Ian took another sip. "Have ye been to Drake?"

"Nay. I caught a ship from Jamestown to London. It took me nearly two months to get there. After a hot bath and a good night's sleep, I boarded a ship to Peterhead."

Alexander hiccupped.

Dughall noticed that his glass was empty. "Ye must go easy on that stuff, lad."

Andrew spoke, "How long are ye back for?"

Dughall frowned. "I'm not sure. It depends upon what's going on at Drake." He changed the subject, "How are Mother and Father?"

Ian grunted. "Father suffers from arthritis pain, especially in his wrists where he was tortured. He's also lame in one leg. He still goes out on the 'Bonnie Fay', but someone has to help him. Mother longs to see the children, but she's resigned to living in Whinnyfold."

This was sad news. "Do they have enough to sustain themselves?"

"Ye left them with a box of gold. It's more than they would need if they lived to a hundred. We will visit them tomorrow."

Dughall sensed that there something else, but he couldn't say it in front of his father-in-law.

Klaas came to the table. "Ian. Yer son Andrew is at the door." He grinned. "Yer wife is calling ye to dinner."

The men stood. Ian frowned. "I wish she wouldn't do that."

"She's a stubborn lass," Andrew said. "Ye're not about to change her."

Dughall addressed the innkeeper, "Reserve me a room for a few nights. I will return later."

They opened the leather flap and began to file out of the back room. Young Alexander was glassy eyed. He tripped on a loose board.

Ian caught him and gazed into his eyes. "Ye're blootered!" He groaned. "There's always a first time for everything. Don't tell yer mother."

Andrew McFarlein chuckled.

Dughall smiled. He missed the interplay between grandfathers and fathers and sons. Drake had provided a perfect place for that. Now, he was split between two countries. Would it ever be the same?

They emerged from 'The Crack' and spotted young Andrew.

***

THE NEXT DAY

The Duke rose at dawn and washed in a basin of cold water. He put on his least dirty clothes and went downstairs to the dining room to eat breakfast. Klaas' plump wife Maartje served him the best food he'd had since leaving Jamestown – eggs, ham, brown bread, and butter. There was even some jam and honey. He wolfed down the food and then asked the woman to wash his dirty laundry.

Dughall left 'The Crack' and began the short walk to Ian's cottage. He turned on to King's Common Gate, passed Walker's place and the fish-house tenement, and arrived at a row of cottages. There was a relatively new one set back off the road, twice as big as the others. He headed for it.

"Nine children," he mused. "Ye beat me, Brother. I would have had nine if those four had lived." Even so, he was grateful. He had Maggie, James, Luc, Rosie, and Duncan. The curse had lifted from them.

Dughall recognized Ian's daughter Morag, hanging clothes on a line. The yellow haired lass looked like a younger version of her mother. "Is yer father inside?"

She clutched a wet towel. "He's waiting for ye." She returned to her duties.

The Duke knocked on the door of the cottage.

Ian answered. "Good morning, Brother! Are ye ready for a walk to Whinnyfold?"

Dughall nodded. "Aye. I'm glad we're walking. It will help me get rid of these sea legs."

Ian came out and closed the door. He was dressed in the same clothes as yesterday. "It will give us a chance to talk. There were things I couldn't say in front of my father-in-law."

Dughall grunted. "I understand."

The brothers walked along King's Common Gate until they came to the harbor. It was a fine summer day, with warm sun, a moderate breeze, and noisy rolling waves. They barely spoke a word as they basked in the weather and each other's presence. After a brief stop, they began the hike south along the coast towards Whinnyfold.

Dughall smiled. "I can feel ye, again."

Ian nodded. "Aye. It must have something to do with this place and being close together."

"I've missed ye, Brother."

"As have I."

Dughall sighed. The smell of the sea, the warmth of the wind on his face, and the magnificent view made this hike special. "I wish I could move back here."

Ian glanced at him. "The King is no longer a threat. Why don't ye?"

"I wish it was that simple. I'm torn between three places - Eden, Drake, and this one. When I was in Jamestown, it seemed right. Maggie and Philip have made a life there, as well as Luc and his new wife. We are prospering as landowners and farmers. Now, I come here and feel the pull of the sea. I can not deny my feelings."

"What about Drake?"

"I will return to Drake in a few days. I don't know how it will affect me."

They were coming upon the village of Boddam, where there were several cottages and the ruins of a castle. They stopped to ask for water. Mrs. Galt provided some and went about her business.

Dughall drank deeply. "Do ye intend to return to Drake, Brother?"

Ian frowned. "I wasn't planning on it. Are ye coming home for good?"

"Nay. I intend to spend time in Scotland and Virginia."

"Then I can not move my family to the castle. We've settled in Peterhead and prospered. The children are thriving. Mary is content to be near her parents. I can keep an eye on ours. I got my chance to be a warrior. But I'm a fisherman at heart."

Dughall hid his disappointment. "I understand. What is going on with Mother and Father?"

Ian frowned. "I couldn't say much in front of Andrew. Father's health is failing. It's not just arthritis. He had the grippe twice last winter and struggles to walk with a cane. Mother says that he forgets things."

Dughall's heart ached. "What about Mother?"

"Her mind is good but she's getting old. It's been tough on her."

They started walking again, along a path that would take them by the Bullers of Buchan. They were silent until they reached the hamlet of cottages. These were built next to a collapsed sea cave which formed a semicircular chasm nearly a hundred feet deep. The sea rushed in through this natural archway. It was enough to give you vertigo. The brothers stood on the lip of the chasm and looked down at the cliffs. They were a nesting site for colonies of seabirds – kittiwakes, puffins, fulmars, and razorbills.

"Just beautiful," Dughall whispered. "My soul belongs here."

They kept moving along the rocky path until they spotted Slains Castle. Another mile and they came upon the big tree that had meant so much in their childhood. It marked the path to Peterhead. They lingered for a minute and then entered the backside of Whinnyfold. After walking through a few rows, they arrived at their parents' cottage.

Ian grinned. "Stand off to the side."

Dughall complied.

Ian rapped on the door with a special knock that identified him. He pushed on the door and entered. "Mother? Father?"

Dughall's heart soared as he heard Jessie's voice. "My son." He looked in and watched them embrace and separate.

Jessie's eyes widened. "Dughall?"

"Aye, Mother." Dughall entered the cottage and hugged her. He held her apart and looked her over. Her face was wrinkled and her hair was white. But she was still his mother. "I've missed ye."

"Oh, Son. We didn't know if we'd see ye again. Then the King went into exile. We hoped. We prayed."

He smiled. "I'm here. Where is Father?"

A troubled look passed over her face. "Down at the water, checking on the 'Bonnie Fay'. He does it every day."

Dughall nodded. "I will find him."

***

The Duke walked through a row of cottages and emerged from the village proper. He took a few strides and arrived at the cliff top. It was just like he remembered it. To his left, he saw Slains Castle, the home of the seat of Clan Hay. To his right was a path that could take him south to Collieston. Beyond that was a stunning sight, the purple mountains at Braemar. Below, was the bay of Whinnyfold, a narrow inlet.

Dughall saw a scaffie on the beach with a man sitting next to it. "Father," he whispered. He found the place where a path was worn and scrambled down the steep slope to join him. As he got closer, he considered what to say. His boots crunched on the rocky beach as he walked the last twenty yards.

Alex must have heard him. The old man stood with difficulty, leaning on a cane. "Who?" He stared. "Dughall?"

The Duke was shocked by his father's appearance. The man favored his right leg. The left one seemed almost useless. His face was lined with wrinkles and his hair was as white as snow. "Father!" He walked to him.

Alex dropped his cane and embraced him. "Son!" His words came in sobs. "I prayed... that I would see ye... before I died."

Dughall hugged him tight. "I missed ye, Father."

They separated.

"I thought that God was punishing me. I put ye in a bad situation.

What ye did to rescue me from prison..."

Dughall sighed. "I did nothing wrong." At least, nothing *he* knew about. "Father, I am home. Is it not proof enough?"

Alex stared. "I suppose so."

Dughall picked up his cane and handed it to him. He noticed that his hands were gnarled with arthritis. He remembered how proud old Maggie had been. He would not offer to help him. "Mother is making tea. Let's go up."

They began to walk along the rocky beach. Alex leaned heavily on his cane and forced his foot forward. The old man grunted. "Don't fret, Son. I start slowly and hobble for twenty yards. Then, everything loosens up." He was right. By the time they got to the cliff side path, he was walking with a slight limp.

Dughall resisted the urge to help him. "Can ye climb?"

Alex scowled. "I do it every day! Yer mother doesn't like it. But it keeps me fit."

They began to walk up the steep slope, first taking a path to left, then to the right. Alex was breathing hard when they got to the top. "See? I made it."

Dughall smiled. He was as stubborn as ever.

They began walking towards the cottages. "Where is yer family?"

"In Virginia. I'm the only one who came. The men are needed on the farm. Maggie and Keira just gave birth to sons."

Alex stared. "Maggie did?"

"Aye, to a son named Donald."

"Good thing she got married!"

Dughall hid a smile.

They arrived at their cottage and entered. Ian and Jessie were seated at the table drinking tea. Dughall and Alex joined them.

Dughall spent the afternoon with them. He told them about Virginia and the plantation called 'Eden'. He talked about their indentured servants. He bragged about his new life and the lives of his wife and children.

Jessie poured more tea. "So, I am a great-grandmother."

Dughall grinned. "Aye. Wee Donald was born in January."

Alex grunted. "It's a fine name."

She seemed sad. "When will ye go back?"

Dughall touched her hand. "Don't fret. I will be here for a while. I must visit James at the Abbey and spend some time at Drake. I don't want to lose my estate."

"Especially now that ye have an heir," said Ian. "Wee Duncan?"

"Aye." He stood to leave and they joined him. Dughall embraced his father, and then his mother. He hugged her tight. "I will be back soon."

The brothers left the cottage and began the walk back to Peterhead.

They hiked in silence until they passed the Bullers of Buchan. At last, Ian spoke, "What did ye think of them?"

Dughall's heart ached. "They seem old. Mother is fine, but Father is failing."

"I know. Is there anything ye can do for him? Mother tries, but he resists her."

Dughall shrugged. "I'll think on it."

Chapter 67
Brother James

June 25th 1652
1 Week Later

THE ABBEY OF DEER

Brother James stood in the honey house, checking on the progress of a batch of mead. He reflected back to when they made it, eleven months ago.

***

The cooking was done in a large iron pot suspended over a steady fire. Monks started the batch with twenty one quarts of spring water and recorded the starting level with a stick. As the water warmed, they stirred in seven quarts of honey and a sprinkle of pungent cloves. Then they brought it to a boil, skimming off impurities.

One monk packed five pounds of dried grapes into a cheesecloth sack and dropped it into the mix. When the fruit swelled and softened, he removed the bag and squeezed the juice into the batch.

They boiled the mix until the level was down to the original mark, put out the fire, and waited. When the liquid cooled, it was strained through cheesecloth into a fermentation bucket and covered with cloth so that nothing could foul it. There it remained for six weeks until the fermentation process started. Finally, the batch was transferred to an oak barrel and stopped up tightly for at least nine months.

***

James suspected that the batch was ready to drink. There was a heady fragrance in the room – of honey and grapes – floral and fruity. He smelled alcohol, too. The batch would be a strong one. He prepared to draw off the clear amber liquid into rows of freshly washed bottles. "I will put aside a quart for Mother and Father."

The door opened.

Brother Adam hobbled inside. He was leaning heavily on his cane this morning. "Ye have a visitor, lad. I'll take over."

"Donald Grant?"

"Nay."

James frowned. No one was supposed to know that he was here. "Who is it?"

"Yer father." The older monk began to tap the barrel.

The lad's mood lightened. "Are ye sure?"

"Aye."

James rolled up his sleeves and washed his hands in a bucket of water. Everything was sticky in the honey house. Cleanliness was close to Godliness. "Is anyone with him?"

Adam grunted. "Nay. Go. He's waiting in the library."

James left the honey house and walked through the gardens. A trail of honey bees left the flowers and followed him to the courtyard. One lit upon his open hand. He spoke to it with affection, "Ye must not follow me, wee one. Tell yer sisters."

The bee did a strange little dance and flew off. Her companions followed.

James crossed the courtyard and arrived at the building that housed the library. It was under a giant yew tree. He climbed the steps and entered. It was cool inside. "Ah. This feels heavenly."

The library was at the end of the corridor, so he took a moment to compose his thoughts. "It's been two years since I saw Father. I wonder what has happened." He smoothed his white robe and walked the long hallway. The door was open, so he entered.

The Duke stood at the end of the room, gazing out an open window.

James read his feelings. The man was glad to be here. But he was torn between places. "Father?"

Dughall turned to face him. "My son."

They came together and embraced.

Dughall stepped back and looked him over. "Ye're so tall! Ye must have grown six inches."

James grinned. "Seven. I fit into the men's robes. I'll be fourteen in September."

"I know. Can we sit and talk?"

"Aye." The lad led him to a couch, where they sat together. "Ye look good, Sir. Tanned and fit."

The Duke smiled. "It's from many days working in the sun. In Virginia, I'm a tobacco farmer."

James nodded. "Ah. Where is Mother?"

"In Virginia. She sends her love. She couldn't make the trip because she just gave birth to a child."

His eyes widened. "Another one?"

"Aye. Ye have a new brother named Duncan."

James felt a momentary pang of regret, and dismissed it. "This means ye have an heir to yer title and property. How are my sisters?"

"Morrigan Rose is two and a half. We call her Rosie. She's a handful." Dughall reddened slightly. "Maggie gave birth to a son named Donald."

James was stunned. The world had gone on without him. "I see. Ye must tell her that I'm happy for her."

"I will."

James sensed that something was amiss. "Donald Grant told me that the King is in exile. Are ye free to return to Scotland?"

"Free?" Dughall sighed. "The King is no longer a problem. But my heart is torn between two countries. I'm back for a while to visit my family and check on my estate. But I must return to Virginia."

James' intuition had been right. He was curious about the new world. "Tell me about the colonies."

Dughall told him about Virginia and the plantation they called 'Eden'. He described his new life and the lives of his wife and children. He mentioned that Luc was married to a buxom girl named Fiona. He talked about tobacco farming and their indentured servants. Lastly, he described the system of government in Virginia. "I must return by early spring at the latest. I got elected to the House of Burgesses. They meet once a year for a few weeks. This year, we met to elect a new Governor."

James was impressed. "It seems that ye belong there."

"I do." Dughall looked sad. "But I am torn. Ye're here. Father and Mother and Ian, too. And I have a duty to Drake that cannot be denied."

James touched his arm. "There are many choices in this life. The Abbey teaches that ye must follow yer heart."

"Good advice."

"I followed mine when I decided to serve God. Now, I am a novitiate. The next step is to take simple vows before God, my fellow monks, and my family. Perhaps I can do this before ye leave for Virginia."

"I would be honored to attend, Son."

James smiled. "Can ye stay the night? I want to show ye the work that I've done with the bees. They are remarkable creatures."

"I can stay."

James sensed that the man truly loved him. He returned the sentiment, "I love ye, Father."

The Duke's eyes misted. "Oh, James. I love ye, too."

He stood. "Come with me. We will get some refreshments in the Refectory and visit the honey house."

Dughall joined him. "The honey house?"

"Aye. It's where we extract the honey and make mead." James smiled. "I have a gift for ye."

Chapter 68
Drake

June 26 1652
1 Day Later

A MILE FROM DRAKE CASTLE

The Duke felt a rush as he neared his castle on horseback. He'd borrowed a mare from Klaas, the keeper of 'The Crack' in Peterhead.

As the castle came into view, he thought about how good it would be to see Black Lightning. How many times had he regretted leaving him? "Perhaps I will take him to Virginia."

There were others he'd sorely missed – Jamison and Murdock and Pratt and Hunter. He would reward them for running the castle in his absence.

Dughall emerged from the woods and made the final approach to the castle. A sharp whistle went up when he was spotted, and the main gate opened.

"My Lord!" Pratt shouted. The servant helped him dismount and took his horse. "Jamison will be glad to see ye."

Dughall grinned. "I hope he got my letter."

"He did. We've been expecting ye."

"Good. Take my sea bag to my quarters. Be careful with it. There is a special bottle of mead inside. But first, give this horse food and water. I must send her back to Peterhead."

"As ye wish."

"Speaking of horses... How is Lightning?"

The servant smiled. "Good! He missed ye! We've been taking him out every day."

"Thank ye, Pratt. I will visit him later."

Dughall's subjects greeted him as he crossed the courtyard. "My Lord!" "Lord Drake!" "The Duke is back!" There were joyful shouts and whistles as they spilled into the courtyard. Small children ran past spinning hoops and chasing a terrier.

Dughall stopped to address them, "My beloved subjects. Spread the word that I am back. I will see ye later." He entered the castle and took the first flight of stairs.

Murdock caught up with him on the second level. "My Lord!"

"Murdock!" Dughall embraced him like a brother. "I'm glad to see ye."

The servant grinned. "I heard that ye arrived. I was searching for ye."

"Where is Jamison?"

"He took Black Lightning for a ride on the moor. He will return soon."

Dughall smiled. "That will give us time to talk. Let's go to the kitchen and order food and a pitcher of ale. I'm parched and starving."

They talked as they walked. The Duke began, "How is the missus?"

"We're still married."

Dughall chuckled. "Ha! Any children?"

"Nay. I think we're too old. But we have fun trying. How is My Lady?"

"Good. She gave birth to a son a few months ago. I have a male heir named Duncan."

"That's great! Yer subjects will be glad to hear it."

They arrived at the kitchen and entered. Old Marcia was tending the pots on the hearth.

The woman's eyes widened. "My Lord!"

"Aye."

Her eyes misted. "Has the family returned?"

Dughall sensed that she meant Gilbert and his family. She was originally his servant. "Nay. I am the only one. But Gilbert is doing well. He send his regards to ye."

"Oh, bless him. How is Bridget?"

"Good. So are the children. George is practically a man and the wee lassies are a help to their mother."

Marcia sniffled. "I miss them." She wiped her hands on her apron. "But where is my head? Can I serve ye something?"

The Duke grinned. "Aye. Murdock and I are going to the breakfast room. Send us some of what ye're cooking and a large pitcher of ale."

"I shall." She returned to her pots.

They left the kitchen.

***

Murdock sent a messenger to the gate to intercept Jamison. The two friends went to the breakfast room and spent the next hour eating, drinking, and talking.

There was a rap on the door and Jamison entered. The man looked sweaty from his morning ride. "My Lord!"

Dughall pushed back his chair and stood to greet him. "Jamison!"

They embraced like brothers. The servant looked him over. "Ye look good. Fit and brown and a bit older."

The Duke nodded. "I've had an interesting life in Virginia." He motioned to the chairs. "Sit. I just opened a bottle of whisky." Dughall sat across from his servants. He poured the spirits generously into three squat leaded glasses. "How is yer family, Jamison?"

"Happy. The marriage was a good thing. My wife is a sweet lass, far less trouble than Jenny. She gave birth to a daughter a few months ago."

"Ah. The wee lassies are certainly different."

The servant grunted. "She has me wrapped around her finger."

"Ha! I understand." Dughall held up his glass and admired the amber color. "The nectar of the Gods. We don't have whisky like this in Virginia." He took a long swallow.

Jamison stared. "Ye don't?"

"Nay. We have rum, a potent spirit made from sugar cane. I like it, but it will never replace whisky."

Murdock grunted. "Sounds like they need a distillery in Virginia."

Dughall made a small sound of agreement. "I've given it some thought. The problem is agriculture. Most of our grains feed people and livestock. We'd have to grow more barley. There's another problem."

"What?"

"We couldn't smoke it with peat. There isn't much around Jamestown. The soil is sandy. We could smoke it with hardwoods like the tobacco. But it would have a different flavor."

Jamison took a swallow. "Donald Grant could advise ye."

They sipped their drinks in silence, basking in each other's presence.

The Duke refilled their glasses.

Murdock smiled. "Tell him what ye told me."

Dughall held up his glass in a toast. "To my new son, Duncan Gordon."

Jamison slapped the table. "An heir for Drake. Congratulations!"

They joined him in the toast. "Long live Duncan!"

The Duke felt homesick. The child would be very different by the time he returned to the colonies. He wouldn't say it now, but his home was in Virginia. The time would come soon enough for the truth. He bolted his whisky and felt it burn a trail to his belly. The emotional relief was instant. *Father was right. Everything looks better through a glass of whisky.*

Jamison put down his glass. "When we regain our senses, there is much to discuss. There have been problems with the castle."

The Duke nodded. "I have been gone two years. It's to be expected."

Jamison seemed relieved. "Thank ye. There is one more thing. Donald Grant wants to see ye. The man has been a loyal friend. There was a time when I could not risk sending letters to ye or James. Donald handled it. He also gave me updates about the King and advised me about problems."

Dughall was grateful. "Donald is a steadfast friend."

Murdock spoke, "It likely helped that ye had his nephew."

"'Tis true. It's been a good marriage for my daughter. She gave birth to a son in January. They named him Donald."

"The Laird of Grant will be pleased."

Dughall stood and the men joined him. "Summon Pratt and Hunter. We will meet at supper to discuss the problems. But for now, there is one other I must visit."

Jamison stared. "Who, my Lord?"

The Duke grinned. "Black Lightning."

"He's in the stables."

They left the breakfast room and walked the long corridor. Dughall stopped at the top of the stairs. "Go about yer business. We will talk later."

Murdock spoke, "We have all the time in the world now that ye're back for good."

Dughall didn't answer. *I can't let this go on much longer.* He would have to tell them. *I've never been so torn. I must go back to Virginia.*

He took the stairs alone to the ground floor and left the castle to visit Lightning.

***

The Duke crossed the courtyard and arrived at the barn that housed the stables. A young lad was coming out, carrying a wooden box with grooming implements.

The boy stopped. "My Lord?"

Dughall smiled. "Aye, lad. I'm here to see Black Lightning."

The lad reddened. "I just wiped him down and combed his mane. He was too hot to do much else."

"That's all right. Ye can finish him later. Go on yer way."

The boy hurried across the courtyard.

The Duke opened the stable door and went inside. There were eight stalls in the barn. The stallion had to be in one of them. "Lightning? Where are ye?"

In the third stall, a horse nickered and stamped his foot. Dughall's heart soared. "Lightning?" He opened the stall and went inside. The stallion stood against the wall, regarding him with wide eyes.

Dughall walked to him, repeating his name in a soothing tone, "Lightning. Lightning. I'm back." He ran a hand between the horse's ears and stroked his forehead. The horse's nose wuffled against his shirt, searching for an apple. He laughed. "Ye remember me or at least my apples." The horse shivered under his touch. "That's better. I love ye, Lightning."

The Duke resisted the urge to ride him. Jamison tended to run a horse hard. The stallion was likely exhausted. He took an apple out of the trough and held it out to him. The horse crunched the apple and licked his hand.

"Oh, Lightning." Dughall's heart swelled with love. At that moment, he knew he would take him to Virginia. "We will never be apart again. I promise."

The horse whinnied in agreement.

CHAPTER 69
GRATITUDE

JUNE 28TH 1652
2 DAYS LATER

CASTLE GRANT, THE HUNTING LODGE

The Duke and his servant arrived at Castle Grant just after midday. As they were escorted to the hunting lodge, he noted that the castle was in disrepair. One section required the services of a stone mason. Another was seriously understaffed. Was Lord Grant in trouble?

Dughall and Jamison followed a boy to the lodge and waited outside while he announced them. The child returned and told them to go inside. They entered the hunting lodge through a massive oak door. The room was dim and smelled of whisky and tobacco smoke.

Donald Grant sat in a comfortable chair, enjoying a dram of whisky. "Lord Drake and Jamison! My friends."

Dughall smiled. "It's good to see ye, Donald."

Jamison reddened. "I will wait outside."

Donald grunted. "Nay. I hope that Lord Drake doesn't mind. Jamison and I have developed a friendship. I'd like him to stay."

Dughall was glad. "I don't mind at all."

They took seats in leather covered chairs opposite the Laird of Grant. Looking down on them were the heads of deer, boars, wildcats, and foxes. Dughall saw the rack of a large buck, but it wasn't as big as the one Luc took down.

Donald had poured them a generous dram of whisky, so they lifted their glasses and took a swallow.

Donald spoke first, "Dughall, my friend. It appears that ye have escaped the hangman."

"Or worse," the Duke said. "They say I was marked for a traitor's death."

Donald scowled. "It's a good thing that son of a snake is no longer King of Scotland!"

"Agreed." Dughall took a sip. "Has there been any word of him?"

"Aye. Charles failed to get support in France from his cousin Louis XIV. Now, he has moved on to the Netherlands to beg his sister and her husband."

Jamison spoke, "They say that she won't support him."

Donald grunted. "I hope that's true. It will take me some time to recover from the battles. I've lost too many men and a good deal of wealth."

The Duke understood the condition of the castle. He considered his next words carefully. "Did ye provide the Prince with troops?"

"I had to. Otherwise, I would be suspect."

"How many men did ye lose?"

His shoulders slumped. "Hundreds. One was a favorite nephew."

Dughall removed a scrap of paper from his jacket. "Are ye referring to Peter Grant?"

"Aye."

"Jamison wrote me about him. I made inquiries. They say that a Peter Grant was captured at Dunbar and sold to Lynn Iron Works in Massachusetts. I can't be sure that it's the same man, but here is the information." He handed him the paper. "Perhaps, ye can buy his contract."

Donald grinned. "Thank ye, my friend!"

Dughall was pleased. "Speaking of nephews, I must tell ye about Philip. He's matured into a man. Hard working, sincere, and now a father."

Grant's eyes widened. "A father?"

"Aye. My daughter gave birth to a son in January. They named him Donald."

The man was stunned. "A namesake? I am honored."

"I will tell him that."

"Good. Is my nephew happy?"

"Happy and prosperous. Philip is a land owner. Each person who settles in Virginia gets fifty acres. That includes women and children. His one hundred and fifty acres are part of a large plantation we call 'Eden'."

"Ah. 'Eden'. Just like in the Bible."

The Duke nodded.

It was an innocent question. "Will ye return there?"

Dughall sighed. He'd explained it to his servants. "Aye. From now on, I shall be a man who lives between two places - Scotland and Virginia."

"Hmmphhh... That's a hard way to live."

"'Tis true." The Duke sipped his whisky. "My friend, I wish to thank ye for yer help. How else would I have contacted my family? I understand that ye offered Jamison valuable advice on occasion."

The older man nodded. "It's what friends do for one another."

"Someday, I will repay ye."

"Just take care of my nephew."

"I shall."

Donald Grant stood and filled their glasses. "Have one more." He took his seat. "Tell me about Virginia."

Dughall and Jamison stayed until supper time, discussing life in the colonies. Donald insisted that they stay for the evening meal. After gorging themselves on beef, bread, and root vegetables, they settled in for a smoke and a wee dram.

Several drinks later, it was too late to safely navigate the forest. They stayed the night and left in the morning.

Chapter 70
A Sea of Feeling

October 4th 1652
14 weeks later

DRAKE CASTLE

The Duke woke with a deep sense of foreboding. Sweating profusely, he threw off the blankets. It wasn't a bad dream. Was something wrong with his family?

Dughall sat up and tried to still his pounding heart. Several breaths did the trick, but the feeling didn't leave him. He pictured his family one by one to inquire if something was wrong with them. Keira – asleep. Wee Duncan – awake and kicking. Ach! The child was in her bed again. Wee Rosie – in a peaceful slumber. Maggie... Donald... Luc... Gilbert... Hmmm... The problem was not in Virginia. He closed his eyes and connected to his family in Scotland. James was at morning prayers. Ian was readying a scaffie in the harbor. Would it be what he feared most? He pictured his mother and father.

"Oh, God!"

Dughall saw his mother standing at the hearth, making a pot of tea. Her thoughts were desperate. *God help us! He suffered an apoplexy.* With tears running down her face, she poured the tea and brought it to the table. "Let me help ye drink this, Husband."

Dughall saw his father sitting at the table, propped against the wall of the cottage. The right side of his body was slackened. The man gazed at her with eyes of love. "My... bonny... lass. I must... leave... ye."

"Nay, Alex!" she cried.

The Duke opened his eyes. He couldn't take any more of this. He jumped out of bed, used the chamber pot, and dressed in his riding clothes. Dughall met Murdock in hall and ordered him to summon Jamison and prepare two horses. Then, he stopped at the kitchen to get some bread and dried meat for his saddlebag. He pulled on a warm jacket, left the castle, and met Jamison at the stables.

The servant looked like he was roused from bed. "Where are we going, my Lord?"

Dughall stuffed the food into Lightning's saddlebag. "Whinnyfold."

"Ye were just there last week."

"Father is dire straits. Mother thinks he suffered an apoplexy."

Jamison stared. "I won't ask ye how ye know that."

"Good. I don't have time to explain it."

They mounted their horses and left the grounds of the castle.

***

LATER THAT DAY

They drove the horses hard, covering forty five miles in nine hours. Riders and beasts were on the verge of exhaustion. It was suppertime when they came upon the backside of Whinnyfold. A raw North Sea wind greeted them and they put up their collars.

Dughall was as tense as a bowstring. "Let's walk the rest of the way in." The men dismounted and led their horses through several rows of cottages. "Some of these must be abandoned. There's no smoke coming from the chimneys." The grippe had taken a few families last winter.

They arrived at his parents' cottage and tied the horses to a hitching post. They would find shelter for them later.

Dughall swallowed hard. He knocked on the door, using a special rap that Ian taught him. Minutes passed before someone answered.

Jessie opened the door. "Dughall! Come in. Yer father.... He had..."

He embraced her. "I know. I sensed it."

They came inside and closed the door.

Dughall looked at her. Her clothes were disheveled, her white hair was wild, and her face was stained with tears. "How is he?"

She sniffled. "He's sleeping. I couldn't make him eat or drink. He wants to join old Maggie."

Dughall walked to the bed where his father was laying. Alex was facing the wall. He reached out and stroked the man's hair. There wasn't a response, but he was breathing. "How bad is he?"

She stifled a sob. "One side of his body is paralyzed. His face looks like a grimace." She began to cry. "He has trouble with words."

Dughall sighed. "He had an apoplexy."

"Aye."

"There is nothing we can do for it."

"I know."

"Did ye send for Ian?"

She wiped her tears on a handkerchief. "I couldn't. The men are out to sea. The women have small children."

Dughall turned to his servant. "Jamison. Go to Peterhead and fetch Ian."

The servant balked, "I can't leave ye unprotected."

"No one will harm me. My father is dying. Fetch my brother."

Without a word, Jamison pulled on his jacket and left the cottage.

Jessie busied herself at the hearth. "I made cock-a-leekie soup.

Would ye like some?"

The Duke's stomach growled at the mention of it. "That would be good."

Jessie ladled the steaming soup into bowls and brought them to the table. She laid down two spoons and took a seat.

Dughall sat opposite her. "Shall we pray?"

"Aye."

"Bless us O Lord, for these thy gifts which we are about to receive from thy bounty, through Christ Our Lord, Amen."

"Amen."

"Let us pray for Father." His voice was strained, "Oh, Lord. We pray for this man – our husband and father. He is a good man, a God fearing man. Take his hand. Let his passing be easy." A single tear slipped down his cheek. He was trying to be strong for his mother, but his heart was breaking. "Amen."

Jessie sniffled. "Amen."

They picked up their spoons and ate their soup in silence. When they were done, she began to clear the dishes.

"Can I help ye, Mother?"

There was a slight rustle from the bed. A voice spoke, rough but familiar, "Dughall?"

The Duke stood and walked to the bed. "I am here, Father."

The old man was laying on his back with his eyes partly closed. His right limbs were drawn up near his body. "Thank... God."

Dughall pulled up a chair and sat by him. *As a child, I thought he was the strongest man in the world. Now, look at him.* He took his father's hand. "I sent my servant to fetch Ian."

Alex spoke through parched lips. "Ah."

Dughall turned to Jessie, "Soak a cloth in water and bring it here."

She did as he asked and brought it to him.

He held the cloth to his lips. "Suck on this, Father."

Alex made a slight sucking sound and choked. "I... canna... swallow. I'm... done... for."

Dughall took the cloth away. The man was right. He couldn't last much longer. He squeezed his hand. "I love ye, Father. Ye've meant so much to me. Ye are my true father, no matter what my bloodline is." He stifled a sob. "I am a good man because of ye."

Alex smiled, but it looked like a strange grimace. "I... love... ye... too. I... can't... wait... for... Ian. Tell... him... that... I... loved... him." He squeezed his hand hard. "Take... care... of... yer... mother."

Dughall heard Jessie sob. The man sensed his impending death. "What can we do for ye, Father?"

Alex opened his eyes fully. "Take... me... to... the... sea. I... want... to... die... there."

Dughall glanced at his mother. Jessie had a look of panic in her eyes. Would she deny him this last request? She nodded slightly. Did she want him to decide? "Fetch his warm clothes, Mother."

The woman gathered his breeks, sweater, boots, and sea coat. They had a hard time dressing Alex as his body wouldn't cooperate. As last, it was done.

Dughall spoke softly, "We must wear warm clothes as well."

They dressed like they were going to sea, with heavy coats, hats, and heavy breeches. Jessie grabbed several wool plaids for the ground.

Dughall went to the bed and looked down at his father. His eyes were closed, but he was breathing. He lifted the man into his arms and was surprised at how heavy he was. "Get the door, Mother."

They left the cottage. It was nightfall, but a full moon illuminated the harbor. The wind was raw but the sky was clear. The sound of the waves hitting the shore was just what Alex needed.

Dughall carried his father out to the Point. Jessie laid down several plaids on the sea grasses. They sat together on the plaids with Alex propped up between them.

Alex opened his eyes and stared at the North Sea. He mumbled a few things to his wife, who hugged him tightly. He thanked his son for being there. Then, he closed his eyes and fell into silence. His breathing was shallow.

The Duke felt a chill. Something cold and powerful moved through him and hovered around his father. He glanced at his mother. She seemed to feel it, too. "Maggie is here for him," he whispered.

Jessie sniffled. "Take good care of him, Maggie."

Alex moved his lips, but no sound came forth. His body slackened as his spirit escaped.

They sat quietly for a moment, unwilling to acknowledge what had happened. The Duke took his father's wrist and checked his pulse. "His life force is gone."

"I know." She began to cry softly.

Dughall longed to comfort her, but there was work to do. "Let's take him home."

They stood. Dughall lifted his father into his arms. Strangely enough, he felt lighter. He carried the body back to the cottage, wrapped it in a blanket, and placed it on the floor with great reverence. Then he attended to Black Lightning by sheltering him in Maggie's abandoned cottage and bringing him apples and water.

Dughall's heart was heavy as he returned to his mother's cottage. The loss of his father was devastating. He consoled himself with the fact that the man got his last wish.

As was their custom, Jessie made pots of tea and they talked about Alex for hours. His strength, his ingenuity, and his patent stubbornness... They would miss him.

Just before midnight, they crawled into bed and fell into a fitful sleep. Jamison would return with Ian soon. They would bury his father tomorrow.

Chapter 71
Changes

October 5th 1652
NEXT DAY

WHINNYFOLD

Dughall struggled with emotion as he stood in the church cemetery. He would never forget his father. The thought of lowering him into the ground ripped his heart to pieces.

The minister closed his book and made the sign of the cross. "So we bury our brother in Christ. Alexander Hay. Beloved husband, father, fisherman, and friend. In the name of the Father, Son, and Holy Ghost. Amen."

"Amen," the family murmured.

The minister shook Dughall's hand and started to walk back to Boddam. The black mortcloth was placed over the body, a plank put in place, and the rough pine box lowered into the ground.

Dughall and Ian shoveled earth into the hole until the coffin was covered, and marked the grave with a granite stone. It was raw outside, but they were sweating. Jamison had offered to take Dughall's place, but he'd refused. It was the last thing he could do for his father.

Well, maybe not the last thing. The Duke was concerned about his mother. He'd talked to Ian that morning to see if he could take her in. Ian had given him excuses. They had no room. A separate cottage must be built. Mary and Jessie didn't get along. It surprised him. Ian promised to check on Mother every two weeks, but that didn't seem likely.

Dughall stayed back while Ian consoled their mother. He watched them embrace and have a short conversation.

"My Lord," Jamison said. "I'm going to take the horses for a run. They've been cooped up in that cottage."

The Duke nodded. "Thank ye, friend. Stop at my mother's place afterwards." Dughall watched the man trudge in the direction of Maggie's old cottage. He saw that his brother was ready to leave. "Ian. Can I talk to ye privately?"

"Aye."

They left their mother with Robert and Colleen and walked a short distance. Dughall stopped and faced him. "I'm concerned about Mother. I understand what ye told me. Would ye object to me taking her to Virginia?"

Ian frowned. "The children will miss her at Christmas. But it could be the best thing for her."

Dughall breathed a sigh of relief. "Thank ye, Brother. I promised Father that I would care for her."

"Then, ye shall keep yer promise. Ye were always a better man than I."

"That's nae true."

"It is."

Dughall wasn't about to argue with him. "We will visit yer family before we leave Scotland."

Ian squeezed his Dughall's shoulder. "Good. I must go." He turned and began the trek back to Peterhead.

The Duke watched him walk away and returned to Jessie. By this time, Robert and Colleen had left her. "Mother?"

Jessie looked sad. "Robert is having a hard time with this."

"It's to be expected. They went through a lot together."

They walked back to her cottage. Once inside, Jessie put on a pot of chamomile tea. "This will settle our nerves." She poured the steaming liquid into two cups and placed them on the table. They sat opposite each other and began to drink.

Jessie started to sob. "I'm sorry... I can't help it... I sat across from him just like this thousands of times. "

"Don't cry, Mother."

Her voice was anguished, "What will I do? Alex is dead. Mary doesn't want me. I have nothing to live for."

Dughall took her hand. "I want ye to come with me."

Her eyes widened. "To Drake?"

He smiled. "Aye, and to Virginia."

There was uncertainty in her eyes. "I'm an old woman. I don't want to be a burden."

Dughall squeezed her hand. "In Virginia, no one is a burden. Everyone does their fair share. Bridget and Keira and Maggie and Fiona care for nearly sixty people. They cook, clean, sew, tend the animals, and raise the children. There are few midwives in Virginia. Another pair of hands would be welcome."

She regarded him hopefully, "Does Ian know?"

"Aye. I talked to him this morning."

Jessie took a sharp breath. "But Alex..."

Dughall finished her sentence, "Asked me to take care of ye."

She managed a smile. "That he did. Thank ye, Son. I will go with ye."

"There is one thing I ask. In two days, James will take his simple vows at the Abbey. I would like ye to attend with me."

"I would be honored." She sipped her tea. "I can't wait to see Maggie and wee Donald and Duncan! When will we leave for Virginia?"

"In a few weeks. They are preparing my ship. It will give us a chance to pack yer things and visit Ian and his family."

"Will we return?"

Dughall nodded. "I will return each year to manage my property and see my son and brother. Ye are welcome to accompany me."

Jessie went to the hearth to get them another cup of tea.

Dughall wondered if she would want to return. He'd neglected to tell her that a winter sea voyage would be a rough one. He decided that it didn't matter. *She will return to see Ian. Nothing will come between a mother and her son.*

CHAPTER 72
VOWS

OCTOBER 7TH 1652

TWO DAYS LATER

ABBEY OF DEER, THE CRUCIFORM-SHAPED CHURCH

Dughall felt close to God as he sat in the pew with his mother. They'd been there for almost an hour, witnessing James take simple vows. It was the last step before taking solemn vows at age sixteen, which would promise stability, obedience, and chastity.

The young man was beautiful. James was dressed in the robes of a Cistercian monk, a white flowing garment that draped to the ground and was barefoot. His long red curls had been tied back in a tail. The lad knelt at the rail, preparing to receive the Holy Eucharist. The Abbott stood before him, uttering the 'Agnus Dei'.

"Agnus Dei, qui tollis peccata mundi, miserere nobis.
Agnus Dei, qui tollis peccata mundi, miserere nobis.
Agnus Dei, qui tollis peccata mundi, dona nobis pacem."

The Duke's mind translated.

*"Lamb of God, you who take away the sins of the world, have mercy upon us.
Lamb of God, you who take away the sins of the world, have mercy upon us.
Lamb of God, you who take away the sins of the world, grant us peace."*

If only it was that easy, Dughall thought. He felt blasphemous. *It is that easy. We just don't see it.*

James spoke in a clear voice, "Lord, I am not worthy to receive ye, but only say the word and I shall be healed." He bowed his head before the Sacrament as a gesture of reverence.

The Abbott continued, "Behold, the body of Christ."

James looked up and smiled. "Amen." He opened his mouth and received the Sacrament.

The Abbott said, "Now, ye are truly a junior brother. From this day forth, we shall address ye as Brother James."

Dughall was conflicted. Part of him was happy for his son. The lad would live in a place dedicated to peace, hard work, and the love of God. He would never have to go to war or torture and execute a man. It wasn't easy being a Duke. But part of him mourned for his son. James would never fall in love and marry. He wouldn't father a child or watch his wife nurse. It wasn't the lad's fault. The blame lay squarely with himself and his wife. He felt guilty about that. *Keira should have let me die. Instead, she bargained with the Morrigan. Oh, why did I agree to it?*

The ceremony concluded. The Abbott attended to his chalice and vestments, while the young monk approached his family.

James embraced his grandmother. "Thank ye for coming. It means a lot to me."

Jessie had tears in her eyes. "Oh, James. It was beautiful."

"I am sorry about Grandfather."

Her lip trembled. "We all are."

The lad turned to his father. "Weep not for me, Father. For I am at peace with my decision. I do not blame ye and Mother."

Dughall blushed. Nothing had changed. It was impossible to hide anything from him. "Oh." He embraced his son with affection. "Thank ye, James. Bless ye."

They separated.

James smiled. "Will ye join us in the Refectory for refreshments? My brothers insisted on a celebration."

"Aye."

The chapel bells rang as they left the church, deep and resonant. It was uplifting. James let down his long red curls and they followed the monks across the courtyard.

Dughall felt like a weight had been lifted from his heart. *My son will be safe and happy here. What a gift to know yer heart so well that ye are free from life's temptations.*

He was almost envious.

Chapter 73
Sea Voyage

October 28th 1652

Three Weeks Later

MORAY FIRTH, THE HARBOR

It had been a busy three weeks. Dughall and Jessie returned to Drake, where he wrapped up outstanding castle business. They took a cart to Whinnyfold to pick up her possessions and say goodbye to the townspeople. They went on to Peterhead, where they spent three days with Ian and his family. Making good time, they stopped at the Abbey to say goodbye to James. Then they continued on to Drake.

There was no rest at the castle. There was a considerable amount of packing to do. Two horse drawn carts were loaded to capacity with sea trunks and other baggage. Black Lightning was coming with them, so his food and implements were loaded.

Jessie talked to old Marcia, who expressed her longing to see Gilbert and his family. The woman considered him a son and his children her grandchildren. So Jessie asked Dughall if they could take her with them.

He'd balked at first. Marcia was ten years older than his mother and might not survive the voyage. After talking to the old woman, he gave in. Just like his father wanted to die by the sea, Marcia wanted to be with Gilbert. She didn't care if she died trying. If she survived, they would have another cook.

They said goodbye to the Duke's subjects and left Drake in a procession of horse drawn carts, heading for Moray Firth.

***

Now, they were staring up at the Black Swan, which was anchored in the harbor. The sailing ship had been recently improved in expectation of the Duke's return trip. Several cabins had been added and others had been refurbished.

The Black Swan was a ninety foot ship powered by the wind. The square-rigged boat had three masts, six sails, and a web of fifty five lines used to direct the boat.

Dughall watched in awe as the white sails were unfurled. They caught in the wind and flapped, adding to his excitement. "I will never tire of seeing this."

Jessie and Marcia stood nearby, stunned by the display.

Captain McGee and several crew members stood on deck, waving. They lowered a dinghy to retrieve their passengers.

Dughall was concerned about Black Lightning. It would be a trick getting him onto the ship, but the captain assured him it could be done. He would take him across last in the dinghy.

The dinghy arrived at shore. Dughall's servants scrambled to load the contents of the carts onto the small boat and then sent it back to the ship. Crew members formed a chain and passed the goods up on deck. The small boat returned to the shore.

Dughall touched his mother's shoulder. "Ye and Marcia are next. Be careful with the rope ladder. Take one step one foot at a time."

Jessie smiled. "We will, Son."

The two women walked a few steps and were helped into the dinghy by a crew member. The boat rowed back to the ship and they were slowly helped up the ladder.

Dughall breathed a sigh of relief when he saw them on deck. "Now, for the hard part." He was nervous. "I will never forgive myself if Lightning breaks a leg." He turned and said goodbye to the servants who had brought them here. "Ye may leave as soon as I am boarded. Thank ye."

The dinghy arrived for a third time with one crew member. Dughall took the stallion by the reins and encouraged him to step into the boat. The stallion stepped in, but he seemed spooked by the dinghy's movement.

Dughall stroked his mane. "Easy, Lightning. Ye're with me. It will be over before ye know it."

The horse nickered.

The crew member started rowing and the dinghy pulled away from the shore. The stallion was getting jittery. Dughall talked to him on the way over. "It's all right, Lightning. I love ye."

They arrived at the Black Swan and pulled alongside. Captain McGee supervised. Crew members dropped the end of a long plank down into the dingy. "Back away until the plank can be climbed!" he ordered.

The man rowed slowly. Dughall kept one hand on the reins and another on the plank as they backed away. At last, it was at an angle where it could be climbed. But only one could go at a time.

McGee shouted, "Come on up, my Lord! I will send a man down to guide the horse."

Dughall balked, "Nay! I want to do it."

McGee frowned. "As ye wish. Here is how it must be done..." He gave a detailed explanation.

The Duke's heart pounded with fear. It seemed dangerous for both man and horse. But Lightning would listen to only him. He extended the reins as far as he could and tried to lower his energy. The horse could detect his anxiety. "Come on, Lightning." He began to pull the horse up the plank, which was at a thirty five degree angle. *I guess it's no worse than a steep hill.* He looked to the sides. *Except a hill path doesn't have a steep drop on each side.*

Captain McGee encouraged him, "Good. Good. Not much farther."

The horse was getting spooked. It whinnied.

"Stay with me, Lightning." Dughall went within and connected to the animal. *Come on, boy. I'll give ye an apple when we get to the top.*

They reached the ship and Dughall stepped off the plank onto a platform of wooden boxes. He encouraged the horse to step onto them. "Come on!"

The stallion shook his head. At first, it looked like he might rear, but he calmed when he saw an apple in his master's hand. He took several shaky steps and was on the platform.

"Thank God!" Dughall cried.

The crew cheered. They scrambled to make steps for the beast of various sizes of boxes. Within minutes, the horse was standing on deck.

Dughall felt weak-kneed. He knew that they'd been lucky. As the dinghy was brought onboard, he spoke to the captain. "Did ye build a stables for him?"

The Captain smiled. "Aye. Just like ye requested. He's going to need it. It's likely to be a rough trip over."

Dughall whispered, "Don't tell the women."

McGee lowered his voice, "They seem old for such a trip."

"They are relatives. There was no choice but to take them."

"Well, we've made their cabin comfortable and taken on plenty of fresh water and food. Some lemon juice as well, to avoid scurvy."

"I appreciate that."

A crew member approached. "We are ready, Sir."

"Draw up the anchor." The Captain walked away to supervise.

Dughall approached his mother and put his arm around her shoulder. "Are ye all right?"

Jessie nodded. "Aye. I'm glad that I've gone to sea before. Otherwise, it would be terrifying."

"Will Marcia be all right?"

"Oh, aye. I sent her below to our cabin. That was quite a trick getting that horse on the ship."

Dughall smiled. She had no idea just how dangerous it was. "Aye. Let's talk about something else."

The anchor was pulled up and the Black Swan began to slowly drift out to sea. Dughall and Jessie went to the rail and watched his servants drive the carts away.

She squeezed his arm. "Let me tell ye about the time that we sailed to Peterhead in the midst of a storm. That was the day the Earl choked ye. Ian sensed that ye were in dire trouble. We should have walked, but yer father insisted that we sail. There were ominous signs – a halo around the sun and swells higher than the wind could explain. Banks of storm clouds loomed to the south. All hell broke loose after we passed Slains Castle. We almost lost Ian..." She told the story with feeling.

Dughall's heart swelled. His family truly loved him. His father was a brave man and his brother was a better man than he believed himself to be. And his mother, oh his mother. It was good to have her with him.

The North Sea wind was raw. Jessie was shaking from the cold. Dughall drew her close to keep her warm. "Do ye want to go below?"

"Nay. I want to watch."

Their eyes never left the shore until they were out to sea. The last landmark disappeared, the ruins of a castle on a mountain. Dughall sighed. *Farewell again, Scotland.*

Chapter 74
Dark Night of the Soul

October 28th 1654

TWO YEARS LATER

ABBEY OF DEER, THE CHURCH, JUST BEFORE DAWN

It was a special day at the Abbey. Their youngest monk, James Gordon, was to take his final vows. His parents had arrived yesterday, but were not allowed to see him. According to their custom, the lad had been in seclusion since the night before, fasting and praying about his decision.

It was just before dawn. The church was illuminated by a single pillar candle that had been burning all night. The flame danced and sputtered. It was about to expire.

James knelt at the rail, imploring the Savior to help him. His legs ached from kneeling so long. He didn't think it possible, but he was conflicted. Oh, he was sure that he wanted to be a monk. He'd lived with these men for four years and considered them his family. He knew that he was destined to serve God and was convinced that he was safe at the Abbey.

Living as a Brother required sacrifice. James had resisted using his powers. He had self-imposed rules. No reading minds or the emotions of others. No moving objects with his thoughts or feelings. No calling upon the forces of nature. The only exception was the bees. He harmonized with their energy and understood their smallest behaviors. When no one was looking, he could coax a swarm into a skep by raising his own vibration. He called the bees his 'wee lassies'. Honey production had soared since he began to assist Brother Adam. They were making enough mead to sell it to surrounding villages. God wouldn't condemn him for that.

So, what was wrong?

James was troubled. Since his sixteenth birthday, he'd been plagued by impure thoughts about making love to a woman. It wasn't Maggie, for he'd given up on that four years ago. It was a nameless, faceless woman who would allow him to do what he wanted. It always ended with him touching his manhood and relieving himself. Wasn't that a mortal sin?

He'd confided in Brother Adam, who told him that it was his cross to bear. While he should try to suppress such thoughts, they should not interfere with him becoming a monk. James wasn't so sure. For a week, he distracted himself by whipping his back with a knotted cord. It worked, but the thoughts came back.

James was having a 'Dark Night of the Soul'. The young man felt lonely and desolate. He folded his hands in prayer, "Oh God! Forgive me for my impure thoughts. I can't control them." He shuddered. "What is wrong with me? How can I take a vow of chastity?"

The sun was rising in the eastern sky, pouring colored light through the stained glass windows. It filled his heart with love of God.

A voice spoke, deep and resonant, "I loved you, James, before you loved Me. I want to give you hope and a future. Give all your worries to Me because I care about you."

James sensed the presence of the Almighty. He prostrated himself on the floor. "Oh, God. Make known to me Yer purpose for my life. As days unfold, let every circumstance of my life lead me to fulfill the purpose of why Ye created me."

There was a pregnant pause. "I shall. But for now, know that all men face temptation, even my beloved Son. Do not be afraid to take your vows. I will protect you."

His heart pounded like a great drum. "I will take my vows."

"Excellent." The voice faded.

James lay there for almost an hour. His body ached from the cold floor.

A familiar voice spoke behind him, "Are ye all right, James?" It was his dearest friend, Brother Adam.

"Is He gone?"

The old man leaned on his cane. "Who?"

"God."

"God is never gone. He is everywhere. Ah... Did He speak to ye?"

James got to his feet. "Aye."

Brother Adam smiled. "Ye truly are a chosen one... Are ye still worried about impure thoughts?"

James reddened. "Aye."

"Don't be. Ye are the youngest novitiate we've had. It's likely that it is normal."

"I'm not evil?"

"Nay, just human. Most men have these thoughts in their youth."

"Even ye?"

"Aye. It was before I entered the Brotherhood."

"Did they go away?"

"They did. Sometime in my late twenties." Adam shifted his cane to his other hand. "What did He tell ye?"

"To take my vows. That He would protect me."

Brother Adam sighed. "I would give my life for such a message."

James blushed. He didn't know what to say.

The old monk smiled. "The Abbott sent me to ask, are ye ready to take yer vows?"

"Aye."

"Good. Then, ye must bathe and dress in a clean robe. This one looks like it has been through an ordeal."

James tried to smooth his garment. "It does."

They walked the aisle towards the exit, passing rows of elaborately carved pews. When they reached the vestibule, they dipped their fingers in the font of holy water and made the sign of the cross.

James felt the power of the moment, "In the name of the Father, Son, and Holy Ghost." It was early morning and he had his decision. He'd survived his 'Dark Night of the Soul'.

***

10AM

Dughall and Keira stood outside of the church, waiting for the monks and the Abbott. They'd been told to gather here to see the ceremonial procession. The Duke was dressed in a kilt, a silk shirt, and a soft wool jacket with gold piping. She was clad in a modest green dress and a black cape, simple but stunning.

The Gordons were lucky to be here. This year's session of the House of Burgesses had run longer than usual. They'd left Virginia on the first day of September and had a rough sea voyage. Upon arrival, there were serious problems at Drake. He had to pry himself away from them.

They arrived at the Abbey yesterday, to be told that they couldn't visit James until after the ceremony. Somehow, he'd imagined that his son would need his advice. But why would he? For the last four years, they'd been absent in his life. This was Keira's first trip to Scotland. Today was her first to the Abbey.

They'd spent the morning helping an old monk update the Drake family book with marriages and progeny. Dughall told him about Maggie's husband Philip Grant, her son Donald and daughter Isobel. Then he mentioned his infant son Duncan. So far, they hadn't noticed anything unusual about the children. It might be the end of their special talents.

The Duke frowned. *I'm glad than James couldn't join us. He will never have a child or a page in the book. I wish I could have counseled him.*

Keira squeezed his hand. "Ye're tense. Are ye all right, Husband?"

Dughall forced himself to relax. "Aye, lass."

Chanting emanated from the courtyard. The couple gazed in that direction. Dozens of monks in white flowing robes were approaching the cruciform-shaped church.

The Duke's heart soared. *There he is! Walking between Brother Adam and Brother Luke, the Abbott. He's beautiful!* Dressed in a long white robe with a wooden cross at his neck, his red locks were loose and his feet were barefoot. Dughall glanced at his wife, who gripped his arm tightly.

Tears streamed down her face. "Oh... He's so tall."

The Duke had been so tied up in his own emotions that he hadn't considered hers. She hadn't seen their son in four years. His words were weak, "He's a man now." The chant was intoxicating.

> ♩♪♩Veni, Creator Spiritus,
> mentes tuorum visita,
> imple superna gratia,
> quae tu creasti pectora.
>
> Qui diceris Paraclitus,
> donum Dei altissimi,
> fons vivus, ignis, caritas
> et spiritalis unctio.
>
> Tu septiformis munere,
> dexterae Dei tu digitus,
> Tu rite promissum Patris,
> sermone ditans guttura.
>
> Accende lumen sensibus,
> infunde amorem cordibus,
> infirma nostri corporis
> virtute firmans perpeti.
>
> Hostem repellas longius,
> pacemque dones protinus;
> ductore sic te praevio
> vitemus omne noxium.
>
> Per te sciamus da Patrem
> noscamus atque Filium,
> te utriusque Spiritum
> credamus omni tempore.
> Amen. ♩♪♩

Dughall's mind translated the Latin.

> *Creator Spirit all divine,*
> *come visit every soul of Thine.*
> *And fill with Thy celestial flame*
> *the hearts which Thou Thyself did frame.*

O gift of God, Thine is the sweet,
consoling name of Paraclete.
And spring of life and fire of love,
and unction flowing from above.

The mystic seven-fold gifts are Thine,
finger of God's right hand divine;
The Father's promise sent to teach,
the tongue a rich and heavenly speech.

Kindle with fire brought from above
each sense, and fill our hearts with love.
And grant our flesh so weak and frail,
the strength of Thine which cannot fail.

Drive far away our ghostly foe,
and grant us Thy truce peace to know.
So we, led by Thy guidance still,
may safely pass through every ill.

To us, through Thee, the grace be shown,
to know the Father and the Son.
And Spirit of them both, may we
forever rest our faith in Thee.
Amen.

James passed by without glancing in their direction.

Dughall heard his wife suppress a sob. He squeezed her hand. "Our son is concentrating on his vows. We will see him later."

She nodded. They followed the procession up the stone steps and into the church's vestibule.

Dughall dipped his fingers into the font of holy water and made the sign of the cross, "In the name of the Father, Son, and Holy Ghost." He encouraged her to do the same.

Keira dipped her fingers into the water and made the sign. She whispered, "May the Goddess bless his actions."

They proceeded into the church proper. Chapel bells rang, deep and resonant. A monk ushered them to a pew that was several rows from the altar. They entered and sat down.

The Abbott stood at the altar. He nodded when they were seated, and began the ceremony, "Brothers and honored guests. We are gathered here today to witness the vows of James Conan Gordon."

Dughall felt a rush of communion. Was he connected to his son? *Oh, aye. The lad is determined to serve God. He doesn't need my advice.*

The Abbott droned on, describing the seriousness of the

commitment. At last, he asked James to come forward.

The young man left the front pew and approached the altar. He lifted his robe slightly and kneeled in front of the Abbott. Brother Luke placed his hands on his head and asked him to say his vows. Then, he stood back.

James spoke with confidence, expressing vows of poverty, obedience, and stability. The young man swallowed hard and included chastity.

Dughall sensed that it would be his greatest challenge. He banished the thought.

The Abbott announced, "Rise, Brother James! For as of this day, ye are a full brother. The Abbey of Deer welcomes ye."

The young man stood and faced his brothers. "I am honored."

The ceremony was over. The monks began to file out of the church.

James approached his parents. He embraced Keira. "Mother. It is good to see ye."

Keira hugged him tightly. "Oh, James. I've missed ye."

He stepped back and smiled. "Thank ye for coming, Father."

Dughall was glad. "I wouldn't have missed it." The last two years had been exhausting, living in two countries. It meant four months on the open seas and four months in each country. He didn't feel like he was doing a good job in either. If it wasn't for James and Ian, he might abandon his estate in Scotland.

Father and son embraced.

Keira asked, "What is the vow of stability?"

James smiled. "This vow means that a monk stays put. Unless he's sent somewhere by his superiors, or gets a dispensation from Rome, a monk must remain in the monastery of his profession." He paused. "By making a vow of stability, a monk renounces the vain hope of wandering off to find a more perfect monastery."

She smiled. "It's like a marriage vow."

James brightened. "Something like that. It implies an act of faith - the recognition that it does not matter where we are or whom we live with. The ordinariness that descends on it after the novelty wears off is one of its most prized aspects."

Dughall nodded. "A sound philosophy. Are ye happy, Son?"

"I am."

"Then, ye have our blessing."

James smiled. "Thank ye. How is Grandmother?"

The Duke grinned. "She's doing well. She was delighted to be back with the family and pitched right in with the daily tasks. There aren't many healers in Virginia. I don't know what I'd do without her."

James looked around. "It seems that everyone has gone to the Refectory for refreshments. Since I am the focus of the day, I should be there. Will ye join us?"

"Can we, Husband?"

Dughall nodded. "Aye. We will entertain the Brothers with stories of Virginia." He took her arm and followed their son to the vestibule where they observed him making the sign of the cross.

They imitated his actions and followed him outside into the bright sunshine. It was a beautiful October morning.

Dughall was inspired. They were together and that was all that mattered. He stopped and stared. It was almost too perfect. He wondered if they were in the eye of a storm.

CHAPTER 75
A WEE BIT OF HISTORY

OCTOBER 1658

FOUR YEARS LATER

A WEE BIT OF HISTORY...

Britain went through a major transformation after the establishment of the Commonwealth. Without a King, members of Parliament engaged in serious infighting. As a military hero, Oliver Cromwell emerged as a natural leader. He demanded three things of Parliament – that they set dates for new elections, unite England, Scotland, and Ireland under one policy, and put in place a national church. The Parliament struggled.

Cromwell was frustrated. Did they form a Republic for nothing? He cleared the chamber by force and dissolved them. His words were harsh, "You are no Parliament! I will put an end to your sitting."

After a brief rule by an interim council, a constitution was drafted which named Oliver Cromwell "Lord Protector" for life. Thus, he became the chief magistrate and administrator of government. He could dissolve ineffective parliaments with the majority vote of the Council of State.

The former military leader had two objectives. The first was healing and settling the nation after the chaos of civil war and the regicide. He instituted reforms to this end and then turned his attention to the colonies. Once they submitted to the Republic, he left them to their own affairs. His second objective was the spiritual and moral reform of government. It was a difficult task that pleased some and alienated others.

In 1657, Cromwell was offered the crown by Parliament. He could have been King, but refused it. He stayed on as Lord Protector, but the position took on the qualities of a monarch. He was allowed to name a successor, and named his son Richard.

The Scots had diverse opinions about Cromwell. Some thought that he was a regicidal dictator. Others believed he was a hero of liberty. Catholics hated him because he persecuted their religion.

He barely lived a year after naming a successor.

***

Now, it was October of 1658. Shock waves were spreading across

Scotland. Oliver Cromwell was dead at age fifty-nine. The man had succumbed to a high fever, the result of a deadly infection. His son Richard was named Lord Protector, but his ability to lead was in question. The young man lacked his father's connections and lost the support of the military. Many feared that Britain would descend into anarchy. Support for the Commonwealth was crumbling.

Chapter 76
Handwriting on the Wall

July 2nd 1659
9 Months Later

DRAKE CASTLE, THE STUDY

When the Duke returned to Scotland for his yearly visit, he found Drake Castle a shadow of its former self. It had suffered greatly in his absence. The weapons range was abandoned and the remainder of his army dispersed. There were reasons for it besides his absence. London had levied taxes on the estate that drained the castle's coffers. The days of excess were over. Drake was operating with less than a third of its staff. It was doubtful that it could defend itself.

If that wasn't bad enough, Britain was in turmoil. Oliver Cromwell was dead and his son had been named Lord Protectorate. Richard Cromwell had no power base in Parliament or the Army and failed to control the government. There was talk of ending the Commonwealth.

***

Dughall was in a terrible state. News had arrived that morning that Richard Cromwell had been forced to resign, ending the Protectorate. Factions in London were jostling for power and the government was teetering on anarchy. The English governor of Scotland, George Monck, was leading the New Model Army on a march on London to restore the Parliament. Rumor was that he intended to urge them to make constitutional adjustments so that Prince Charles could be restored to the monarchy.

The Duke sat at his desk, pouring over the ledgers. Drake wasn't consuming what it used to and that was a good thing. He reviewed the last item and signed the bottom of the page with a scrawl.

Dughall was almost forty. He'd been traveling between Scotland and Virginia for nine years. He'd given up his seat in the House of Burgesses years ago because he felt he could no longer do it justice. There was no doubt that living two distinct lives was taking a toll on him.

This time the handwriting was on the wall. He would have to leave Scotland for good. There was much to do to achieve that. He had to conclude his affairs at Drake, relocate a few of his subjects, and say goodbye to his son and brother. He also intended to liquidate some wealth to bring it to Virginia. 'Eden' needed it. Every five years, they had to replace their freed indentured servants.

These things could take a while. Every day he stayed in Scotland put him in mortal danger. "The King intends to execute me as a traitor! How can I stay here?"

Jamison sat across from him. "Donald Grant says that ye will have a year before the King comes back. They haven't even begun to talk to him. There will be lengthy negotiations."

"Thank God!" Dughall breathed a sigh of relief. "I'm glad that I didn't bring my wife. I shall write her and tell her that I will be a while." He felt the muscles in his back tighten. "There is much to do."

"Where shall we start, my Lord?"

Dughall turned to a new page in the ledger. "Let's make a list." He inked a quill and poised it over the paper. "This estate will pass to a new lord when Charles is crowned. Some of my subjects will not be safe here. Cameron Hunter must move his wife and her people back to their original village to avoid persecution."

Jamison grunted, "Agreed."

Dughall made a note to talk to the archer. "The rest of my inner circle will have a choice – to join Donald Grant or accompany me to Virginia. Of course, their families are welcome."

The servant reddened. "I had this conversation with them months ago. Pratt and Suttie intend to go to Castle Grant. Murdock will go to Virginia."

Dughall wrote these things down. There was only one other man who knew about his life in the colonies. "And ye?"

Jamison's voice was laced with emotion, "My Lord. I have served ye and yer grandfather before ye. It has been my honor and pleasure, though the last few years have been difficult. I have thought long and hard on this. I can not leave Scotland."

Dughall's heart sank. He would miss this man. "Where will ye go?"

"Donald Grant made me an offer." He seemed uncomfortable. "But I will stay until ye leave."

The Duke wrote it down and forced a smile. "Thank ye, my friend." He opened a crystal decanter and filled two squat glasses with whisky. "Drink with me for old times sake." They drank in silence, basking in each other's company. "The Black Swan is due to return to Moray Firth in September. I want her to remain there fully provisioned until I am ready to leave. We must tell the captain to prepare for more passengers."

"Will ye ask yer brother to accompany ye?"

"I will ask him." Dughall sighed. "Ian will never come. He is comfortable living with his wife's people. And he loves the North Sea. I will miss him."

"What about yer son?"

The Duke frowned. "The monks have endured persecution since Cromwell came to power. Even so, James is determined to stay there. The King's mother is Catholic. Perhaps, he will ignore them."

Jamison scowled. "I wouldn't bet on that."

Dughall sipped his whisky. "I will miss this place. Drake has been my home. There are things that I want to take with me."

"What, my Lord?"

"The books and maps in my library. The globe. My telescope, stand, and star charts. The contents of the Surgery – it hasn't been used since Mother left it. And some of Grandfather's things – the chair with the lion's head, his carved boxes, his cane, spectacles, and rosary." He added them to the list.

The servant sipped his whisky. "We should move them to the Black Swan when she returns to the harbor. Ye might have to make a quick getaway."

"'Tis true." The Duke tossed back his drink. "There's one more thing. I must liquidate some of my wealth to take to Virginia. I own a horse farm and a mill. I will try to sell them."

"That's a tall order."

"Indeed. We will do it covertly to avoid suspicion. Of course, I will leave enough wealth to sustain the castle until a new lord takes over."

Jamison grunted. "The staff will appreciate that."

Dughall stood. "Let's get started. The list will get no shorter by us looking at it."

CHAPTER 77
ROYAL NEGOTIATIONS

OCTOBER 10TH 1659

THREE MONTHS LATER

BREDA, THE NETHERLANDS

Charles Stuart strutted across his quarters and stopped to admire his reflection in a mirror. The young man was impeccably groomed and dressed like a royal. He was twenty nine but looked much older.

The Prince was feeling smug. He had just returned from a meeting with George Monck, the English governor of Scotland and the leader of the New Model Army. The man had practically begged him to return to London and accept his crown. Of course, there were conditions.

Charles already knew about Cromwell's death and the anarchy that followed. He had spies in London who kept him abreast of politics. He'd suspected that they might ask him to return and so had devised his own conditions. He'd sent Monck away with a list of them. "They expect me to forgive them for my father's execution! I may pardon some but the ringleaders will suffer. Some things I simply cannot agree to."

Sir Monck had been apologetic. He'd listened patiently to his demands and promised to present them to Parliament. They were making constitutional adjustments so that Prince Charles could be restored to the monarchy. He stated that this was the first in a series of meetings that would lead to his reinstatement. All he needed to know today was if the Prince was open to an offer.

Charles smiled. "Open to an offer? Idiot! It was everything I'd hoped for." He felt that his terms were reasonable. Any man directly involved in his father's death would be executed as a traitor. This would include the Chief Judge and the commissioners who voted for his demise. Those who participated to a lesser degree would be imprisoned or barred from holding office. Cromwell's son would be killed and the rest of his family banished from the country.

"Oh, how I wish I could execute Cromwell! I would hang, draw, and quarter him. I should do it posthumously and bury the parts in unhallowed ground."

The Prince felt better about the Scots. They had invited him back and fought at his side at Dunbar and Worcester. There was only one Scot he wanted to kill, and that was Lord Dughall Gordon. "I will get him, Father, before he can leave Scotland."

Charles had been keeping tabs on Gordon through a loose network of spies. According to his sources, the man lived part of the year in Scotland and the other part in France. He wondered if that was true. He had contacts in France and no one had encountered him. But this did not matter, because he knew about the man's son. James Gordon was a monk at Deer Abbey. Abduct the son, and the father would come to him. It was justice in a macabre sort of way. "Father specified a traitor's death for him. I shall make his son watch."

"Father. Oh, Father. It won't be long now." Charles pinched the bridge of his nose with his thumb and forefinger to curb a headache. It happened every time he thought about his family. "Soon I will regain my throne - no thanks to any of them."

His cousin Louis XIV laughed when he requested troops to regain his throne. His sister Mary, wife of William of Orange, offered him refuge, but her husband refused to support him militarily. Of his relatives, his mother was his only ardent supporter. She was a loyal woman. He wondered why his father hated her.

Points of light danced before his eyes, a sign that the headache was worsening. He lay down on a brocade couch and tried to relax. "Breathe, Charles! Imagine the gardens at Whitehall. They will soon be yours. Breathe!" He took several breaths and his headache began to subside.

"It doesn't matter what my family thinks. I shall soon be King of England, Scotland, and Ireland." He managed a weak smile. "I will recall Mother from France and wait for Monck's next offer."

CHAPTER 78
THE LETTER

OCTOBER 17TH 1659

ONE WEEK LATER

JAMESTOWN, VIRGINIA

Gilbert Gordon had a feeling of foreboding as he approached the general store on horseback. A ship had arrived that morning from London, but Dughall wasn't on it. They had agreed that winter ocean crossings were dangerous and that he would start out by September. The captain had told him that he'd brought a box of letters and that these had been picked up by Fergus.

Virginia wasn't in the dark about what was happening in Britain. They were just a few months behind on the news. The colonists knew about the death of Cromwell, the naming of his son as successor, and Richard's resignation. A few commissioners had received letters from London stating that England was descending into anarchy. There was talk of asking the Prince to come back.

Gilbert was worried about his brother. He had hoped that he would take the first ship out of Scotland. "Does he not have enough sense to come back?" But sense was not what his brother was known for. He reached the store, dismounted, and tied his horse to a hitching post. He took the stairs and entered.

Fergus was busy with a matronly woman with a large floppy hat. He was packing her items into a woven basket. He handed it to her, "Thank ye, Anne. Stop by next week. I'm expecting a shipment of fine cloth and notions."

The woman nodded. "I will return next week with my daughters." She left the store.

Fergus grinned. "George Gordon! I haven't seen ye in weeks."

Gilbert wanted to ask about the letters, but he knew that he had to answer a few questions. It was what happened in the general store. "I'm working on the plantation more now that I'm solely a commissioner." The commissioners were on a rotation. They took turns being Sheriff.

"How is my lovely daughter?"

Gilbert smiled. "Fiona is doing well. The lass certainly has her hands full."

"And my grandchildren?"

"Young Fergus has grown an inch this month. The wee lassie twins are thriving. They look like their mother."

"I will have to come out and see them."

Gilbert nodded. "Any time, Fergus."

The shopkeeper grinned. "What can I do for ye?"

"There is a ship in the harbor. The captain said that he gave ye some letters. Are there any for us?"

Fergus opened a drawer and began to sort through the contents. There had to be thirty envelopes. He slapped one on the counter and sorted through the rest. "That's the only one addressed to ye. It's from Scotland."

Gilbert saw that it came from Castle Grant. But it bore the wax seal of Drake Castle. It had to be from his brother. He picked it up and slid it in his jacket. "Thank ye, Fergus. I will be back next week to pick up supplies."

"Goodbye, my friend."

Gilbert left the store and walked to his horse. He'd planned to read the letter at home, but curiosity was getting the best of him. He extracted the envelope from his jacket and opened it with his boot knife. It was in Dughall's handwriting.

My dear brother. I hope that this letter finds ye well and that our families are thriving. I know that I promised to return by October because of the possibility of a dangerous crossing, but it seems that I will have to stay here a while. As ye may have heard, Cromwell is dead, Britain is floundering, and the Parliament is negotiating with the Prince to come back and assume his crown.

I know that my life is in danger, but there are a few things I must accomplish before I leave Scotland. I must see Ian and James and relocate some of my subjects. I also need a few months to liquidate some wealth to take to Virginia. The plantation needs it.

Gilbert tasted fear. "No amount of wealth is worth yer life!"

I know that this will upset ye. But understand that I have my ship provisioned and ready to sail. Donald Grant says that it will take up to a year before the Prince returns to England. I will flee Scotland at the first sign of trouble.

Even so, dear brother, there is something I must ask. Ye once asked me to care for yer wife and children after yer death. Now, I ask ye to do the same. There is a slight chance that I will face the Prince's wrath and suffer a traitor's death in Scotland. I am not afraid of death, but I am afraid to die that way. It is all the more reason for me to leave as soon as possible.

Give my love to my wife, my children, my grandchildren, my mother, and yer family. Tell them the truth but try not to worry them. Ask them to pray for me.

I must go now. Jamison and I are transporting a cart of goods to the ship.

Ye can tell Mother that I am bringing her medical books and the contents of the Surgery.

As always, write to me care of our good friend, Donald. 'Tis the only safe way to contact me.

Ye've been a good brother. Love, Dughall

Gilbert was on the verge of tears. "Of course, I will care for yer family." He felt frustrated. "Dughall has risked his life too many times! First for Alex, then for me, now for Eden? Forget the wealth! Come home, Brother."

Gilbert placed the letter in the envelope and stuffed it in his jacket. He untied his stallion and mounted. His heart was heavy as he rode towards 'Eden'. He'd been assigned an ugly task. "How will I tell his family?"

He decided to show them the letter.

Chapter 79
Winter Blues

January 31st 1660

Fifteen Weeks Later

DRAKE CASTLE, SCOTLAND

The Duke stood in his study, gazing out a frosty window. It was a typical wintry day in the Highlands. Fierce winds buffeted the castle and falling snow made travel difficult. Occasionally, a servant or a tradesman braved the weather and crossed the courtyard with their coat flapping. There were few children left at the castle.

Dughall was feeling discouraged. He'd hoped to be sailing to Virginia by now. He'd made progress on his goals, but some of them seemed hopeless.

With Jamison's help, he'd moved most of his belongings to the Black Swan. Books and scrolls and maps from the library... The globe... The telescope and star charts... The contents of the Surgery... Grandfather's prized possessions... Jamison had convinced him to move more – the leaded glassware and his hunting clothes. There was so little left that he felt like he was camping. The moves were all made in the dark of night so that no one would suspect them. As an afterthought, he acquired a male and female deerhound and took them to the ship. The captain wasn't happy.

Cameron Hunter moved his wife and her people back to their original village, taking cartloads of tools and livestock with them. Pratt and Suttie moved their families to Donald Grant's castle and began to serve him. Drake became more of a ghost town without their presence.

Dughall traveled to Peterhead to offer his brother a place in the colonies. He tried to make the case that Scotland could become too hostile. Ian wished him well, but showed no interest in his offer. Dughall could only plant the seed and hope to see him someday.

The Duke visited his son at the monastery and explained his precarious position. James had been understanding, and encouraged him to leave the country immediately. Dughall promised to see him one more time before he fled Scotland.

What was holding him up was the sale of his properties. Donald

Grant was interested in the mill, if he could get it for next to nothing. No one was interested in the horse farm. These were uncertain times in Scotland. No one dared to predict the future. They held onto their wealth and hid it.

Dughall sighed. He missed his wife and family in Virginia. It had been torture to spend Christmas without them. Every day, he hoped for a letter. Had he angered them? Nay. He sensed that they were praying for him.

There was a knock on the door and Jamison entered. The servant had been gone for a day, taking a cartload of Murdock's belongings to the ship.

Jamison removed his snow covered coat and hung it by the fire. "I'm back, my Lord."

The Duke smiled. "It's good to see ye. It gets lonely around here."

The servant nodded. "Murdock and I stayed at Castle Grant last night. He gave me a letter for ye." He reached in his pocket and extracted it.

The envelope looked like it had been through hell. It was smudged and dirty and a bit wet. It was a miracle that the address was readable.

Dughall accepted the envelope, opened it with his boot knife, and extracted a letter.

Jamison grunted. "I should get home to my wife."

"Go, friend. Thank ye for bringing it."

The servant grabbed his coat and left the room.

Dughall's hands shook slightly as he unfolded the letter. He couldn't bear any bad news. To his surprise, it was in five distinct handwritings.

My dear brother. I hope and pray that this letter finds ye well. I received yer letter and shared it with our families. We all agree on one thing – that no amount of wealth is worth yer life. I beg you to leave Scotland immediately and return to the safety of Eden. - Yer loving brother, Gilbert

My son. Gilbert showed us yer letter. Say yer goodbyes to Ian and James and take the first ship out of there. No wealth is worth yer life. – Love, Mother

Dearest Husband. Gilbert is right. Come home to us! I would rather work hard for a hundred years than know that ye suffered a terrible death. Do not make me a widow and leave yer children fatherless. I love ye with all my heart, Keira.

Come home to us, Father. Ye and I have shared a special connection since even before my birth. I could not bear to lose ye in such a horrible way. I need ye, the children need ye... Great Goddess! Come home to us. – Love, Maggie

Father. I cannot begin to describe what ye mean to me. My life before I became yer son was unbearable. Now, I know what it is like to grow up in a loving family, and have gone on to create my own. Do not tarry for the sake of gold. Come back to us! We need ye and the children need their grandfather. – Love, yer son, Luc

There were other markings on the paper that looked like they were from the wee children – a scrawl, a drawing of a hen, and a heart.

The Duke was close to tears - tears of joy. The fire in the hearth popped and crackled. Dughall walked to the hearth and stoked it with a bundle of apple wood. The sweet fragrance lifted his spirits. He made a decision, "I will sell the mill to Donald for a pittance and give him the horse farm. I belong in Virginia."

***

DEER ABBEY

Brother James finished his afternoon prayers and stood stiffly. It was cold in the church and the marble kneeler was freezing. "Ow... But it is nothing compared to what Jesus suffered."

The young monk straightened his robe and walked the aisle to the back exit. He threw a wool wrap over his shoulders, opened the heavy door, and stepped outside. Wind whipped through the trees and a light snow was falling. He went down the icy steps and proceeded across the courtyard. He had been summoned to a meeting with the Abbott.

James was feeling melancholy. He missed his honey bees. Winter was the time when the colony stayed inside the skep to remain alive. They would not come out until the first warm day of spring. He knew that they were alive. He sensed their vibrations and communications. They were his friends... His allies... His wee lassies...

James was lonely without his bees. At times like this, he missed his family – his mother, his father, and his sister. Except for one more visit by his father, he would never see them again. He resolved to carry them in his heart, like a memory of one passed on.

The young monk arrived at the Abbott's house and knocked on the narrow door.

After a moment, Brother Luke fumbled with the bolt and let him in. "Thank ye for coming. Take a seat, Brother James."

They sat at the desk opposite each other. The Abbott spoke, "I have brought ye here for a reason." He sighed. "I have recently learned that my health is failing."

James didn't know what to say. He nodded.

"'Tis quite serious. They don't expect me to last a year."

James asked, "What is wrong?"

The Abbott shook his head. "It doesn't matter. There is nothing ye can do. Serving as Abbott has taken a toll on me."

James sensed that he had something to ask him. "Then what do ye want?"

Brother Luke smiled. "Ah. The Sight again. I have not seen it for a long time. Ye are a remarkable man, James." He paused. "I am concerned about what will happen to the Abbey after my death. Many of our brothers are old and feeble. They will need a leader. I have thought long and hard on this. I want ye to succeed me as Abbott."

James was stunned. "I'm only twenty-one!"

"But a truly old soul. Ah... I know. Catholics are not supposed to believe such things. The Gnostic gospels talked about reincarnation."

The young man was riveted to his words. He didn't realize that he was holding his breath. "And so... ye think..."

"That ye have been here before... living at this Abbey..." Brother Luke opened a cabinet and took out a bottle of honey wine and two crystal glasses. He poured them each a generous portion. "Drink with me."

They sipped the sweet nectar in silence.

The Abbott spoke, "I would like ye to succeed me as Abbott. This would involve training. Ye would have to understudy me."

James stared, "Can I still raise my bees and make mead?"

Brother Luke seemed surprised. "Aye. Most Abbotts have preferred activities." He took a sip of wine. "Ye don't have to answer me today. I will give ye a month to think on it."

The young man finished his drink and place the glass on the desk. "Ah. This was from a sweet batch."

The Abbott nodded. "It was. Will ye think about what I asked?"

James smiled. "I will think and pray. Ye will have yer answer in a month."

Chapter 80
Royal Preparations

February 15th 1660
Two Weeks Later

BREDA, THE NETHERLANDS

Charles Stuart sat at a desk in his elaborate chamber, planning his next moves. He had just come from a meeting with George Monck, the leader of the New Model Army. The man had finally presented him with an offer that was acceptable to both parties.

Charles was to come to London sometime during the month of May. They anticipated that he would be crowned King at Whitehall on May 29th, his 30th birthday.

The terms were thus – Charles would be required to grant amnesty to Cromwell's supporters according to the 'Act of Indemnity and Oblivion'. The Prince could name fifty one people who would specifically be excluded from this. Charles had already crafted such a list and was able to give it to Monck. It included the regicides who'd voted for his father's demise. It also specified that they were to be arrested immediately and await their fate in the Tower of London.

He grinned maniacally, "I have great plans for them! Nine will be publicly hanged, drawn, and quartered. Others will suffer life imprisonment or be excluded from office for life."

The Prince had negotiated one more term – the bodies of Oliver Cromwell, Henry Ireton, and John Bradshaw would be subjected to the indignity of posthumous decapitation and buried in unhallowed ground.

Only one man on his list came from Scotland, and that was Lord Dughall Gordon. Charles had extracted a promise from Monck that he would be allowed to pick him up ahead of time.

The Prince agreed that he would not enter England or Scotland before May. This he was willing to honor. But he was concerned that Gordon would leave the country on his yearly trip to France. He would have to send soldiers to pick him up sooner. This would be done with his brother-in-law's men, whom he trusted not. He would send someone to supervise them, and that person would be his mother.

There was a knock on the door. He answered, "Come in."

***

Henrietta Maria stood outside her son's chambers, waiting for him to answer. She'd been recalled from France late last year and summoned to his chambers this morning. It was a pleasure living in the Netherlands with her son, daughter, and her daughter's young family. Here, she wasn't treated like a poor relative by her spoiled and arrogant nephew.

Henrietta was fifty-one years old. She was beautiful and had never remarried. Several men had attempted to court her, but they always came up empty handed. They'd gossiped that she was still in love with her deceased husband.

Henrietta resented such stories. They ruined her chance for a relationship. It was true that she had rejected them. Only she knew the real reason. They didn't measure up to a sexually intuitive Scot by the name of Dughall Gordon. Perhaps, she would have more opportunities in the Netherlands.

The former Queen heard her son bid her enter. *What does Charles want?* she wondered. She enter his chambers and bowed slightly. "My son."

Charles did not stand to greet her. To her, it was an act of disrespect. But what could she do? He would soon be King of England, Scotland, and Ireland. She shuddered slightly. He reminded her of her husband.

He motioned for her to sit across from him. "Sit, Mother."

Henrietta lifted her black silk skirts slightly and sat in a chair opposite him. "I came as you requested."

Charles grinned. "I have good news. I have been able to come to a compromise with the Parliament. I will be crowned as King on my birthday."

She smiled. "That is good news, my son. Your father would have been proud of you."

He pounded the desk. "That brings me to my point. I owe Father a debt that I can finally repay. The last time I saw him, he gave me a directive. Father said that my first act as King must be to execute Lord Dughall Gordon as a traitor."

Henrietta swallowed hard. She was glad that she was wearing a high collar. "Who?"

"Lord Dughall Gordon. Perhaps you know him as Lord Drake. I'm told that he visited the Queen's House."

Henrietta reddened. *How much does he know? Am I being baited?* She opened a fan and fanned herself. "Forgive me. It is so hot in here. It must be the change I am going through." She took a moment to gather her thoughts. "I remember Lord Drake. There wasn't anything remarkable about him. The man was uneducated. He could barely keep a conversation."

Charles frowned slightly. "I wonder why Father hated him."

She offered a reason, "His brother was a royalist. Lord Drake supported the rebels."

"Hmmphhh... I guess we'll never know the reason."

She breathed a sigh of relief. "No, my son."

Charles leaned back in his chair and gripped the arms. "Nonetheless, I must see to his demise. Perhaps if I torture him, he will tell me." He smiled. "Which brings me to the point of our meeting. I have agreed to not enter England or Scotland before May. I am concerned that Gordon will flee the country. I intend to send soldiers to pick him up."

Her heart pounded. "Where will you get the troops?"

"William said that he would provide the men. But, I do not entirely trust them. I must send someone to supervise them, and that would be you."

"Moi?"

"Yes, you Mother! And for God's sake, speak English! You are not in France."

She was properly chastised. "Forgive me, Son. I do not think that I am the proper choice for this mission. I am an old woman..."

He cut her off. "You *will* do it. You are the only one I can trust."

Henrietta knew that the conversation was over. She didn't dare to say another word. At least, he didn't suspect her of what really had happened. But what could she do for Lord Gordon? She didn't want to be involved in this.

Charles scowled. "Are you listening, Mother?"

The former Queen blushed. "Oui. I mean, yes, my son."

"I will ask William to gather his troops. You will leave for Scotland next week."

James Conan Gordon – Brother James

CHAPTER 81
TROUBLE

MARCH 1ST 1660

TWO WEEKS LATER

INSIDE DRAKE CASTLE, 6AM

The Duke sat in the dining room, eating breakfast with Jamison and Murdock. His heart ached as he looked around the table. This was the last day that they would be at Drake and the last time they would take a meal together. One month had passed since he decided to go to Virginia. It had taken him longer than expected to transfer his properties to Donald. Now that was settled and he could leave Scotland.

Dughall lay down his fork. "Ye have been brave and loyal friends. It has been my honor to know ye."

Jamison reddened. "'Tis been our honor to serve ye."

Murdock swallowed his food. "I second that."

Dughall forced a smile. "Jamison. Are ye ready to take yer last load to Castle Grant?"

"Aye, my Lord. I moved my wife and children last night. All that remains is three trunks of clothes."

"Keep yer horse and the cart."

"Thank ye, my Lord."

The Duke turned to the other man. "Murdock. Take yer last cartload to the ship and yer wife with it. Ask the captain to load the horse on board. He can do what he wants with the cart."

"What will *ye* do?"

"I must visit my son one last time. I will stay the night at the Abbey and start out for the ship in the morning. It might take me two days to get there."

Jamison frowned. "Murdock should accompany ye to the Abbey. It's dangerous to travel alone."

Dughall sighed. "I've been alone at Drake three times this month. The guard at the gate is useless. It won't be any different."

Jamison grunted. "I guess so. I won't rest until ye're on that ship, sailing away from Scotland."

"Check the harbor next week. If the Black Swan is gone, I'm on it."

"Will ye write me?"

"Of course." Dughall looked around the table. Everyone seemed to be done with breakfast. He stood. "Let's get started."

They joined him.

Dughall embraced Jamison like a brother. "I will never forget ye."

The servant's voice was heavy with emotion, "Nor I." He turned to Murdock, "Take care of him."

The three men left the dining room and walked a corridor to a stairway. They took the steps to the ground floor, put on their wraps, and left the castle proper. They went to the barn, where they met up with Murdock's wife Sara, who had three sacks of bread and scones for them. The buxom lass wished the Duke well and joined her husband. They retrieved their horses and carts and left the grounds through the main gate. The guard was sleeping.

When they reached the woods, the three parties separated and went in different directions. No one at Drake noticed.

***

ONE MILE FROM DRAKE CASTLE, 8AM

It was a cold windy morning in the Highlands. Twenty soldiers, a commander, and an exquisitely clad woman approached Drake Castle on horseback. They'd been riding since dawn, from the tiny sea port of Garmouth.

The former Queen pulled off her hood. She'd been informed that they were nearing Drake and didn't want to miss anything. Henrietta felt a knot in the pit of her stomach. She didn't want to trap Lord Gordon. But if she refused, her son might learn about their tryst. She was caught in a bad situation.

The soldiers stopped short of the gate and dismounted. The commander, a tall man named Janssen, studied the imposing structure. "Something is not right. This is a big place. There should be more active chimneys."

A soldier frowned. "Ja." They began to converse excitedly in Dutch, a language Henrietta did not understand.

Janssen held up a hand. "Let me speak. The lady does not understand Dutch." The soldiers grew quiet. He looked up at her. "Madam. The place looks somewhat deserted. It could be to our advantage. We will breach the wall and attempt to find our target. We could use you as bait. You won't be in danger." He looked to her for approval.

Henrietta swallowed hard. "It's a reasonable plan. Proceed."

The commander addressed his men in Dutch. They checked their weapons, light flintlock muskets called fusils. The former Queen was included in the plot. She stayed on her horse with one unarmed escort, while the others moved to the wall and spread out around the gate. The commander rapped on the wall.

Minutes passed. To their surprise, a guard looked over the top of the wall. The burly man looked like he'd been roused from bed. "Who is there?"

Henrietta called out, "I am a friend of Lord Dughall Gordon. Surely, he told you to expect me."

The guard stared at the woman and her escort. "Where are ye from?"

Henrietta named the place they had come from, "Garmouth, a village on the sea. Please, Sir. I assure you, we are harmless."

The man left the wall. For a few minutes, they thought that they'd lost the advantage. Then they heard fumbling with a lock. Could he be that stupid?

The gate opened a crack. Twenty Dutch soldiers stormed through the wall and killed the man who admitted them.

***

DEER ABBEY, 11AM

Brother James stood in his bee yard, checking on his wee lassies. The snow had finally melted. The skep hives were starting to show signs of life. There were hundreds of bees flying! A few had succumbed to the cold and were laying on the ground unable to fly.

The monk picked them up and warmed them in his cupped hands. "My precious wee lassies. Ye survived winter. Surely ye can live another day." He prayed for them.

After a minute of warming, they fanned their wings and flew back to the hive. James' heart soared. He loved nature. These bees were his tiniest friends.

Brother Adam, now deceased, had taught him to feed the bees for a few weeks after a difficult winter.

James followed his advice, and laid out shallow trays of honey water. No one was watching, so he went into a 'purple meditation', connected to the creatures, and imitated their summoning vibrations. After a minute, bees streamed out of the hives to the honey trays. He grinned. "That's right. Drink and thrive!"

When they finished feeding, hundreds flew to him and alighted on his white robe. He had absolutely no fear of them.

"Brother James!"

James saw an elderly monk limping through the gardens. He raised a hand and yelled, "Over here!" The old man came to the edge of the garden, but stopped when he spotted the bees. James sensed that he was afraid of the creatures. "I will come to ye, Brother Simon." He turned his back to the old monk, closed his eyes, and signaled to the bees to leave his clothes. They fanned their wings and flew to the hives.

James approached the monk. "What do ye want?"

Brother Simon coughed, "Ye have a visitor, lad."

"Who is it?"

"The Duke of Seaford."

James was surprised. His father visited him every few weeks since he made the decision to flee Scotland. Last time, they'd said farewell for good. What was he doing here? "Where is he?"

Brother Simon leaned heavily on his cane. "In the library."

James nodded. "Thank ye. Can I help ye walk back?"

"Nay, young one. It does these old bones good to struggle."

James squeezed his shoulder with affection. "I will see ye at the evening meal." He watched the old monk limp away. He knew that there would be an announcement tonight. That morning, he'd told Brother Luke that he would understudy him to become the Abbott. He was a bit nervous about how the older monks would receive this.

James walked through the gardens to get to the courtyard. Most of the plants were brown and shriveled, but a few had new growth peeking through. Spring was coming! He crossed the courtyard and took the steps up to the building that housed the library. His senses heightened as he entered. Father had something important to tell him.

The young monk walked the hall and entered the library. As he expected, the Duke was at the window. "Father!"

Dughall turned and walked to him. "My son."

James led him to a couch, where they sat together. "I thought I would never see ye again."

The Duke sighed. "I know. I am leaving Scotland tomorrow. I had to see ye one last time."

James felt a twinge in his heart. The man really loved him. "Oh, Father. Ye must not risk yer life for me. We will always be together. All ye have to do is reach out and feel me."

Dughall smiled. "I will do that."

"I have something to tell ye. But ye must promise to keep it secret until it is announced."

"I promise."

"I accepted an offer from Brother Luke to understudy him. The man is dying. I will soon be Abbott."

Dughall looked stunned. "That's wonderful. Ye're so young."

James nodded. "I know. It makes me nervous. What will the older monks will think? Some of them still call me 'lad'."

The Duke chuckled. "Are ye happy, Son?"

"Oh, aye. Can ye stay the night? The Abbott plans to announce it at supper."

"I wouldn't miss it for the world."

They left the library and headed for the Refectory.

***

INSIDE DRAKE CASTLE, 12 NOON

The King's soldiers took charge of Drake Castle building by building and room by room. They even searched outbuildings, looking for the Duke of Seaford. The soldiers didn't encounter resistance. The place was staffed by a few dozen servants who claimed to know nothing about the Duke's whereabouts. Janssen was busy torturing one of them to see if they changed their story.

Henrietta Maria wanted no part of it. She sat in the formal dining room, partaking of a light meal brought by a terrified servant girl. There was tea, too strong for her taste... Stale scones... Grainy breads... and butter. It was hardly a meal for a former Queen. She sipped the bitter tea. *Lord Gordon is not here. Merci Dieu! We did our part. We should leave this pathetic place and return to the Netherlands.*

There was a knock on the door.

Janssen entered and bowed slightly. "Madam. We are finished with the prisoner. He claims that the Duke was here yesterday, but does not know where Gordon went. I ransacked the Lord's chamber. The Duke's clothes are gone. It appears that he fled the country."

Henrietta feigned irritation, "That is unfortunate. My son, the Prince, will be displeased.

The man scowled, "We have one more place to check. The Prince told us that Gordon has a son in a nearby monastery. The Abbey of Deer is a half day's ride from here."

The former Queen placed a hand on her lower back. "I'm not used to riding a horse. This morning's ride crippled me. You will have to go without me."

Janssen grunted. "As you wish. We will make this place our base of operations and leave ten men here to defend it. The rest will travel with me to the Abbey."

She glared at him. "These are Catholic monks. You must not hurt them."

The commander grunted. "We will try our best to avoid a conflict." The man started for the door.

Henrietta stood. "Wait! What did the Prince say about Gordon's son?"

Janssen turned. "If we find them together, we are to arrest both of them." He opened the door and left the dining room.

Henrietta was upset. She wanted no part of an operation that arrested one of God's holy monks. The very idea bordered on blasphemy.

***

DEER ABBEY, 5PM

The Refectory was a free-standing stone building near the monk's cloister. The main chamber was illuminated by narrow windows and torches on inner walls. One long carved oak table was graced with matching chairs and pewter dinnerware. The air was moist and filled with the smell of chicken stew and fresh bread. Water and ale flowed freely.

The Duke sat near the head of the table, next to the Abbott and across from his son. He was grateful to partake in this modest meal. Dughall looked around the table. It had been years since he'd shared an evening meal with these men. It was an aging order and their numbers were dwindling. Several men had died. Two, including the Abbott, were in their late fifties. The rest were in their sixties and seventies. Three men appeared to be suffering from senility. It made sense that they'd chosen James to succeed the Abbott.

Brother Luke looked haggard. "Dear Brothers... Lord Drake... I have an announcement. I have been ill of late. My heart is weak. A physician says that it is quite serious. They don't expect me to last a year." He stopped to let it sink in and continued when all eyes were on him. "This morning, I chose a monk to understudy me. He shall succeed me as Abbott. Ye know him as Brother James."

There was shocked silence. The Abbott continued, "I asked him to speak to ye."

James smiled. "Dear Abbott... My beloved Brothers... Father... I am honored and humbled to be chosen. I am young, but I will do my best to serve God and the interests of this monastery. I will need yer support, but most of all yer love, for that will sustain me."

One by one, the Brothers congratulated him.

Dughall was glad. There didn't seem to be a problem. "Congratulations, Son."

"Thank ye, Father."

They raised their glasses in a toast.

There was a sudden commotion outside the Refectory. A man shouted and a woman screamed. It sounded like a gun fired.

Dughall stood and grabbed his boot knife. He'd left his sword in his quarters. His heart pounded with fear. Was it the King?

The Abbott sent everyone to the back of the room. Then, he stood alone and waited.

The door flung open. Eleven armed soldiers entered wearing unfamiliar uniforms - a strange combination of red, white, and blue. They had the cook in a hold, with a knife to her throat.

The woman looked terrified. "They breached the wall!" she screamed.

The Abbott reddened. "The woman is a cook. Let her go!"

The commander of the troops stepped forward. "We will release her when you give up Lord Dughall Gordon."

Brother Luke was livid. "This is a house of God! We provide sanctuary here. Ye dare to violate it? Who are ye?"

"We are agents of the future King, Charles Stuart." The man raised his musket and pointed it at the Abbott's chest. "Give up Gordon or we'll kill ye!"

Dughall could stand it no longer. *No one should die because of me.* He hid his knife in his boot and stepped forward. "Stop! I'm Dughall Gordon."

Four soldiers grabbed him and pinned his arms behind his back. Others let the cook go and she slid to the ground. The Abbott rushed to her and signaled to the monks to get her.

The commander glared, "Which one of these monks is his son?"

Dughall struggled, "Don't tell him!"

Brother Luke stood. "Those who violate a house of God risk eternal damnation."

Once again, a gun was aimed at him.

"I am willing to die to protect my flock."

A young monk stepped forward. "Don't shoot him! I am James Gordon."

Two soldiers grabbed him roughly. The commander spoke, "We shall take him as collateral. We might return him if his father cooperates."

The Abbott clutched his chest and collapsed to the floor. Several monks attended him. The man reached out to his understudy in desperation. "I... have... failed."

Miraculously, the soldiers allowed James to approach him. The young monk kneeled and squeezed the Abbott's hand. "Don't worry, Sir. God will protect me." He paused and spoke softly, "Perhaps it is my destiny."

The soldiers grabbed him. The prisoners were searched and bound with their hands in front of them. Dughall knew that they were in grave danger. He had lost his boot knife during the search. Now, he was under arrest. Worse yet, his son was with him. What could they do?

The soldiers pushed them out the door. They were prodded across the courtyard, through the church, and out the main entrance. The prisoners were forced onto horses and led away from the Abbey. It seemed like they were headed back to Drake.

Dughall was confused. Had the castle fallen? Would the Prince be there? Would he meet his fate tomorrow? He swallowed hard. *My life doesn't matter. I have to save my son.*

Chapter 82
Confrontations

March 2nd 1660
The Next Day

DRAKE CASTLE, THE BREAKFAST ROOM, 7AM

The former Queen sat at the breakfast table, enjoying a cup of raspberry tea. She had instructed a girl to make the tea from a stash she brought in her saddlebag. This was a primitive place by royal standards. At least she could have her tea.

Yesterday had been tedious. The search party set out at midday, leaving her alone to amuse herself. She walked through the main part of the castle, but found that it had been stripped. There were no books, globes, telescopes, or musical instruments. How could someone intelligent live here? She settled for a hot bath, but even that unsatisfactory. The soaps were crude and the towels were stiff. Obviously, no lady lived here. She'd gone to bed at 10pm, and slept through until morning.

Henrietta sipped her tea. "Did the search party find Lord Gordon?" She sighed. "I would do a thousand penances to see him one more time."

The door opened and Janssen entered. "Good morning, Madam. The search party returned last night. We got him."

She was careful to disguise her emotions. "Lord Gordon?"

"Yes. And his son."

Henrietta frowned. "Did you hurt those monks?"

"No, madam. They gave Gordon up willingly."

She suspected that the man was lying, but she had to be careful. "What will we do with them?"

"The Prince said to take them to the Tower of London. He will deal with them when he is crowned."

Deal with them... She knew what would happen to them. Her lover would be hung, drawn, and quartered. His son would be forced to watch. She herself might be required to witness it. It was a frightening prospect. "I must talk to Lord Gordon. Bring him to me."

The commander stared. "Nay, Madam. He is a desperate man. It's dangerous."

She stood suddenly and raised her voice, "Am I not in charge of this operation?"

Janssen stammered, "Yes, but..."

"Do not invoke my anger. Bind him if you must, but bring him here." She stamped her foot. "Now!"

***

IN A HOLDING CELL IN THE BOWELS OF THE CASTLE, 7:30AM

Dughall sat on a hard bunk, contemplating his situation. They'd arrived at Drake after midnight and were taken to this holding cell. There wasn't much light in the room, just a narrow beam from a door window. At least, they'd removed his bindings.

Imprisoned in my own castle! He looked across the dim room and saw his son sleeping in a bunk. The lad hadn't said much since the incident at the monastery.

Dughall wondered if he understood the seriousness of their situation. It was likely that he would suffer a traitor's death – to be hanged, drawn, and quartered. At least he would be in good company. Better men than he had died that way, William Wallace among them. But the thought gave him no solace. To tell the truth, he was terrified. His thoughts ran wild. *Is the Prince here? Will I die today? What will happen to my son?*

James sat up and wiped the sleep from his eyes. "I will survive, Father. The King will not execute a monk."

Dughall was embarrassed. The lad had been reading his mind. "James... I'm sorry that ye are involved."

The young man was calm. "What ye fear... Is it true? Would the King kill ye in such an unspeakable manner?"

Dughall's blood ran cold. "Aye."

"Then, we cannot let that happen."

"He is a powerful man, Son. Ye cannot stop it."

They were distracted by a rattling of keys. The door opened and three soldiers entered. One of them was the commander.

The Duke was hauled roughly to his feet. "Where are ye taking me?"

Janssen snapped iron manacles on his hands and fitted them tightly. "Someone wants to see you."

Dughall's heart pounded with fear. "Who?"

"You will find out when you get there."

They prodded him out of the holding cell.

***

THE BREAKFAST ROOM, 8:00AM

The former Queen stood at the window, gazing at the courtyard. Except for activity around the bake house, it was deserted. It puzzled her that Lord Gordon had been living in poverty. She knew that Drake had once been a thriving concern. Where did his wealth go?

The door opened and Janssen entered. She turned to greet him.

The commander spoke first, "Madam. Lord Gordon is in the hall. I will escort him in with two armed soldiers. They will guard him while you speak to him."

Henrietta frowned. "The guards will not be necessary. Did you bind him?"

Janssen reddened. "Yes. There are manacles on his hands, but you can not trust him. I say that the guards stay."

Her dark eyes flashed. "And I say that they will not!"

Janssen's eyes narrowed. "Then, I cannot be responsible for what might happen to you."

She spat the words, "So be it." Henrietta handed him a black silk scarf. "Take this. Blindfold him before you bring him in."

The commander was visibly angry. He arranged a chair and left the room.

***

Dughall stood between two armed guards awaiting his fate. He was so upset that he was nauseous. It didn't help that he'd had nothing to drink since leaving the Abbey. He knew that he would need water soon or he might suffer a seizure. His condition had worsened over the decades. Stress or lack of water had been known to trigger them. *God, help me!*

The breakfast room door opened. The commander walked into the hall with a scowl on his face. Dughall sensed that he was angry. But, at whom?

"Stay here!" Janssen barked to his soldiers. He approached the Duke, grabbed his arm, and led him down the hall. They stopped at the open door. "You will behave in there or your son will suffer." The man blindfolded him and took him through to a chair that sat in the open. "Sit!"

The Duke's heart pounded against his ribs as he sat in the chair. The angry man left, slamming the door behind him. Dughall was afraid and the blindfold was making him nauseous. He thought he heard the swishing of skirts. Was he going crazy?

Delicate hands untied the blindfold and removed it.

Dughall gazed into the face of his captor. *Henrietta. But how could it be? She looks as young as she did before. The woman is ageless.* He found his tongue, "My Queen."

Henrietta smiled. "It's been eleven years. You must be forty. But let's not talk about age."

Dughall glanced behind him. "Where is the Prince?"

"My son is in the Netherlands. He sent me to retrieve you."

He tasted fear. "What does he want with me?"

She clicked her tongue. "Charles intends to execute you as a traitor. You already know that. I informed you in a letter years ago. Did you not receive it?"

Dughall reddened. "I did."

"Then why did you not answer me?"

He stayed silent.

She walked around the back of his chair and placed her hands on his shoulders. "I never forgot you, Lord Gordon. You spoiled me for all other men." She whispered in his ear, "I never remarried." Her tongue followed.

Dughall stiffened. "Henrietta, please! Do not do this. Not while I am trussed like a pheasant."

She pulled back his hair and kissed his neck. "Ah. The manacles. They could be a problem – or an interesting challenge. Perhaps it is your turn to be restrained."

Dughall closed his eyes. Her tongue was busy at his neck, tasting him. His manhood had a mind of its own, but he couldn't allow it to happen. "I can't do this! I must stay faithful to my wife."

"Faithful? Bah! Tell the truth. Did you think about me?"

He hung his head. "Oh, aye. Especially, at first. It was torture."

She walked around the front of his chair. "That is what I want to hear." She softened, "It can be just as it was that day. A man in as much trouble as you should seize the opportunity."

A chill ran down his spine. "My Queen. If ye care for me, let me go. Do ye want me to suffer a traitor's death?"

Henrietta hesitated. "No." She smiled. "I like it when you beg."

"This is not a game!"

"No, it is not. Make love to me. I might be inclined to let you go."

The Duke was conflicted. He didn't want to die a traitor's death - but he could not betray Keira. It wasn't just his wife. He'd promised God he would be faithful. His soul hung in balance. He gulped, "I can't do it."

She was angry. "Then I cannot help you. They will take you to London tomorrow."

Dughall felt his heart drop. She meant the Tower. "What about my son?"

"He goes with you. He will be forced to watch you die."

He struggled with his bindings. "Nay! Henrietta, please! I beg you. Let my son go!"

The woman was unaffected. "I expected this to go better. How unfortunate for you and your son. I'm a reasonable woman. I will give you until tonight to reconsider." She walked to the door and opened it.

He heard her say, "You can take him back to his cell."

***

THE HOLDING CELL, 9AM

James sat cross legged on the cold stone floor. Rodents scurried along the walls, but he didn't fear them. To the monk, they were God's lesser creatures. All living things had a place in nature. James had been sitting still for an hour, connecting to his father. The man wasn't in mortal danger yet, but soon would be. Tomorrow, they would be transported to the Tower of London. He wondered about the woman and what she meant to his father. It was obvious they'd had a sexual encounter. Father called her 'My Queen'. Was she the mother of the Prince? If so, the woman was powerful. Could she save his father?

He took a cleansing breath and got to his feet. *There are things I don't know about my father. I hope he's willing to talk. I have questions.*

James sensed that they were bringing him back to the cell. The Duke was being prodded down a dim corridor and he was begging them for water. The man was in danger of seizing.

Keys rattled. The door opened and two soldiers entered, pushing his father before them. One of them sat him roughly on a bunk and removed his manacles.

James sensed that his father was ill. "Please, Sir. We need water."

One soldier sneered, "When we're damn good and ready."

The other seemed amenable. "I will inquire about it." They left the cell and locked the door.

Dughall massaged his wrists. "Ach! They were on too tight. I can barely feel them." He spent a long moment staring at the wall and cradled his head in his hands. "I'm sorry, Son. Oh, God. I'm sorry. I should have left Scotland months ago! We are in grave danger."

James sat and put an arm around his shoulder. He sensed the depth and power of the man's emotions. "We will survive this."

The Duke sniffled. "I won't. Perhaps ye will. 'Tis the thing I dare to hope for."

The young man was touched. "Don't give up hope. I shall try to reason with them. But to do so, I must know everything. I have been connected to ye this past hour. Who is the woman?"

The Duke hung his head. "I am so ashamed." He told the story in pieces. Dughall described their trip to London and the Queen's proposition. He emphasized that he never intended to come to her bed. He'd been relieved to leave London. The Duke stopped talking and massaged his arm muscles. He was sweating. "Listen carefully. I might suffer a fit. It would be best to let me choke on my tongue. It's better than what they plan for me."

James stiffened. "Please continue the story, Father."

The Duke took a ragged breath. He proceeded to talk about the trials of the Covenanters, the skirmishes and battles, and his father's arrest and torture in the Tower. He'd offered the Queen his body for the safe return of his father.

James was stunned. "Ye made love to her?"

"Aye, in her own bed."

The lad sensed that there was more to this. Scandalous images flooded his mind. He would ask about them later. "The woman kept her bargain and let him go?"

"Aye. She also released Uncle Robert."

James considered this for a moment. "So the Queen is a woman of her word." He tried to be kind, "Tell me, Father. Did ye ever regret it?"

Dughall's eyes filled with tears. "Aye and nay. It was the only time I was unfaithful to yer mother. I felt guilty, but I couldn't tell her. Worse yet, I kept thinking about the Queen. It was torture. But one thing is sure... I never regretted saving my father." Dughall was beginning to twitch.

"Ye must rest." James helped his father lay down and kneeled on the floor beside him. His thoughts were desperate. *This man, who I once hated but now love, is to suffer an unspeakable death. Can I stand by and let it happen? Be expected to watch? My vows prevent me from interfering in worldly matters. Yet, I have the power to change it. What should I do?* He clasped his hands and prayed, *Oh, God. Ye once said ye would protect me. I do not fear for my own life, only the life of my father. Should I stand by idly while he is hanged, drawn, and quartered?* There was no answer. He recalled the trials of Jesus. *God, if thou be willing, take this cup from me. Nevertheless not my will, but thine, be done.*

They were distracted by a rattling of keys. The door creaked opened. A soldier entered, carrying a flask of water. It was a sign from God.

James stood and accepted it. "Bless ye, Sir!" He handed it to Dughall. "Drink, Father."

The Duke frowned. "I would rather seize and die."

"Trust me. Ye will need yer strength. Drink!" He gazed into the face of the soldier. The man's eyes were fixed on his crucifix. It was an opportunity. James did something that Skene had taught him and pushed a thought into the man's mind.

The former Queen requires this man's presence. I do not need to bind one of God's holy monks. He will not hurt us.

James cupped his crucifix in his hand and kissed it. "Shall we go?"

The soldier nodded. He grabbed James by the arm and led him out of the cell.

Dughall cried, "Where are ye taking him?"

The man answered blankly, "To the former Queen."

"James, be careful!"

The soldier locked the cell door and they proceeded to the main floor of the castle.

***

THE LADIES RETIRING ROOM, 10AM

Henrietta sat in a comfortable chair, partaking of a cup of raspberry tea. After the encounter with Lord Gordon, she needed to calm herself. She'd located one room that wasn't stripped of niceties. It had four stuffed chairs, a couch, a writing desk, and pieces of unfinished needlework.

She'd left instructions that Lord Gordon was to be brought here as soon as he requested to see her. She fully expected that he would reconsider. What man would endure a traitor's death for the sake of a moral dilemma? She looked around and smiled. This room was better suited for their encounter.

She examined the piece of needlework on her lap. "It's been years since I've done embroidery. Still, it is something to do."

There was a timid knock and a servant girl entered. She brought forth a crystal water glass and a plate of freshly baked scones. The girl bowed slightly as she arranged the service for her mistress. "Will there be... anything else, Ma'am?"

Henrietta shook her head. "No. You may go."

The girl stammered, "A soldier... said to tell ye. A prisoner wants... to see ye."

Her heart began to beat rapidly. "Where is the prisoner?"

"In the corridor."

"Is there a lock on this door?"

The servant nodded. "Aye, Ma'am. My mistress sometimes used it."

"Go now." The former Queen smiled. "Send the prisoner to me."

The servant left the chamber.

Henrietta stood and smoothed her silk skirts. She was prepared for an intense encounter. She'd stopped by her chambers and removed her underwear. "Mère de Dieu! Grant me one more time with him."

A young monk entered the chamber and closed the door behind him. They stood for a moment studying each other.

Henrietta was stunned. Was this her lover's son? He appeared to be in his early twenties. The lad had fiery red locks and startling blue eyes. But the nose... the mouth... He looked like Lord Gordon. Such a strong masculine neck! She wished she could see the rest of him. *C'est une pensée scandaleux!*

She found her tongue, "Who are you?"

James approached her. "I am the son of Dughall Gordon."

She tried to act disinterested, but her body betrayed her. Her heart was pounding like a drum and her skin was flushing. "Your name?"

"James Gordon."

"Why are you here?"

The lad's voice had a hypnotizing quality, "To plead for the life of my father."

She walked to the window to gain composure. "Do you know who I am?"

The voice again, "Aye. Queen Henrietta."

She turned and faced him. "That is correct. My son is Charles Stuart, heir to the throne of England, Scotland, and Ireland. Your father is in dire trouble. The late King ordered his execution. My son is determined to carry it out."

The monk seemed unimpressed. "What crime is my father accused of?"

She reddened. "Lord Gordon violated the King's trust."

"How so?"

She lied, "I am not privy to the reason."

James took a step towards her. "Oh, but ye are. Why would ye condemn him to death for a sin that ye participated in?"

Her heart dropped. "I swore him to secrecy!"

The monk frowned. "My father didn't tell me. I am like him and more. I can read minds and discern intentions. 'Tis why he was a good lover. He is a broken man now. They say that he has the Sacred Disease. He cannot grant your request. I left him in our cell - seizing."

Her mind went wild. *Lord Gordon is epileptic! No wonder he denied me. But all is not lost. The son is like the father. I must be sure of his talents.* She turned away and heard his voice.

"Ye are thinking that I might be as talented as my father." He paused. "That it would be scandalous to rut with one of God's holy monks. That ye would do a thousand penances to make it happen."

"How dare you!" She turned and gasped. The monk was undressing. He dropped his rope belt, removed his crucifix, and stripped off his long white robe. He was naked underneath. Her eyes widened with desire. *He is Adonis!*

His eyes were cold. "Will ye let us go if I make love to ye?"

"I will."

"Swear it."

"I swear." She walked to the door and latched it.

***

James was a bundle of conflicting emotions. He was glad he found a way to save his father. But he was grossly unhappy with the way. He would have to break his vow of chastity. This woman wasn't worth it. She was totally bereft of morals. He watched her undress. First her delicate shoes... her stockings... her wide lace collar... the indigo silk dress... He blushed. She was naked beneath and beautiful. It didn't seem possible that she was fifty. His manhood had a mind of its own. It responded.

He didn't know how to begin. "I've never done this before."

This seemed to please her. She smiled knowingly and came to him. "I will think about what I want and you will do it. But first... I will get you ready." She pressed her naked body against him. Her hands sought his buttocks and squeezed them. "It's been decades since I've had a hard young man."

James sensed what she intended to do, but he didn't believe it. Was it normal to make love this way? He held his breath as she sank to her knees and took his manhood in her mouth. *Dear God!* But God had nothing to do with this. He groaned as she sucked him, teasing his manhood. *I can't control it! What does she want?*

He forced himself to focus on her. She wanted him to take her to the couch. She wanted him to do the same for her. He held her head, "Stop, lass." She complied. Then he picked her up and carried her to the couch.

James kneeled and examined her. The woman was petite and practically hairless. There was a slight patch of hair around her privates and this he parted. She guided him with her desires, so it was easy. James spread her soft petals and began to suck her womanhood. He did what she wanted – first vigorously, then easy, in a circle – she loved to be teased. He stopped to catch his breath.

She cried, "Ne vous arrêtez pas!"

There was a frantic knock at the door. A soldier called out, "Are you in trouble, Madam?"

She yelled, "No! Go away. We are praying." She was breathing hard. "Our time together is growing short. Do what your father could not do. Enter me."

James frowned. He didn't want to father a child.

She seemed to sense his discomfort. "Don't worry. I'm too old to get pregnant."

His manhood felt like it was about to burst. James crawled onto the couch, straddled and entered her. The feeling was overwhelming. *Her insides feel like silk.* He moved instinctively, stroking slowly, then pumping faster. His heartbeat quickened.

After a few minutes, the woman shuddered and grasped him tightly. "Now, it is your turn."

A bead of sweat dropped from his forehead. James pumped slowly at first, increasing the rhythm until she shuddered. His control was lost and he ejaculated. The deed was done. He lowered himself and held her. His senses were returning. "The soldier is worried about ye."

They got up and began to dress. When they were done, he came to her. "Now, ye must let us go."

The former Queen hesitated. "I'm not sure that I can arrange it."

James could hardly believe it. She was thinking of breaking her promise. He threatened, "Do not cross me."

She flushed with anger. "I am in control here."

He had to scare her. "I said that I am like my father – and more." James pointed to the crystal water glass. "Watch me break this." He extended his hand, closed his eyes, and concentrated. The glass made a high pitched sound and shattered.

She had her fingers in her ears. "Mon Dieu!"

He opened his eyes. "This is why I was banished to a monastery. See that glass? Ye will honor our bargain or I will burst yer heart."

The woman was frightened. She slipped on her shoes. "I will accompany the guard when they take you to the cell." She opened a drawer and handed him a dagger. "Kill the guard with this, then strike me with your fist. This cannot appear to be my fault."

He nodded. "I will not need this weapon, but I will take it for my father."

"I will get you out of the cell. Then you are on your own." She went to the desk and scribbled on a scrap of paper. "When you are safe, write me at this address. We will do this again. There are hundreds of ways to make love. You won't be sorry."

James accepted the paper but said nothing. She had fulfilled his wildest dream, but he hated her for it. It would be a cold day in hell before he returned to her.

They straightened their clothes, unlatched the door, and left the chamber.

***

THE HOLDING CELL, 11:30AM

The Duke sat on the bunk, drinking from the flask of water. He was starting to feel better. The water had revived him to the point where his muscles stopped twitching.

Dughall had tried to connect to his son, but the lad was blocking him. Only glimpses of the encounter came through, and these frightened him. He made the sign of the cross. "God in heaven! Protect him." He sensed people coming down the hall – a soldier, a woman, and his beloved son. There was a scuffle and a thud. What was happening? He readied himself for a fight.

There was a rattling of keys. The door opened wide and remained open. From his bunk, he spied the silhouette of a man and a woman.

James beckoned, "Come out, Father."

Dughall stood on wobbly legs. It took him a moment to get his balance. Then he walked out of the cell into the corridor. What he saw confused him.

The guard was face down on the floor, senseless. Henrietta stood by, pale and speechless. His son handed him a dagger.

Dughall frowned. "Did ye kill him?"

James shook his head. "Nay. I squeezed the vessels around his heart until he fainted."

Henrietta's eyes were wide. "I got you this far. You must get out of the castle."

Dughall was grateful. "Thank ye."

She ignored him and looked to his son. "Do what you promised."

The young man backhanded her across the face. She fell to the ground, whimpering.

Dughall was appalled. "James!"

The lad crouched and stroked her hair. "Forgive me, lass." He looked up. "'Tis what she wanted, Father. Now, she cannot be blamed for our escape. We must go. Which is the best way out?"

***

OUTSIDE THE GATE, 12:30PM

Dughall knew just what to do. Years ago, he'd restored a secret passage that ran underground from the castle to an outbuilding twenty yards outside the wall. Only his inner circle knew about it. The tiny building was off limits to the staff and could only be unlocked from the inside.

Father and son emerged from a trap door into the building. The only room was dimly lit by sunlight streaming through a crack near the ceiling. They were dirty and sweaty.

Dughall retrieved a small bag of silver and then began to feel along the wall. He ran his hand over a burr in the wood and moved lower. There was a hole in the wall with a key in it. "Thank God!" he grabbed the key and showed it to his son. "Let's get out of here."

They opened the rough hewn door and stepped outside. It was a rare sunny day and for that they were grateful.

The Duke listened carefully. "I don't hear a commotion. Perhaps, they haven't discovered us."

James had his eyes closed. "They just found the woman."

Dughall felt a rush of fear. "We had better get going. The Black Swan is moored in Moray Firth. They've been instructed to wait for me."

They set off on foot, going due west through the woods. Taking the road was too risky. Dughall estimated that it was about twenty-three miles to Elgin and thirty-three miles to the Firth. He'd never tried to make it on foot. By 2pm, they'd covered four miles. They reached a stream, refilled their flask, and sat down to take a rest.

Dughall was exhausted, but fear drove him forward. He gazed at his son. There was a mark on his neck that looked suspiciously like a love bite. "James. Why did the Queen release us?"

The young man reddened. "Do not ask me, Father."

"I must know."

"I made a bargain with her. Like ye, I did it to save my father."

The Duke was in agony. "Did she seduce ye?"

"What's done is done. I will not talk about it."

Dughall pleaded, "When this is over, ye can enter another monastery. Ye can live the life ye want."

The young man hung his head. "I can not go back. I have broken a vow." He stood, brushed off his robe, and listened. "Quiet, Father. We are in danger. They used yer dogs to find our trail."

"Run through the stream!" Dughall cried. "They may lose track of us."

"It's too late, Father."

They heard the sound of deerhounds barking in the distance.

"How many are there?"

James closed his eyes, "Eight. They are armed with muskets and bayonets."

Dughall swallowed hard. "I will turn myself in. Run, my son. Save yer life."

***

James inhaled sharply. "I will not leave ye! We will find a way out of this." He would not allow his father to be executed.

"Son..."

"Let me be, Father. I am considering our options." When the soldiers got closer, he could affect their hearts. But it was a feat that took a lot of energy. It was likely he wouldn't affect them all. They would be captured. He needed help and he couldn't rely on his father. The man's state was fragile.

James sighed. There was an alternative. The things he learned from Lord Skene could save them. He could call upon the forces of nature to destroy them. But was it murder? Or self defense? What was the difference?

"They're getting closer!"

James heard their voices. It was time to make a decision. "Trust me, Father." He sank to the ground cross legged and began an orange meditation. He called to the ravens. He called to the crows. And he called to his wee lassies.

They came from miles around. Ravens, crows, and swarms of honey bees, both kept and feral.

***

The Duke saw eight soldiers burst into a distant clearing, led by two howling deerhounds. He grasped his dagger and prepared for a skirmish. It would be best if he died defending them.

The soldiers spotted him. "It's the Duke! Get him!"

The Duke stood guard behind his son. *If James can't save us, we will go down together.*

Dughall sensed something supernatural building. Raucous cries and low throaty rattles emanated from the trees. He looked up and saw them. Hundreds of ravens and crows sat on branches, stretching and awaiting orders.

James raised his hands. "Get them!" The birds swooped down on the attackers, shrieking as they pecked their head and shoulders. Six soldiers were enveloped in clouds of birds. They screamed and staggered blindly, as their eyes were picked to the sockets. Two soldiers fought off the birds and advanced on them with bayonets.

The Duke's heart raced. "There are two left!"

James raised his hands. "Now, wee sisters!"

Dughall heard a deafening buzz. He watched in awe as tens of thousands of bees descended upon the remaining soldiers. The men were stung thousands of times. There was no way they could survive it.

James raised his hands again. "Disperse!" The birds and bees left the clearing. The lad stood and embraced his father. "We are safe."

"Thank ye, Son. I will never forget this."

James turned and saw the carnage. He stood in shock for a moment, then bent over and vomited. "Oh, God!"

Dughall held his shoulders. "Seasoned soldiers do this after battle. Get it out. It's normal."

The young man wiped his mouth. "I didn't want to kill them. I read their thoughts. They gave me no choice."

"It was self-defense, lad."

James noticed a dead bee on the ground and picked it up and stroked it.

Dughall saw that he was weeping. "Ye're crying."

"Aye. My wee lassies gave their lives for me. They die when they lose their stinger."

Two deerhounds emerged from the woods. They loped to James and nuzzled his fingers. Dughall was glad. "Ye spared them."

"Of course. They are innocent creatures."

"We will bring them to Virginia."

James managed a smile. "Luc will want them. Oh, Father. It will be good to see him."

They examined the dead and took some things – flasks, knives, and two muskets. James discarded his robe and changed into a soldier's breeks and under shirt. But he kept his crucifix close to his bosom. He'd spent nine years walking between the worlds. No matter what he did, God would be with him.

Father and son filled the flasks and headed west towards Elgin.

Murdock

CHAPTER 83
ESCAPE

MARCH 5TH 1660

THREE DAYS LATER

MORAY FIRTH, THE HARBOR, 10AM

Murdock stood on the deck of the Black Swan with his wife, Sara. A brisk North Sea gale was blowing. The servant was uneasy about his master. This was the fourth day since he last saw him. Dughall should have reached the ship. "I'm worried, lass."

Sara squeezed his arm. "I know."

"Jamison was right. I should have gone with him to the Abbey."

Women didn't argue with their husbands. Instead, she changed the subject. "The Duke said that we will be landowners in Virginia. They will award us one hundred acres."

"Aye." Murdock grunted. "But I will always serve him, even if it's as a friend."

She smiled. "Agreed. The Duke has been good to us."

Murdock took out a mariner's spyglass and held it to his right eye. "Ach! I can't get this to work! It makes me dizzy."

Sara said, "Let me try it." She took it from him, held it to her eye, and pointed it at the forest. "It helps to close the other eye." She spent a minute making minor adjustments. "I see two men coming out of the woods. I think it's the Duke and his son. There are dogs with them."

Murdock was excited. "Let me see that!" He grabbed the spyglass and held it to his eye, but all he saw was tree branches. "This damn thing!" He put it down. "Let's walk out to greet them."

The plank was down, so they took it to the dock. They hurried towards the place where she spotted them.

***

Dughall and James emerged from the forest near Moray Firth. The harbor was a welcome sight. They'd walked more than thirty miles in three days. Father and son were exhausted.

Fortune had smiled upon them. They'd found lodging at inns in Elgin and Forres. At first, they'd been tempted to buy a horse, but nothing cheap was available. The long walk served a purpose. It helped them get reacquainted.

The Black Swan came into view. It was by far the largest ship in the harbor. Dughall's heart soared. "That's my ship!"

James was impressed. "How long is she?"

"Ninety feet."

"That makes me feel better about sailing the ocean."

"Ha!"

They spotted two people coming towards them, waving handkerchiefs.

The Duke strained his eyes. "It's Murdock and Sara! Let's run out to meet them." They picked up the pace and met halfway between the ship and the forest.

Murdock grinned. "My Lord! We were worried about ye."

They embraced like brothers.

Dughall stepped back and smiled. "Sara. Murdock. I'm glad to see ye! We almost didn't make it. We were captured by the Prince's soldiers."

Murdock frowned. "God in heaven! I see that yer son is with ye."

"Aye. They took him to make sure that I would cooperate."

"How did ye get away?"

Dughall clapped him on the back. "It's a long story. We will tell it later. First, let's board the Black Swan. I won't feel safe until we leave the harbor."

They hurried back to the ship and boarded. Dughall spoke to the captain and the crew pulled up the anchor. The men worked with purpose, dragging up the plank and releasing the sails. After a series of adjustments to the rigging, they began to drift out to sea.

Dughall stood on deck, watching landmarks grow smaller. He'd made this trip a dozen times, but this time it had a different significance. He was leaving the land of his birth forever.

James stood with him. "Are ye sad, Father?"

Dughall smiled. "Nay. It's bittersweet. My property and title are forfeit. I don't know if I'll ever see Ian. But my son is with me. I can't wait to show ye Virginia. Yer mother will be pleased. Maggie and Luc will welcome ye. Ye must meet yer brother, Duncan. Oh, and now ye're an uncle."

James chuckled. "Ha! The world has gone on without me."

The last landmark faded from sight. The North Sea waves swelled as they merged with the Atlantic Ocean. Dughall began to sing a seafaring song.

♩ ♪ ♩The letter came late yesterday
The ship must sail the morn
'Alas', then cried my own true love
'That ever I was born.'

And it's braw sailing on the sea
When wind and weather is fair
It's better being in my love's arms
And oh that I were there

The moon rose full o'er the deep
Where sea and sky do meet
But naught I heard but a murmuring wave
That broke upon my feet

And it's braw sailing on the sea
When wind and weather is fair
It's better being in my love's arms
And oh that I were there

Distant shores be fair and wild
And friends in ports be dear
But in every song and every glass
I wish my love were near

And it's braw sailing on the sea
When wind and weather is fair
It's better being in my love's arms
And oh that I were there ♩ ♪♩

James sighed. "It's a beautiful song."

Dughall smiled. "Aye." Soon, he would see his own true love. They would always be together. "Let's go below. We have a story to tell. Murdock is dying to hear it."

Epilogue

April 1661

One Year Later

LONDON, ENGLAND, WHITEHALL PLACE

Charles Stuart had been King for almost a year. He'd set out for England in May and reached London on May 29th, his 30th birthday. Shortly thereafter, he was crowned King of England, Scotland, and Ireland.

Charles had set about getting revenge for the humiliating death of his father. Although Charles and Parliament granted amnesty to Cromwell's supporters with the 'Act of Indemnity and Oblivion', fifty-one people were excluded. As he requested, most of these were already imprisoned in the Tower. He didn't wait long to get revenge. Within a month, nine of the regicides were hanged, drawn, and quartered in a gruesome display on Tower Hill. The rest were given life imprisonment or excluded from holding public office. The bodies of Oliver Cromwell, Henry Ireton, and John Bradshaw were subjected to posthumous decapitation. Their remains were buried in unhallowed ground.

***

Now, King Charles II strolled through the royal gardens with his two year old spaniel 'Shakespeare'. The canine was a great-grandson of his father's dog, the beloved 'Rogue'. The gardens were coming to life, after a cold and soggy winter. Early flowers were in bloom and many of the trees were budding. The King's protectors followed at a distance - armed and silent.

Charles crouched and stroked the spaniel's head. "Father would have loved you, boy. I wish you could have known him." The mention of his sire made him melancholy. The young King frowned. The only task he'd failed to complete was the execution of the Scot, Lord Dughall Gordon. He'd come close. "His life was in my hands!" Unfortunately, he'd placed his trust in imbeciles, who captured and then lost him.

He was especially angry at his mother, whose incompetence led to the traitor's escape. It would be the last time he trusted a woman. Charles had allowed her to attend his coronation and then banished her to the Netherlands. His sister Mary could support her.

The King stood and looked to heaven. "Forgive me, Father. This isn't over. I will find Lord Gordon if I have to look under every rock in Scotland!"

Just then, the sun's rays peeked out from behind a cloud. Charles smiled. It was a sign from God. His father heard him.

With an air of satisfaction, he led his spaniel back to Whitehall Palace.

THE NETHERLANDS

Henrietta Maria stood at an elaborate cradle, admiring her youngest granddaughter. The six month old child was a joy and comfort.

She'd left London shortly after her son's coronation. Charles had made it crystal clear that he was disappointed in her. Lord Gordon had been in her hands – and she lost him.

The former Queen didn't regret her actions. The woman no longer pined for Lord Gordon. She was obsessed with his son, the handsome young monk from Deer Abbey. The lad exuded raw sexuality. There was a cruelty about him that excited her.

Henrietta sighed. "I would do five thousand penances to be in his bed."

The former Queen had tried to locate the young monk. She learned that the Abbey closed after the untimely death of the Abbott. The monks had been placed under the care of the Vatican and scattered to other monasteries. James was likely among them. "What a terrible waste of a virile man!" All she could do was wait for his letter.

Henrietta played with her granddaughter's dainty fingers. "Precious child," she crooned. "May you find a man as skilled as that one."

VIRGINIA, EDEN PLANTATION

James Gordon stripped off his Sunday clothes and dressed in breeks and a clean shirt. They'd been to church. Now, visitors were coming.

***

Father and son left Scotland in early March and sailed across the ocean. It was an easy voyage, and they arrived in Jamestown ten weeks later. On board ship, they discussed a plan of action. It was likely that both men were wanted for treason. Dughall was known in the colonies as Duncan Gordon. James would need a new identity. He chose his middle name and assumed the name of Conan Gordon.

His family welcomed him with open arms. All was good. All was forgiven. He was surprised by the prosperity of the plantation as well as the number of children. Maggie had five, Luc had four, George had three, and his parents had Rosie and Duncan. James was a brother and a favorite uncle. What a surprise! He loved children. In spite of his gifts, he longed to be a father.

Living in Virginia was a change from Scotland. The weather was almost tropical and there was a long growing season. There were interesting trees, birds, and animals. He even found honey bees! They'd been introduced to Virginia decades ago by the early settlers. The young man liked plantation life. He worked hard – and loved it!

***

Now, James walked out of the main house in time to observe his parents. Dughall and Keira were embracing on the porch. He cupped her face in his hands and kissed her tenderly. She smiled and wrapped her arms around him.

James was glad. If he lived to be one hundred, he would never regret saving his father. They were the best of friends.

He left the porch to give his parents some privacy. As he approached the fire pit, Luc yelled to him.

"Look, Brother! Kelsey is coming!"

James' heart leaped with joy. He'd been courting the lass for five months and was desperately in love with her. He watched as she came into view – an Irish lass with red hair and eyes as green as a peacock's feather. Clad in a white flowing dress, she was riding a mare - bareback.

The young man sensed that she had something to tell him. He ran to her and helped her dismount. They tethered her horse to a fence post.

James took her delicate hand. Kelsey looked up at him. He saw beauty in her eyes. They were indeed the doorway to her heart. The lass had his undivided attention.

She was not one to waste words. "Conan. I have something tell ye." Her green eyes misted. "I am with child."

James was stunned. How could he not have sensed it? "Don't cry, lass. I will marry ye."

Kelsey's voice was timid, "There is something ye must know. I come from a long line of women who are 'fey'. Do ye know what that is?"

His thoughts ran wild. They both had supernatural gifts. For a moment, he was speechless.

Her fair nose wrinkled. "I see things that have happened. Sometimes I see things that *will* happen. 'Tis why we were driven from Ireland."

James understood. "I know what ye are, lass. It doesn't matter."

She smiled. "Oh, Conan. I will love ye forever."

This was the first time she'd said this and it made his heart flutter. James took her in his arms and kissed her. His right hand sought her belly. "There are two, here. A sister and a brother."

They gazed at one other, as young couples had done from the beginning of time.

Kelsey's eyes were wide. "Ye have the gift?"

"Aye." He wasn't about to tell her that he had more than one.

"Such unions are forbidden in my country."

He reassured her, "They are common in my family."

"Oh, Conan. Two parents with the gift? What will become of our children?"

James wasn't worried. "Don't fret, lass. We will deal with it. Let's go tell my father."

"Will he understand?"

"Trust me, lass. He will."

James had found his one true love. They would always be together. He took her delicate hand in his and together they walked to the main house.

THE END

AUTHOR NOTES

THE STATE OF MEDICINE AND HEALING

If you lived in a major city like Edinburgh and had money and stature, you could have engaged a trained physician. Healers, midwives, and bonesetters were available for common folk. They were skilled in the use of herbs and other natural materials such as tar or honey to cure disease or treat wounds. In Dark Destiny, I tried to make the healing and midwifery scenes authentic, given the time and place and resources available. However, my advice to the reader is to not try them at home without formal training. Just a note... In the book, both Brother Lazarus and Alex Hay suffer an apoplexy. This is what we commonly call a stroke.

RELIGION AND WAR

Dark Destiny was not meant to be an endorsement or criticism of any religion. The religious and political upheaval in the book was true to that period.

THE GEOGRAPHY

"Dark Destiny" is a work of historical fiction. It takes place during 1648-1660, and is set in Scotland, England, and the British colony of Virginia. See the maps in the beginning of the book. Most locations in the book exist today or existed in the 17th century. Here are a few exceptions. Drake Castle is a fabrication of the author's mind. The Abbey of Deer's life as a religious institution came to an end with the Reformation in 1560.

HISTORICAL CHARACTERS

"Dark Destiny" is a work of fiction. Names, characters, places, and incidents are either the product of the author's imagination or are used fictitiously. Any resemblance to actual events or persons, living or dead, is entirely coincidental.

Some characters' names and the events depicted in this novel have been extracted from historical records; however, neither these characters nor the descriptions of events are held to accurately represent real people or their conduct. Every effort has been made to present readers with an exciting, interesting story set in a reasonably authentic environment. No other purpose than entertainment was intended or should be implied.

That being said:

The execution of Charles I was a well documented event. Several accounts described his activities on that day. His speech was recorded by scribes.

The Marquess of Montrose led an effort to restore the Prince to his throne. He was captured and met his death as described.

Historically, from 1562-1636, George Gordon served as the 1st Marquess of Huntly. The novel portrays an alternate reality for the Gordon clan if George had succumbed to the madness of the sword of Red Conan, to be succeeded by a mythical brother Robert. Robert then spawned a son named Robert, who became the cruel and powerful Earl of Huntly in Dark Birthright. His son Gilbert, who succeeded him after death, is the Earl of Huntly in Dark Lord and Dark Destiny. Even though Gilbert Gordon is a mythical character, I tried to portray what happened to the real Lord Huntly. There is a notable exception. The real Lord Huntly had no brother to exchange clothes with in Edinburgh's notorious prison. He was beheaded at the Market Cross.

Historical records show that Lord Alexander Skene died in 1724. A popular myth portrays him as a wizard and a warlock. It was said that he never cast a shadow and was followed everywhere by ravens and crows. He had the power to reest anyone who annoyed him - in other words, he could force them to remain rooted to the spot or bend their will to his own.

There are stories about the 'Wizard Laird'. One concerns when he was studying the Dark Arts in Padua, playing cards with the devil. Whoever lost would pay for the other students with his soul. As the last hand was played, the students dashed for the door and the devil grabbed Skene's shoulder. He quickly shouted that the loser was behind him, pointing to his shadow – and the devil grabbed it instead. Thereafter, Skene cast no shadow.

Another story concerns a wild ride across the frozen Loch of Skene. One night, Lord Skene instructed his coachman Kilgour to ride the coach and horses across the loch, but not to look back at the laird's passenger. Kilgour waited at the water's edge as his master and the unknown passenger climbed into the black coach behind him. He cracked the whip and the two horses trotted onto the sheet ice. They got underway, crossing the frozen loch. Hearing low whispers, the coachman turned to see Alexander Skene and 'Auld Cloven Hoddie', the Earl of Hell himself deep in conversation. Kilgour suddenly realized that he was riding the heavy coach into the middle of the frozen loch. The ice broke, but magically the coach made it to the other side.

On a more recent note, a local resident remembers seeing an ancient portrait of Lord Skene with a raven on his shoulder when she worked as a maid at Skene House after World War II.

Of course, my portrayal of Lord Skene is pure fantasy.

NOTE ON THE USE OF THE SCOTS DIALECT

Some may wonder why I used only a bit of the Scots dialect in this book. I decided to lightly salt the manuscript with Scots to make it authentic, but easy for the reader. In this novel, you will find a lot of ye's, scores of lads and lassies, and a few self-explanatory words. Forgive me if it's not more widespread. I will leave that to Sir Walter Scott.

HONORABLE MENTION

There are a few songs referenced in this book, taken from traditional Scottish and English folk music. These compositions are over 100 years old and in the public domain. I also referenced some Gregorian Chant - in the original Latin and translated.

RESOURCES:

"Braw Sailing On The Sea" - music and lyrics traditional, arrangement and additional verses © by Eileen McGann /Dragonwing Music available on the CD "Journeys" DRGN 113   www.eileenmcgann.com

"Hush-a-ba, Burdie, Croon, Croon" – lyrics traditional - www.mamalisa.com

"Chant, Music for the Soul" - The Cistercian Monks of Stift Heiligenkreuz

"Chant Compendium 1" – www.chantcd.com

BIBLIOGRAPHY

Books

"A Land Afflicted- Scotland and the Covenanter Wars 1638-1690" – Raymond Campbell Paterson – published by John Donald Publishers LTD

"Colonial Living" – Edwin Tunis – published by Thomas Y. Crowell Company

"The Jamestowne Century" – Julien Ravenel Marshall, Jr – published by Washington & Northern Virginia Company Jamestown Society

"Winthrop's Boston – a Portrait of a Puritan Town, 1630-1649" – Darrett Rutman – published by W W Norton & Company Inc

Occasional online resources

http://www.englishmonarchs.co.uk

http://www.british-civil-wars.co.uk

http://www.en.wikipedia.org

CPSIA information can be obtained at www.ICGtesting.com
Printed in the USA
LVOW061512210212

269749LV00004B/11/P